Comfort Songs

A Novel by Kimberly Fish

Comfort Songs

Published by Fish Tales
303 West Loop 281, STE 110
PMB 316
Longview, Texas 75605

Cover Design: Holly Forbes
Back Cover Photo Credit: Bryan Boyd
Formatted by Enterprise Book Services, LLC

ISBN-13: 978-1732338654

Acknowledgments

Though the plot for *Comfort Songs* has long been brewing in my mind and heart, it took seventeen years to bring it to the page—but who's counting. I'm grateful for friends Kelly and Carl Caton, who introduced me to the best of the Texas Hill Country. I can't reveal those adventures here, but there's a reason that people say laughter is the best medicine. After Mel and I had settled into East Texas, their daughter, Brooke, spent a whole day photographing buildings and streets in Comfort, Texas, so that I could have evidence of a town I couldn't forget. Those old snapshots have helped me craft this novel. In addition, Sherry Klein and the 8th Street Market in Comfort, Texas, indulged my first book release of *Comfort Plans*, and that treasure box of a store has plenty of vintage farm implements that inspired me for this book. The good folks at the Comfort Public Library have taken my questions and wanderings with graciousness, and I've never met a stranger inside their doors. But if you want to see the garden center that inspired this book, drive to Edom, Texas, and discover Blue Moon Gardens. Trust me, it's worth the mileage.

I'm sending oodles of thanks to Marti Patten, Esther Begle, Lisa Ross, and Betty Johnson (thanks, Mom) for their early reads of *Comfort Songs* and their encouragement in the crafting process. I'm grateful for my friendship with fellow author Jill Haymaker, and that we can meet for tea, or out walking Merlin, for craft conversations. Thanks to Carol Blair for her editing and to Holly Forbes of Forbes and Butler for the rock-star cover design. I'm forever grateful to my patient husband, Mel, and to Mike and Laura, who indulge me lugging a laptop on family vacations.

You readers who encourage me with your comments, reviews, and enthusiasm, please know that your words are invaluable. Thank you.

P.S. You're going to meet a lot of friendly characters in this book—among them are those who have made appearances in other books I've written. If you'd like to know more about their stories, visit my website, www.kimberlyfish.com. While you're there, you can subscribe to my newsletter and receive a **totally free e-book**, *Emeralds Mark the Spot*. It's a novella that tells the story of Kali Cavanaugh and Jake Hamilton—two college sweethearts who get a second chance to find out if a love set free ever circles back. While you are at the site, take a look at the first book in this Comfort series, *Comfort Plans*. If you've ever binged watched HGTV, you're going to zip through this novel, and along the way you'll fall in love with Colette Sheridan and Beau Jefferson.

With sweet memories of Jean Fant Fish and Curtis Dudley Fish—

Alzheimer's disease was such a small part of your love story.

Prologue

In a move calculated to break more hearts than her long list of number-one singles, July Sands announced today she was retiring from the industry that made her name synonymous with broken-winged angels and love gone wrong. After thirty-two years as an artist who has won multiple Grammy awards and made the top ten on a variety of music charts, she looked out across the faithful who'd followed her to a Louisiana casino and told them she was stepping off the stage for good.

Luke English dropped the press release to his blotter and stretched back in his chair, making the hinges groan. He let his gaze wander to the window revealing an April shower drenching the tree branching over the recording company's parking lot. His mind stretched the words of the announcement and rearranged their order to find the hidden meaning.

How did one stop a star falling from the sky?

July Sands would create a vacuum for fans who'd followed her through a—what, three-decade career? Yes. Thirty years, five presidents, and countless lifetimes.

The Nashville news stations would allow a few seconds for the power of the shock to resonate with their viewers, much as they did when Garth Brooks said he was taking the wheels off his tour bus. Icons didn't get to step down from their pedestals without considerable speculation from the press, industry peers, and everyone else who had an opinion about what celebrities got to do with their fame.

Luke rubbed his thumb over his chin, hoping the grazing of stubble would revive his brain. Nothing about this announcement made sense. No one takes a pen away from a poet except to punish her. So, what could be responsible for July walking away from a talent honed in the era of radio disc jockeys and album sales defined by who'd make the Top 40?

He flipped the rewind on his memories, taking him back to an evening where, as a nineteen-year-old, he'd stood backstage of a charity dinner, spellbound like everyone else in that North Georgia country club, as July Sands's voice swept the floor and lifted every unattached molecule to the ceiling, casting melodies to the stars as if she strummed moonlight. She and her Gibson guitar had transformed everyone's idea of what Southern tunes built on blessings and blues could do to a heart—none more so than his own.

Before the stage came down that night, Luke had joined on as production grip for the rest of July's tour across the South. A summer marked by miles, questionable promoters, and dusty arenas still ranked as one of the high points in his life. It channeled his career and gave him the grit for his dream of helping artists achieve their goals.

His gaze darted across his office to the wall marked with his accolades: photos snapped with winners at the Grammy and Dove award shows, letters from grateful celebrities who had found their success because of Luke's insight and marketing savvy, and there at the bottom, still in the dingy frame he'd bought at a garage sale, a faded Polaroid snapshot showing his loopy smile, beaming as July Sands thanked him for detailing her tour bus after a mudslide in Alabama.

July's uneven embrace of fame had created a source for lyrics that had pushed every boundary known to producers. She'd woven soul, pop, gospel, and country into a collection that refused to fit into any classification and brought on the anger of studio heads who'd tried to dictate her choices. She had bank accounts to prove that her authenticity was what fans adored.

Luke had watched from afar as her revolving door spun out agents, managers, one husband, countless lovers, and some of the best and worst producers in Nashville, as she stayed true to her soul. When the TV Christmas specials began, the rest of the country fell in love with her Tennessee farm and her easy nature before the cameras. She was America's best friend, and she could sing their woes and joys like none other.

So, why quit now?

He stood and walked to the window. Staring down at umbrellas bustling among the cars, he replayed what he remembered of her media exposure. Sure, July had her share of bad press—some reports were so scathing he was sure that a publicist had been stoking the paparazzi. She'd also had her run-ins with the law over DUIs. Her divorce from Roger Worthington had been the fuel for an endless supply of rag magazines and gossip shows. But her music was still dynamic and relevant all these years later. And she was unquestionably photogenic. Great roots for a gold-label marketing campaign.

Could July Sands really be retiring?

Luke picked up the press release and stared at the fine print until the type blurred into the fragments of a plan—maybe more of a benediction for a life song that had ended mid-note. He'd not be worth the salary he earned if he didn't at least consider there was another way forward for someone with this much talent. Though he'd be breaking company policy and changing protocol, he would find a way, if July wanted to save her career.

Chapter One

Before choosing plants for your garden, you must first decide on the perfect patch of earth. Look at the soil, study the sunlight, and judge the ease for watering or installing irrigation before you till the ground. It's better to thoroughly plan first than have to pay twice later. – "Lessons from Lavender Hill," a gardener's manual

"You got a man on the phone."

Autumn Joy Worthington closed the hatch for a customer who'd purchased lavender, rosemary, and lantana plants that didn't fit well inside the BMW's back end. She glanced at her shopkeeper, who was pinching the portable phone. Betty's cheeks bloomed pink, as if she were moments away from a heatstroke.

"Is this like that old Prince-Albert-in-a-can joke?" AJ—as she preferred—wiped a bandanna around her neck and spied a caravan of SUVs pulling into the parking lot.

Betty's brow arched. "I'd take a prince over a salesman—which is probably what this call is about. Your grandmother gave me the phone on her way to the greenhouse. God only knows what she may have told him."

Yesterday, her grandmother, Inez Worthington, former San Antonio Junior League president, stuck her tongue out at a customer who had complained about the price of coreopsis. The customer had not thought it charming and demanded a full refund.

A breeze rustled the tops of lavender growing in rows behind the shop, sending fragrance and cooler weather through the outdoor rooms of her garden store. *A cool breeze.* Stunned, AJ's gaze shot north. The only way a cold front could ease the late April heat swirling over Comfort was if one of those strange, blustery weather patterns whirled over the Hill Country and surprised them with rainfall. Forecasters were stumped to explain the phenomenon, but locals prophesied the northern wind always brought disaster.

Betty held the phone forward. "Dang, a blue norther," she said, glancing at the clouds.

AJ took the phone.

"This means trouble." Betty sighed. "I better check the till. This is not the day I want to stay late if the receipts are off. My grandkids are coming for supper."

"If the receipts are off, it's not because of a wind." AJ raised her arms so the air would refresh her skin. "It's because someone let Gran work the register."

Betty opened her mouth, as if to start in on a retread of Inez's erratic behavior. AJ held the phone to her ear, preferring to take a call than hear the latest. It was a flimsy defense, but the Inez stories were tiresome. Her grandmother was in her mid-eighties and had simply lost her mental filter. It wasn't the end of the world, but every day the staff relished comparing notes. Climbing the steps of the porch that served as visitor central for those who came to explore Lavender Hill, the garden center and lavender farm, she glanced again to the horizon. Surprise buzzed among customers as they realized the change in temperature. She hoped the clouds brought rain. One significant change had already hit smack in the middle of her busiest sales season. The thought of another gave her heartburn.

Opening the periwinkle door, she closed it gently so as not to set off the bell that tinkled every time someone passed through. She sidestepped a customer breathing in the fragrances of candles. Shoppers lingered in this room filled with sachets and potpourri, telling her it was like an aromatic spa treatment. It didn't smell special to her, but she'd been working this room for six years and figured she'd gone nose blind.

She passed a couple scanning artwork and headed through to the kitchen. Despite peeling linoleum and a sink that burped fumes, the room was command central for her staff. Craning her neck to one side to relieve the strain of a morning's worth of work, she sat down on a chair. Propping her feet on a box, she tilted her face to the ceiling fan and connected the line. "This is AJ, how may I help you?"

The crackle of the phone line lingered, and she wondered if the caller had put her on a speaker and then walked away. Fine. She had more work to do than she even wanted to imagine. Just as she was about to push the "disconnect" button, a voice jumped to attention, and a baritone rushed her ears.

"Hello there, I'm Luke English. I understand you're in charge at Lavender Hill, and I believe in going right to the top if you want the best information."

She stilled with the awareness that this was not the usual twang of her seed supplier. This man's Southern accent implied he did business at fox hunts or debutante balls. She didn't have a lot of experience with those types, and she counted that lack of refinement as one of her better assets. Lavender Hill's mailbox was stuck deep into the limestone hills of Central Texas—if foxes roamed these spaces, someone gave them a free pass, providing they could survive the bobcats.

"I'd always heard the most reliable information came out of the mail room." AJ rubbed her palm across the hem of her shorts, trying to remove rosemary sap.

"I started there, but the lady warned me she had a tendency to lose messages. I had a request that was too important to not try for someone with more authority."

It figured. He was a salesman with a voice that oozed slow summer nights. She lifted her braid from her shoulder to let air circulate around her collar. "What makes you think I would be any more informative than the mail clerk?"

Luke paused. "I've been looking for someone, and the latest information leads to Texas, specifically Comfort and your business, Lavender Hill. I would appreciate any information you have regarding July Sands."

AJ bolted to her feet, her blood cooling with no need for air-conditioning.

She pushed the curtain aside, wondering if some customers were paparazzi in disguise. "Then you should have stuck with the mail room," she said, with a calm that belied the clench in her stomach. "Contrary to what you may have heard, Lavender Hill is not a lost and found."

"Well, that's an improvement over what the other lady said."

Luke English must be a private investigator or — worse — a bill collector with a mint-julep tongue. "Did she tell you we were a nursing home?"

"A juvenile detention center."

That's a new one. "Did she say anything else?" AJ asked, listening for any salacious innuendo that her grandmother might have let slip.

"The more I asked about Ms. Sands, the more she said I needed to talk to you."

AJ didn't have time to ponder her grandmother's unusual restraint because she was more worried Gran had given away a lot with what she *didn't* say.

"Miz Sa-ands?"

AJ stalled as she tried to think of a clever way to steer this man away from Comfort. "Are you selling a new brand of fertilizer?"

7

"Excuse me?"

The media hounds would be right behind this guy. "We're a gardening center and a lavender farm, Mr. English. If you're not a salesman or a client, there's really nothing for us to talk about."

"But I thought—"

Rapping her knuckles against the tabletop, she said, "Oh, someone's knocking, I have to go. Thanks for calling." She disconnected the line with more oomph than necessary.

Squeezing her eyes together, she knew that any moment now *Entertainment Tonight* would accost her employees for gossip.

"Hi."

AJ spun, facing the man standing inside the kitchen door. The air trapped between her heart and her lungs released. He wasn't a reporter. He was a youth pastor. She set the phone on its base and squeezed her fingers like there was still the possibility of residual electrocution. "Ethan, I didn't hear you walk in."

Ethan Ross shrugged his shoulders as if the freshly pumped muscles underneath the Comfort BBQ T-shirt weighed nothing. "You must give things away. There were so many cars in your parking lot I had to park down by the cemetery and walk." He stepped into the small kitchen space, stopped without getting too close, and studied her face. "Your nose is sunburnt."

AJ touched the tip, regretting that even more freckles would soon appear. "I'm trying an organic sunscreen. I guess the ingredients aren't working too well."

"Sun kissed." Ethan brushed long bangs from his eyes. "I believe that's the term."

"It's better than fried, which is what my grandmother would say." Thinking of Inez made her itchy. She moved toward the counter, where cans of lemonade sat piled in a tin filled with ice. "Would you like a drink?"

"No, thanks." Ethan paused as he watched her, then folded his fingers together. "Say, I, uh, heard some interesting news today."

And just that fast, she knew. She'd not had a lot of time to form her plans for fortifying walls around her mother, but the bricks were falling regardless. Surely the people of Comfort had better things to gossip about? Wasn't there some national crisis that everyone should worry over at the library or, now that AJ thought about it, some rumor that a developer had purchased a vacant shopping center? That had to be better conversation than what was going on at Lavender Hill.

"Can't believe everything you hear," she said. She'd learned how to fend off curiosity-seekers and paparazzi before most of her contemporaries had mastered bikes without training wheels.

"I think you're the victim this time around."

AJ popped the top of the can and took a long sip, buying seconds. *Victim?* That was an interesting term. All the locals knew her family dynamic. They'd watched her father ride his motorbike across these hills, called the sheriff when he scared their cows, and harnessed their daughters when he came to spend his summers at the farm. But July was a ghost to most folks here. She'd fly in on a private jet to drop off or pick up AJ periodically, maybe spend the night if forced, but kept a low profile in a town loyal to the Worthingtons.

Only a few of those closest to AJ knew who'd slept in her guest room the last two weeks, but they had strict orders to feign amnesia if questioned.

Apparently, she had a leak in her organization.

"I've heard that you have a visitor," Ethan said, giving a pious tilt to his head.

She reached for a cookie on a tray. "And with that, you came straight to Lavender Hill?"

Ethan relaxed. "I did some checking first. I couldn't believe my momma's favorite singer had fallen into such dire straits."

AJ had been thankful there wasn't a photographer around when July, unrecognizable to most as one of *People* magazine's most beautiful celebrities of the 1980s, crawled off a Greyhound bus.

As she debated whether to continue the charade that her mother wasn't at the farm, AJ looked more carefully at Ethan. He was a youth minister at her church. Surely, he had to have taken a confidentiality vow. "Don't believe everything you read. Dollar signs drive those stories."

"Some have said July Sands has made her bed, and now she has to sleep in it."

"That would be my grandmother talking. She's convinced Mom has slept in too many beds as it is. But Dad isn't without his share of the blame."

Ethan propped his hands in the back pockets of his jeans and rocked back on his heels. "Sounds like you might need to talk. You want to grab burgers tonight?"

His eyes looked sincere, but she knew the temptation celebrity played even on the most noble. "Sorry, but I've got to sort through some end-of-the-month statements before my accountant drops me. I also have to write text for a gardening manual my publicist says I need to produce, but tell the gang to think of me next time."

He shuffled in his boots. "This would not be a night with the others from the singles' group." His voice dropped to a husky level. "I was thinking just you and I could go out. You know, as—special friends."

AJ glanced at the soul patch under Ethan's lip. She'd suspected he was interested in her months ago. Her best friend, Kali, had been teasing her about puppy love because he was twenty-four to her twenty-nine.

She'd lived through so much in her lifetime, she felt about forty. She was sure it would take a man with burglar skills to unlock the rooms in her soul. Or maybe those were just lingering scars from the one man she'd let close enough to engage her heart. Her ideas of romance had been jaded by a golden-voiced heartbreaker—a category that pumped singers, musicians, and their assorted ilk into one classification she'd vowed to avoid for the rest of her life.

Then she remembered. Ethan played the guitar. And led the youth choir. He was one of them. Yes, Ethan would need to be let down, too.

"I've been gone too long, AJ. I didn't know you had 'special friends.'"

AJ's circling thoughts derailed, and she turned toward that honey-and-bourbon-soaked voice with the same dismay she felt when frost killed off her spring blooms.

July Sands leaned against the doorjamb as if she were holding up the wall instead of the other way around. Life on the road had decimated her willowy frame—first as half of a famous singing duo with AJ's father, then as a solo artist. Well, music tours and the steady diet of vodka, pills, and cigarettes. Even with faded auburn hair, a papery complexion, and shoulders that looked as frail as a sparrow's wings, AJ saw beauty in her mother, but, she amended, she also saw splendor in compost, so that might not be saying much.

"Ethan's just a friend, Mom, and a youth minister. So, be kind."

July exaggerated a shiver. "Yikes. You should never be friends with a minister. Perfection is a communicable disease."

Ethan moved so fast he tripped on a peeling corner of linoleum. "Ms. Sands, I'm like one of your biggest fans." Enthusiasm crammed his words into a sandwich. "My mother used to put me to sleep at night playing your records."

"And doesn't that make me feel ancient." July wagged her finger, pointing at Ethan. "AJ, this grown man was a baby during the peak of my fame."

AJ ignored her mother's pout and handed her a can of lemonade. "Here, you look dehydrated." A steady infusion of protein and an IV of vitamins would be good too, but she'd start with what she could get her hands on.

July took the can, but she did little more than hold it as an accessory. "That girl, she's always taking care of people." July winked at Ethan. "When she was a child, she adopted every stray that wandered into the yard. Be sure and have her tell you about the round-robin of animals she's named 'Sassy.'"

July was still controlling the stage, even if it was in a kitchen surrounded by an ugly cookie canister collection and rooster wallpaper. The problem with having celebrities for parents was that there was a fragile veil between real living and performance. Almost no one understood this except other children of superstars. All those kids in private prep schools in Nashville knew they were one or two chess moves away from the dark bleed of scandal every time their parents hit the road. She'd known it when she'd been staring at a blackboard too but was powerless to control the outcome.

Until now.

Now, she had her mother in a place where maybe, finally, the madness could end.

AJ could see the skin around Ethan's eyes soften, and his mouth drop open like July's wit enchanted him. By tonight, Ethan would tell everyone how misunderstood July was by the critics, and that if people knew her — blah, blah. Blah.

Wiping her hands on the back of her cut-off shorts, AJ knew it was time to throw herself down as a roadblock. The move protected everyone. "You don't get to tell Ethan stories if you don't pull your weight around the farm, Mom. Remember? You swore you wanted to learn how to water the seedlings. I assume that's why you're here. *In public.*"

July's glib expression melted right off her face. "You've made such a success of your life, AJ. I wish I had a reason to get up every morning like you do."

AJ glanced at the ceiling fan. She fully expected a lightning bolt through her roof. When it didn't happen, she figured the angels had grown immune to July's pity party.

"Ms. Sands," Ethan asked as he stepped between mother and daughter, "would you like to come hang with the youth group this Friday night? You could bring your guitar and play a few songs."

"Tempting though that sounds—"

"Mom's retired," AJ interrupted. She would let nothing wreck July's first seclusion that didn't involve medical supervision. It was a classic example of a prodigal returning, and if she had to erect an electric gate to keep her mom at home, she would. "She told me she's burning her guitar on the pyre of her past. The ceremony is tonight at midnight. Sorry. Find another singer to impress the teenagers."

Ethan folded his arms and narrowed his gaze on AJ. "I didn't think you had such a cold heart."

AJ never realized Ethan struggled with idol crushes, either.

"AJ's heart isn't cold. She's the only pragmatic one in a family full of dreamers." July heaved a sigh from the depths of a hollowed soul. "Now, are you two dating or what?"

They both chorused, "No," and then looked sheepish that they'd said the same thing—AJ more emphatically than Ethan.

"Oh, that's right. AJ is married to her precious Lavender Hill." July ambled toward a chair. "She ran from Nashville the moment she heard this farm was available."

A broken heart, thousands of dollars of debt charged to her credit card by a former almost-fiancé, and a distinct distaste for people who could hum the tune "Tangled in Delight"—her parents' breakout hit—but let her mother have her quips. No one ever cared what the real reason was for AJ leaving. They'd just let her go.

AJ saw July's bunions poking through her sandals. As a child, those bumps had scared her as she rubbed coconut oil into her mother's feet after shows. "Mom, Ethan is a man of the cloth. We're not supposed to lie to him."

July's shoulders lifted along with a yenta inflection, "Who's lying?"

AJ saw her mother's cheeks had brightened. Must have been the attention of a male fan. "If you're bored," she said to distract July from Ethan's awe, "you can inventory that new shipment of candles that came in this morning."

July beguiled Ethan with her smile. "AJ's trying to put me to work because she thinks if I'm busy I won't dwell on the wasteland my life has become. Worthingtons don't do depression."

"AJ needs cheap labor." Plopping a well-worn cowboy hat over her braids, AJ wished she'd done a better job expecting when July would tire of the farmhouse. She should have come up with a plan B before the weekend. "Mom, since you're here, you might as well keep an eye out for my accountant, Keisha Dawes. She's supposed to swing by any minute to collect the sales records for this month. Apparently, I'm behind on tracking my quarterly revenue."

July popped the top of the lemonade, and the hiss circled the room. "You have an accountant on staff?"

AJ gulped her lemonade, knowing that her mother did not understand retail business, and maybe she'd been selfish in not letting either of her parents touch this part of her life. It had seemed prudent to keep them far removed from the groundwork needed for her dream; their shine had a way of spoiling her independence. But they weren't those people anymore. Hadn't been for a long time. And she still hadn't told them all that she created on the old family farm. They didn't ask either, so there was that.

"Keisha owns her own firm, but I keep her on retainer for my math emergencies. So, maybe she can sort through your checkbook. Be prepared for bill collectors. I think they have this number."

"Ouch," July cooed. "The kitten has claws."

The real challenge of having July home was putting up with the fragments of woman weaned on adulation. That was a hundred percent behind why AJ loved gardening. Plants didn't feel entitled, dismiss your heartaches as insignificant, gloss over your troubles, or ding your dreams for not being big enough.

"As you can see, Ethan," AJ stopped at the doorframe and glanced back at them, "Gran overrated the gossip here at Lavender Hill. So, don't worry about me. You sort through the issues of high school and unrequited loves. We will settle into a new routine around here. Something far removed from music." AJ saw her mother staring out the window. "Right, Mom?"

July turned back to AJ, but her eyes were glassy. "Whatever you say, honey."

Chapter Two

Austin, Texas   February 5, 1954

Seventeen-year-old Inez McCall gripped the microphone stand for all she was worth, and for a girl coming off an asthma attack that wasn't saying much. She cut her gaze to the pianist to see if he was worried about the fracas going on at the back of the fraternity party. After wrapping an awful rendition of "Cold, Cold Heart," Denny was too busy wiping sweat off his forehead to see the boys dragging a young black girl toward a smoke-filled room. This wasn't the first time their band had played at a fraternity party, but it was the first time the crowd turned ugly before they even got to their ukulele version of "The Eyes of Texas."

Inez scanned the room, hoping there was an exit close to the stage.

The last time she'd been singing to a drunken group her father had manhandled a bunch of roughnecks away from his bar and interrupted the sheriff from his poker game—a situation that complicated an already dangerous mix of cards, gin, and gunplay. She didn't run then, and she'd not run now. Her daddy bragged to his customers that nothing scared his daughter. But he was wrong. Dead wrong.

Denny nodded to the drummer to begin their version of "How High the Moon."

Inez tapped her toe to the timing and caught sight of the girl being thrown over some boy's shoulder. Was no one going to step in and help?

Opening her mouth, she readied her vocal cords to lead with the lyrics. Someone jerked on her skirt. She glanced toward the space below the stage and dodged the hands of the boy who had reached for her legs. She yanked the fabric of her new poodle skirt from his grip. Singing despite this hindrance proved harder than she'd thought. Glancing at Denny, she raised her brow, asking if he would stop the song. Another man clawed for her ankle. Denny continued to play. Inez decided that she was done with this gig. Yes, their band needed the money. Rent was due. But her entertainment was limited to what she produced with her voice and did not involve games with the customers. Kicking out at the man who had crawled onto the stage and was reaching for her skirt again, she stepped backward and crashed into the trumpet player. He gave her a shove forward. The drunk had crawled onto the platform and caught her, lifting her up and dropping her over his shoulder. She let go of the mic and screamed. Pounding his back with her fist, she yelled for Denny.

The man jumped to the floor with such force that her shoes fell from her feet. "It's about time someone taught you a lesson," he growled, wrapping an arm around her neck.

Inez knew well what this man had in mind. She'd grown up watching hookers work the stage at her daddy's bar, and ,more times than not, things got feisty. Bruises and broken bones were patched up and disguised by makeup.

Kicking and screaming seemed to make the man shackle her more. Inez blinked against the smoky haze and bit the guy on his hand. Her skirt had been flipped over her head, and she felt multiple hands hitting her bottom, tearing at her hosiery. Tears poured from her eyes. She'd heard the stories;

she knew what men would do to a girl, but she never knew she'd be so powerless to confront it. Slapping his chest didn't make him stop either. Flailing her arms at anyone she could, Inez jerked, trying to free herself from the clutches of the man who was calling his friends to join him in the back room.

The loud crack of glass hitting bone caused her assailant to drop to his knees. As soon as her feet touched the carpet, she jackknifed off his shoulder and spun, looking for an escape. A hand reached for her arm, jerking her through the wall of bodies. Inez fought off the grip, even as she felt the weave of carpet burn the bottoms of her feet. She saw the slight man who had brought her captor to his knees.

"Follow me," he demanded. "I'll get you out going this way."

Cold air blasted her face as she realized that the man had dragged her into the winter night instead of a back room at the hall. Her nylons caught on the rocks of the roadway, but she didn't cry for the pain on her heels. The fear of rape was still running down her cheeks in a stream of black mascara.

"There's another girl!" Inez looked back toward the metal door marked "Staff Only." "There's a black girl in there."

The man released Inez's arm, bent over at his waist, and vomited into the parking lot. Standing up, greenish in the eerie light of a streetlamp, he wiped his lips with the back of his sleeve. "One guy has already called the cops, another went in after that girl, I hope they can get to her in time."

Inez shook. Her soul was taking on frostbite. "Who are you?"

"A nobody."

"You saved my life. You ain't no nobody."

The man sized up Inez like he wasn't sure she was real. "I can't believe I just walked in there. I've never hit anyone in my life. But something told me to run into this mob. I'd like to think it was God, because I've been praying about getting my life pulled together, but this—well, I just don't know what came over me. I might get arrested."

Inez didn't trust that the man was going to be any kinder than the mob at the fraternity party. She'd known her share of church folk back in East Texas, and they picked and chose from the good book to suit their causes. She started scurrying toward the streetlamp, hearing car traffic a block away. She'd rather take her chances with being run over than mauled by a crowd or a do-gooder.

"Hey, don't go that way." The man caught up to her. "There was a riot at a black church, and it's going to get worse tonight before it gets better."

Inez stopped, listening to the chaos going on around her. Despite common sense telling her to be aware of her surroundings, she couldn't hear more than the reverberation of panic in her head. No one was checking on her, for sure not even Denny, who had promised her daddy that he'd watch out for her.

Inez had never felt more alone than she did in that parking lot.

The man, no more than a kid himself based on his smooth skin and slicked-back hair, rubbed his hands down the arms of a sport coat a size too big for his shoulders. "I'll take you back to the student council hall. We were having a meeting, and when someone heard on the radio what was happening, we came out to see what we could do."

"For a fraternity party?"

"The riot. It was close to campus."

Inez knew more than she cared to admit about riots. Her small town was no easy place for colored people—or a white girl whose daddy played both sides of the law. "How can I trust that you're not going to hurt me once you get me away from this place?"

He held his hand toward her. "I'm George Worthington, and to hear my mother tell it, I've never hurt a fly. You'll be safe with me."

Chapter Three

Luke English steered the rental car away from the haze hovering over the concrete ribbon of Interstate 10 and slowed for the exit directing travelers to Comfort, Texas. He'd been chasing the golden grasses, chalky limestone patches of hilltops, and endless sky since he'd left San Antonio. Somewhere among the mile markers and the May sunshine, bits and pieces of the stress he'd brought with him from Nashville seemed to roll away. He pulled into Bubba's Bust-A-Gut gas station and parked so he could read the notes he'd printed about what he'd find in Comfort. Glancing beyond the building to the trees so twisted they could inhabit nightmares, he wasn't sure what he'd really find. He lowered the window, and the heat whipped into the car, bringing with it odors of diesel, cow manure, and the kind of cooking oil perfect for donuts. He stepped out, stretched his back, and watched an eighteen-wheeler speed by on the overpass. He could count the number of vehicles on this stretch of interstate.

Even if nothing came of his search, at least he could say he spent these few days doing something 180 degrees different from pecking away at his laptop and video conferencing with record producers. Tempted by the blinking donuts sign, he climbed back into the driver's seat.

Luke set his iPhone to play one of July Sands's romantic hits "Tangled in Delight," a duet she sang with Roger Worthington. When his gaze shifted to his bare left hand clutching the steering wheel, he felt his heart being sucker punched by their lyrics of love everlasting. He knew about despair, heartache, and grief, but he'd never known that blinding fireworks of desire they'd sung about.

Not wanting to linger in that wasteland, he upped the fan on the air conditioner and set the car in motion. It was time to find out why July was hiding at a garden store. He still hadn't ruled out that Lavender Hill was a cover for an addiction center, but the website had looked authentic and oriented to products one might produce with lavender and its oil. Someone was working the lavender business from every angle.

Work. This he understood. Romance was a worn-out word that he'd have to delete from his vocabulary.

No one understood why he wanted to drive into Central Texas and track down a woman who had publicly announced she was done performing. The CEO of the record company where Luke was a vice president certainly didn't understand. He'd thought Luke had lost his mind to chase down a performer — one not even under contract to them — and explore talking her out of her retirement. July Sands was an expensive risk; not only because of a career that had skittered off the rails, music catalogs owned by who knows whom, and an aging fan base, but also because of a temperament that had too long been fed by adulation. Rumor had it she was broke. They'd argued about rescuing talent, new avenues for old musicians, and independent artists in the music industry, but in the end, it was determined that if Luke was going to pursue this fool's mission, he was doing it on his own time.

So, he was on vacation and touring the Hill Country.

His playlist switched over to an Alan Jackson tune about the Chattahoochee River. He grinned and couldn't help himself. Alan Jackson wasn't under contract to their firm either. Maybe he was tired from the recent calendar of events he'd managed, but he felt like it was time to start looking at the Nashville business model through a different lens.

He'd been thinking about those ideas ever since he'd wiped his calendar free for a sudden two-week vacation. Now was not the time to contemplate a career refresh, but this compulsion to pursue July Sands needled him in a way that nothing had in years. The challenge had invigorated his brain cells. She'd been difficult seventeen years ago, so he'd guess she was what the media like to call a "diva" now, but strip away the packaging, and he'd bet everything that she was still an artist. And now, she was an artist with a story to tell.

He wiped his brow. There would be a book deal in her life story, a re-release of her greatest hits, and maybe a made-for-TV movie. Yes, as a marketing expert, he was absolutely right about taking the risk.

Heat was flowing under his skin, and he placed a palm in front of the air-conditioner vent, wondering if he was really right, or if he was just looking for a way out of his rut at work.

Sunshine radiated off the road leading into town, giving a Norman Rockwell vibe to the 1950s-era gas station, supermarket, and lumberyard on the outskirts of Comfort. Distracted by the landmarks, he hit a pothole. Feeling the car's alignment buckle, he slowed down and eased past the chamber of commerce and a few shops that looked like they catered to tourists. He turned onto a street a sign identified as the historic downtown district. If someone needed a place to hide, this town would suffice.

Mildewed buildings, ivy-covered walls, and awnings with stripes that had been sunbaked to beige were the first hallmarks of Main Street. He turned left at Sixth Street and right onto High Street. Here were the charming stores.

Two ladies were window-shopping.

A boy was trying to hang on to a leash as his dog chased a squirrel.

A shopkeeper was sweeping her stoop.

The few parking spaces outside the bank building were empty save for one wood grain-paneled Jeep Grand Cherokee, a model sold about twenty years ago.

He pushed the button to drop his window and thought the temperature had dropped ten degrees from the interstate. He silenced the music on his phone and listened to the rumblings of old pickup trucks and a barking dog.

Did he smell bacon?

Looking across the street, he saw a red sign advertising High's Cafe dangling among some green vines.

A few minutes later, he was standing inside the bright café outfitted with bookshelves and gifts, waiting behind a wiry, silver-haired woman, who was talking loudly to the employee working the register. He read through the menu offerings a second time. The chicken-salad sandwich or the vegetable wrap would be in line with his usual workday menu. But when it was his turn to order, he opened his mouth and, thinking chicken salad, said the words, "triple-cheese-and-bacon quesadilla." The worker scribbled his words onto a notepad. *So much for the usual,* he thought. And, vowing to go on a run later, he added, "And a side of curly sweet potato fries too."

He moved aside and took a cup to the soft-drink dispenser. Standing behind the same wiry woman, he read a poster advertising the Comfort Street Fair on July 3. It was a fundraiser for the local library and promised a sunset dance and fireworks. With little provocation, he could smell sawdust and hear the hoofbeats of a rodeo. There'd be a steel-guitar band. There always was. Maybe he could scout local talent while he burned through his personal days in Comfort. That might justify his time in Texas.

"You passing through?" the woman asked, sizing up his casual-Friday attire.

Luke glanced down at his wrinkled slacks, knowing he should have worn his jeans and boots to blend in. "I'm on a hunt," he said. "I could be here a while."

"You don't look like any game hunter I've ever seen." She leaned closer to his arm, seeming to sniff his custom-mixed cologne. "Most men don't wear loafers in the field."

"I'll keep that in mind." Luke aligned his cup to the ice dispenser. The lady kept staring at his head, like his hair gel hadn't dried into the style he'd perfected. Maybe he should have checked his reflection. He had driven with the window down. As much to distract her as to help his cause, he asked, "You wouldn't know where I could find a place called Lavender Hill, would you?"

The lady chuckled then reached to hold the front of her T-shirt out for his inspection. A purple logo bracketed by sheaves of lavender flattened between her fingertips. "Now, I guess I would, wouldn't I?"

Bacon wasn't his only win at High's.

"Are you an employee at Lavender Hill or just a fan?" he asked, a little too reluctant to believe he'd hit a home run this soon after crossing the city limits.

"My granddaughter owns the place. I work for her in the mornings to keep myself agile. Plus, I taught her everything she knows about displays, so she needs me to hang around and give her pointers."

His knees had that funny sizzle, like something poised them to either run or leap in the air, kicking his heels together. Steadying his voice to sound as if he was only vaguely interested in a garden store, he suggested, "Then you can give me directions. I'm heading that way as soon as I finish lunch."

She waved to someone behind him. "It's not too far outside of town," she said, returning her attention to him.

"Just past the cemetery up North Creek Road. You can't miss it. The house next door is a real dump."

"Look for the eyesore," he echoed. "Then do I turn left?"

Inez Worthington shook her head, revealing she'd stuck butterfly pins into her silvery hair. "No, you look for the place with all the lavender fields rolling on behind it. There's a picket fence along the road. And if you get to the ... uh ... the," her eyes glazed over as she fought to find her words. "It's a ... a, uh, oh, there's a sign on a gate."

He wondered if her directions were solid. Before she looked away, he asked, "What if I want to say hello to your granddaughter, to tell her I met you in High's? Is she working today?"

"She works every day. She doesn't hide. Not like other people I know. Since you're a handsome fella, I might want to go with you—to make sure you don't get lost." Inez winked as if she were about fifty years younger. "We get a commission if someone buys things. You feel like buying a lot of plants today?"

He pulled his cup away from the dispenser and wondered how best to play this opportunity. "Well, I like to go to arboretums and gardens back home, but I don't live around here. Getting flowers onto the plane might be a problem."

Inez's eyes narrowed. "You could still have things shipped to your house. A lot of folks are so crazy about the plants she sells they pay her to drive to, uh, to—well, to wherever it is they live and hand deliver the stuff. She's got a steep price tag, I'm not going to kid you, it's outrageous, but folks buy her plants like they're stealing candy."

This granddaughter sounded interesting, but he needed to avoid getting off track. With only a few days to find July Sands, he would not linger at the garden store. He would find out why July claimed to have an association and then find out where she was really hiding.

"I live in a condo in Nash—far away from here," he said, realizing that he shouldn't give away his identity. Folks around here might protect July.

"Then what in the world are you doing going to Lavender Hill?"

The way her pale-blue eyes bored into Luke made him realize he had less time than he needed to figure out his strategy. "Let's say I'm open to exploring new ideas."

"Nobody comes out here chasing an idea, mister." Inez pursed her lips as she seemed to grade the label on his shirt. "Are you a reporter?"

Luke heard his order number called over the loudspeaker. "I'm a wanderer this weekend. Just here to look around."

Inez pursed her lips. "I can't quite put my finger on it, but something about you doesn't add up. Despite our friendly nature in Comfort, we don't take kindly to being thought rubes by city slickers."

He wasn't here to defame the town. Once his rental car pointed south again, he'd have no cause to return.

Her gaze drifted to his expensive shoes. "We have ways of dealing with folks who try to expose us to the world. Try to change who we are—" she blinked, "around here."

Luke guessed that this grandmother would be packing a pistol in her handbag. He hoped she had medication, because she was getting a little scary in her tourism approach.

He backed up a step.

Then with no warning, she smiled and tapped his cheek with her arthritic fingers. "I'm just joshing you. You're too cute to look so worried."

"Heartburn." He tapped his ribs, where motives and his conscience had collided. "It's the by-product of my work."

Before she stepped away, Inez winked at him and added, "You need a new job. Good thing you came to Comfort. We specialize in changing folks' lives."

Chapter Four

To achieve healthy and abundant blooms in your garden, you must be prepared to sacrifice quiet hours cultivating your plants. Dirt under your fingernails is the sign of progress. – "Lessons from Lavender Hill"

AJ lifted a scoop of soil to her nose and tried to guess if there was a chemical reaction affecting the hybrid basil she'd been testing in the greenhouse, besides the obvious lack of watering. The screened door at one end of the greenhouse opened, and she turned toward the fresh air.

July crossed the threshold, carefully placing her flip-flops over the pea gravel that carpeted the space, considering her daughter's expression. "I'd say you look like something the cat dragged in, but that's rude to the cat. What gives?"

AJ dropped the baby roots to the tray. "I'm about to lose a batch of experimental herbs. This was a cross-pollinated variety of basil I'd invested in, so I don't have a lot of experience with its peculiarities, but yesterday these were brimming with health."

"Maybe there's something in the air." July crept closer toward the table covered in peaty soil. She dusted an edge clean before leaning her hip into the frame. "I've felt horrible all morning. It could be the temperatures. The first time Roger brought me to Comfort, I thought I'd have heatstroke before nightfall." She lifted her fingers to her nose. "Your dirt smells like espresso."

Something tempted AJ to comment on how often her dad's name found its way into conversation this past week, but she didn't. She preferred to contain her disasters to manageable spurts. "I mix the compost with used grounds given to me by the local coffee shop." She walked over to the hose attachment and turned the sprinkler to a gentle flow. "Headache from the nicotine patch?"

"Maybe. But could be a stomach bug." July grimaced. "I've been ill since I drank that tea Penny made for me, and I'm supposed to meet your accountant in a few minutes. She said she'd take me on as a client. If I have any money left." July clutched the belt holding up the broomstick skirt. Regardless of her outfit, she wore the trademark orangey-red lipstick the manufacturer renamed "July" in her honor. "Do you think Penny has a vindictive streak?"

Strange things had been happening since her mother returned. She hoped this wasn't the beginning of a plague. A frog invasion would freak out the customers.

AJ felt a furrow between her brows and rubbed at it to keep it from setting grooves. Penny King, AJ's housekeeper-cook, was one of Roger Worthington's former groupies. Hiring her three years ago had been a twist in irony, but July rarely visited Comfort, and Penny worked hard, didn't need a huge salary, and could cook like a chef—skills that trumped her fascination with a man who hadn't called the home phone in six months.

"Tea? Penny always brews a pot of coffee first thing."

"Penny said Inez brought the tea over from the cabin because the brand used to be my favorite back in the day— that would be the days that Inez even cared what I liked." July stepped out of the way of the automatic mister spraying water over petunias. "I guess I'm surprised your grandmother moved out here to live with you. When did that happen?"

And this was one more item on a long list of reasons they needed to talk more often. Things like … what finally made her mother — once and for all — ditch touring and, with it, her entire career. Or, things like why hadn't they talked before her mother sold the Tennessee farm to some developer who would put in a subdivision. Or why they'd not seen each other in almost a year. Or what happened to the last lover who supposedly stole July's new lyrics and offered them to a competitor. Or anything that would lead to them treating each other in a kinder, more mature way.

Developing a true friendship with her mother was a dream she'd babied almost as much as these basil roots.

But first, she had to keep her mother and grandmother from spending too much time near each other. Inez was irrational around July, and there was no love lost from the ex-daughter-in-law either. They say a marriage is both the strongest bond and the most fragile. The divorce from Roger Worthington shattered their little family of three, but the residual bitterness also broke the brittle bonds stretched between Texas and Tennessee. So far, keeping Inez from personal contact with July was a working strategy.

"I moved Gran here last autumn. I bought the cabin near the back of Granddad's property line and finally convinced her to leave the big house in San Antonio. She hated it here at first, said it brought back too many painful memories, but now she seems fine. It's like she's forgotten why she ever stayed away from Comfort."

July studied AJ for a long moment then walked over to another bin fostering baby plants. "So." She picked up the soil and lifted it to her nose, as if trying to determine the roast. "You're collecting human strays now?"

Stung, AJ pointed the hose toward the hybrid basil, letting the water shower the plants. If what her mother said was true, it went a long way toward explaining why AJ had always left a porch light on for both of her parents. "Gran was getting a little forgetful, and I needed help at the shop, so it worked out for both of us."

"I wonder how she's adjusted to not having symphony galas to plan."

When AJ was a child, she'd spent summers with her grandparents in San Antonio. Granddaddy George would always let her work at the dealerships, polishing the chrome on the new models, then he'd take her to the Worthington family farm on the weekends, just the two of them. Inez was too busy in the city to spend the weekend away. They had leased the Comfort pastures to local cattlemen by then, so she and her grandfather had few tasks. They'd fish in the creek, ride horses across the hills, and check off a list of odd jobs to preserve the two-story, limestone-bricked house he'd inherited from his mother. They'd eat at the local diner, where her grandfather still seemed to know everyone by name. Inez would welcome them back on Sunday nights with a fancy dinner and some trinket that would ensure her status as the favorite grandmother.

That had been a small competition as July's mother died when AJ was eight.

Regardless, AJ had fallen a little more in love with Comfort on every trip. The gray-blue hills, the town that still boasted a general store, and the old Worthington family home that creaked with every footstep—it was all an elixir that Nashville could never compete with. Even in high school, she'd chosen this destination over some exotic locales her parents would tour, and it was devastating when her grandfather died and the final heartache realized—that access to Comfort was over. Inez arranged for those who leased the land to lease the farmhouse, too.

Inez eventually transferred the deed for the land and the house to Roger, to get him to stay put in one place, but days before his bankruptcy hearing, he shuttled the deed to AJ. That silver lining to a dark period in their family dramas had become the greatest gift she'd ever received from a parent. The timing couldn't have been more perfect. Being recently dumped by a man she'd planned on marrying, she left behind the pieces of her broken heart, her unimpressive education, and the purposelessness she'd felt in a city of singers and songwriters. Claiming the keys to the abandoned family home had been a godsend.

She'd experimented with growing lavender on the land that her German ancestors had planted generations before. One row of Dutch lavender become another, and then she deviated to Royal Velvet and Hidcote varietals, until she found a heartiness and color that could weather the brutal extremes of the Texas Hill Country. Processing the oils and selling the bundles had led to her buying the caretaker's house on North Creek Road and opening the shop, Lavender Hill.

She'd never stopped treasuring the second chance for both the farm and her future. Inez had been there to cheer her on when no one else thought this idea had a chance to survive.

But July had asked about Inez. AJ had to wonder if moving her grandmother to Comfort had really been the best idea. The grandmother who loved her social gatherings, her palatial home, and nitpicking the man who'd bought the Worthington Chevrolet dealerships from her nine years ago had grown desolate in the last few months. Her housekeeper had called AJ to say Miss Inez would sleep in the recliner for days at a time and not remember to eat. Inez had not wanted to live "on the backside of the moon"—as she referred to Comfort—but there weren't a lot of options for an eighty-something woman who'd worked her entire life and was running out of things to give her a sense of purpose.

"I guess Gran contradicts the 'old dogs, a new trick' adage, and I like her company, so it works out," AJ said, thinking the words summed up their relationship.

July sighed with dramatic flair. "Are you saying I haven't been good company?"

The curse of working with plants all the time was that it made a person careless with people—particularly people who were more fragile than dandelions. "Mom, you're always good company. When you're around. But your condo is in Nashville, and you've traveled for years. Our relationship is what it is. Or was. Those days are history now, and with your retirement, we can have fun again. Want to play spades?"

July propped her hand on her hip. "You're such a Pollyanna. I don't know how you're my daughter."

Neither of her parents appreciated her simplistic approach to life.

They didn't recognize contentment because it wasn't born in angst and accompanied by a microphone and a soundboard. AJ avoided anything that appeared snarled with celebrity. She didn't even do crossword puzzles anymore, because "disgraced female Grammy-winner named after a summer month" would make a logical prompt.

"I don't mean silliness; I mean peacefulness." AJ had thought through a list of chores guaranteed to give her mother time to test life while doing something meaningful with her hands. Gardening was cheap therapy. "Without the scrutiny of Nashville, we can get to know each other again and, who knows, maybe become friends."

July bit her lip as if to keep tears from falling. "I need a friend, AJ. I have no one left."

AJ walked closer, dusting her hands on her shorts.

July glanced out the window to the yard fenced with aged oak trees. Her chin wobbled. "I have had little practice in saying this, but I appreciate what you've done for me over the last few days. You've rescued me."

It was moments like this that drove AJ to the garden. Dirt, roots, water, and sunshine, that's what made sense to her.

Confessions from a woman who had sung before sold-out stadiums and had dinners with the president weren't in her frame of reference. Thankfully, a life of music and fame was behind them. Forever.

That press release had been her second greatest gift from a parent.

AJ rubbed her left earlobe. "It was no big deal, Mom. You were flexible about trying the new products. I think the lavender and eucalyptus lotion you like will be a big seller. I will offer those as the special next week."

July's voice cracked as she said, "Everything is finally over."

AJ reached into her back pocket for a bandana. Since she didn't know the words to say, she brushed tears away from July's cheek.

July collapsed into AJ's arms with a sob. "You know, there's more to me than just the image on those record covers. I'm not sure what, but I hope I find out soon."

Before AJ could respond, July bolted. She heard the screen thud as her mother's shape faded into the haze of garden light reflected through the plastic liner over the door. Maybe the sun would bake out some of her mother's depression, but she suspected it would require a prescription.

AJ bent to search under the table for evidence someone had poured too much plant food into the water mix for the basil. The organic fertilizer had disappeared, and a box of rat-poison pellets was in its place. AJ removed the box and stood upright, wondering how *that* had gotten there.

"Reporting for duty," Inez announced from the opposite end of the greenhouse.

If July's voice was an indulgent whisky, Inez's was tumbling granite.

AJ double-checked her watch. Almost two o'clock. "You're late, water girl. I was expecting you during the morning rush. That's always been your favorite time to work."

Inez walked over to the sink and filled a watering can. "Oh, you know, I've been here and there."

"Don't bother watering today." AJ set the rat pellets on a high shelf. "Just turn on the drip irrigation for the established plants on the south end. We're going to lose this crop of basil."

"They look fine to me."

AJ turned the faucet off. "Gran, did you even water in here yesterday morning? I wrote your schedule on the blackboard."

"I wasn't here yesterday."

"You were here when Hector and Betty left last night. She told me you said you were going to the movies. Which I thought was odd because you haven't been to the movies since *Twister* gave you nightmares."

Inez ran her fingers into the dirt. "I didn't go to the movies."

AJ placed the hose on its hook and took one last look at the basil inventory. Before AJ could glance again to Gran, wondering why a woman with an opinion on everything was so quiet, she'd vanished.

The screen door bounced against its jamb, echoing the thud.

"Don't act surprised when you don't make your bonus this month," AJ called out, suspecting that only the plants heard her threat. Between her grandmother's erratic behavior and her mother's emotional chaos, she felt as drained as the succulents she kept along the dry creek bed.

Wiping her forehead, she checked the thermometer—it must be ninety degrees in the greenhouse. She'd heard that one employee had brought a keg filled with homemade lemonade and peach tea to keep everyone hydrated, so AJ decided she'd stop by the break room before she dug out the chemistry set she kept in the office, the one to analyze the pH of the soil.

Pushing through the door, AJ scanned the acre of land she'd transformed into a mixed-use outdoor room that acted as both storefront and how-to center for the native plants she sold at Lavender Hill. The mix of sunshine, mint, petunias, mulch, and lavender was heady for first-time customers, but try as she might, she almost never recognized the scent anymore unless someone commented on it.

And her customers raved about their experience at Lavender Hill. Many came from over a hundred-mile radius to make this shop part of their Texas Hill Country tour. The rows of cultivated lavender—particularly when they were at their peak—were the subjects of countless photographs and had become the backdrop for several marriage proposals.

The tourists strolled her lavender fields, admired the converted house that had become a studio for local art and organic treats, and inevitably left with plants, paintings, and gifts that had kept her financially solvent since the day she'd opened. Several customers wrote glowing endorsements on social media and travel sites, bragging about the walkable art space with the unique Texas garden aesthetic. But to her, it was just another day at work.

A man was standing under the carport where she presented those hand-mixed soils in chardonnay casks, and various plant tonics were propped on the shelves of a pharmacy cabinet she'd bought at an auction. He wasn't the most unusual customer she'd ever seen at Lavender Hill, but he was a standout from the tourists. His slacks and polo shirt contrasted with everyone else's shorts and ball caps. He was tall enough that, if he didn't duck his head soon, he'd get beaned by a hummingbird feeder.

Because he was a customer and not the yin to her garden's yang, she crossed the trail and approached him. "Hi. Those composted mixed soils are our special house blends. We have dark roast and mild. Which do you prefer?"

As he turned to see who was speaking to him, his warm brown eyes smiled, the creases fanning deep into his skin, advertising that he laughed often. "The dirt is like coffee?"

His Southern accent delighted her ears. It had been ages since she'd heard that sound, and his voice brought back those days growing up in Tennessee when syrup dripped from vowels. He really was off the beaten path. Almost no one with that background made it this far into Kendall County, unless they were on someone's deer lease.

Her hand drifted to one of the casks filled with crumbling black peat and let the silky mix filter between her fingers. "I create an organic compost with leftover grounds from Cup of Joe's coffee shop on High Street. I'm inclined to believe it's what gives a garden an extra boost."

He watched her hand sift the compost. "I thought I was looking at drums of ordinary dirt."

AJ stuffed down her sudden reaction, thinking he sounded like a ringer for a modern Rhett Butler. "There's nothing ordinary here."

His lips lifted higher on one side than the other. "I can tell."

AJ sizzled. She could almost see a plantation behind him. Snapping out of her fantasy, she wouldn't bother thinking about her sweat-stained T-shirt, socks draping over the mud-stained clogs, or the curling ends of her twin braids underneath her cowboy hat.

Oddly nervous, considering she always shared the Cup of Joe's secret, she tugged on one of her hoop earrings. She tried to be unobtrusive as she took in his wavy brown hair, broad shoulders, and sparkling eyes. "Are you looking for something in particular? Besides the lavender varieties we sell, there's also a large selection of herbs and native plants well suited to central Texas."

His gaze swept AJ, the oddly charming carport room, and the lavender fields rolling across acres beyond. "I'm not sure what the best way is to describe what I was looking for. I guess I was hoping just to recognize it."

A bumblebee reminded her of the pink rose growing up toward the roof of the carport. "We also have several antique varieties of rosebushes."

"No, nothing like that." He turned on his heel, seeming to take in the full measure of the cultivated yard and bedding plants in front of the house. "I guess I'll keep looking and enjoy the scenery. Those lavender fields are amazing."

"Then I encourage you to wander around." She brushed perspiration off her palms against her backside. Her heart was in her throat, and she felt as if she'd say something stupid if she didn't find breathing room away from this man. With absolutely no cheesy come-on, he'd sent her imagination straight to a dance hall and a slow-moving waltz. She knew by looking at him that he could do justice to a Pat Green ballad and a full moon. "Browse as long as you'd like," she blurted. "There's no rush at Lavender Hill."

Except for me, she thought, as she scurried past customers. *I haven't talked to an unfamiliar man in so long I'm like a junior high girl.* Taking the cottage porch steps two at a time, she dashed into the store, swearing she'd return that *Gone with the Wind* DVD to the library and pay the ridiculous fine.

She closed the front door gently, to not set off the tinkling bell, and eased through the rooms displaying art—and deep leather chairs for those who didn't derive their life's pleasure from wandering endlessly around a garden store—to the kitchen. She saw her mother and Keisha sitting together at the table. She set her sunglasses on the counter and took off her hat. Reaching for an insulated tumbler, AJ held it under the keg's spout, watching the peach-tea lemonade fill the cup. "The numbers must not be as bad as you first thought," AJ said, as July and Keisha turned to watch.

"Keisha assures me I'm not destitute."

Keisha tapped a pencil against the checkbook. "You know, if they still play your songs on the radio, someone's getting a royalty check. It's supposed to be you."

AJ had already attended Keisha's school of money management. Inherent distaste for carnage prevented her from witnessing her mother's indoctrination. "This will be a long and possibly painful conversation, since Keisha doesn't understand the Worthington-family approach to paperwork, so I'll just go stir the compost. I think I saw ladies interested in the bags of Provence Farms goat manure. Can't let it go to waste. Get it? Kali's goats' manure, from her farm; here, with my soil?"

July stared at AJ. "It's been so long since I'd been here, I'd almost forgotten you'd inherited your father's sense of humor."

AJ toasted her mother with the tea.

"Better than your grandmother's—" July looked down at the bankbook and added. "She doesn't have one."

Keisha held up a pencil. "Don't go far, AJ. I've got payroll checks needing a signature, and some publicist, a lady named Elizabeth, is running around the shop looking for you. She asked me if I knew where the first pages were. You have pages?"

She had no pages.

Elizabeth Adams would be furious. AJ regretted that she'd let herself get talked into doing a book about the mystique at Lavender Hill. She was the Worthington with zero talent for words—and that proof would be on display for all the world to see—and mock—if the book on learning to garden the Lavender Hill way ever made it to press.

"Leave the checks in the register, and I'll sign them later," AJ said, ignoring the tug on her conscience that she'd promised a rough draft this month.

Weaving behind customers, she stepped through the front door and stopped for a moment on the porch, practicing the excuse she'd give Elizabeth about the book. Could she invent statistics about her customers that painted them as just wanting to hire a landscaper, not needing an inspiration book?

Elizabeth had tracked AJ down at a county-wide lavender festival with a local winery and begged AJ to consider the book idea. Caught up in the moment and maybe relaxed by a sparkling wine, she agreed to the contract before she ever realized she was a disaster with writing instruments. She'd have to learn from this disaster that she was an easy mark for people with an overly developed persuasive skill. Like she'd not learned that already with the managers and agents that stalked Roger and July around Tennessee. But still, it was wise to be reminded of one's weaknesses.

A hand waved in front of her face.

"Hi, again."

AJ turned, without the protection of her sunglasses, and tried to look unfazed by her second brush with the handsome stranger. "Did you find what you were looking for?"

"Not yet, but I don't mind waiting. The experts say the best part of a treasure hunt is the journey." He leaned closer and dropped his voice. "I love a good hunt."

A fragile spark arced from her soul and seemed to connect with this man. Instantaneous attraction hadn't happened to her in a very long time.

"Maybe if you could tell me a little about what you want, I could steer you in the right direction," she said.

He slipped his hands deep into his pockets and looked at her with an intelligent gaze. "That's a tricky question. I thought I knew what I wanted, but now I'm not so sure."

"Annual or perennial?"

"Excuse me?" he asked.

"Do you want something temporary, a seasonal bloom, or do you want something long lasting?"

"There's a choice?"

"There's always a choice."

39

"I guess I want what lasts the longest," he said. "I don't enjoy short-term arrangements."

Imaginary innuendoes about midnight trysts and bridal bouquets flooded her brain.

"I'll be honest with you," he said wistfully. "I've never thought about a garden until today. You have, well, this place too, it has inspired me."

AJ covered the fires in her belly with folded arms. "Why don't we talk about a container garden and go from there?"

"Sure, let's start there. I should know your name if we'll do business together."

Stepping off the porch, she stood in a circle of sunshine outlined by parsley, thyme, and the soft, pale herb everyone called "lamb's ear," and wondered how best to introduce herself. Did she play down her role at Lavender Hill or go with the "Ms. Worthington" approach? Since he seemed to reach into his pocket for a business card, maybe she should polish her introduction.

"AJ?" a familiar voice called from the porch.

She looked beyond the man to where her mother leaned out the front door. A ratty cowboy hat was pinched between July's fingers, as if it might breed cooties.

"You left this in the kitchen," her mother said, lifting it for inspection.

In glancing back to the man, she saw his gaze was no longer fastened on her. AJ watched the lights in the stranger's eyes brighten to stadium intensity, while the anticipation bubbling in her stomach turned to acid. She didn't know how to label his interest in her mother, but he'd found what he was looking for at Lavender Hill.

He stepped over the cat near his feet. "July Sands?"

AJ saw her mother's face stiffen with wariness.

As she watched the man ease over to grip July's hands in an embrace, AJ wondered what was at stake besides the obvious. After all the years and the insulting flirtations she'd endured, she should have learned every trick men used to

40

get to her famous mother. How foolish had she been to think this one might be different?

Customers brushed past, and AJ reached toward a pot of begonias, pinching off the spent blooms as if they were traitors.

It was time to use the control she'd honed from keeping rodents, particularly that sneaky armadillo, out of her lavender fields. If she was going to let July stay in Comfort and, hopefully, restore herself to something befitting an actual mother, then AJ would have to implement a containment plan.

She gazed across the tops of parked cars, planning a strategy for keeping her mother safe from those who might gawk. Locking July in at the house seemed drastic, but AJ had waited for years for her mother to tire of the road, and now that she was finally here, there wasn't anything she wouldn't do to fortify the walls of a sanctuary.

Turning, AJ decided the first thing she needed to do was find her .12-gauge.

That was how she had finally gotten rid of that armadillo.

Chapter Five

July hurried down the cottage steps, calling out, "AJ!"

Luke followed July, stunned that the beautiful woman he'd been talking to about dirt turned around in response to the name. That wholesome, farm girl-meets-*Sports-Illustrated* model was Autumn Joy Worthington? Only child of the world's sexiest singing duo and heir to a catalog of music that would be the envy of every recording company in the nation? *That* Autumn Joy?

When he talked to her on the phone the other day, he'd pictured a woman in starched scrubs, grumpy from nursing celebrities at a wellness facility. Something tickled his nose with a stringent aroma. The scorching heat, bumblebees, and butterflies proved what his head had not wanted to accept. Lavender Hill really was a garden store with acres of lavender fields behind it, and that woman really was a complete surprise.

Luke's blood had caught fire the moment he met AJ's flashing eyes, easy smile, and honeyed skin that made him hear a loop from his memory of the Beach Boys' classic song about California girls. He hadn't felt that kind of reaction in a very long time. Too long, if he was being truthful. He'd wondered if there was a girl alive who'd pique his interest anymore after dating an endless string of women who'd chased him because of the financial portfolio that would follow a wedding ring.

Jaded by pop star wannabees and their entourages, and the pretense of their attitudes, he'd been so stunned by this woman's effortless beauty that he didn't even take a minute to connect the dots of who she was. The daughter of July Sands and Roger Worthington looked nothing like her parents, yet now, as he studied her body fleeing across the pebbled walkway, he could see the willowy frame she'd inherited from her mother and the bearing that mimicked Roger Worthington's swagger.

"AJ, don't act like you can't hear me call your name." July skipped down the steps, trying to keep up with her daughter.

This rebuke sounded familiar. He chuckled, remembering his mother and sister in just this tiff. He stepped down to the ground again, stunned by what was happening here in a yard filled with cultivated flower beds, graveled paths, and plants growing from pots that looked rescued from some farm surplus store. July and her daughter—and he hadn't even had to work that hard to find them.

He dropped his hands into his pockets, knowing he'd be staying in Comfort for a while. Easy though this first round had been, he'd bet he'd have to earn his crazy, stupid salary to get July to agree to hear him out. It was a good thing he'd left his hotel reservation at the Comfort Commons open-ended. There was a five-foot-six female that looked like she might have an opinion on anything that her mother signed, and it intrigued him to consider what bartering with the daughter might involve.

"Thanks for bringing my hat." AJ turned around with lightning-strike precision to grab the straw brim.

July latched onto her daughter's arm. "I want you to meet Luke English. He's a friend of my old agent."

AJ's gaze shifted from her mother and hardened to stone as it landed on him. "Luke ... *English*?"

He crossed the pathway, wondering if he'd ever heard his name pronounced with such disdain. Usually, family members view him more like the leprechaun carrying a pot of gold. He wasn't sure what he'd done to merit this disapproval, but if he did nothing else today, he would get that girl to smile at him again like she had five minutes before.

AJ straightened her shoulders. "Mr. English called for you a few days ago. Out of respect for your privacy, I told him I didn't know who you were."

He'd enjoyed the sass and vinegar from her banter that day. "She'd said Lavender Hill was not a 'lost and found.'"

July turned to face Luke. "AJ protects me. I decided to think it's charming."

"No one knows exactly why you're here, Mr. English. It's obvious you're not looking for plants. Oh, wait, you said you were on a treasure hunt. For the record, Mom's broke."

Two customers, standing close enough to hear the conversation, dropped the pretense they weren't eavesdropping and looked at him as if he'd become a sociopath or a thief — or both.

"Maybe my first inclination wasn't to buy plants," he defended. "But now I could spend hours wandering this place." He spread his arm in a wide arc. "You've created a masterpiece. It's inspiring."

AJ folded her arms across her chest. Her glare dared him to be honest.

He was truthful, but he could tell by the set to her shoulders she'd believe a spaceship was landing on a rosebush before she believed him. "But I was looking for July Sands. I'd like to talk to her about how she got to this point of retirement and if it has to remain permanent."

AJ's green eyes turned to jade. "She's finished. The music business burned her, chewed her up, and now she's turned her back on the road and moved in with me."

Those two customers were looking at July with new scrutiny.

"I read the press release," he said, closing the gap. "But things aren't always what they seem. It would be a crime to silence July's voice and cut her off from creating new music."

"Oh, Luke," July sighed, collapsing against his shoulder. "I feel so confused. My manager said it was time to retire because no one was coming to my shows anymore. But I don't know, I can't promise I really feel done. I've been itching to get my guitar out and play ever since I arrived. I guess I don't know what else to do with myself."

AJ moved toe-to-toe with Luke. "My mother's not well, Mr. English. She needs her rest. She might even be contagious."

"AJ!" July looked around to see who might spread this rumor.

"You said you were feeling bad," AJ countered.

"Because of the spoiled tea." July's eyes grew wistful. "I'd like to talk to Luke about my career. It might be easier to put it all in perspective, now that I'm officially off the road."

"Don't rush into anything, Mom. Give yourself some time to think this through. Maybe talk again after the holidays?"

Luke saw no relaxing to AJ's stance. "By holidays, do you mean Christmas?"

"Is that too soon?" AJ asked.

By Christmas he'd have five or six new clients on an alarming schedule of talk shows and TV specials, three albums that needed splashy events, not to mention the day-to-day work of marketing efforts to maintain the company's established performers. "Well, I only have a few days to spend in Texas, and I'd like to find out if July has any interest in writing a memoir or some compilation of favorite songs. As a marketing guy, I'm supposed to be on the lookout for ways to showcase talent, and here is, without a doubt, one of the best voices we've ever had in the industry."

July's eyes rounded with surprise. "A book! Who knew?"

AJ threw her hands into the air. "There'll be no end to the madness."

Luke chuckled. July's daughter, standing in a bed of pink flowers, was the most vivid person he'd seen in months. "What exactly are you afraid of, AJ?"

"Who says I'm afraid of anything?"

The set of your posture, the flares in your eyes, the tension radiating through your fingertips. Maybe because he was altogether too aware of her legs and the blond hair woven into braids, and maybe because he had enough years in the trade, he knew there'd be no easy answer. There were scars attached to her attitude.

"It's obvious you care for your mother," Luke said, running through his dossier on July. "But I'm not here to hurt her. I want to help. I want to celebrate everything your mother did to make contemporary music memorable."

"You don't want to celebrate anything but the commission you'll make when Mom is tossed back onto the trampoline of has-been music stars. I swear, if you even say the words 'reality show,' I'll have you thrown out of Comfort faster than you can say fifty thousand dollars." AJ heaved a breath. "And don't think I won't. The county judge is one of my best customers."

July's head pinged between them like she was watching tennis.

Luke almost faltered. AJ had to know, one professional to another, that money was a natural outgrowth, but it didn't have to be the motivation. Honestly, if July Sands had been his client all those years ago, he'd have had her in rehab long before it was popular. He could have saved her, if only he'd had the right.

Obviously, the only way to spend time with July would be at the whims of a suntanned woman in a shabby hat. He would have to fight for the opportunity to get close to July. For a man known at his company as "the Fixer," having to get creative again was heady.

"I'm staying in Comfort for as long as it takes to talk to July about this idea." Luke enjoyed seeing the disbelief splash across AJ's face. "And to convince you I won't ruin your mother."

Her eyes blinked, and a sash closed over the windows that revealed her heartache. "She's already ruined," AJ said, stepping out of their circle of conflict. "But I won't let the jackals pick at her bones. She's in Comfort to recover, find herself, and become something new. Something far, far away from the long country roads of Tennessee."

"AJ," July sighed. "Don't–"

Luke put his hand on July's arm. "Let her have her say."

AJ put her hat on her head as if it were a crown. "And you, Mr. English, need to leave. There's no glory for you to gain here."

Chapter Six

Comfort, Texas   May 4, 1954

Inez leaned her head out the window of the car George had bought and breathed in the Hill Country air. She'd grown so accustomed to the cigarette odor of Austin that she'd almost forgotten what purity smelled like.

"We'll not visit in town just yet." George winked at her. "It's nice enough, but if Momma gets wind we stopped for a soda before going to the house, she'd have my head."

Inez had heard so many stories of Momma Worthington that she prepared to meet the First Lady of Texas. "You should tell me the history of Comfort, since there's a fair this weekend."

George shrugged. "Oh, it's not much of a story. Just a bunch of German settlers who decided they'd had enough of the government telling them what to do, so they settled this area and vowed everyone could do what they wanted. Liked to call themselves freethinkers."

She'd come from a county settled by outlaws, and they were proud of their free thinking, too. Maybe the Germans were better citizens. "Sounds respectable."

"Momma and Daddy are staunch Lutherans and revere their German traditions, although one of the great-grands changed the family name, since it was hard to pronounce."

"So, they're like these freethinkers?" Inez had heard a lot of talk in Austin about people wanting to break free from the confines of society, but she didn't know if it was the same as those here in Comfort. Judging by the buildings, nothing much had changed here in a long time. "Are they kind of progressive?"

George laughed, and it cracked the seriousness in the car. "They're as rigid as the day is long. They mean well, but they're hardworking folks. And church is important to them — me too."

"I understand about hard work." She rubbed at a knife scar on her finger. "My daddy worked hard all the time, taught me everything I know about showbiz."

George cut his gaze to her. "We're not talking about the same thing. And don't tell Momma that your daddy owns a bar. She gets bent out of shape about nightclubs, the people who spend their bucks on booze."

Inez rubbed her earlobe. "Well, dang, what am I supposed to tell her? I sing in a club."

"Don't tell her anything. All you have to do is sit there, smile, and look pretty."

Inez wasn't sure how that would go over, because they were here for the whole weekend, and she couldn't keep a secret for nothing.

They'd been lucky to get two days off in a row, between George's classes and her work schedule, but thanks to the influenza outbreak, they'd both had their work schedules shortened. George had big news to tell his parents, and he said he needed to do it in person.

Inez saw the folks of Comfort turning to watch them drive past. She wasn't sure what they were thinking, because they all looked as if a new car was some strange thing, but maybe it was because the couple in the coupe were so young and beautiful.

She glanced over at George.

He was really almost too pretty to be a man. She was jealous sometimes of his perfect blond hair and smooth skin. He might not look a lot like the rough-and-tumble men from her world, but George was safe. He was kind, smart, and didn't even once threaten to hit her. That counted for a lot in her book.

As they turned down a road outside of town, paved streets gave way to dirt roads and endless miles of ranches. Untamed hills in the distance and short, scrappy trees broke up what was a landscape for coyotes.

"I thought you said your family grew peas."

George chuckled again. "Momma grows peas, corn, and many vegetables. But they mostly raise cattle to sell. Daddy keeps a stocked pond, chickens, and pigs to have food to put on the table, because we sell everything he raises."

Inez frowned. "So, no steak dinner for us?"

"I didn't eat my first steak until I went to Austin."

Inez looked again at the man she'd recently promised to marry. She'd thought his family was better-off than this. Not that it mattered. George sold cars at the Chevrolet dealership, and they would make a lot of money once his commissions added up. As they turned off one dirt track onto another, she saw the fence posts carve out a path for them. Following the ruts, they eased around a few turns, and the valley opened before them like a picture. Hills had materialized from nowhere, and there was an easy river, tilled farm fields, and barns that looked just like the ones she'd known back in Gladewater.

Peace settled over Inez. The country air was working its magic on her.

George parked the car in front of a two-story limestone house that had floor-to-ceiling windows and a wraparound porch. The limestone had faded to a buttery yellow, but the green shutters were crisp, and the porch swept clean. This place bore no resemblance to the tiny walk-up apartment she and George shared over the dry cleaners.

The thin shade of the tree covered the car as George leaned over the gearshift and took her hand. "I'm so happy to bring you home. There's nothing so special as this place. I hope you love it like I do."

Inez smelled freshly turned dirt in the air. "I already do."

She waited for George to walk around and open her car door. As she put her heels in the soil of the Worthington ranch, Inez glanced up to the porch where she saw two older people standing in the doorway. Neither of them looked like they were expecting company. The woman was wiping her big hands on an apron. Her lips looked straighter than two-by-fours.

George drew in a ragged breath. "This will be harder than I thought."

She didn't think they looked all that awful. Sure, they were glowering and wore funeral clothes, but George was their darling. He'd told her so himself.

The story was that he was the last of the four Worthington brothers, the only one not killed in the war. That was only because he'd been too young to be drafted. He'd said he had grown up hearing the gossip that painted him as a "momma's boy." But George said he couldn't control his momma's mind any more than he could bring a smile back to his father's face.

As Inez stood taller, smoothing out the wrinkles in her red skirt, she wasn't sure the woman standing at the front door looked much like the doting mother she'd imagined. But she did admit she didn't have a lot of experience with mothers, devoted or otherwise. She'd have to give this one a try and hoped she'd fit.

Chapter Seven

Sometimes while tilling the soil, a gardener encounters rocks and clay. Work patiently around the hard spots. They'll break up eventually, and you'll appreciate the ease you made for new roots.
— "Lessons from Lavender Hill"

As AJ drove over the tar-topped road running behind the shop, past the lavender fields, and toward the house, she critically gazed at the mounds growing in neat, oyster-shell-lined rows. Her goldendoodle loped between the mounds, rubbing his fur against the stalks and inviting lavender oil onto his coat.

Slowing down, she propped her elbow on the windowsill and waved, calling out, "Hey, Beans," to redirect the dog out of the fields. Though he'd smell fantastic, he was too gregarious to watch his step. Tomorrow she'd send one of the yard crew out to check the plants. Someone must have gone into the fields for cuttings and accidentally let the dog tag along.

She screened her eyes from the sunset as she drove the mile and a half separating the shop of Lavender Hill from the Worthington family farmhouse. Her great-great-grandfather inherited a land grant in the 1910s—turning it into an active cattle ranch. Over the years, family members had sold off the acres until this spindly twenty-acre tract was all that remained. She was grateful, as the one who now held the purse strings of the property, that she didn't have to pay taxes on what had been. If she hadn't figured out how to make the garden store flourish, she doubted she could have held onto any of it.

At the base of a gentle hill where the road forked from the lavender fields on the left and a barren valley on the right, she followed the road and made sure Beans stayed center in her rearview mirror. His tongue lapped at his mouth, as the sunlight painted him in the glow of happiness.

The two-story farmhouse, a remnant of the original land grant, rose from the soil near the creek tributary and a small stand of live oak trees. A few years back, she'd re-painted the shutters dark green and painstakingly stripped and oiled the iron hinges. She'd built and painted white flower boxes. Against the yellowed limestone, the pop of seasonal color gave a timelessness to the house. She couldn't imagine living anywhere else.

As soon as she'd been able to afford the expense, she'd torn out a few interior walls and remodeled the kitchen and upstairs bathrooms, leaving everything else as close to original as possible. Pulling into a ramshackle garage built in the '70s, she vowed that if she made a profit from that silly book Elizabeth Adams wanted to publish, she would treat herself to an attached garage, complete with a spacious laundry room, a walk-in pantry, and dog-grooming station.

Climbing out of her truck, AJ bent to run her hands through Beans's lavender-scented fur, relishing that he smelled like a bar of French soap. "Love to you, too," she murmured, enjoying the licks across her wrist. "You have some explaining to do, Beans, but here," she reached into her tote bag and pulled out a treat. "One of the product reps remembered you from her last trip out and brought a present."

The dog barked his approval and snatched the beef-scented cookie before leaping toward the fading sunshine. She followed his path, thankful to close the door on a day that had outlasted her energy reserves. She turned back when a question wiggled her memory. Looking over her shoulder to the corner of the garage where she stored bug spray, tablets for the septic system, and rat pellets, she saw there was a vacant space on the shelf. The rat poison she'd found in the greenhouse had been the box she kept here at the house.

AJ rubbed her earlobe, wondering who'd have known she kept the pellets here and who'd have taken them to the greenhouse. And why? There was a slew of cats on the company payroll whose only job was to entertain the Lavender Hill customers and chase off rodents.

While walking toward the house, she almost overlooked the assortment of vehicles parked under the oak tree near the front porch. AJ stopped. Beans came back to nudge her knees forward. The lights she'd strung for last year's outdoor Thanksgiving dinner now twinkled with fresh bulbs. George Strait crooned from portable speakers.

AJ glanced over her shoulder, waiting for her friends to jump from behind the propane tank and yell "surprise," but it wasn't her birthday. Nor was it anyone's birthday in her little clan of women.

The sound of tires crushing gravel drew AJ's attention to the driveway. A small SUV parked behind an unfamiliar sedan.

"Keisha?" she asked, looking twice at the driver.

Keisha climbed from her vehicle. "My goodness, girl. I would have thought you'd have at least showered. I can smell you from here."

"The last customers left the shop fifteen minutes ago." AJ glanced down to the dirt stains on her shirt. She reached into her pocket for her cell phone and saw she'd missed several calls from Penny. Resetting the mute button, she asked, "Is there a party I didn't know about?"

"July invited me for dinner after I asked if could pick up her bank statements and royalty reports, but I heard nothing that sounded like a party."

"Mom has royalties?"

"I sure hope so, because if she's this behind on her bills, the taxman probably hasn't been paid either."

AJ noticed her favorite tablecloth and candles styled on a table set on the front porch. She climbed the shallow steps and opened the front door. Penny was standing next to the entry table, holding a platter of prosciutto-wrapped cantaloupe, shards of curling parmesan, nuts, and strawberries sitting proudly on a bed of lavender buds.

Penny stepped backward, allowing Keisha to enter. "It's about time you showed up," she growled to AJ. "I was this close to closing that store myself." AJ glanced at where Penny pinched her finger and thumb together and saw a shred of parmesan trapped between the emphasis.

AJ kicked off her clogs before she stepped onto the rug that divided the living and dining areas. "Sorry, I didn't realize I'd muted my phone until now. It's been a wild day."

Penny winked. "I heard all about it. Miss Inez has been gaga about the man who dropped into Lavender Hill today. She stopped by on her way to her cabin to tell me about him, and you'd have thought she'd seen Elvis."

AJ set her tote on the round entry table, catalogs and reports spilling out and knocking into the vase filled with bachelor buttons, buttercups, lavender stems, and wild mustard. She didn't even have to work hard to guess the identity of that mystery man. She glanced into the living room. "Is Gran still here, or has she gone to her place?"

"She said she had to go home to freshen up." Penny moved to set the platter on the coffee table. "And don't scare off our guest, either. He's in the kitchen getting down the good dishes from the cupboard. We will eat on the porch, and I've got to keep him around at least through dessert. I made cheesecake."

AJ's nervous stomach gave birth to butterflies—or maybe wasps. She wouldn't deny the thought of Luke English ignited a reaction, one that made her itch for her insect repellant. "Care to tell me why *this person* is in my home?"

Keisha reached for a napkin. "And is it too soon to sample your appetizers?"

Penny wiped her hands on her apron. "Well, I couldn't offer him the usual chips and salsa, now could I? A man with this much sophistication is used to the best. I wonder if they'll have some of Kali's goat cheese tomorrow at the farmers' market?"

Glancing up the staircase, AJ ached for her shower. Not that she wanted to bathe to make a good impression on anyone, but because she could stretch a shower out to include a pedicure and manicure—a veritable spa experience. He'd leave by nine, right?

"Didn't your mother tell you?" Penny smirked. "Luke is here to talk July out of retiring. He wants her to write a book. I told him he should interview me for a behind-the-scenes glimpse into July's lifestyle. Boy, do I have stories."

Keisha laughed, but AJ felt her gaze lured past Keisha and drawn to the man leaning against the antique buffet table in her dining room. He had changed his polo shirt for what appeared to be an expensive dress shirt. His smile offered a million apologies.

If she was being honest, she could see where her mother might have been deceived by a smile and fine clothing. This man wouldn't even have to work hard to get exactly what he wanted. But he was not welcome in her world, not after she'd found out who he worked for. He'd have to find some other celebrity to save.

Luke approached her with a confident stride. "I know you've had a long day, AJ, and the last thing you wanted was a houseful of people, but July was insistent that I see what you've done in remodeling your family's farmhouse and stay for supper. So, if it's any consolation, I promise to cater lunch for your entire Lavender Hill staff tomorrow to make up for this inconvenience."

AJ glanced at Keisha and watched Penny re-enter the hallway. Was anyone else put off by his arrogance? Did he think that coming in and waving a magic wand of money and big gestures would erase the knowledge of what the music business really created? "That's nice, Mr. English," she said through gritted molars. "As hard as they work, they'd appreciate the lunch. But I'd be grateful if you didn't lobby my staff to help you win your cause to lure Mom back on the road. They don't know the wringer Nashville puts a person through."

"Please call me Luke." He shrugged in the way a spider might to a fly. "We got off to a rocky start, but I want to do everything in my power to make sure you understand I'm not here to lobby anyone but July. She and I have an important conversation brewing. Everything else about my time in Comfort is different."

AJ rolled her shoulders, feeling new knots form over the familiar ones as she put on her armor. "People in town either love or hate July Sands. They will see everything you do as manipulation."

July stepped between the swinging doors that kept the butler's pantry separate, a breadstick propped between her fingers in place of a cigarette. "Really, AJ, you mean you will see everything Luke does as a conspiracy. I know you have my best interests at heart, but Luke is just here to talk. I'm a big girl. I can decide what I want."

"Last month you decided you wanted to retire," she said, regretting the sarcasm.

July sighed. "A woman has the prerogative to change her mind, right?"

AJ let the weight of a long day settle deep into her muscles instead of on her tongue. Sometimes that worked.

"I'm grabbing an iced tea, and I'm taking a shower," she said, deciding to postpone battle until they were on a level field. "Y'all do whatever you want. You're going to, anyway."

"But I've made a chicken, with that shallot sauce and orzo, and your favorite steamed veggies." Penny trailed behind her like a kite's tail. "Here's a pomegranate spritzer to get the evening started."

AJ stared at the crystal. With condensation on the glass, she was tempted to gulp the drink. As it was, she'd seen the ravages of too many tours, bad press, and sleazy managers to capitulate over a wine cooler. Though no one else seemed to care, she would stand up to this no-good, smooth-talking executive and stop the insanity sure to follow in the aftermath of his deals.

After her shower.

Chapter Eight

The beauty of a well-planned garden is the surprises that bloom every season — the flowers left behind by bird droppings or a windblown seed. Nature is mischievous. — "Lessons from Lavender Hill"

AJ was halfway up the stairs when she heard the swoosh of the front door opening and turned around.

"I'm here," Inez Worthington sang, as if she were walking out onto the stage of the Grand Ole Opry.

AJ clutched the smooth banister. Panic created a tighter grip. She'd been so careful to keep Inez and July distracted from crossing paths for the last two weeks. Gran's cabin was a good quarter mile down the other side of the fork in the road, you couldn't even see the rooftop from here. July was reluctant to leave the farmhouse, or her bed for that matter, so it had worked.

Her grandmother swirled her Christmas-plaid taffeta skirt around her ankles like she was a schoolgirl showing off a prom dress. An edgy grin twisted her bubblegum-pink lipstick. "Let the games begin."

"Gran," AJ cajoled, as she hurried down the stairs. "What are you doing dressed like that?"

Inez sparkled with a gleam that seemed too diabolical for AJ's comfort.

"I've come for the party. I came to see that good-looking man that followed me around town today. And to eat Penny's cooking. But mostly, for the man. I felt I should dress up."

"I told you." AJ scooted down the last step, glancing into the living room where Keisha and Luke were sipping cocktails. "We'll organize a welcome-home dinner for Mom in a neutral setting."

"What are you squawking about?" Inez asked. "I've got myself a date with a handsome man. They told me to be here at seven sharp, and I'm here."

It was 7:30, but she would not correct her grandmother.

AJ felt the collective stares of people moving into the hallway. She'd never told Keisha the whole messy family history. It hadn't seemed necessary, because for the last few years she'd been living a quiet, productive life in a town where everyone knew the family name—but no one ever held her in contempt for it. A prize she valued beyond measure. Now, Keisha would see July's checkbook and discover that her mother was living beyond her means and too proud to be honest about the faith she'd put in shoddy advisers. Even AJ had cut off the handouts to her mother, because more times than not there was no logical explanation for where the money went.

Penny knew most of the details as she was the one who collected the mail, answered the house phone, and played Bunco with a group from the library. Plus, she'd known July and Roger from before their fall from fame, picked the parts of their story that put Roger in the best light, and then answered questions accordingly. That meant July was always cast as the devil. But few in town asked about the former music stars anymore, and that's the way AJ preferred things to continue.

Once word got out that Gran was wearing Christmas clothes in April, that might change. It was bad enough that her staff was keeping a tally of Inez stories, but a new flare-up between Inez and July would send everything through the roof. She'd need time to formulate a strategy—since the two women were known to have loud, heated words about everything from the color of the sky to whose idea it was to name a baby girl "Autumn Joy."

"You know what, Gran?" AJ said, feeling her own filter tilt. "This is my house, and no one asked me if I wanted a party. I think it's time everybody went home. How did you get here? Did you walk or drive? I'll drive you home."

In what should have been a power rush for her, she realized that she might as well have been talking to Beans.

Inez waltzed into Luke's welcoming embrace like he was her beau.

AJ turned around to see who else just witnessed this weird behavior, but July must have ducked into the kitchen, because Keisha was the only other person standing close enough to hear.

"Are you kicking us out just because you weren't consulted for dinner?"

"I'm not being a brat." Then thought maybe she was. "I'm exhausted."

"So, go shower. Put on some fresh clothes." Keisha sized her up. "Lord knows you need to eat. Once you get a little food in you, we'll figure out what's going on in your household. Okay?"

A tattoo pounded under AJ's left eyebrow. All she wanted was a shower and a pass to go straight to bed.

"Seriously, you're still standing here?" Keisha's gaze tallied the levels of AJ's dirt stains. "Go, with your old smelly self, and get cleaned up. You'll feel so much better after you wash your hair."

AJ glanced at the curling ends of her braids and saw compost where there should be blonde. "There's no way this day could get any worse, right?"

"Once you put this in perspective, you'll see that there are reasons to smile, not to cry." Keisha's gaze drifted to Luke. "Lots of reasons."

"Just when I was feeling good about things," AJ muttered as she turned back for the stairs. "You fall for him too."

Keisha's chuckle was as warm as hot fudge.

AJ closed the door on the bathroom with more force than necessary, but that act of petulance helped release steam. She folded her clothes into the laundry basket, careful not to shake dirt onto the extravagant floor mat she'd given herself last year for Christmas.

Standing under hot water, AJ turned this way and that, trying to find a set of muscles that didn't need comfort. Turning the shower massage on, she stood and let the pulsing water work out the kinks. One half of her brain wanted to tussle with the dichotomy going on in her house. The other half wanted to set all that aside and enjoy the profits of a day that topped a similar day from last year's sales by 25 percent. As she squeezed lavender-geranium-eucalyptus shampoo into her palm, she attributed the increase to the Lavender Hill product line she'd developed over the winter.

She smelled the shampoo lather, letting the scent permeate her brain. Many people asked her if she was sick of fragrance after all the time she spent cultivating it, but she knew the varietals of flowers much like a winemaker knows the differences in grapes. The challenge to mix pleasing scents and essential oils was as exacting for her as she imagined Meritage was for a vintner.

She stared at the white tiles.

That thought about mixing scents might work well in Elizabeth's book. Not that she'd scribbled anything down as of yet, but she hoped she'd remember the idea when she had a few minutes to stare at the blank pages. What was it she'd just thought of — challenging mix? Like wine?

Capping the bottle, she ran her thumb along the edge of the periwinkle label. The print was too small to read, and customers with bad eyesight might not know which bottle was conditioner and which was shampoo. Maybe she should try different sized bottles to distinguish the two or —

"How much longer are you going to be in there?"

AJ dropped the bottle on her big toe, crying out in surprise at hearing Penny's voice in the bathroom.

"You okay?" Penny asked, sounding much closer to the shower than she had a second ago.

"A knock would have been nice." AJ peered around the curtain. "I feel like I live in the dorms again."

"Price you pay for having women in the house." Penny folded her arms over her apron. "Am I holding dinner for you or not?"

"Not!" AJ yanked the curtain closed. "I didn't plan this party, so don't wait on me. I may drive into town for a burger."

Penny harrumphed. "This dinner was your mother's idea. You know she can't resist a pretty face. Although what Luke sees in her is beyond me. Do you know how demanding she is? This morning she insisted I make her an egg-white omelet. Who eats just the egg white? And, I overheard her on the phone with some man. She was stringing him along, telling him she needed more money. Could it have been her drug dealer?"

AJ gritted her teeth. "I'm not having this argument with you."

"If you'd exercised a little more caution before turning this place into the Betty Ford Center, we might not have an argument at all."

"Go downstairs, Penny. It's your job to keep Gran from hitting Mom."

"She's not my grandmother."

"Yeah, well, I'm willing to bet you're the one who told Gran to dress for dinner, so you get to deal with her."

When the door slammed shut, AJ let out her breath.

Water sluiced over her face, and she wiped her eyes. There would be no tears now, but she'd be reckless to think someone wouldn't be crying before tonight was over.

She hoped it wasn't her.

She hadn't cried in years, and she didn't want to start now.

Chapter Nine

Luke seated Inez at the table and then claimed the chair positioned between her and July, going into buffer mode.

He caught Keisha's gaze over the candles and saw the first flicker of amusement since everyone had moved to the porch. This didn't feel funny to him. There was a weird vibe in the air, and it was bitter. Like maybe he was the only one not clued in to the big secret—the one where at this address they hold a man hostage, torture him, and flambé his parts on the barbecue.

July inspected the empty stemware.

Penny set the platters on the table before sitting down next to Keisha.

Luke glanced toward the French doors, hoping AJ would materialize.

"You're a gutsy fella, I'll say that." Inez offered him the tea pitcher.

"Does anyone have something stronger than tea?" July asked. "Wine, bourbon?"

Penny handed the platter of chicken to Keisha and whispered loudly, "Stock up. When this plate gets to Miss Inez, she takes enough for two grown men."

Keisha speared a few slices of meat. "Thanks for the warning."

July pushed fingers into her forehead as if she had a headache. "I'm going in for a Chardonnay. Can I bring one back for anyone else?"

Keisha waved her hand.

Luke watched July nod in response but saw that she didn't seem to know which cabinet they stored the wine in, based on the fact that she was randomly opening cupboards in the butler's pantry.

His internet search that afternoon had yielded tons of celebrity photos of the Worthingtons but was skimpy on the details he wanted to know—like did Roger and July raise AJ in Texas or at their farm in Tennessee? Why was a beautiful single woman so comfortable fifty miles away from modern civilization? He'd read that July and Roger wrote their song "Autumn Joy" based on their feelings at the birth of their only child, but there'd been few scant photos of AJ since that album cover of her as an infant, and most of those that popped up were when she was a teenager, attending events with one of her parents. He'd thought she looked out of place, wearing homespun-styled clothing while someone in Hollywood had dressed her parents, but maybe July and Roger had a different code for their child.

Knowing there had to be more details, he'd left a message with one of his friends who worked at *The Tennessean* to get family background, but so far, all he had to work with was what he saw at this table, and he was receiving mixed signals.

Penny winked at him. Was that her foot kicking his shin under the table?

Keisha took a wineglass from July, but she spoke to Luke. "So, tell us about your life in Nashville. There must be many glamorous things going on in the music capital."

Luke dusted off his patented answer. "Nashville earned its reputation with a lot of grace and guts."

Keisha leaned forward. "Do you know Keith Urban or Faith Hill?"

Luke smiled like this was the first time someone had asked him this question. "No, I haven't had the pleasure."

"I do." July sipped from her glass. "I even worked with Faith once. She was a studio singer for me back in the day."

Keisha's eyes widened. "How cool is that? Tell me all about her. Is she as sweet as she seems? And what about that cute husband of hers?"

July shrugged. "Can someone pass the orzo?"

Keisha leaned forward, "And what about—"

Inez waved her fingers to interrupt. "You know she'd be nothing without Roger Worthington, so don't even get her going about who she might know and who she doesn't. If she had an ounce of graciousness, she'd give credit where credit is due. Isn't that right, Penny?"

Penny drew an imaginary line over her mouth and threw away the key.

Luke saw a flash of hatred in Inez's eyes. Such a tiny woman to pack so much resentment.

July looked as if they had wrung her out, and she was drying in the sun.

He glanced again to his right. Inez's eyes glowed with indignation, so he'd guess that the issues in Roger and July's acrimonious divorce were still unsettled. Penny seemed to be on Inez's side of things. Keisha, well, he did not know what part she played in the dynamic. Did she work at Lavender Hill too?

He regretted that he'd flown out of the office with such pitiful preparation.

As the silence around the table turned frosty, Luke sipped his tea and then leaned back in his chair. "July, you might not even remember this, but I once worked on your road crew, the Tangled Southern Tour."

July's eyes narrowed like she was filing through the notecards in her memory bank.

Maybe she'd blocked that summer, because that was when she fell in love with the new guitarist in her band and all her marital problems hit the press, with paparazzi photos to corroborate. "I rode with the crew on their bus, so you probably thought I was just one of the many guys in a T-shirt and jeans."

July stared at him like she was trying to place him. "Which tour?"

He shrugged, hoping he would not dredge up some memory that would make her want to kick him out, too. "You were going through North Georgia with that new country album, and I was in between college semesters. It was just for a few weeks." He regretted bringing this up. "It was so long ago, I barely remember."

Keisha's fork dangled over a plate. "If you were in college, AJ was probably in high school."

"Yeah." Didn't he hate himself for clueing everyone in to the time AJ's parents had their cataclysmic fight. "But July's album went through the roof, and from then on, our road crew members had to go through a screening process. I'm glad I got in during the early days."

July studied him over the rim of her wineglass. She seemed more focused now than she had been when he first arrived, and he wondered if she were contemplating their earlier conversations with this new information, or if she was tired of being reminded of all the ways her life had skidded off the rails.

Inez wagged her finger at him. "My Roger should have been the one to fly off the charts. He was being courted by all the big record companies, but he couldn't deal with their politics. Said he wanted to keep it real. I can't remember what finally got him noticed, but when he was, *he* became the famous one."

Luke stared at his plate. Surely Inez was joking. Roger's fame was built on the back of hit duets with July. They were the James Taylor and Carly Simon of their day. Not for the first time, he wondered if there was something off about Inez.

July pushed back from the table. "I've lost my appetite."

"Whatever." Penny shrugged. "I can't do tofu or whatever else you vegans demand."

He'd responded to July's invitation to dinner because he was expecting it to be like all his other family encounters — gushing relatives and unrealistic expectations. This meal made him see he'd underestimated the people involved in July's story. They were all mourning things they'd lost.

Reaching for the tea glass, he bought a moment to form a new strategy. July was one of the most talented singer-songwriters living today, but whether she was in a place to be creative again was anyone's guess. Luke remembered a snapshot of the office calendar that his assistant had wiped clean for him to be on vacation. He couldn't afford much time away beyond his two weeks, but if he could wriggle himself into this world a few extra days, maybe he could convince July — and anyone else who would care to listen — that life was better when you treasured what you still had — not what was gone. If she could really appreciate this scene, or this town, or even just the relationship AJ was offering, maybe she'd feel inclined to take a second look at her career and what they could do to make it fun again.

July stood like a queen announcing an end to the festivities.

Setting down his glass and standing, because she did, he asked, "July, do you have a phone number I can call later? I have a few days off and I'd like to — at the least — hear your thoughts on why you retired and if you're inclined to think about your music."

July gripped the back of the chair, staring at him like she wasn't sure how to answer the question

"She's staying here, Mr. English."

His head spun toward that voice. AJ held onto the French door between her dining room and the porch. "My home is her home, her refuge, and we don't take kindly to people from Nashville sneaking in and offering false schemes. Mom has retired. You're a professional, you know what that means."

Luke stared at AJ, wondering how she could sound exactly like the woman who walked into this house dirtier than a hound dog, but now, a mere half hour later, appeared a goddess.

The air in his lungs seemed to evaporate. Had his blood pressure spiked?

The chandelier glowing in the dining room cast her in an angelic light, sparkling beams of light off the cloudy waves of blonde hair spilling over her shoulders. Her skin was warm and rosy, and she wore not even a wand of mascara, yet looked like a photographer's dream model. He pictured her standing in the middle of one of those blooming lavender fields, wearing a chiffon dress that would billow from her waist, a basket in her arms and a wreath of flowers in her hair—she'd be the perfect cover model for an album or a book.

He blinked, fully aware that people were waiting for him to respond.

AJ was not, however, standing in a field of lavender but in a doorway, her hands propped on her hips like she was ready to go to war.

"I—" Luke stuttered, his image of her as a lavender queen drifting away like wisps of charred paper. "I have no schemes. Just a conviction that your mother's music is not over, and her voice has not shriveled. She still has much to offer the world, even if it's in a venue other than a concert hall."

AJ quirked her head to one side, which sent a trail of gold down her shoulder. "You want to be her agent?"

He could hear the resonance of a southern accent in her voice and guessed they had raised her in Tennessee. "No, I'm not an agent. I'm just an ideas guy, who earns a salary in marketing. But I am here as a friend—to tell her I can see down the road, and that she's nowhere near done."

"Oh, Luke!" July hurried toward him, squeezing his hand like it was a lifeboat.

Inez growled. "She's so done you can stick a fork in her."

"She can't even sing in the shower." Penny nodded. "The cigarettes killed her vocal cords."

Luke shifted his gaze from July to AJ. "I'm in Comfort, using my vacation days, not in any official capacity representing my company. And I will convince you I have your mother's tender soul in the palm of my hand, when I suggest she at least consider that the retirement was a mistake."

A shutter fell over AJ's eyes, but her voice was as firm as any general. "My mother has been on the road since she was a seventeen-year-old. It's time for her to know a life that doesn't involve lights, sound booths, and ticket stubs. She's here to heal, and I will let nothing interfere with that."

Luke had seen lines drawn in the sand before. He'd met fathers who'd carried rifles to protect their daughters from image-makers. Before he stepped over that line, he'd have to review all his resources. There was no room for error with AJ, or July.

Penny held up the platter of chicken. "Sit down, AJ, and eat. We have plenty."

Inez scooped vegetables into her mouth and winked at him. "Yeah, before Luke finishes it all. I can't believe he has room to eat, after what he put away at lunch."

Maybe the grandmother wasn't off at all. Maybe Inez was the craftiest woman in the room.

"You had lunch with my grandmother *before* you came to Lavender Hill?"

He should have explained that to AJ at their first encounter. "It was a fluke. I ran into Mrs. Worthington at High's Cafe. I'd never have known who she was if she hadn't shown me her shirt and bragged about her wonderful granddaughter."

Inez smiled. "I told him, I taught you everything you know. Although, technically, you got your green thumb from George's mother. That woman could grow peas from rock bed."

AJ's gaze swiveled to her grandmother before coming back to rest on Luke. "Who have you overlooked in contacting my family? If you tell me you've called my father, I will throttle you."

Penny twisted her napkin. "Roger hasn't phoned in months. Last I heard, he's still wandering around Hawaii. I'm just dying to see him."

"I have no interest in your father." Luke meant that earnestly. He'd watched how Roger let July wither in the face of public analysis, and he'd lost respect for the man who wouldn't at least shoulder half of the blame for the marriage. "And not because he's not an incredible songwriter," he added for Inez's benefit. "But he wasn't the one who garnered headlines with a retirement announcement."

July rocked back on her heels. "I've just told everyone I'm quitting. I have nothing left to offer anyone. I've come here to find myself. Maybe discover if I can knit or paint or something."

Luke had no intentions of suggesting a grueling schedule. She looked far more melancholy than he'd have thought for an artist with a fan base that still watched reruns of her Christmas specials. "I want a conversation. To see if there're any wells of poetry left untapped."

"She stole her best songs from my son, so if you want a real musician you need to talk to him," Inez said with a sneer. "I've got Roger's number."

"As you can see, Mr. English," AJ said, as she leaned over the table to snatch a bite of chicken, "all the poetry has evaporated. We're just a run-of-the-mill working family, and that's the way we intend to stay. I hope you won't think unkindly of me, but I will show you the way out. Penny can fix you a to-go plate. I hear she's made cheesecake."

Chapter Ten

In planning your flower or herb garden, leave plenty of room for growth. Expecting a perennial's spreading leaves or bushy blooms is critical to maintain form and shape in the bed. — "Lessons from Lavender Hill"

Though her nerves were zinging with tension, she swallowed every reservation she felt about confronting people and fixed her gaze on the candlesticks. Not looking her enemy in the eye was weak, but she had little experience going to war for her mother, and she wouldn't push herself to extremes with this being only the second battle. "Penny, will you prepare Luke's to-go plate?"

Penny stood, but her face radiated defiance. "My cheesecake hasn't set yet."

"Slice him some for the road. There's too much for us to eat, anyway."

Inez pushed back from the table. "Speak for yourself. I love cheesecake. I'd eat the whole thing if you weren't so stingy."

"You are lactose intolerant," AJ said, reminding her grandmother of the list of ailments that might be behind her grumpiness.

Though the sun was sinking low and leaving a beautiful velvet wake across the sky, Luke's expression implied he'd rather be anywhere other than the porch dinner party. His misery made her feel victorious. It had been his mistake to come to Texas. Knights in shining armor should survey the landscape before rushing in. If he'd been honest when he called a few days ago, she could have saved him the airplane fees and the resulting indigestion.

There was plenty of talent in today's music industry. Some TV show contestant would cover July's songs, and they'd fan-girl all over again. AJ wasn't heartless about her mother's music. She was just tired of picking up the pieces left behind by critics, slow sales, and shady managers. Luke should know that. This couldn't be the first "retired" singer he'd ever chased down.

Inez sent AJ a withering glance. "You've protected your mother all these years. If she's going to hide out on this farm, she has to deal with the truth. And the truth is—" Inez pointed a fingernail at July. "I could just kill her for breaking my son's heart."

An empty shelf and rat poison glowed in her memory. *Tea.* Had Inez poisoned July? AJ couldn't process that notion at the moment, so she'd do the one thing she *could* accomplish. She stepped around a chair and reached for Luke's elbow. "Come on, it's time to get you on the road."

Luke nodded, like he was grateful for the escape. "Good night, ladies. Thank you for dinner."

AJ led the way toward the steps that eased down to the yard. "When exactly did you meet my grandmother?" she asked, over her shoulder.

"About noon today, at High's." Luke stopped in the grass and glanced back at the dinner scene. Then he turned to AJ, saying, "I'm so sorry. I did not understand there was so much hurt in July's family. I guess, if I thought about it at all, I figured the drama was so long ago wounds would have healed by now."

She was tempted to blast him for his naiveté, but the lights strung between the limbs caught a shadow on his face and revealed that he wasn't quite the confident man she'd first met. "Scars don't mend in our family. They take on a life of their own." She folded her arms around her waist. A gentle breeze stirred hair into her face. "You had to have known she's not the same July Sands that used to fill arenas. The papers haven't been shy about her rides with fame."

Luke looked down as if to watch the shades of dark play over the grass. "But peel away the trappings from the last few years, and she still has an incomparable voice."

"Those trappings aren't coming off without some serious lifestyle rehabilitation. Comfort is as far removed from the stage as one can get. I know that personally because I ran here to find myself too. She's safe now. She can recover. But you coming all this way waving contracts at her will not help."

Luke searched AJ's face. "She needs the money."

"She needs peace."

"She needs something to stimulate her creativity."

"She needs to forget the spiral of the last few years." AJ pushed her hands through her hair, feeling a tangle of anger, resentment, and the sharp edges of broken dreams. "Writing new songs will bring that front and center."

"Writing is a proven therapy," he breathed. "She should do a memoir."

"Books!" AJ spun away. "What is it with everyone thinking that writing a book is the answer to everything?"

Luke stepped closer to AJ. "I hated watching her spin out of control, but she wasn't my client. Now she's free from contracts. I could make a difference."

His audacity made blood boil under her skin. "Who are you?"

He took another step closer. "Just someone who cares."

AJ felt the draw of his magnetic gaze but had enough experience to ignore the sizzle. "Leave Mom alone. She doesn't need your kind of interest."

His smile tilted up like he was enjoying an irony. "Funny thing, mentioning interest. I'm feeling something I haven't felt in a long time."

"It could be Penny's orzo."

"It's you. This place." His eyes softened, as if he was thinking of something that had nothing to do with July Sands. "I took a chance on coming to Texas, and everything here has been a total surprise. Including you."

Oh, she wanted to believe she had impacted a man, but she knew he was using her like all the others who wanted to open the back door on July's world. "You took a chance? That sounds like a line from a bad country song."

"It sounded corny, didn't it?"

She'd never been able to resist someone who could laugh at himself. It was the one thing her parents could never do. Taking a step back, she wanted to disappear into the shadows and figure out how she was going to keep people like Luke from talking to her mother. She was selfish. She knew that, but this return to Comfort was the open door that was going to give AJ the mother she'd always wanted, and she'd kick and scream to make sure that dream could finally have life. She needed it. All these years of making it on her own, she'd longed to have a mom who could help shoulder the burden or just be there for a long chat. But July had never had the time. Some concert, some tour, a record to be made, always took precedence over baking cookies together.

"AJ, I—"

Instead of softening her heart toward someone who maybe didn't have the world by the tail, she channeled the anger she'd felt when she saw her mother turn to putty in this man's attention. Luke didn't know July like she did, and he couldn't possibly understand how her mother caved the moment someone waved a contract. It always seemed to AJ that her mother couldn't resist a quick fix to her problems. But after years of working soil and amendments, she'd learned that patience was more than a virtue; it was the reward of struggle. And pain and disappointments were an important part of becoming virtuous. Like her garden. And that's what AJ wanted for her mother. A desire to do the hard, patient work of recovery.

Because in the process, they'd become close.

"Don't say anything," she insisted. "I don't want to hear your plans."

"I have suggestions, not plans. She's free to make her own choices and pursue her own dreams."

"She's an addict, and you're offering her drugs of choice."

Luke folded his arms over his chest, his eyes reading AJ for a clue to her motives. "Your mom is just in a midlife crisis."

Oh, for it to be that simple. "You've really never seen someone—like her—at the end of her career, have you? What you want to give her is more adulation, so she'll find some untapped reserve to write music. Something you could sell. What she needs is healing."

"Unlike you, I don't think she's washed up. Where you see disaster, I see potential."

The sting of his words would be hard to erase. "I've lived with her through some tough benders, so I guess I know her limits better than you. She's given all she has, and now she needs to find something else."

"Does she? Or is that what Roger wants her to do?"

Blinking fast, AJ wasn't sure how her dad got into this discussion. "My father has little to no influence on my mother. They don't even speak to each other."

"All the more reason for July to set aside the past and create something new."

AJ froze. He'd just echoed her own argument, but with a different outcome. "She's fifty-three years old. I think she set the patterns."

"And you will fix her with fresh air and hard work?" Luke looked beyond her shoulder, his gaze taking in the indigo-dusted hillsides. "You must think a lot of your abilities."

AJ bristled. Creating Lavender Hill had given her a future when all she had were a broken heart, a meaningless degree, and no one to guide her. She was sure it could save others too. "Who do you think you are to come in here and judge me because I love my mother and want the best for her?"

"You don't want the best for her. You want the best for you."

He might as well have slapped her cheek. AJ turned to go back inside. "I don't have to take this from you. Even my friends don't talk with this much judgment."

Luke reached for her arm. "Then don't think of me as a friend. Think of me as the one who can make a difference."

Like a fireball run amok, his self-righteousness cut a path in her thinking and made her realize that maybe July would choose *him*—instead of being with her. The five-year-old in her soul didn't have a word of rebuttal, because once again she wasn't enough.

She stared into his eyes like she'd been shocked senseless, or maybe that was the effect of headlights cresting the driveway behind him.

Someone new would intercede in this farce and, hopefully, keep her from saying something she'd regret. AJ pulled her gaze away from Luke's and watched an unfamiliar car hit every pothole before it came to a stop behind the line of vehicles parked in the circular drive.

The moment bought her time to process her thoughts.

Luke breathed heavily. "I don't want to argue with you. I'm sorry, I've hurt your feelings. But your mother is too young to retire from singing and songwriting."

AJ searched the sky instead of being drawn back into his gaze. "My feelings have developed a thick skin. Occupational hazard of being Roger and July's child."

"Your mom looks like an angel compared to your dad. Something tells me you needed armor just to get through the years he went on the road 'to find himself.'"

"Oh, so you know both my parents?"

"Anyone who worked in the music industry remembers Roger's reputation. He gave the term 'bad boy' its platinum layer."

She suspected her father's journey to find himself was really more about how to lose himself. Considering the chaos of failed contracts, drugs, alcohol, and indulging the women who followed him from concert to concert, she'd say he did a fine job. "Just because you have an inside track on knowing the garbage in my family does not mean I will ever forgive you for stirring up the insanity."

He cupped her elbow. "I've seen worse. Your parents aren't without hope."

"Spoken like someone who wants to see July in a recording studio."

A breeze, reminiscent of yesterday's blue norther, chilled the air between them. For one weird moment, she wondered if Betty's legend was true. But the disaster of Luke and July was almost over. He'd return to Nashville, and AJ could hide her mother's cell phone. She almost smiled. Maybe Inez wasn't the only devious one in this family.

Luke turned toward the sound of a car door slamming, and she remembered that she wasn't destined to spar with Luke English all night long. The weariness she would have expected with that thought was oddly energized. Though she never wanted to see this man again, there was no denying that he'd made her think and react in a way that she hadn't had to do for a long time. And she was going to miss that thrill.

"Well, I'd always expected to sneak up on my daughter smooching in the dark when she was sixteen, not twenty-nine."

The chemistry she felt zipping through her blood took a right turn into an abyss of madness. "Dad?" Her voice choked in her throat, and she wondered if that blue norther was responsible for this surprise.

From the shadows of the trees, a lanky man with hair to his shoulders stepped toward the twinkle lights. "The prodigal has returned," Roger Worthington announced with his arms thrown wide.

Chapter Eleven

The Roger Worthington who'd been featured on magazine covers didn't resemble the man standing in the yard. The Jack London of the country music scene was fifty pounds lighter, his nose broken and reset badly, and his mane of hair was a stringy, gray mess. Roger looked more like Inez than anything resembling the glowing health of his daughter—a woman who couldn't be more shocked if God had parted the skies and rained down a plague.

Luke picked up on the tension swirling between father and daughter and realized that AJ carried an unfair burden of responsibility. Both her parents seemed ill-suited to be the adults in this family, and the one woman who should be enjoying life to the hilt was, in fact, carrying all the weight. Even her grandmother depended on her. Scratching at his beard stubble, he was fascinated by AJ and wanted to know why she was the anchor for them all. But first, he had to help. She might not appreciate it, but AJ looked overwhelmed. "Mr. Worthington, the women inside have firearms. Think twice about announcing your arrival."

Roger nodded like he wasn't that surprised. "That's just Momma's way of welcoming me home. She called and told me to take care of business. That AJ was about the lose the house to July."

AJ ran her fingers through her hair as if she were looking for something to hold on to. "You need to leave now. Mom is here. Penny is here, and Gran has taken a weird turn for instability."

Roger seemed to count the women on the porch, and his eyes narrowed as he couldn't recognize the fourth woman sitting at the table.

Luke thought Inez's condition copied his grandfather's early days with dementia, but he'd play along if they wanted to label it instability instead. "I'm staying in town, Worthington," he offered. "You can follow me to Comfort Commons. They might have a spare room."

Roger kicked at the grass much like a bull might before a matador. "I don't know who you are or why you're acting like this is a big deal, but AJ always makes room for me."

"Gran is getting careless with rat poison." AJ grimaced. "Mom drank bad tea. I can't swear that she won't come after you. And, my house is full. You'll either have to take the couch or bunk with Gran at the cabin."

Roger's eyes widened. "Momma had talked about slipping July some barbiturates years ago, but I thought that was just to get her to stop bragging about how grand our life was back in Tennessee, back in the good days."

At least he'd gotten that part right, Luke thought. He knew quickly that Inez and July were enemies. What he couldn't figure out was how AJ was able to keep them living peaceably within such close proximity to each other. She must have skills in psychology that tag teamed with her gardening expertise. Maybe she was right about the soil therapy. He'd give her the credit if July started doing manual labor — a feat he'd have to see to believe.

"Dad, believe me. Gran is not herself. I can't imagine why she called you, but there is nothing going on here." AJ caught her breath. "Save trying to rehabilitate Mom."

"Roger?" July's thin voice carried from the porch like cheap cotton that was unraveling.

Penny's voice was shrill in comparison. "Roger, baby! You're home."

"Well, look what finally turned up," Inez grunted. "Took you long enough."

"This is like a rewind of my high school memories." AJ groaned, dropping her forehead into her hand. "I can't watch."

"Memories can't be trusted," Inez muttered from the steps. "I should know."

If he was nervous and confused, he imagined AJ was too. Luke held out his card and lowered his voice, saying, "I should probably leave now, since that's what you asked me to do. But if you need anything, anything at all, please call me. I'm good at running interference."

AJ took the card reluctantly.

Roger grabbed Luke's arm. "You're not leaving here without some explanation for why my mother, my ex-wife, and an old girlfriend are coming toward me with teeth bared."

AJ sighed, and it sounded like bones rattling. "Gran has dentures now; she won't bite."

Luke held his hands in surrender, as if getting involved in Greek dramas was not his preferred after-dinner entertainment. "I'm used to some resistance when working with a performer's families, but this is a new level. For the record," he said to Roger, "if you can make it to Keisha, you're home free."

Penny flew off the steps and raced to Roger's arms, wrapping herself around him like she was clinging to a tree in a storm. Luke glanced at the old man's expression and could see her enthusiasm had winded him

Inez followed behind, but as she got close to her son, her eyes cleared and she smiled as big as a kid at Christmas. "My baby boy, I've missed you so much."

"Hi, Momma." Roger set Penny on the ground and reached out to hug his mother.

Luke thought the resemblance was uncanny but, of the two, he'd take his chances with Inez. Roger had earned the reputation of a mean drunk.

With Roger and Inez catching up, he watched AJ standing there like she was little more than a fan waiting in line for the moment the star glanced her way. This was her father, a man she often entertained, so why was there a reluctance on either of their parts to embrace? Why had he not even touched her?

"I'm going to bed," July announced from the porch. "Reunions make me nauseated."

Luke watched her pause at the doorway, her eyes resting on Roger in a way that implied more sorrow than jealousy.

AJ patted her dad's shoulder. "Welcome home, stranger."

Finally, hugging his daughter, he replied, "Sorry I've been so bad about keeping in touch. I lost my phone and kind of got used to being untethered. I bought a new one when I got back to LA, and Momma was one of the first ones to call me on it."

Penny was clinging to Roger's arm. "I've got so much to tell you. Have you had dinner? Are you thirsty?"

Inez swatted at Penny. "Good Lord, why are you always trying to feed everybody?"

"It's my love language, Inez." Penny patted Roger's sleeve. "And he likes my cooking. Says I'm the best, don't you, baby?"

"Penny King, you get your hands off my son. He's not your pet. He's not even interested in you anymore. He told me you were some trashy fling from his past that just wouldn't let him go."

Luke felt the ice wave strike the yard and watched the expressions on Roger, Penny, and AJ's faces react accordingly. This little dynamic was not something needing his finesse. He was—for all intents and purposes—an outsider. While he knew he should flee, the urge to stay and fix the broken angel wings on AJ's shoulders was almost too much to resist.

He climbed the porch steps, nodding to Keisha. "Let's get coffee going."

Keisha's dark skin blanched. "I'm thinking we need to sneak out the back door."

Inez propped her hands on her hips, her voice carrying across the distance. "I don't know why y'all are staring at me. Roger always asks if Penny's still hanging around, like he's not coming back to the farm until she takes her winter trip back to see her relatives."

Penny took three giant steps away from the family circle.

Roger turned toward her, his chin dropped sheepishly low. "Penny, it's not like that."

Penny covered her mouth with her hand. "You hate me. You really don't want me here."

Luke tugged Keisha back toward the French doors. "We need to do something. Let's hide in the kitchen while we figure out a plan that doesn't involve notifying the police. The paparazzi wouldn't be far behind. AJ's hair will catch fire if someone with a camera shows up—I know that much."

Keisha led the way off the porch back into the dining room decorated with antiques and brass wall sconces.

He'd walked into this house two hours ago and immediately felt at home in the comfortable balance of old walls, mixed furnishings, and art. This place echoed AJ's design flair from the shop but had the weight of expensive hand-me-downs and thick rugs to create a cocoon that anyone would want to linger in, and he'd admired her bookcases the moment he saw the crowded shelves.

But no one would brag about her design talents tonight.

They'd be lucky to be even speaking to each other by morning.

"I'll collect the plates," he said to Keisha, as she passed through the butler's pantry. "You get the sink ready. We'll at least wash the dishes."

She nodded but looked yearningly for her friend standing shell-shocked in the yard.

Luke tried to be unobtrusive as he gathered the plates and silverware, but Inez was unleashing a lot of frustration on a man who'd abandoned his family on more than one occasion.

Carrying his load into the kitchen, Luke set a stack on the counter and got smacked on the cheeks by bubbles.

Keisha smiled. "I got a little carried away with the lavender soap. It's more concentrated than what I'm used to."

He glanced around the kitchen and saw piles of pans on the stove. "I'm not sure where everything goes, but we can at least wash and dry, right?"

Keisha tied on an apron. "I'm hating all that drama for them. Penny's a good helper to AJ. This will not end well."

Luke walked over to the breakfast table and surveyed the cheesecake poised for dessert. "What do you think will happen?"

Reaching for the glassware, she said, "I'm guessing Penny will run off tonight in a huff. Roger will drive Inez back to her cabin and give her a double dose of a nightcap, and AJ will walk the lavender fields, praying for a way to sort all this out."

"She does that a lot?"

Keisha glanced over her shoulder at him. "She says she does her best praying at night, because sometimes she's too exhausted to sleep and the lavender soothes her. Kind of thinking this will be one of those nights."

Luke brought in the platters and could see that Penny was sitting on the swing dangling from an old oak tree, and AJ and Roger were trying to get Inez into the rental car.

Walking back into the kitchen, he nodded to his co-worker. "You were right. They're trying to get Inez to go home."

Keisha's smile was disarmingly wise. "Maybe this will wake them up to the truth. No one wants to admit that Miss Inez is losing it."

"AJ can't see it?"

"AJ doesn't want to see it." Keisha picked up the soaking silverware and ran it under hot water. "That woman has been the only stability AJ has known for a while. They're tight."

Luke held up a pan of table scraps. "Can I give this to the dog?"

"Beans will love you forever. He's a chump for leftovers." Keisha nodded toward a screened door. "His pen is right outside."

"Beans?"

"You'd have had to be there, but Kali, one of AJ's friends, gave her the puppy a few years ago. He was the runt of the litter and sickly, and the only thing the dog would eat were canned pinto beans."

Luke scraped the pan into the dog's bowl. His reward was an enthusiastic lick on his wrist. When he came back into the kitchen, he saw Keisha peeking through the kitchen window.

"We should probably skedaddle," she said. "There's crying going on out there, and they will not want to explain to us what's going down."

Luke knew she was right, but he felt a pull to AJ that urged him to want to go out there and shake Roger's head. How could a man with such a daughter treat her hospitality so carelessly?

"Do you think July will finish up in here?" he asked, drying the dinner plates quickly.

"That woman didn't even know where her investments were located. I don't see her knowing her way around a kitchen, either."

Luke nodded, feeling a little foolish that he'd forgotten July had been a diva even when he was on her tour all those years ago. AJ said she'd been performing since she was seventeen. That's a few lifetimes of adrenaline and privilege. He doubted July was going to ever adapt to housework.

"You seem like a nice guy, Luke." Keisha untied the apron. "So, there's probably something you should know about AJ. She's private. As an only child, she's used to being self-sufficient. She built this whole business on her reputation, and never once did she trade on the fame of her parents."

"She doesn't want to be stained by association?"

"She wants respect for her own talents."

He unfolded the towel and reached for a clean plate, thinking he'd had a similar epiphany when he'd been in college and his dad had insisted the family insurance business was the path to take.

"Yeah, I get that." Luke pictured AJ as he'd first seen her, glowing and beautiful, like they had crowned her from a national competition of farmers' daughters. Having known her parents, or at least their types, it was easy to see that nothing of Lavender Hill, or even this house, testified to a Grammy-award-winning past. "I think she accomplished her goal."

"You're smart, I saw that right away." Keisha came close to him. "So, don't mess with AJ."

He'd not been warned away from a girl in a long time—most people were trying to set him up with their friends. "If it's any consolation, we're probably never going to speak again."

"Most likely not." Keisha handed him the tea pitcher to dry. "But she has an unhealthy fascination for the sick and wounded, and you seem to be on the other side of her mother's issues, so consider yourself warned."

As it was, she'd probably kick him to the curb and slam the door behind him. "I'm really not here to create problems.

I wanted to offer a way forward for July, not get tangled in family dysfunction."

"It sounds like you've been in the industry a while, so you want me to believe you didn't at least expect pushback?" Keisha cut her gaze to him. "Seriously?"

It was like she'd peeked at his client roster. "Truthfully, I expected July to be in a rehab hospital, and I'd have to bribe the nurses to get close — not the staff of a garden store."

"And that was before Miss Inez called Roger in from God knows where."

Luke closed his eyes to pause the memory of AJ's expression when she saw her father walk across the yard. Heartache and horror all in one blink of the eye.

Keisha patted his arm with her wet hand. "Go easy with my friend. Her courage chips as easily as this china. And she's the nicest person on the planet. If you mess with her, there'll be a whole posse of Comfort women who will come after you."

Though it wasn't intentional, and he had no justification for it, he decided — right then, right there — that he wanted to be included in the group that circled AJ. He was drawn to her in a way that was personal, intimate, and destined to be unforgettable. No other woman in his lifetime had ever seared him with such an instant attraction, and he wasn't sure what he could do with it, seeing as there was a fifty-three-year-old woman standing between them. But he still had several weeks of vacation to use, and it might be wise to spend time in the gardens of Comfort, seeing what might grow.

Chapter Twelve

Comfort, Texas   September 16, 1954

Inez unpinned the lace veil from her hair and laid it over the chair in the room assigned for brides. She was glad to have ten minutes of privacy after the wedding. Of the twenty guests who witnessed the ceremony at Immanuel Lutheran Church, none had been from home. They'd all been friends of George's parents and seemed to share the same sentiments for the bride.

The door opened without a knock. Inez glanced into the mirror and saw Mrs. Worthington step in and close the door quietly. Inez's stomach dropped. It did every time Mrs. Worthington wanted a conversation with her, private or otherwise.

"Wearing white was an interesting choice," Mrs. Worthington said, as she folded her arms across her chest. "I would have thought you'd have more respect for spiritual traditions, but I guess with your upbringing that's too much to hope for."

Some burlesque girls in Gladewater had offered to take her to church when she was little, but she didn't think Mrs. Worthington would appreciate that memory. "I had hoped that you would be happy for George and me today."

"How can I be happy when my precious son has fallen in with a woman who sings in nightclubs and has corrupted him with her evil ways?"

Though her knees were quaking, Inez would remember the words George had given her for courage. She would do everything she could to stand up to his mother. "I'm not evil and I have not corrupted George. He's a man who knows his own mind, and he's happy now."

"Is that what is fashionable to call it today?" Mrs. Worthington stepped away from the doorway and came to stand close to Inez. "You've caused him to drop his plans for the law, and for what? Selling cars. I know he can become a judge."

Inez squeezed her fingers into the fabric of her wedding gown. She hadn't asked for George to love her. She'd pushed him away so many times, he had bruises. But he'd won her over with his goodness, and she'd not do anything to tarnish him. Even if that meant smiling at his mean mother. "He's good at selling cars. His boss is giving him a promotion."

"I don't care if he's good at selling ice to Eskimos. That's not the respectable line of work his father and I mapped out for him. At the very least, we would have expected him to come back to the ranch."

Inez knew enough to know this was not the time to mention how much George hated weeding the vegetable patches or chasing the wayward cows. "He will make something good of himself. And I'll be right there beside him to help."

"You?" Mrs. Worthington scoffed. "You're responsible for his downslide into sinful behavior. He was on his way to being president of the debate club before you derailed him. You will never be welcome in my home as long as you keep up this pride and shameful behavior."

Tears blurred her vision. She'd always felt like trash. That's what her daddy's lady friends called her—trailer trash. But she'd run away from the pawn shops and bars and made something of herself. Something that George thought was worth his heart. "I'm not shameful."

A gnarled finger pointed into her face. "You're the most disgraceful person I've ever met. I wrote my cousin in Tyler, and he told me all about your father and his criminal activities."

Her lips trembled, knowing how many times her father had spent a night in jail. Had it not been for his friendship with the sheriff, he'd have been locked up forever. "My daddy has never been convicted."

"You're a reprobate. You've tainted my son."

Inez was sure the floor of the church was quaking. "We love each other."

"Love—" Mrs. Worthington seemed to gag on the word. "Love is for cheap women and summer flings." She flagged her hand in front of Inez. "You are not worthy of George or the Worthington name. You're nothing but a floozy. If you loved him, you would leave him."

Her stomach clenched so hard it became a bowling ball. Inez didn't have a lot of schooling, but she knew what she would become, and it was not someone who'd bring shame to the one man who loved her. "You'll see. George and I are meant for each other. We will have a future."

"Over my dead body."

Chapter Thirteen

When choosing bedding plants, always think through your garden's goals and go to the nursery with a list. It's too easy to be swayed by specialty flowers and purchase the wrong plant when you make spontaneous choices. What looks pretty at a garden store might be all wrong for your specific bed. — "Lessons from Lavender Hill"

AJ held her coffee mug to her nose, breathing in the dark roast of Cup of Joe's house blend. Unlike Kali and her fellow Monday morning regulars at Comfort's only coffee shop, AJ took whatever the barista brewed as the daily special for her order. She didn't care to know the origin of the beans or the time attributed to their roasting—all she knew was that she liked her coffee strong, hot, and extra creamy.

AJ leaned back into the chair and hugged her mug closer to her lips as she stared out the window, watching Comfort stretch and get ready for its day.

Kali Hamilton set a plate of scones on the table, and the resulting clatter shook AJ from watching the bachelor farmers and the widows spill out of High's Cafe, none of whom seemed to enjoy eating breakfast in their home. It tempted her to cross the street and eat at the cafe, but her friends insisted they'd rather be over-caffeinated than take the risk of hardening of the arteries with the sunrise special.

She was interested to find out if there was as much chatter and laughter in the café as there was at Joe's. Well, it was mostly her friend group that provided the noise. Glancing around, she saw several people trying to read the *San Antonio Express-News*.

Jake Hamilton held the chair for Kali to sit down as she glanced at AJ. "I see you got here before me again. Either I'm slowing down, or you didn't want to hang around your house this morning."

AJ offered a half-hearted smile. "As you so accurately guessed, I was miserable at home."

"Who knows you better than me?" Kali asked, contentedly patting her baby bump.

Jake, the token male in the Monday morning friend group, stepped away from the table. "Since this sounds personal, I'm going for our mugs. AJ, you need a refill?"

"No, thanks," she said, regretting that he bolted so soon. With Jake gone, Kali wouldn't hold back.

"What did you end up doing with your parents yesterday? I still can't believe you have your mom and your dad at the same address." Kali's gaze shot from her husband's retreating form to AJ in one split second.

There was no way to avoid this conversation. Kali was one of the few people who knew almost all the gory details of AJ's past and why natural disasters created less fear than seeing her parents forced into the same room.

"Dad is staying with Gran at her house. Said he couldn't take being close to Mom without some wickedness rubbing off on him. He likes to blame his corrupted soul on Mom's influence."

Kali chuckled then covered her mouth with her hand. "Oh, sorry. I guess that wasn't hilarious."

AJ had spent hours analyzing how unfunny her life had become. "I don't know what I will do with them all. Gran says Dad won't get out of bed, citing jet lag. But I need him to run interference with me on Gran. She's gone to a dark place, and I don't know if it's permanent or just her prerogative now that she's old enough to not get her hand slapped."

"I saw Keisha yesterday, and she said you got surprised by a party you didn't ask for. So, I'm guessing this means your mom's not playing fair either?"

"Mom thinks Dad is here to rub it in that she was forced into a retirement because she couldn't support herself as an artist anymore, and the few times they're in the same space, they're circling each other like hyenas about to pounce."

"What is Beans doing?"

"Beans?" AJ asked, wondering if Kali's nature for nurturing animals had grown to the next level.

"Dogs are intuitive." Kali rubbed her belly. "He doesn't know either of them well, so watch his behavior, and at least you'll know which one is the kinder human."

"Or keeps snacks in their pocket. You know how that dog is around food."

Kali nodded, her gaze drifting to the window, but she wasn't watching the shopkeepers, she was fitting puzzle pieces together in her mind. "This doesn't have to be your problem to solve. They are, chronologically speaking, grown-ups."

AJ rubbed her earlobe. She'd often wondered if she'd gotten an extra dose of some enabler gene, because despite common sense, she still tried to get everyone to behave and play nice. It was a doomed effort, and she knew it, but she couldn't seem to resist any more than she could resist seed catalogs in the winter.

"So, with all the moody silence in the house this weekend, you wrote five chapters in your garden manual, right?"

AJ appreciated Kali's flair for distraction. As tired as she was already from the drama at home, she imagined the still-empty notebook on her desk. "Define chapters."

Kali groaned.

"I'm seeing this gardening book turn into more of a picture book," AJ said, sounding convinced of her own good idea. "Once I get past the basic stuff like good dirt, sunshine, and watering schedules, I don't know what else to say about creating a garden. How long can I go on about compost?"

Kali pursed her lips and stared at AJ like she was trying to figure out the chemical equation for nitrogen. "You could talk to Elizabeth. She said she'd help you find a — what's the word I'm looking for? — I'm giving my memory cells to this baby. Ghostwriter! That's it. Someone to help you write."

AJ would have more time to give to this project once the June accounts were closed. The store became more of a browser's paradise after June, when it was too hot to plant anymore. "What I need is someone objective about what I do but still connected to the media industry. Someone who can see what I've scribbled and decide if there's any hope for the words. Someone like —" Her mind conjured an image of a brown-haired music executive who had suggested a memoir. "Nope, I need no one. I'll figure this out for myself."

Jake folded his tall body into the cane chair. "Am I the only one at this table who's not sleeping well? It will take three cups to get me moving this morning."

Kali fixed a dead-eyed stare on her husband's face.

"You snore." Jake pointed a finger back at his wife. "And I don't care if that baby is sitting on your ribs all night. I wish I'd known a year ago that you would be this much trouble. I'd have sold that emerald ring."

AJ waited for Kali to rise to the bait. Jake and Kali delighted in arguing about who best remembered the details of their whirlwind second courtship.

Kali's face brightened instead. She turned back to AJ with a wide grin. "We think it's a boy. Not that I'm doing an ultrasound, because I want to be surprised at the birth. But

Jake and I both have had dreams the baby is a boy, and so we've called the baby Maximus Brutus. Max, for short."

AJ kept her expression serious. Kali named her goats for literary characters, so anything was possible between now and the due date. "How interesting."

"On account of how he kicks Kali like he's going for a field goal," Jake explained.

"And I'm feeling quite bruised." Kali's smile shifted to Mona Lisa contentment. "Ergo, Maximus Brutus."

AJ was about to respond, but she saw the profile of the man walking up the steps and pulling open Cup of Joe's glass door.

The breath seeped out of her body. "Oh, no. No. No. No."

Kali's head whipped around to follow AJ's gaze. "Is it your mom or your dad?"

"I'll bet it's that youth director, Ethan." Jake sipped coffee from his mug. "He turns up everywhere AJ goes."

AJ pushed away from the table so she could hide but thought better as the chair legs would only scrape against the concrete floor and reverberate a calling card around the room. Better to duck down below Jake's shoulder and hope people at the counter didn't feel an overwhelming need to check out the corner seating arrangements.

Maybe Luke wouldn't recognize her.

She'd not bound her hair into the braids she wore for work, and after she'd slept with it tied into a topknot last night, it had crimped into waves. From this angle, she probably looked like a teenager in serious need of a hairbrush. AJ stroked her clammy hands down her thighs, wishing she'd worn something a little more inconspicuous than the bright red tank top and khaki shorts. But how was she to know Luke was an early bird with a penchant for coffee?

"AJ?" Kali stared like there was an unreported outbreak of fever in the air.

"I can't stay," AJ mumbled. "I've got to run by the general store and see if they have any more orange oil in stock."

Jake glanced again between the door and AJ. "Are you okay? You look kind of sick."

"Fine." She slinked down farther on her spine when a voice from behind Kali's shoulder stopped her cold.

"AJ, what a surprise. May I join you?"

The man who had wrecked her world was now staring at her — like she had cinnamon, instead of freckles, dusting her nose. "Luke, I, uh, didn't expect to see you again, or even here, you know, this morning."

Kali coughed as if she was choking down the most interesting tidbit.

Luke smiled his million-watt executive grin to those gathered around the table. She was sure Kali was smitten, and Jake leaned back in his chair like he'd finally seen another one of his kind live in the wild.

AJ wanted to shout — he's not a billionaire, too! Or at least she didn't think Luke had the same portfolio as Jake, although, to be fair, she wasn't exactly sure what or who he was. But since he'd arrived Saturday and tossed around super-expensive projects to lure July into a studio, maybe he had resources that came with bottomless wells.

She should have researched his company, but she was too angry with him for ignoring her mother's end-of-the-road press release to be that thorough.

"AJ, I promise I'm not stalking you." Luke said, with the tone of an apology. "But I've been up for a while, on the phone with the folks back at my office, and needed a caffeine fix." He smiled at the duo staring at him. "I'm Luke English. And that office is in Nashville."

Jake offered his hand. "Hi, Jake Hamilton. This is my wife, Kali. We're close friends of AJ's. Not that you'd know that based on the lack of introductions."

Kali turned in her chair to offer a smile. "Please join us. We have plenty of room," she said, pointing to an empty chair across from AJ.

"Except that's Anna's chair." AJ knew she sounded strident, but she didn't want to include him. Luke was the thief of her mother's recovery plan. "Anna will be here soon. We can't give up her chair. You know how particular she is about that chair by the window. And Lacy. Where would Lacy sit?"

Kali's brow quirked over her eye, as if asking, "What gives?" But she said instead, "Anna left for Austin last night, remember? She's doing research at the LBJ library. And Henry's in town, so we won't see Lacy today."

AJ knew when she'd lost an argument, and if she didn't give up, Kali would grill her with questions about why she was being antisocial to an attractive and reasonably intelligent male. "Oh, well, then I guess the chair is free."

Luke pulled against the cane back, moving the chair far away from Kali and the windowpane. He settled in the seat much like Jake—legs knocking the table and elbows going everywhere.

AJ tried to avoid his gaze, but much to her chagrin, she knew of his every movement. Even as he inspected the scones, she thought his movement was a deliberate attempt to brush his hand against her arm. She'd jerked her arm back, sloshing coffee on the table.

Kali nailed her with an unspoken question.

"So, Luke, what brings you to Comfort?" Jake leaned forward, apparently grateful for testosterone at the table.

"Luke is in the record—"

Luke interrupted AJ. "I handle special interest projects."

"And this brings you to Comfort, how?" Jake's eyebrows drew together.

AJ remembered him as he stood in her yard Saturday night, offering to run interference with her family. Then later, when she finally had her parents and Inez sorted for the night, she walked into the kitchen to find that Luke and Keisha had cleaned pots and pans, stacked dried dishes on a table, and put away the leftovers.

She'd laid her head on the breakfast table and cried. As much from sheer emotional overload as from that gift of service. Which was odd, because she'd not cried in years. Not since she wasted buckets of tears on an almost-fiancé who'd chosen a tour opportunity over staying in Tennessee with her.

She was the one who took care of people—having someone do something for *her*, well, it left her speechless. And humbled. On Sunday, when she'd called Keisha to thank her for the cleanup, Keisha said she'd left after they washed the dishes. Anything else done in that kitchen was all Luke's effort. She'd quickly dismissed his kindness to sway her over to his side, but when he didn't call her mother Sunday—and July didn't call him—AJ had hoped the worst was behind them.

Luke held his coffee mug, blowing steam from the top. "I'm collecting old songs."

Kali's hand froze mid-reach for a scone. "How do you know AJ?"

"He came to meet Mo—"

"Lavender Hill." Luke interrupted again. "Folks said I'd be nuts to miss out on a local attraction. I found myself there Saturday, and I met AJ in the dirt area." He winked at her. "I want the extra-dark-roast variety. Whatever the plants don't need I can just sprinkle on my patio and get a caffeine boost without having to fire up the coffeemaker."

AJ defrosted for the first time since she'd seen him amble up the cracked steps of the coffee shop.

As the conversation turned to Nashville, AJ waited. This would be when he spelled out his intentions. Knowing Kali and Jake and their unflinching loyalty, they'd scorch Luke for his scheme to wreck the first foothold in normal family life that AJ had seen in years.

Kali asked, "How long are you here?"

"I will stay in the area for a week or so." Luke poured a sugar packet into the espresso and stirred it through the swirl foam. "Call it a working vacation, if you will."

Jake nodded. "More emphasis on work, I'm sure, because we don't have a lot of vacation sites around Comfort. There's tubing on some rivers and tennis is good around here, but the golf courses are closer to San Antonio. Most of what would probably appeal to you is in San Antonio, or Austin."

Luke smiled. "I've had plenty of busy activity for a while. I'm looking for a slower pace."

"Must be nice to take a break." Kali split a scone in half and smeared the sides with lemon curd. "Jake and I work year-round managing two businesses a hundred miles apart."

Jake handed her a napkin. "While we're expecting, we're staying closer to Kali's gourmet cheese company at Provence Farms. Apparently, she can't separate from her goats, even though we have a staff to run her business."

"And they won't let me herd the kids either. Afraid that I might trip, but who will pamper those goats like I do?" Kali giggled. "I meant the actual four-legged goats, not my staff."

"How far along are you," Luke asked.

"Six months," Kali picked up her scone and bit into it like someone who did not need to count calories.

AJ could see that Luke's nosiness would transfer to her friends, and she didn't want him investigating the Hamiltons anymore than she wanted him getting close to her mother, or—God forbid—her father. He'd already charmed Keisha, Inez, and Penny. She'd keep the collateral damage to a minimum if she could. "Well, that was fun. Now we all have to go to work. So, see ya. Bye."

"We're not leaving yet." Jake glanced between the two like he enjoyed the show. "Luke, tell us what you've found so interesting here in Comfort."

Luke's gaze collided with AJ's.

She felt her skin flush and knew that giving him an inch into her personal life was setting back her advantage in the war. On top of a busy day at the shop, she still needed to figure out how to manage her parents, undo whatever stories Inez had spread, and stall the book publisher for another few weeks. But ignoring Luke English might be the most important task of all. He seemed harmless with a cup of coffee in his hand, but she'd met his type before. Snakes slithered into places where people rarely looked.

"I need to head over to the store," AJ said, pushing back her chair. "I've got to collect new merchandise, recruit staff to help with inventory, and make sure the sprinklers all came on during the night. It will be another scorcher today."

Luke stopped AJ from picking up her coffee mug. "Can you stay one quick minute? I'd like to talk with you about our mutual interest in a project."

Kali swallowed her bite of scone. "Oh, my word, you're the one who will help AJ with her book, aren't you?" Kali swung her gaze to AJ. "No wonder you didn't need Elizabeth's help. You'd already lined up your expert."

"I don't know what you're talking about," AJ stammered. She felt Luke's eyes boring into her, and if she could have taped her friend's mouth shut, she would have. "Kali, look over there. I think it's Beau Jefferson. Is Beau finished with that house yet?"

Luke turned to face Kali. "AJ's been reluctant to explore 'the project.' What has she told you?"

"Just that she's supposed to have that gardening manual rough draft finished by August, and at the rate she's plodding along, she'll miss the date entirely." Kali looked over her shoulder. "That's not Beau, AJ. I swear you need glasses."

Luke leaned forward, his gaze resting on July's daughter. "A gardening manual sounds like a great marketing tool. Why aren't you interested?"

Not even a hiccup of a surprise. That was probably how he'd helped some of those high-grossing acts that July said had earned him his reputation in the music industry. She was tempted to lie, but Kali would spell everything out, and she'd look like a fool for not being honest.

Standing, AJ said, "Oh, I'm interested, particularly if someone else would do it. I can't write a pretty sentence to save my life. Everything I jot down sounds like a textbook. I was telling Kali we should just hire a photographer, turn it into a picture book of plants, and leave it at that."

"But why would anyone want to buy one of those?" Luke sipped his coffee. "As one recently at Lavender Hill, I can tell you what people want to know is how they can recreate that same beautiful, peaceful feel you've generated by laying out your gardens in a particular order and choosing the right plants for the right place. What you've made to look like it sprouted from the ground was, I'm sure, a deliberate and well-conceived plan. That's what your customers want to know. *The secret.*"

AJ stared at Luke, stunned that he'd nailed the aim. "That's what Elizabeth said."

"Well, this Elizabeth must be brilliant," he said with a smile.

Kali nudged Jake. "I like this fella. Can we hire him to do a book about Provence Farms too?"

"If you wish." Jake nodded. "Sounds like he knows what he's talking about."

Luke stepped back to give AJ space. "I'd love to spend time with you, AJ. Giving book advice."

The only way to break this spell was to tip over the cold, bracing truth. "He's not here to see me, Kali. He's here to throw Mom back into the recording industry. Do not fall for his charm."

Kali turned, her face blanched white. "You're here for July Sands?"

103

Luke shifted, as if something sharp was poking him in the back. "Well, July Sands has phenomenal talent. How do we know she's finished with her music?"

Jake settled in his chair, crossing his arms over his chest. "And I was about to ask you to go fishing this weekend."

Luke glanced to his cup where the foam had dissipated into the milky coffee. "I'm guessing no one wants to see July succeed, even though she's just moved into one of the most significant periods of life. So many artists do their best work after they've crossed into middle age."

AJ folded her arms, thrilled to be back in an anger zone instead of the perilous one where she turned to him for help. "It's obvious we will not agree on the issue. So, I recommend you leave. Staying in Comfort will only confuse my mother. She's torn as it is with my dad showing up."

"I know you think the worst of my motives, but here's the deal," Luke said, rising from his chair. "Your mother has lived a rich and some might say, perverse, life. It's from such ashes that some of the best poetry and music come, and I would not be the professional I am if I walked away from the challenge of seeing something good come from the life July has led."

AJ fisted her hands at her waist. "I hardly think that's for you to decide."

"It's not," Luke replied. "But it is *July's* call to make. She doesn't need a jailer locking away her guitar."

Chapter Fourteen

"I messed up big time," Luke said, settling back into the chair as he watched from the window as Kali and AJ stormed down the sidewalk.

Jake sipped his coffee. "Yep."

Luke watched them stop at a familiar beat-up truck, Kali waving like AJ needed big hand gestures to understand whatever was being said. "She will not forget this conversation soon, will she?"

"Nope."

Luke pushed his coffee mug toward the center of the table. "Do you think there's any hope she can overlook the July Sands issue and go to dinner with me?"

"Couldn't say."

"And your wife," Luke cut his gaze back to Jake. "Following AJ out of the coffee shop, does that mean she will talk her into giving me a second chance, or reveal the location of a stash of weapons guaranteed to cause a slow and painful death?"

Jake scratched his beard. "So, you like AJ?"

Looking out the window to the pedestrians meandering along High Street, he said the first thing that came to mind. "I don't understand it myself, but she's taken over my head.

I could hardly sleep last night for thinking of a way to get her to stop seeing me as the enemy."

"Running into AJ this morning was a bonus, not a real plan?"

Luke pushed a crumb around on the table. "Nothing about being in Texas is going according to plan."

"Ah," Jake grinned. "The heart wants what it wants."

Shifting his gaze to the man who looked as if he could wrestle a bull and win, Luke asked, "Did you quote poetry?"

Jake shrugged. "That's how Kali explained the relationship she and I had, one that had an eight-year gap before I sealed it. Sometimes attraction can't be rationalized."

Luke had underestimated the people of Comfort. Wasn't that exactly what Inez had warned him about in the cafe? "Is everyone in this town running from something?"

"Hey, whatever is in the air benefited me, so I will not knock it." Jake leaned forward on the table. "Rethink your strategy with AJ. Most of the single guys here have been in love with her. She might be immune to the air."

That flirtation at her shop still ranked as one highlight of his month, and AJ had responded. If July hadn't walked out at that moment, he would have been well on his way to having the most interesting conversation with a single woman he'd had in years.

Luke knew some of the most gorgeous female artists in the industry, but after the stage lights dimmed and the makeup came off, they were unremarkable—and most times, boring.

AJ, with her sass and sparkle, had captivated him from the first moment, and he'd not known that she was July's daughter. If he could just convince AJ of that, maybe they could have a conversation that didn't deteriorate into battle lines.

Not that either lady would appreciate being reduced to a prize. But in the clear light of day, he had to ask himself if he could choose only one Worthington woman, which one would it be?

Luke watched a shopkeeper across the street open the front door to an art gallery. There was a wreath on the door, and a cat sniffed at a pot of flowers nearby. He wished he could define what made this village so appealing, because if he could get a handle on what made Comfort distinctive, maybe he could use that to help win more time with the local gardening entrepreneur.

Luke glanced back to Jake. "Any chance I could call in that fishing offer?"

Chapter Fifteen

It is simple to repair a broken plant. Take the fallen stem, clip the end, and dip the stem in a container of powdery root stimulator. Tuck the powdered stem into a small pot of prepared potting soil, keep it moist, and in a few weeks, you'll see new growth sprout from damage. — "Lessons from Lavender Hill"

AJ unlocked the back door of Lavender Hill's cottage, stepping over the previous day's delivery of merchandise. Years ago, she'd been reluctant to sell home accessories, because anything that distracted her from producing the best quality plants was, in her mind, a bad thing. Kali had insisted customers were seeking to copy the romance of Lavender Hill's shabby chic aesthetic in their own homes and selling products and gifts would provide additional income for the lean winter months.

Elizabeth had echoed that sentiment when advising her on the Lavender Hill book idea, and sales figures had justified all her risks so far. So, why was she worried that listening to Kali's advice now would drive her off the deep end?

Because brown eyes would be hardest things she'd ever had to resist.

Even as AJ bolted down High Street, Kali had pleaded with her to keep an open mind about Luke. July's press release had been her manager's idea—a man who was long past ready to retire himself. Maybe, if AJ was willing to listen to new ideas, there could be a way for July to ease out of the life she'd led, not stop cold turkey.

AJ paused at the thermostat and readjusted the temperature to combat the predicted heat. Punching the keypad with too much effort, she pulled her fingers back and considered all the times she'd had to surrender her preferences for her mother's.

Like someone had opened a photo album and scattered pictures to the floor, she revisited the summers spent with tutors and sitters on her parents' tour buses. Their bitter divorce, and the resulting tug-of-war over whom she'd spend the seasons with and where. She'd played along, until she enrolled at Vanderbilt. Though she wasn't far from home, she enjoyed the independence of college life. Until she met Cullen Smith at his piano recital.

AJ bit her back molars, forcing the images of her one real romance back into the pages of her memory. No need to indulge that disaster. July had hated Cullen the moment they'd met, but AJ had always thought it was professional jealousy and not any real insight regarding the potential of adding another musician into their already complicated family. But ultimately, July had been right about Cullen's character.

And maybe she was right about needing to explore her options too.

Though the press release had stunned AJ, it had felt like a beacon of light. Lavender Hill was thriving, and once the heavy sales season was over, AJ could take time off to travel with July. They could learn to live together. They could find out what they had in common, not the laundry list of things they didn't.

It was her childhood fantasy come true. July becoming a real mom. Just like the women who'd driven carpool in high school or followed their daughters to sorority events in college. Or helped salvage the tear-stained wreckage when an almost-fiancé dumped a girl.

Dust bursting out with the blast of cold air-conditioning caused her to sneeze. Thankfully, her thoughts of Cullen flew away too.

AJ walked down the hall, turning on lights, and hung her tote bag on the vintage knob nailed to the wall inside the small office. She paused, leaning out the door again, hearing voices from the kitchen area.

"Knock, knock," she called out, wondering who had shown up for work early on a weekday. She looked again to the back door she'd just walked through and knew it had been locked. Had there been a car in the drive when she pulled in?

"AJ, is that you?"

She stepped into the kitchen crowded with Christmas accessories needing to be inventoried. She saw Penny and Inez standing over an open box of ornaments.

"Well, color me shocked. I'd never have expected the two of you in the shop before opening hours." AJ kicked at the packing peanuts scattered over the floor. "Had I mentioned needing help this morning?"

They both pointed accusing fingers at the other.

Finally, Inez spoke. "Well, I had this dream. I knew someone had robbed you. Robbed blind, I say. Before I even had my coffee, I drove down here to the shop, and who do I find going through your supplies?"

AJ shifted her gaze to the window and saw Inez's Cadillac parked under a tree near the greenhouses. "Uh, Penny?"

Penny threw her hands in the air. "*July* had come here early. I followed her here, because I'd yet to see that woman leave the house before nine, and I was mighty suspicious of what she might be doing. I was on the way to the farmers' market after that. I want peaches for a dessert."

AJ glanced around but didn't see evidence that her mother had been on site. "Mom came to the shop and now is—?"

"Out in the gardens," Penny said, pointing an accusatory finger to the other window. "She asked to borrow your bike this morning, she said she needed the exercise. Knowing her, I thought she might meet someone. Someone she has no business talking to, if you catch my drift."

AJ scratched her forehead, confused by the disarray in the stockroom. "You two helped unpack Christmas products while waiting for Mom to come back?"

"No, I'm telling you they have robbed you." Inez waved a hand around the room. "I'm not sure what they have taken. But you'd better talk to Sheriff Weston, because something's gone missing."

AJ steadied her grandmother's hand. "I think it's safe to keep him out of this little drama."

Inez jerked away. "I've already called him," she snarled. "You know he's always had a sweet spot for me, and he said he'd swing by this morning to check in on the situation."

Inez had some strange connection to the Sheriff of Kendall County, and he treated her like she was his favorite aunt, but AJ was never clear on what their connection was, because until she'd moved here, Inez had rarely stepped foot in Comfort.

"Gran, come walk with me. Let's make sure everything is okay in the store. I think you can call Sheriff Weston and tell him he doesn't need to stop by."

Penny picked up her purse. "Now you're here, I'm going on to the farmers' market. The peaches will be gone before I can blink. We both know Roger loves my cobbler. Or at least he used to."

"Thanks for stopping by to check on everyone." And by everyone, she felt sure Penny knew she meant Inez. AJ glanced to her grandmother, noting the worry lines pinched between her artificially darkened brows. "What's going on here, Gran? Are you dizzy? Is your heart giving you fits again?"

"No! It's . . . her ... it is. . ." Inez couldn't seem to find her words, but her brows tightened into a V. "*That woman* is stealing from you. She's wanted the house for years, but since she can't get her hands on that, she's going after your first love, this store. I saw her with her hand in the cookie jar."

AJ kept a cookie jar collection in the break room, but July's past visits to Lavender Hill were usually limited to long weekends, and she doubted if her mother even paid attention to any of the details inside the shop. She'd complained that the lavender fields gave her a headache. "Let's go look at the cookie jars, Gran. You think someone has moved them?"

"I'm not talking about stealing a real cookie jar, AJ. I'm talking about your business. *She's* after something. That's why she's been rummaging in your attic."

AJ peeped through the miniblinds. She could make out the oak tree beyond the greenhouse where she grew seedlings. If Penny was right, July was sitting under an arbor on one of the twig chairs and listening to the bluebirds sing as they danced over the lavender tops in the field beyond.

This moment did not feel like a nefarious plot to overthrow Lavender Hill, but judging by Inez's expression, there was no convincing her grandmother otherwise. "Gran, maybe you're right. I'll keep an eye on things."

Inez's shoulders slumped. Her eyes lost their sheen. "I need something to drink." She walked out of the kitchen and down the hallway toward the back door.

AJ followed, turning on ceiling fans along the way. When she came to the door, she saw her grandmother staring at the keys in her hands like she didn't know what she was to do with them. "I thought you were thirsty?"

"I am." Inez looked twice at AJ, like she was considering confessing something. "I'm going to the Burger Barn and get a Coke."

"Are you sure you don't want coffee instead? Joe's has a nice blend this morning."

"That stuff costs a fortune. I'll hit the drive-through and grab me a Coke in my refillable cup. That's why I support the local businesses, because they take care of their own, with refillable cups."

"Joe's is locally owned," AJ defended.

"Is not."

"Is too." AJ felt like a kid taunting another kindergartner. "You used to tell me Joe's granddaddy was the butcher here when you married Granddad."

"Maybe he was. I always liked the butcher. He gave the Worthingtons a good deal on chops. Anyway, keep an eye on you-know-who. She's up to something, I can feel it."

Everybody was an expert on July Sands.

"Sure, Gran. I'll probably walk out there and see what she's doing," AJ said, checking the return address on the deliveries. "Maybe take her a cup of tea."

"Don't take care of her. She'll never leave if you treat her kindly."

"I'm thinking kindness wouldn't be amiss. Mom's had to put up with a lot from reporters this year. Maybe she'd like to have a conversation that didn't involve words like 'platinum records.'"

Inez sighed. "I give up. I tell you how to deal with her, and you ignore me. Don't you know I know what I'm talking about? I didn't get to this age without knowing how to manage people."

AJ had seen Inez master the San Antonio social scene like a professional. Inez and George Worthington had owned and operated three Chevrolet dealerships, and that feel-good relationship they'd built with their customers carried over to a variety of settings. "You were always the most popular lady at any party. I assumed that was your wit drawing everyone in close."

"Ha!"

"I'm sure you were the sorority president in college." AJ hadn't seen many pictures of Inez in her youth, but judging by the few she'd found of Roger when he was a baby, her grandmother was a beauty on top of being so well liked. "You will have to teach me your ways."

Inez picked up a stack of mail as if she'd take it with her. "I don't think that will work out so well."

AJ's heart sank. This vagueness about her grandmother was one of the most unsettling of all the changes. Maybe there was more going on than just losing her mental filter.

"I hardly recognize anything anymore," Inez whispered.

AJ put her arm around Inez's shoulders. "You don't recognize me, seriously?"

"Autumn Joy Worthington, I recognize you. I meant in the more, you know, what's the word, uh ... that other sort of way."

AJ leaned into her grandmother's shoulder. Inez wasn't one of those warm, fuzzy grandmothers, so a hug wouldn't be welcomed, but she'd squeeze her close regardless. "Well, maybe we're all getting a little fuzzy around the edges. Sometimes I don't recognize you, either."

"I can see that in your eyes and it just scares the fool out of me." Inez clutched the doorjamb. "I'm going into town. I'll be back later for my shift."

"Leave the mail here for me, will you?"

AJ stared at her grandmother's wake, wondering what was happening and how she could help. Hadn't she seen a magazine article about the pitfalls of aging? Could this be the sign of a disease?

Maybe she should call Inez's internist. Thinking of what she'd say if she got up the nerve to call the doctor, she wished she had someone to bounce all this off of—someone who didn't have a preconceived idea of Inez. Someone who could hear the story without making a snap judgement.

Someone with experience dealing with difficult people.

AJ stepped into her office with more oomph than needed. She knew exactly the person who could give her advice about dealing with her grandmother—most likely even offer insight into navigating the world of celebrity and the pitfalls of coming off a fame-bender, but she was not talking to him. Luke English, with his amiable smile and J. Crew attire, could go find another person to fix.

Her gaze settled on the giant ceramic frog sitting in the middle of the desk.

AJ stepped back stunned. That cookie jar was always on the top of the refrigerator.

Had someone broken into the store?

With more care than an inexpensive cookie jar warranted, AJ lifted the green frog's painted crown and stared down into the gulley where she kept $500 for emergencies. She found the spare keys to her house, spare keys to her truck, and the key to her safe deposit box. But the money and her list of computer passwords was gone.

Stunned, she rocked back on her heels.

With those passwords, a thief could clean out her bank accounts, ruin her credit, and scramble her inventory shipments for the next year.

Inez was right. She had been robbed.

Chapter Sixteen

Never underestimate the power of preparing a good bed for developing future blooms. Whether placing new plants in your garden or caring for established ones, invest in the details that will enhance growth — nutrients for health and mulch to choke out the weeds. — "Lessons from Lavender Hill"

Pushing her clogs against the wooden porch, AJ set the swing in motion and watched a customer drive off into the orangey-gold haze over the ribbon of asphalt leading back into town. Though there were still a few cars in the parking lot, most folks weren't staying until sunset anymore; it was too hot in the late afternoons. And serious gardeners were working their own beds by now. She leaned her head against the support of the swing's wicker back. With the rocking motion, she closed her eyes, grabbing a few minutes of ease from the last hours of a day she hoped never to repeat.

A cat rubbed its nose against her ankles, but she didn't stir. That was too insignificant a distraction to interrupt the hoops her mind was chasing. Betty and Hector argued nearby over whose turn it was to check the gates around the lavender farm. Still she kept her eyes closed. Dozens of wind chimes were tinkling, jostled in a warm breeze, but that presented no danger of dislodging the burdens that had become irreversibly apparent today.

"You look like you could use one of these."

She opened one heavy eyelid. Luke stood to her right, holding two icy cans of Dr Pepper. His chin was dark from a few days of missed contact with a razor, and his eyes were as warm as the horizon. Had his hair always had that much curl?

Maybe she was dreaming. He did look like a poster for sexy guy-next-door.

"May I join you?" he asked, with some trepidation.

So, she wasn't dreaming. She sat up and rolled her head to relieve the pressure she'd put on her neck. "A cold drink is always welcome. But we didn't part this morning on the best of terms."

Luke sat down on the swing. He settled in next to her, their shoulders, elbows, hips, and knees touching. It was way too close, too much into her personal space, and she felt singed from the contact.

He popped open a Dr Pepper, letting the fizzy hiss diffuse into the air. "I come in peace," he said, offering her the can.

AJ glanced at the horizon, chiding herself for reading too much into a reaction to his body. She smiled her thanks and took the can, enjoying a long drink as if she'd been dehydrated. The carbonation burn woke her up again, and the sugar softened her thoughts, making her aware of her shortcomings. Ever since Saturday, she'd been some strange version of herself, and she wasn't keen to see the pattern continue.

She had no idea what she was supposed to do about Luke, since he clearly hadn't left town, but she didn't want to always do battle either. She had bigger problems to deal with, and whether or not July decided to settle down here with her was not her most pressing concern.

"Do I get a prize if I guess you've already lured July back into your record company? She's not the rich woman she once was. I can see where your dollar figures would be a lot more appealing than my promises of quiet evenings and the annual summer street fair."

"I have no prize, and you've lost your guess."

AJ studied his profile. He might have the straightest nose she'd ever seen. There wasn't one hitch or dent to testify to his ever having lost a fight. "It's six o'clock on a Monday night. Maybe it is a little early for a victory dance."

"Is it that late? I've lost track of time."

She saw his Rolex. She'd put good money down he could account for every minute of his day. "Must be the country air getting to you."

"Could be." Luke stared across the garden. "I drove with the windows down today."

That wasn't something most folks around here commented on. It was a common enough occurrence. "A lot of heavy pollution in Nashville?"

"Noise. You can't go anywhere without traffic. It's so annoying to hide inside a car."

"For a music man, you like peace?" AJ would add that to her list of oddities about this man.

"I'm a complex person, AJ."

As he turned his face toward her, she sucked in her breath. His mouth was just inches from hers. And he was grinning.

"I, uh—"

"Admit it. You were prejudiced against me from the moment you saw my business card."

She couldn't remember much from their earliest meeting. Other than her mouth had dried to cotton. Her hands had tingled. Stars floated in her vision. And she'd wondered if she'd had a tiny heart attack.

"I didn't see your card," she said quickly, sitting up straighter. "Your cover was blown the moment you looked at my mother."

Luke stopped the swing's sway with his foot. "I'm sorry for ruining the nice time with your friends this morning. I didn't want to bring July's name into the mix, because I know how you feel about that business. Since everything tanked with the mention of her name, I wanted you to know I felt bad about you being the one to leave the coffee shop."

She searched his gaze, looking for something that would show he was trying to manipulate her. Few people associated with July ever apologized for inconveniencing her.

"But on the upside," he said brightly, "Jake and I are going fishing Saturday morning. He said he knows a lake where we can haul in largemouth bass just by dropping sink-worms. He also said, if you're interested, you girls can bring us a picnic. I have to say, I like the way Jake thinks."

Surprise knocked a dent in her preconceptions. "You fish?"

He nudged her shoulder with his. "See, you had pegged me as a desk jockey. Just because I work with musicians doesn't mean I don't know how to have a real life."

AJ gulped more of the soft drink to keep from imagining him in Ralph Lauren casual wear along the banks of the Guadalupe.

"If I catch fish Saturday, can I store them at your house? I don't have a freezer in the cottage I'm renting. And we can even have a fish fry next week. I love to share the catch. Do you cook fish?"

"You rented a cottage? You're staying?"

"I told you I was on vacation."

A spinning wheel of pictures she'd never seen fanned out in her mind. Luke fished? He'd made friends with a highly skeptical businessman? He enjoyed being in the sleepiest town in the Texas Hill Country? None of this made sense.

She'd have to rethink judgment calls she'd made, but first he'd asked if she could cook.

She almost laughed out loud, remembering the summer she'd started the Culinary Institute of Art thinking she would attempt becoming a chef, since she didn't know what else she could do. She'd never mastered cutting an onion and was one of the first to flunk out that semester.

"I can cover the basics," she stammered, wondering how this conversation had spiraled into a fish fry at her house. "But I haven't fished in years, maybe since my grandfather died."

"If you didn't have Penny, would you cook at all?"

She'd invested in a high-end gas stove when she remodeled her home four years ago because she'd still enjoyed playing with recipes, but she only got control of the kitchen in the winter when the garden store was silent, and Penny returned to Tennessee to fulfill her rotation with her invalid mother's care. It was dismal cooking for one person, so when she proposed that Inez move to Comfort, she added meal service to sweeten the deal. Inez hated being in the kitchen, and they'd worked out a nice routine ever since.

"I can make a few things. Gran says my pancakes are to die for."

His eyes widened. "I'm a discriminating pancake aficionado. Comes from staying in a lot of hotels. But I'd have to see proof before I believed a blanket statement like that."

AJ took another slow drag of soda and tried to put this weird moment in perspective. He was flirting with her.

"Sorry," AJ said, flattening her voice to put him off. She wasn't about to indulge yet another man who only wanted to use her to access her connections. "Penny doesn't let me in the kitchen if guests are around. She likes to show off her skills, hoping she can persuade someone with deep pockets to open a restaurant."

"I've seen her knives. They're scary sharp." He shuddered. "I bet that's why you really keep her around. She's your security detail."

AJ chuckled. "Penny has many skills, but Comfort's not a hotbed for crime."

"I didn't mean from thieves. Just people that wanted to get close to you."

Luke must have "psychotherapist" on that business card she'd not as yet seen. "Okay, since you're begging, I'll make you pancakes."

Luke turned toward her, knocking her knees with his.

"AJ, I'm not trying to undermine you. I want to spend time with you. And it's not because I want you to approve of July writing new music. If she refused to hear me out, my life would go on. I won't get a commission for securing her to any deal, I'm not her agent. And I don't want to be." Luke's gaze tracked a butterfly as it darted near their swing. "Derailing her retirement was more of a personal interest of mine than anything that came with a contract."

She wondered when he'd fallen for July. He wasn't that much older than she was, and it must have been another case of him growing up listening to her songs on the radio. "You don't look like one of Mom's usual fans. They tend to wear girdles."

Beans barked at someone driving through Lavender Hill's gate.

A Kendall County vehicle pulled into her driveway, followed by a late-model compact.

"You were expecting customers?" Luke asked, after a quick glance at his watch. "I thought I had timed my arrival better."

AJ stood from the swing, unsure of how she'd explain the sheriff's arrival. "I've had a little situation here today, and Sheriff Weston suggested I change the locks and all my computer passwords."

"What happened?"

She returned the sheriff's wave and wished Beans wouldn't sniff the tires that particular way; it was a sure sign he was about to do something disrespectful. "Nothing more than mischievousness, I'm sure."

Luke analyzed the man double-checking his holster. "This looks serious."

AJ suspected, if push came to shove, that Weston would shoot first and ask questions later. "And that's why he's so good in public service."

Luke stood from the swing. "I'll wait for you to get done with the sheriff. I'm in no hurry. If I can be of help, please let me know. I want you to know you can trust me."

Trust? No one from the music business was trustworthy.

"This could take a while. I have a lot of doors." She waved her arm toward the greenhouse. "But there are some nice restaurants in town. You should go ahead to dinner."

Luke called to Beans, and the dog came loping toward the porch. "I'm counting on a local girl to show me the ropes," he said.

Annoyance flared under her heart, and she tapped it down. Hard. "Well, don't let me keep you. And thanks for the cold drink. I couldn't have asked for a better way to end a long, strange day."

Luke grinned as he bent down to pet the dog's fur. "AJ, you're the local girl I want to have dinner with. But since lock replacement might take a while, how about if I order a to-go meal and come back in half an hour? That way you don't feel rushed."

She bristled from this roller coaster of reactions, including how besotted her dog looked at Luke's side. "You know, we're not going to be friends."

Luke stepped close enough to ease into AJ's comfort zone. "Oh, we don't have to be just friends."

"AJ!"

She tore her gaze from Luke's, seeing the sheriff crossing over the compact thyme like the leaves disguised mortar shells. "I've brought Walter to replace your locks," Sheriff Weston said, as he stopped at the base of the porch steps. "And, we need to talk about your grandmother. Have there been any more incidents since this morning?"

Luke introduced himself, and the two men shook hands like there was more at stake than name exchanging. "Is there a connection between Inez and the security around here, Sheriff?"

"Lack of security, don't you mean?" Weston folded his hands behind his waist and stood at attention. "I've investigated the property this afternoon, and AJ has one of the loosest operations in town. She needs to double down on security. Cameras would at least confirm that Inez is the one you should be watching."

"Gran is angry that I've let Mom move in, but she will not harm us." AJ remembered poisoned basil plants, and almost said something about the tea July drank, but thought better of that idea. "Or, at least I've never known her to have a mean streak. She kept to a list of polite behaviors when I was growing up."

"I interviewed several of your staff this afternoon, and they confirm that Inez has been coming and going with irregularity. She's not herself. And I've known that lady since the day she found her backbone against the original Mrs. Worthington."

"Please don't read too much into this, Sheriff. She's just a little confused."

Luke reached for his business cards. "I've taken an extended leave from work, and I'm here for a few more days. If I can help you with Inez, then count me in," he said. "Here's how to reach me."

The sheriff took his card and nodded. "Another set of male eyes is always smart. Women are way too trusting."

AJ watched Beans sniff the sheriff's pants, feeling oddly outnumbered by the solidarity of chromosomes. This wasn't the time to defend herself, because she thought the sheriff might be right. She'd been way too trusting. Someone was taking advantage of that. If Luke was committed to vacationing here, she wouldn't stop him. She didn't understand why he'd want to spend his days off in Comfort, around her crazy family, but twenty-four more hours here would probably shoot him straight to the airport and the first flight back to Nashville.

AJ pulled her dog's collar, drawing him closer to her side of the porch. "Though I'm insulted on behalf of all women, and I think you're wrong about Gran, I will accept Luke's help in keeping an eye around the house. Things are nuts with Mom, Dad, and Gran all in proximity to each other."

"Roger is home now, too?" Sheriff Weston whistled like the twists of fate stunned him. "Then he can take your grandmother to the doctor. I think what you're seeing here is the beginning of something with no known cure. I hate that more than I can say. Inez was kind to me when I was just starting out as a deputy. She and your granddad sold me my first car when I came home from Kuwait. They practically gave it to me, at the price they charged."

"I have a lot on my plate, but Gran is my priority now." AJ stepped between the two men as she moved toward the steps. "I just need to figure out a way to manage it all."

"Technically, AJ, you're not responsible for your family." Luke stuffed his hands in his pockets. "Well, except for maybe your grandmother. My grandpa needed a chaperone as he got older, because he liked to take walks and couldn't remember how to get home. But everyone took turns to keep him safe — that's the answer."

The sheriff stepped into the yard, careful to bypass the thyme. "Walter charges by the hour. See that you get that barn and greenhouse done too. I saw rat killer in there, and we don't want that getting into the wrong hands."

She saluted. "Yes, sir."

Words were swirling in her head, and she knew she had to say something to Luke. He'd seen every one of her personal disasters in the space of one weekend. She owed him for cleaning up her kitchen and not making an issue of her tantrum this morning.

"The Burger Barn makes a great cheeseburger, if the dinner offer is still on."

Chapter Seventeen

Comfort, Texas   April 4, 1955

Inez rubbed her swollen belly as she sat on the Worthingtons' porch swing. She set the rocker in motion, hoping a slight breeze would cool her skin of the astonishing heat that seemed to be part and parcel of this pregnancy. She'd resisted coming with George for his seasonal visit to his parents, but with the baby so close to its due date, he'd insisted he couldn't leave her alone in their apartment in San Antonio.

Inez sighed. It was easier to pretend she liked these people when she wasn't in Comfort.

No one had mentioned Mrs. Worthington since they'd arrived an hour ago. Maybe her mother-in-law had gone into town.

Inez picked her fingernail.

The screen door opened, and her husband walked onto the porch. His expression looked defeated.

George set a lemonade on the side table. "Thought something cool might help."

Smiling weakly she asked, "Is it spiked?"

"Funny." George gazed out over the tilled soil beyond the driveway. "We won't stay long. I told my father I needed to get you back to the city in case you went into labor."

"I'm sure that was too much information for him to hear."

George sighed. "Maybe you do understand my family after all."

The screen door squeaked again as someone else stepped out. Inez straightened her shoulders, knowing it would be one of her in-laws. No one else lived in this musty old house.

"George, darling, go into the kitchen and bring out that pot of coffee I made." Mrs. Worthington sat on the porch swing next to Inez. "I'm sure we could all use a little refreshment."

Inez cut her gaze to Mrs. Worthington wearing a black dress and apron in the middle of the summer's heat. In one failed attempt at conversation last year, she'd asked her mother-in-law why she always wore black, and was given a steely answer regarding mothers who lost three sons to war. Inez didn't ask those questions anymore.

She stared across the driveway, wishing a troll or something interesting would pop up from the rows of peas growing in the garden. Anything that would break the tension that grew taut with each of Mrs. Worthington's breaths.

"I see your manners haven't improved with impending motherhood." Mrs. Worthington stopped the porch swing's movements. "I'd have thought you'd be a little more charitable with such happy days ahead."

Inez felt bloated to the size of a whale, the summer heat was almost a hundred degrees in the shade, and she had a baby that delighted in kicking her bladder. She wasn't sure what happiness Mrs. Worthington referred to, seeing as how they were bringing a baby home to a one-room studio and a crib made from the drawer of a dresser.

Because she'd rather die than admit any weakness to her mother-in-law, she pasted on a smile. "Forgive my lapse in conversation. I was just daydreaming about baby names. We thought we would ask you for suggestions."

Though Inez would have thought it wasn't possible, Mrs. Worthington smiled. The effort was strained and made her eyes pinch, but it was an upward movement of lips that were usually as straight as iron rail lines.

"Oh, what an enterprising notion. I must put thought into that," Mrs. Worthington said, glancing off to the pasture.

Inez hoped she took the better part of a week.

"I've always been fond of Rupert," she said, bringing that resolute gaze back to Inez's forehead. "It was my father's name, and he was such an honorable man."

And yet, none of George's brothers had carried that name. "Interesting."

"If the baby is a girl, name her Elizabeth. For the queen."

Inez lifted one of her brows. "You mean, the queen of England?"

"Yes, what a remarkable young woman. She's taken on such a beastly set of responsibilities. You wouldn't go wrong naming the baby after someone that respected."

She shrugged and said, "I was thinking of Elvis. I met him a few years ago in Gladewater. He's popular."

Mrs. Worthington scowled. "That's the most disgusting thing I've ever heard. Why would you even suggest such a name? I swear I don't know what George sees in you. You have no taste."

Inez bit the inside of her mouth to keep from giggling.

Since she knew she would never change her mother-in-law's prejudices, she indulged them. It was her private revenge. "Well, we didn't have much exposure to taste when working the oil fields of East Texas, and with my mother dying so young, it's a wonder I even learned how to be a girl at all."

"I should say so."

"If it weren't for the showgirls who came through daddy's bar, I doubt I'd know the first thing about womanhood."

Mrs. Worthington stood, her back as straight as the fence post on the other side of the drive. "You are revolting," she hissed.

George pushed through the screen door with a large tray in his hands. "Here you go, Mother. Coffee, just as you requested."

"Set it here, dear." She pointed to a table as far away from the swing as possible. "We'll have Inez serve for us."

Inez, who could not see her feet anymore, wasn't sure she could stand without help. "I'm not able to get out of the swing."

"Nonsense, child. A good housewife always puts the needs of her husband above her own. It's in the Bible."

Inez looked at George. "Are you thirsty for coffee?"

"Only if Mother says I am."

As she struggled to maneuver herself out of the porch swing—because, by God, she would not give Mrs. Worthington one more fault to accuse her of—she wobbled and lost her balance. Her knees gave out, and she fell to the porch, rolling onto her side to protect the baby. Groaning in instant misery, she cradled her belly and ignored the pain in her shoulder for the worry of protecting that melon-sized human.

George folded down beside her, reaching for her wrist like that was the easiest thing for him to grab. But as Inez opened her eyes, she saw Mrs. Worthington staring down, a glint of hatred in her eyes.

"How unfortunate, George. Inez will need to be put up in the guest room. I really don't see how you can travel until a doctor has seen her. I hope you brought luggage. You will be here for several days."

Chapter Eighteen

When beginning a garden, don't be disappointed by the slow growth of your plants. Roots take time to develop. — *"Lessons from Lavender Hill"*

AJ parked her truck underneath the arms of a generous oak tree and let the cooler air circulate through the open windows of the cab. Tucking Walter's business card into her tote, she glanced around the yard and recognized the vehicles. Beans pawed across her lap, in a hurry to see what he was missing at home. She, on the other hand, could wait.

Dread curled around her ribs. Her mom had texted half an hour ago that Luke had arrived with hamburgers, and she was going to eat with him since AJ was running late. She'd not bothered to tell her mom those burgers were meant for her, because standing up against her parents was an ingrained no-no. But maybe it was time for all that to change. Hearing the sheriff warn her about the pitfalls of letting Inez go without a diagnosis had rearranged her mindset.

If Roger and July wanted to stay in Comfort, then fine. But she couldn't justify placating their moods while Gran was slipping away from them faster than moonlight. She glanced to the inky sky. It was time to prove that if she could make lavender grow in rocky soil, she could define a new relationship with her parents. One that was based on evenness and respect. And maybe . . . distance.

Heaviness settled into her shoulders. Her life was so much easier when they weren't around.

AJ followed Beans across the yard, watching as he happily circled the two rental cars and peed on her father's bumper. Whistling for him, she climbed the shallow steps and paused at the front door. Drawing in a breath scented with freshly mown grass, she leaned her ear toward the glass pane, listening for the sounds of arguments. She would assume if Roger were here, Penny must be also, and with the addition of Luke, that made four adults and four distinctly different agendas at work. She glanced backwards, looking for her grandmother's car and wondered if she was alone at the cabin.

She bit her lip and entered the foyer. Leaving Gran alone was going to be the first thing to change.

The bathroom door at the top of the stairs tempted her. She imagined they'd seen her truck drive in, so there was no hiding under the guise of a shower. Pinching a sprig of rosemary from the arrangement on the table, she tucked it behind her ear as she set her tote on the floor. There were no sounds of breaking glassware, so that was a nice surprise. AJ slipped off her shoes and walked across the carpet in the dining room, smelling the lingering fragrance of fried onion rings. Peeking through the butler's pantry, she counted three people in her kitchen, and they all appeared normal. No tears. No accusations. No broken china.

Luke and her parents were haggling about the talents of a current pop music star and whether she could make it for the long haul. Luke was washing one of the dinner plates, and nearby were paper remnants of the Burger Barn feast. Her stomach leapt and she regretted being so late.

"I'm wondering if I've stepped into a parallel universe," she said, mostly to herself.

Luke turned to her, a bit sheepish that he'd made himself at home in her kitchen. "Strange as this may seem, it is real. I've made them sign waivers preventing bloodshed."

July toasted Luke with a tea glass. "Actually, he made us swear that if we had an ounce of affection for you, we'd put aside our differences for this one night and behave."

Roger tore off the edge of a paper napkin. "You don't have to make it sound like he negotiated world peace."

"I've known you for thirty-two years, Roger Worthington. This is as good as world peace."

Roger scooted back in his chair and crossed his ankles. "I'm not the one with the Irish temper, but I do have affection for my daughter."

Luke pulled a drying cloth from the end of the counter. "See, AJ, they can be reasonable. Biting and caustic, but still sensible."

AJ entered the kitchen, drawn as much by the sight of the food as her parents' truce. She crossed the room and unwrapped the burger from the paper. "Okay, well, Luke, I guess I owe you. You *can* work miracles."

She wasn't about to elaborate on the tremendous gift of getting her parents together. That was just spooky.

He shrugged. "It's just fast food."

July blew out a breath of disdain. "It's not like he had to twist our arms to get us to have a meal together."

AJ slid the fat cheeseburger onto a plate and into the microwave. "The last time you two were in this kitchen, there were tears. And Dad's not often driven to cry."

"I've hit middle age." Roger lifted one shoulder. "It's done crazy things to my system. I cried last week over an orphanage commercial, so don't read too much into the emotion. I just leak."

AJ set the timer on the microwave and snitched an onion ring. Even cold, these were the best vice in all of Comfort.

Luke handed her a tall glass of tea. "I called your Dad because I knew you wanted to talk about your grandmother.

Penny is staying with her at the cabin tonight. We think they're watching reruns of *Golden Girls*."

The onion ring didn't taste as good when seasoned with apprehension. Who was this guy, and why did he feel obligated to get involved? "I'm kind of thinking that was my call to make."

"From what the sheriff said, there's not a lot of time to lose." Luke laid the towel along the sink's rim. "I'm a take-charge kind of guy. Sorry for stepping on your toes."

The silence stretched his apology out longer than it deserved. Part of the shift in her thinking today might include making room for others to help.

After the acrimony of the other night, she didn't think her parents could say two civil words to each other. Luke had them assembled in the first peaceful co-existence she'd seen in forever, and that meant he could bring about difficult interpersonal meetings. She'd not begrudge him that skill. Lord knows *she* didn't have it. "Stepped on toes I can live with. You got my parents here, and that makes up for a lot."

July punched Roger's arm. "I think she insulted us."

"I think we haven't been very nice over the last few decades, and she's paying us back." Roger tucked a strand of hair behind his ear. "

July chuckled. "Go figure. You've developed a sensitive streak. I wish I'd known that was coming. I might have held on a little longer."

"Something tells me you wouldn't have held on had I promised you a gold mine. You were determined to fly, and nothing I could say would change that." Roger leaned toward her like a belligerent kid on a playground. "Am I right, or am I right?"

"*I'm* not the one who filed for divorce." July folded her arms across her bony ribs. "Or demanded sole custody."

"And *I'm* not the one who stole lyrics from somebody else's notebook."

The microwave timer buzzed, and AJ slammed her finger against the door, reaching in for the warm plate. "Obviously, the good times will be short lived, so before you sling mud in front of Luke, a man who need not know about the ugly details of Worthington family history, let's talk about something else. Namely, Gran."

July groaned. "Going from the frying pan to the fire."

AJ pinched a bite from the burger, savoring the cheese and beef. She would not guess how Luke knew she loved mustard on her burger, she'd just be grateful that he did.

"Dad, Gran has come to a weird place in her life. She's showing symptoms of something that's not her normal self. I read that people's personalities can change with dementia, so I'm trying not to panic."

Roger rubbed a finger against his temple. "Mom has always been gruff with people she considers inept. That's just not usually her family. She was great to Dad and me, and we all know she doted on you. But she was brutal to my grandmother. And to be fair, my grandmother dished it right back."

"This is more than impatience—" AJ glanced at her mother and decided not to complicate an already-strained relationship. "She's acting out in dangerous patterns. We'll need to keep a close eye on her until she gets some medication. I don't think we can leave her unsupervised."

July tilted her head to the side. "They have medication for orneriness? I wish I had known that years ago. She's hated me from the first day I walked into her house. Said I wasn't good enough for her son. She had the gall to imply I was a gold digger."

Roger grimaced. "That was because I had the bright idea to let you meet my parents after that concert in Luckenbach. Neither of us was sober."

"Still, it took years for her to be civil. Things got better only after AJ came along."

"She wanted us to have more babies, since AJ turned out so sweet, but you wanted no more kids. Said you couldn't be a mother and an artist."

"I never said that!" July slammed her hand on the table. "AJ, I swear I never said that. I loved being your mother. It was your father who was gone all the time, chasing his muse."

AJ rolled her gaze to the ceiling and said, "We're done hashing out old insults. Tonight, we rally around Gran."

Luke stepped forward, his hands held open in front of him. "Seriously, you both were a mess for many years, and you're not doing anyone a favor by dragging that trash to AJ's doorstep. Now, listen to her and then let her decide what needs to be done."

AJ wasn't sure when he'd moved over to her team, but she'd be grateful for the reinforcement. Unclenching her teeth, she said, "Dad, you couldn't have come home at a better time. You're her closest relative and the one who can get her in to see the doctor. Be her advocate."

Roger held his hands in the air in surrender. "I didn't come all this way to take care of my mother. I'm the last person she'd take help from, anyway. She reminds me I'm the one who left and never came back."

"You're her only child. You may be the one she really trusts." AJ tested the heat of her hamburger. "At least until you take her keys away from her."

"I'm not telling Inez Worthington she can't drive. She'll beat me with a stick." Roger flattened his hands on the table. "You're the one my mother relies on. She moved out here to be with you. She'll listen to you. She still thinks I'm a deadbeat dad because I wasn't around to pay for your last few years of college."

AJ would not touch that hotbed memory. "The thing is, we've got to get Gran to an internist before we can get her in to see a specialist. Just tell her she's due for her physical."

Luke set a platter of cookies on the table and seated himself between July and Roger. He reached for a coconut-and-chocolate-chip and said, "Call me cold, but I see one person in this kitchen with a full-time job and responsibility for feeding a whole family. Two of her adult dependents are temporarily unemployed. Wonder who has the most time to devote to this situation?"

AJ turned toward him, stunned that he kept coming to her defense. This was not the path to winning July to his point of view.

Roger, who'd always been able to resist Penny's cookies, pushed the plate away. "Unless you're secretly engaged to my daughter, English, I'm not even sure why you're at this meeting, and you don't get to have an opinion."

Hacking on cookie crumbs, Luke said, "AJ has only just started speaking to me without flames shooting from her eyes, so I'd rather not rush the ring."

She swallowed another bite of her burger, feeling a warm glow in her heart that had nothing to do with potential indigestion.

Luke pushed away from the table. "Looks like you two have catching up to do. AJ and I will leave and go somewhere far away from the claws."

No one had ever closed the door on her parents. Not in the history of ever.

"It's late, Luke." AJ glanced at her watch, amazed it was only eight o'clock.

"The night's young." Luke glanced at the wall clock. "At the least, Cup of Joe's should still be open."

"I'd love an espresso," July sighed.

Roger harrumphed. "You weren't invited."

"Not invited? Are you kidding? Luke wants me to come out of retirement. He's got some big ideas for me."

Luke moved to stand beside AJ, even though his words were for July. "But you said you didn't want to talk. That you were here to find yourself."

July nodded. "Even though I don't want to record another greatest hits album, it might be cathartic to do the memoir."

AJ's shoulder felt warm and protected, as if Luke wanted to shield her from something. Licking mustard off her finger, she savored—even for the briefest of moments—how nice it was to have a partner in dealing with her parents.

They were exhausting.

"Mom, maybe your retirement was more about shifting gears instead of quitting altogether. Give yourself some time to consider your options." The words sounded stiff coming off her tongue, but there was a measure of candidness. She had questioned Luke's motives all week, but there was no denying her mother needed something creative to process her career. Maybe a book would satisfy her need to play with verses.

"You also said I needed to get off Prozac. Are you doing an about face on that too?" July smirked.

"This isn't flexible, AJ," Roger said. "It's ludicrous. No one wants to rehash July Sands's old songs, or her life."

Luke folded his arms across his chest. "Roger's right."

AJ stared at Luke, wondering if he'd spiked his own tea. "He is?"

Luke nodded. "Don't get me wrong. I think July's original music was powerful. But I've heard some incredible new music flowing from her guitar today. I realize I'm backtracking, but I don't think a re-release of her hits is a good idea. If her fans heard what I've heard, they'd clamor to buy the new songs."

Bitterness flared behind AJ's eyes.

She should have followed her first instincts. "I knew it was too good to be true. You're playing us to satisfy your own agenda."

"That is not true. My agenda is currently under evaluation and has no binding elements. All I'm saying is there's still a well of talent inside July Sands. If she records an album, or not, it is her call. But above all else, she's not a has-been."

Tears trickled off July's eyelashes. "Thank you, Luke. Those words mean more than you'll ever know."

Roger placed his hands over his ears. "Please tell me I didn't hear what I think I heard."

July's eyes flashed when she stared at Roger. "Is sympathy so hard for you to endure?"

Roger stood from the chair, knocking it over in his haste. "It is when it always happens to you. You're like a duck. No matter what kind of mud lands on you, it rolls off. How come my life isn't like that? How come when the bad stuff happens, it sticks?"

"Dad?"

Roger's eyes burned bright as he looked at AJ. "Don't *Dad* me now, AJ. I can't be the paragon you want me to be, okay? I'm not that kind of person. I never have been. And I hate it that July always has the luck."

"Roger Worthington, I do not have good luck," July pleaded. "I have suffered mightily because of my choices, just like you have, and because this man says something nice about my playing guitar does not mean I will have a reversal of fortune."

AJ stared at her mother, amazed by the candor.

"You're insane, July," Roger pronounced. "I've always suspected it."

Luke wrapped his hand around AJ's elbow. "Do you want to get out of here?"

AJ pulled her arm free. "I can't leave now. They need me."

Luke glanced around the room. "This looks fairly healthy. In therapy circles they call this closure. So, come on. If we don't get coffee, lets at least go for that walk in the moonlight."

A day's worth of tension came unloosed on her tongue. "You don't get it, do you? They hate each other. They despise anything that has to do with the other. They'd rather spit than say anything nice about the years we had together as a family, and they will not agree with anything that involves me, or Gran. They are bitter people."

The words pinged off the kitchen walls.

AJ stared at the uneaten burger, because she couldn't bring herself to look at her parents; she was afraid to see what might reflect in their expressions. She turned toward the sink, creating racket when she tossed her plate against the stainless steel.

July's voice broke the strain. "I don't hate Roger anymore. I mean, there were years, well, I seethed with it, but a few summers ago I went to that wellness spa, and the counselor there helped me find a way forward. And then I fell on God. I'm not ready to give up my old hurts—there's comfort in nursing the wounds, but I know if I do, it's just me being me. That's not what God would have for me."

Roger picked up his chair and righted it next to the table. "I have hated your mom for years. But if we're being honest here, and I think we are, then you know that despite my emotional reactions to her, as a professional, I have a grudging respect for her. July is a survivor."

AJ heard a loop of static where logic should be. "You respect Mom?"

July reached across and touched his sleeve. "Roger."

He shook off her hand. "Well, it's not something I broadcast. Imagine what it would do for my reputation as an embittered ex."

AJ looked at her parents, really searched their faces. The faded colors and papery textures were tangible, but nothing else about the picture made sense.

Luke leaned close enough to whisper. "Come with me. Let's leave them to talk."

She shook her head. "I can't."

"You mean, you won't."

She turned a fraction, meeting his eyes, the gaze more steel than she preferred. "This is a breakthrough. I want to see what comes next."

Luke scrubbed at the day's growth of beard on his chin like he wondered, too. She found the action oddly fascinating. When AJ dragged her gaze away from Luke, she saw her parents facing each other, arms folded across their chests, the familiar daggers drawn again.

July took a step back. "I can't believe you can question Luke's motives. He's a gentleman and a business associate. AJ doesn't think he's a mercenary."

AJ had missed something important while thinking Luke had become far more attractive for his imperfections.

"Okay, Luke. Twenty questions." Roger pulled out his chair, collapsing into it with no grace. "My little girl has reservations about you, and since she's running this operation, I think we need to set the matter straight. For her peace of mind, if nothing else. Put away your poker face, we're about to get real."

Chapter Nineteen

"Dad, you've lost your mind." Panic pulled AJ's vocal cords taut. "Really, Luke, I didn't ask him to do this. I've hardly talked to him at all today, and I certainly don't know where he's come up with this bizarre idea."

Luke watched her movements, aching for her in that she'd been going strong since dawn, and here she was, still working and worrying, fourteen hours later. Did these people even see the layers of effort she put into an ordinary day? He doubted they had any notion of what she created on the other side of this hill. They only saw what she could do for them.

If he were AJ, he'd have changed his address years ago and not given it out.

Luke glanced at Roger and July, staring back at him like he was a blemish in their little circle of codependency. Roger acted like he was some sort of patriarch, but everyone knew he'd lost all authority the day he walked out on his family. Luke had a hard time even seeing Roger as one of the most talented musicians of the '80s, though the gold records were there. Honestly, the shine was wearing off July, too.

"It's not too late to go outside," he said, leaning against AJ's shoulder and loudly whispering, "I could use some fresh air."

Her eyes were puzzled, but she was wary. He understood. Crashes were hard to ignore.

Roger motioned to the empty chair. "Have a seat, Luke. This could take a few minutes."

Luke folded his arms across his chest, daring Roger to amend the order. He'd be a lot more cooperative had he seen actual concern for AJ, but it appeared Roger acted on his impulses. That explained a lot about the lack of structure in this family and the way AJ had to react whenever Roger and July rode into town. If he wasn't so attracted to the man's daughter, he'd have told Roger where he could shove it.

Smiling at the thought, he realized that he'd come a little unglued here in Comfort. He was strangely energized by the freedom he felt out here where no one knew him or had any level of expectation for what he could produce. The liberty was going to his head. It made him want to woo this woman, who until two hours ago most likely detested him.

"All right, stand," Roger said. "But know I can go on like this all night. I used to win at Trivial Pursuit because I could outlast everyone."

Luke nodded, surprised that Roger would play games. Maybe there was hope for the man to come around.

"Roger, don't do this," July pleaded. "AJ's nervous because she's worried about me getting sucked back into the industry. It's not personal. She'd be this way about you, too. Leave Luke out."

Roger leveled his gaze on Luke. "Oh, I think it's personal. I've seen the way that man looks at my daughter."

He squirmed. Was it possible that below the grizzled exterior was a man who felt protective of his cub? Luke wouldn't bet on it. Roger probably just wanted to prove a point to July, justifying his superiority in the ongoing war of ego.

"I've never liked a confrontation," July said sullenly. "I'm going to my room."

"No, you need to stick around and verify his answers." Roger grabbed her arm as she moved past. "You're the only one in the room with enough insider knowledge of Nashville to know if he's telling the truth or not."

July quirked her head to one side. "You know, you sound just like Inez when you talk like that."

Roger dropped his hand as if electrocuted. "That was low, but I will forgive you for hitting below the belt because you're still coming off diva status. Now, help me think up twenty questions."

Luke leaned against the sink. This would get dirty. "AJ, you wouldn't have any bourbon, would you?"

Roger leaned his elbows on the table. "Okay, here we go. Are you in fact Luke English, an executive with my old music company, the one that shall not be named?"

"I'm in charge of the marketing department at, well, you-know-where," Luke said. "I can give you references, if you need them."

"They robbed me of my copyrights—I never want to speak of them again. Moving on," Roger said with venom. "So, Luke, are you that desperate for Christmas album sales that you would drag back the mistress of slush hits to churn out another run on her Tennessee sleigh ride?"

A few days ago, he'd spoken that very plan to the CEO of his company, complete with a holiday television special. Now, having talked to July and studied the jagged edges that gave her voice such a touchstone to so many people's tragedies and hopes—he wasn't sure if that was the right path. The twists in her life were steep, the grades so sharp that there were entire valleys of new material waiting to be cultivated. He'd already imagined the verses she could create, if she were of a mind to write.

As he glanced at the acrimonious steel cutting into the hearts of Roger and July, he knew it wasn't their marriage that created such loathing—it was the vagaries of talent. They were too much alike.

Too artistic.

Too self-centered.

Too destructive.

Too removed from the one great thing they created together. The miracle of their gifts — their daughter.

Seemingly the only person on the planet willing to take them in when they were wounded, lost, and scarred beyond recognition.

Luke felt the wheels that had been spinning since he saw that press release slow to a halt. AJ knew, had known for years, that their talent had spawned a madness. That's why she was so desperate to protect them from themselves.

He rubbed at the vein throbbing below his forehead. He'd jumped at an opportunity that was all wrong. Repeating what had gone before would just continue the cycle. Did July, and Roger too, need something to challenge them? Yes. Did they need to write and perform again? Without a doubt. Did they need to do it with the Nashville machine at their back?

No. They didn't have the energy or the drive to work in that hyper-sensitized environment.

Glancing to his side, he saw AJ as more than a beautiful woman with an allure that beguiled him. He saw a fierce and protective woman who knew Roger and July needed stability. Though it ran counter to their marketed personas, they had to have a box. Like overgrown children, they needed boundaries. What AJ never realized, would deny if asked, was that it was pushing against the edges that excited their creativity. The boundaries at issue tonight were related to aging and losing one's sense of purpose. That was a powerful motivation.

He was going to rethink his purposes.

And, maybe, entertain ideas that would rock his master plan. First, he had to salvage this moment.

"I will not force July into a record deal, but I stand by my belief that she's not performed her last song," Luke said, hearing a new perspective whisper in his ear. "And if she ever does something about the lyrics brewing inside her, then I hope she'll call a reputable agent. But I'm not an agent. And I won't hound her."

"Fair enough." Roger glanced at the ceiling for inspiration. "If you're not coming out here to badger July, why are you hanging around? Is it AJ you want to see?"

"Dad!" AJ almost dropped her cup.

Luke grinned, feeling better than he had in the last five minutes. "Can I plead the Fifth on that one? A man doesn't like to play his hand so early in the game."

AJ scowled as she whipped around to pick up a dishcloth and wipe at the counter. "This is absurd."

"I'm going somewhere with this," Roger said in defense. "Luke, are you married?"

He was thirty-five years old, and in all his fantasies of success and goals met, he'd missed filling a big hole in his heart.

"I vote, Roger. I obey the law, and I even drive the speed limit. If I had a wife at home, please know that I'd never offer to take AJ out for a walk in the moonlight. I'm not that kind of guy."

"Okay, good enough. Have you ever been married?"

A flood of antiseptic memories unwound from his heart and wrapped around the emptiness on his left hand. In the past, he'd glossed over this question with few details, using clichés about being married to his work to cover the truth. But if he wanted AJ to trust him, then he had to be honest. Exposing a story that upended his world ten years ago was the only way she'd ever see that — even if he messed up the details — he operated from a noble starting point.

"I was married for about seven months," he said, with a weight that came from shifting a deep scar onto center stage. His mind snapped back to the first time he'd fully realized how life could kick a person in the teeth. "I had this amazing friend group back in my twenties. We met in college and ran headlong toward frat parties and service projects as easily as we'd take off hiking for the weekend. No one had paired off in the group, but a few had met others and were getting married. I was wrapping up my masters and planning how to create a name for myself in the advertising business."

He paused, trying to string thoughts together that would sum up what had been a tumultuous few months.

"The summer after I graduated, I moved to Nashville and reconnected with Roni—she was the unofficial mom of our friend group, the one who remembered everyone's birthday and made sure everyone had a place to go for Thanksgiving. She was a freelance graphic artist and took on a lot of jobs that couldn't pay but were for great causes. I chalked her pale color and weight loss to the long hours she worked, supporting herself while trying to get hired by an agency that matched her ideals. Eventually, I talked her into going to a doctor— thinking she'd get iron pills and be back to her usual self. But she had stage four breast cancer."

He heard the gasp from AJ, but he couldn't slow the memories from filling his brain or rolling off his tongue. "Roni took the diagnosis in stride, while I was screaming from the top of my head. She wouldn't let me call her parents or any of our friends. Said she didn't want to depress them. I called a psychiatrist, thinking she was in denial and we needed to stage an intervention." Luke paused, remembering those meteoric days.

"The doctor," he continued, "told me she was handling this in the way she wanted, and that if I were one of her best friends, I'd respect her wishes and do everything I could to make her comfortable for the road ahead." Luke glanced at the empty ring finger on his left hand. "By then, I had landed a dream job and had great health benefits. Somewhere along the way of trying to get her into a treatment program, we made a deal to get married so she could have access to my insurance. It seemed like the only way to help her get well. We were good friends and figured we'd fall in love along the way. Unfortunately, I didn't move fast enough to get us down the aisle, because by the time we came back from her bucket list honeymoon, she was so sick she didn't qualify for experimental drug trials."

July walked over to him, tears spilling from her lashes as she reached for his hands. "Oh, my word. I can't even imagine how someone does something so unselfish for another person."

Luke looked at her pale hands covering his. He would not tell a Grammy-award-winning songwriter about the wild, unpredictable emotions he'd felt that summer. He didn't want to hear this story in a song. Ever. "Save your tears for her family. They had no idea about the cancer until after the wedding. Roni insisted that she didn't want pity."

AJ's gaze was boring into his shoulder. He could feel her laser cutting through his bone and sinew, and he regretted spilling this heartbreak on an evening already fraught with emotions.

Roger leaned back in the chair, lifting the front legs off the floor. "Wow. So, do you always play the hero, English? Or are you only drawn to women with unfixable problems?"

"Roger Worthington," July hissed. "You apologize this minute."

Roger dropped the legs of the chair to the floor suddenly. "I think this is important to understand. It would explain why he's hanging around you."

Luke steadied his breath, ready for battle with a man who was testing him at the core of his character. Thankfully, his parents gave him the gift of multiple sessions with a licensed counselor after the funeral, and he'd been able to work out his impulsiveness.

"Roni died peacefully, surrounded by people who loved her deeply. I wasn't the hero. She was." Luke swallowed the reactions that arose every time he thought about how brave it was that Roni had heard her diagnosis and lived vibrantly until she couldn't anymore. "And I'm drawn to women with an inner strength and conviction that far outweighs anything this world can throw at them."

July stepped back, her mouth unhinged. "That's good."

Roger stood and stretched his back. "Or, a script for a television show."

"Dad, you need to leave this house right now." AJ whipped around, her eyes flaming with a tension that was nearly tangible. "I don't like you very much when you get so cynical that you can't even see what's standing right before you. Go to Gran's. Now."

July covered her mouth.

"This is my home." Roger said, daring AJ to back down as he cast his gaze around the kitchen. "It's my family's legacy."

AJ's fingers twisted the dishcloth into a knot. "Your home is wherever your guitar lands, and it's currently at Gran's cottage. You need to leave this kitchen, and we'll figure out the rest in the morning."

"I'm not done with my questions for Luke. It's clear he's set his sights on getting July back into the business, and that's something you've said you wouldn't let happen on your watch."

AJ tossed the cloth into the sink. "Penny has loose lips, as you well know. But as with anything else that happens around here, we do best when we let things work themselves out naturally."

Roger stepped close to Luke, staring into his eyes like an old lion. "I don't know what your endgame is here, but consider yourself warned. If you mess with the women in the Worthington family, I will not make life easy for you."

"Duly noted." Luke saw lifelong regret, and possibly cataracts, in those eyes. He didn't feel threatened, though. Roger's MO was to leave the minute life got messy. "But you need to know, you're not done with the music either. It's running through your veins, and you walk with a beat in your step. I'd put my entire life savings on a bet that if you and July could put down your swords for one day, you could write and sing together to stun you both. Maybe even help you forgive each other and find a healthy way forward."

AJ's gasp almost sent him reeling. He'd not planned to say those words, out loud, ever. And now she would question his motives and see dollar signs at every turn.

"When hell freezes over," Roger said, backing away. "But I like your spirit. You're a surprise from all the other suits I've ever met."

July stood next to Roger. "I'm not sure what's happened here tonight either, but I agree that you're not at all what we're used to. You take our girl into the moonlight and help her remember that there's a big world out there. She needs to enjoy it."

AJ turned around, rapping her forehead against the cupboard. "I. Am. So. Confused."

July patted her shoulder. "You're the smartest one in the bunch. You'll figure everything out after a good night's sleep."

"I hope so," Luke said, feeling lighter than he had in months. Maybe they'd broken through a wall tonight. Maybe he'd finally put Roni's ghost behind him. Maybe, just maybe, it had inspired him to chase a new dream. "Because I want to hear more about her gardening book."

July's eyes widened. "AJ's writing a book?"

Chapter Twenty

Luke splayed his arms along the back of a park bench at the perimeter of Comfort's postage-stamp sized park and smiled. He couldn't help himself; just thinking about the crazy turn of events of the last few days made him feel like a teenager who was hitting his prime.

Scooting down on his spine, he leaned his neck back and closed his eyes, thinking this past week ranked as one of the best in his recent life. The crazy thing was, except for commandeering a corner of AJ's sunroom for a temporary office, he'd been doing a lot of physical labor. His shoulders pinched to remind him he'd moved three truckloads of composted manure from Jake and Kali's farm to Lavender Hill yesterday. He'd also fired up a tractor this week and tilled under a whole acre of dirt on AJ's back pasture.

Luke Payne English on a tractor. His mother would pass out from the shock of hearing he could find his way around a choke, a fussy carburetor, and a backhoe.

He breathed deeply. It must be the air. Since driving off the interstate, he'd entered a world where a man's character was judged by how well he could navigate heavy equipment and a fishing rod. And he'd not totally flunked.

Luke rubbed his jaw, feeling the whiskers he'd not shaved in a week. His beard was growing in, and though he wasn't ready for a *GQ* photo spread, there was lumberman potential. Was it too soon to order flannel?

Sweat dripped down his neck, reminding him that this was the time to be dreaming of tubing down the river towing a cooler, not dressing for snow.

AJ had been too busy to notice what he wore. Beans was the only one who seemed to get excited when he drove up to the house every morning to hang out with July and log on to the house Wi-Fi. Roger would usually clomp into the kitchen about an hour later with a list of farm chores for them all. July didn't want AJ to know they were doing the work, because she might misunderstand their motives.

Luke wasn't sure what Roger and July's motives were, but his were plain. He would pursue AJ, if she'd slow down long enough to let him.

He still couldn't believe busloads of tourists made a stop at Lavender Hill during their driving tours of the Hill Country, but he'd seen it with his own eyes and witnessed the labor she put into being both shopkeeper, saleswoman, and farmer of photogenic fields.

She was a lavender queen. Whenever he saw her walking through the fields, it took absolutely no effort to imagine her in a flowing dress, a basket under her arm, and her hair billowing like spun gold. That image should be the cover of her book.

Yes, he thought, imagining the conversation with the artist at a publishing company: late afternoon sunlight, that seven o'clock haze between blue and purple, the stalks raising their lavender swords in her tribute, and AJ wearing—what should she wear? Something white.

Icy water dripped onto his forehead.

His eyes sprung open, and he saw a melting cube dangling precariously over his forehead. "I will not complain. That felt good."

AJ sat next to him on the bench, tossing the ice cube to melt into the grass. "*That* was my attempt at sabotage. You looked way too peaceful for someone on security detail."

Scurrying to file his images back into the folder labeled with her name, he sat upright and pointed to the playground equipment. "Your grandmother refused to sit on the park bench, saying it hurt her legs. So, she's on the swing, singing old songs."

AJ leaned back into the bench. "I heard her singing when I walked up, and for a moment, I didn't know who that was with you. I've never heard my grandmother sing—outside of a church service."

Luke liked the way AJ wore her hair twisted into a clip today. With the blue sundress and sandals showing pink toenails, she looked almost relaxed. "How did it go with your parents this morning?"

AJ shuddered. "Keisha was kind to them both. Once she convinced my dad that Mom didn't have access to my money, nor was she able to steal the house away from me, we had a productive meeting. I think Dad wants Keisha to look at his bank statement, too."

He was glad the necessary but ugly money conversation had been handled by a professional third party. "So, July was right. Getting money out of the way would clear up a lot of problems for your parents."

"I never appreciated how childish they both were about the accounts," she mumbled. "But they admitted that there had been some serious trust issues in the past over who might or might not have spent the royalty money. Who put what amount into the family checkbook, and a lot of other dirt I didn't need to know. Now that they're both broke, maybe they can be more tolerable to each other. And I didn't even squirm when they said they both needed to find a way to earn money. Mom said all she knows how to do is to perform, and maybe you were right about her being too young to quit. She's going to need to do something profitable to replenish her retirement account."

Money was at the root of just about every performer's demise. A sinking star was almost never about the brightness of the light. "I won't gloat at hearing you say I'm right. But I am glad Keisha could help. She's a smart lady."

"I will owe her a serious paycheck for getting involved with all this." AJ opened a brown sack and gave him a cookie. "She's been tracking my accounts too. Whoever stole my passwords hasn't done anything with them. My credit history is still good. So maybe I shouldn't have called the sheriff."

"Inez called the sheriff, remember?" Luke studied the chocolate chip cookie. He held it up to the sunlight. "Are we comparing and contrasting here? I'm sure Penny made something just like this yesterday."

"Penny is perfecting a new recipe. She thinks Dad will take her with him when he eventually leaves, if she can hook him with her cooking."

Luke bit off an edge and savored the gooey flavor. He'd eaten more food in ten days than he had all month. "Tasty."

AJ chewed her bite. She was quiet while she watched a mom push a stroller down the sidewalk. "Do you think they will ever get better?"

"These are fabulous. Her best batch ever."

AJ playfully slapped at his arm. "My parents. You're their new best friend. What do you really think?"

Judging by the softness around her eyes, he thought maybe he'd been forgiven for sticking his nose into their family business. "Your folks have weathered a lot of storms. They'll get through this too, and — fingers crossed — be better for the time spent together. But I stand by my theory: they don't need to live off your income. They need to define themselves with their own skills."

He braced for the tongue-lashing AJ was sure to give him. He'd overstepped his boundaries again and making up for it by sitting with her grandmother during lunch was not going to win him enough points.

AJ folded the brown bag closed. "I used to think I could handle them. That coming home and sitting on the front porch was therapy enough to make up for the road, but now I'm not so sure. They're out of my league."

Luke stopped chewing.

Over the last week, he and AJ had snatched conversations about Comfort forefathers, argued about barbecue sauces, debated the merits of cellular technology, smelled a dozen or more candles to figure out which one was making Inez sneeze, and considered the prospects for the next *American Idol* competition, but they'd never talked about real stuff. Not since the night her father started the questions.

"That's because you're above their league," he said.

Her eyes widened.

Normally, he had to convince family members to back off from living vicariously through their celebrity. He'd never had to talk to one so unimpressed by fame. "You've lived your life in balance. You never once asked for their help, or anyone else's that I can tell. You've expanded on your talents and made a rip-roaring success out of a tired piece of property. That's awesome, AJ. Few people get to do what you've accomplished."

Her gaze drifted to the park, where Inez was swaying on a swing and singing to no one in particular.

He could almost hear the whoosh of thoughts turning over in her brain, and he wondered if her parents ever told her how proud they were of her—that she'd created Lavender Hill from sweat and daydreams.

"They, too, are living with the natural outcome of choices made." Luke was itching to put his arm around her shoulders but resisted. Timing and circumstances weren't favoring him these days. "You made better choices."

"But how can I help them find their way back to normal?"

He had a hundred different answers zinging through his head, one of which was an address for a counseling center outside Nashville.

"Who's saying you've not done enough? Some things they have to do for themselves, like going to see Keisha today. The best part is, they know you love them. You've made them comfortable in your home, and you don't judge them. Sounds like a recipe for success, if you ask me."

AJ bounced away from the bench. "Do you make that stuff up?"

He blinked, wondering if the sunlight had blinded his ability to read her mood. "I'm usually accused of being too smart for my own good."

"At the least, we need to call in a professional mediator, maybe two." AJ paced in front of the bench. "And you said 'love' is all they need. Do you believe all the songs that come out of Nashville, or just the ones my mother wrote?"

The sun was burning a small hole in the back of his neck, but it didn't compare to the heat under his heart. "Look, I'm on your side. I want to help your parents."

AJ took two steps away from the bench. "If you want to help, go back to Nashville." She gestured her hand like a bird flying away. "Nothing good will come of you staying in Comfort."

He watched her skirt kick around her knees as she marched to where her grandmother sat on the swing.

As if a cloud had passed over the sun, he felt the cooling breath of realization.

She was scared.

But he didn't think it was about the music business anymore.

Anticipation zinged through his system, and he stood to join Inez and AJ. Maybe she'd noticed more than he gave her credit for seeing. Maybe AJ finally understood that the reason he hung around was because he was desperate for time with her. She was fidgeting with the cookie bag.

Kids were kicking around a soccer ball nearby, but he focused on the two women, their heads bent close together. It was a beautiful thing to watch a granddaughter stroke the older woman's white hair.

As he approached, his shoes crunching the dry grass, he heard Inez singing a spot-on version of the old '50s classic, "Mr. Sandman." She hit the notes of the chorus flawlessly.

"I didn't know you sang so well, Gran," AJ was saying as she gave her grandmother a small push, setting the swing in motion again. "I'll turn on the radio as we drive to the dentist's office, and we can see what other songs you know."

Though he wanted to, he did his best not to stand too close to AJ. "Yeah, I guess this is where Roger got his talent."

"Hush now," Inez scolded. "I don't know what you're talking about."

"You." Luke prodded, seeing a glimpse of AJ in the woman's profile. "*You're* the one with the real singing gift."

Inez turned to stare at him. "Who are you?"

AJ nudged her grandmother's shoulder. "He will see through that flirting technique, since you were practically throwing yourself at him last weekend."

Inez looked back at AJ. "I've never met that man in my life."

Chapter Twenty-One

Annuals are short lived, but they can pack dazzling color into a small package. — "Lessons from Lavender Hill"

"Friend, you need fun in your life." Kali bit into an apple, while AJ flitted around the store with a dust cloth. "I'm serious. You're wearing me out just watching you. And Elizabeth says you're finding busy work to keep from writing your first draft of the gardening manual. She's out of patience and furious at what she's supposed to tell the printer."

Setting down a porcelain cat figurine, AJ turned to see her friend lounging against the doorway. It was 5:30; most of her customers were on their way home, and she had, for the first time all day, taken time to do a chore usually assigned to her grandmother. When the dentist called with an opening to check Inez's complaint about having a toothache, she'd run home to change and get Gran into Kerrville. She'd been racing the clock ever since they returned.

"Why don't you tell me why you're really here?" AJ asked.

"I can't visit my best friend whom I haven't seen all week?" Kali waited a long moment, then continued. "But I do have a plan."

"You picked up the keys to the house next door, and we'll do a walk-through for exploring our idea about buying the property and turning it into a tearoom?"

"Right. Like you will leap at creating a tearoom for customers when you won't even sit down to finish a book?" Kali tossed her apple core into a trashcan. "We're going out to dinner."

In the old days, her group of four friends—Kali, Lacy, and Anna—had a standing Thursday night dinner date. Now, with two husbands in the mix, the standing date had been watered down to periodic special occasions.

"I'd love to, but—"

Kali interrupted. "No buts. You've been overwhelmed with your parents and figuring out what to do with your grandmother. Consider this a kidnapping."

"Penny has made Dad's favorite dish, and he promised to be civil if we'd eat before 6 p.m. Apparently, he has an acid reflux problem now and can't eat too late."

Kali's face twisted into dismay.

"Obviously, I gave you too much information about my father," AJ said, wincing at the details she'd discovered about him over the last few days.

"I see I've come at just the right time." Kali walked over to the front door and flipped the closed sign toward the window. "Don't worry about your work clothes. Where we're going, you'll be fine."

AJ glanced down at her faded T-shirt, blue-jean shorts, and clogs. She had a silver ankle bracelet around her leg that sparkled in the sunlight. Penny had teased her about the bracelet this morning. It was typically her party jewelry, but she'd seen it in her dresser drawer and decided she wanted to feel a little prettier than normal.

"I'm not fit company for any restaurant. I've been working outside all afternoon." AJ lifted her shirt's hem. "This smells like compost."

Kali shook her head. "You'll be fine."

"Can I at least brush out my hair?"

Kali offered her a bag emblazoned with the name of one of Fredericksburg's trendy clothing stores. "Sure. But first go put this swimsuit on under your clothes."

AJ stared at the bag swinging from Kali's hand. "You don't have a pool."

"We're going to the city pool we used to swim in when we were kids. Remember how icy that spring-fed water felt on a hot day? I think it will be just the thing to invigorate us."

AJ hadn't jumped into a pool in ages.

"The pregnancy hormones are making you do crazy things, but I won't complain." AJ glanced into the bag and saw a yellow-and-red polka-dot suit between the tissue folds. "You didn't go by the house and ask Penny to dig out my old suit?"

"It was my dearest prayer you'd thrown out that ratty thing you wore tubing last year. And on the possibility that you hadn't, I thought a new swimsuit seemed a nice tradeoff for being kidnapped. Don't you agree?"

Half an hour later, after she'd climbed over the locked fence and stood with her best friend, staring into the dark blue water of Comfort's public pool, she wondered if a new swimsuit was worth a jail stay.

The hair twisted into a bun on top of her head let air circulate around her throat, and her pink toenails glowed in the late afternoon sun. She felt like a kid again, more the kid she always wanted to be instead of the Goody Two-shoes she had to act to counterbalance the image of having been parented by two hippies.

AJ grabbed Kali's hand, much like they used to do fifteen years prior when they had to steel their nerves to jump into the frigid water. "If the sheriff comes screeching in here to arrest us for trespassing, I will throw you under the bus."

"I promise, I didn't know it was closed because of a lifeguard shortage." Kali glanced around the park as if expecting the law to spring from behind the live oak trees. "Someone should publish those kinds of notices in town."

AJ drew in her breath, thrilled to be doing something dangerous, and possibly illegal. Adrenaline coursed through her blood like a lava flow.

Almost thirty years old and flouting the law, really, who had she become?

All those years—when she'd obeyed the rules and been so reliable, she got 'atta girls' from librarians; when she'd been religious about being well behaved every summer so that no one would ever have reason to write the awful things they wrote about other celebrity kids; when she felt sheer joy from people never guessing she was July and Roger's offspring because, well, she was respectful and nice. All that seemed to hinge on whether she jumped into this pool.

Like this baptism might be more about unleashing her spirit than surrendering responsibility for an hour.

AJ squeezed Kali's hand. "Tell me again why we're here?"

"Because you need to do something spontaneous and not be the uptight person who is happy only when you've exhausted a to-do list that is twice what most normal people ever dream up."

"Thanks for clearing that up."

"I love you, friend."

"Love you too." AJ's toes itched for the water. "And the trouble we will get in is what ... icing on the cake?"

"This isn't a military invasion. It's about cooling off. And speaking as one whose body temperature is at broiling levels, it's a kind of therapy."

AJ suspected jumping into a forbidden pool was more than therapy, but in her weird state of mind she didn't want to over analyze it.

Kali counted one-two, but before she got to three, AJ jumped, pulling Kali with her. Icy water quickly doused their collective screams.

Floating to the top, she heard Kali sputtering.

"I can't believe how cold the water is. This can't be good for the baby."

AJ laughed, wiped water from her eyes and flipped to float on her back. The weights she'd dragged around for weeks stayed on the floor of the pool, and she drifted carefree, her eyes closed against the sun.

A big splash of water shocked her out of peacefulness. "Kali!" she screeched, swimming to get away from her friend who'd taken a second dunk. Wiping water off her face, it wasn't a petite, smiling face that was grinning back at her like a mischievous child. It was one brown-eyed man with a farmer's tan. She gasped, inhaling water.

Coughing, she dog-paddled to the pool's edge where she could touch her feet to the bottom. "What are you doing here?"

Luke nosedived under the water. When he came up again, he was inches from her. "Surprised?"

He had water running from his flattened hair. He looked twelve. "Stunned is more like it. How did you know we were here?"

A body exploded the water in cannon-ball style, and she saw Jake bounce back to the surface. Luke whipped his head around to swing water from his hair.

AJ stared at the two men, who were laughing like boys and splashing each other. She could barely make sense of this bizarre turn of events.

"Hamilton, are you wearing a man-kini?" Luke asked askance.

"Dude, I don't know you well enough to bring out the tiny suit." Jake laughed.

AJ tried to regain her composure and asked, "How did you two end up here also?"

Luke wiped his eyes. "I asked Kali to kidnap you while Jake and I hit Popo's Restaurant for fried chicken." He glanced around at the cloudless sky. "It seemed like a perfect night for a picnic."

"Are you nuts? We could get arrested."

"You keep questioning my intelligence. Is this going to be a trend?"

AJ gulped shots of nervy excitement. "Possibly. You seem to be drawn to the unexpected."

The light in his eyes shifted from laughter to something more intimate. "In all honesty, I've always followed a carefully planned course." His voice dropped for her ears alone. "But you make me want to be a better version of myself, and apparently that means letting go of agendas."

She tried very hard to keep her gaze on his eyes, but his shoulders were so broad, and she was curious about the cross necklace dangling against his chest. With extreme self-control, she focused on his irises. "Everything about you is unexpected. I can't pin you into any category."

"That's good to know, because I was sure you'd decided I could only be the adversary."

She'd thought about him in so many contexts since he first arrived at Lavender Hill, that she couldn't remember what her first reactions had been. All she knew for sure was that he was the bloom in her garden she couldn't name and doubted she could ever duplicate.

He swam closer.

AJ stared at his smile, wondering if he knew his lips had a bow shape. It would be hard to notice once his beard grew in, but color had rushed into his lips with the startling cold water, and she suddenly had a compulsion to find out if he was as good at kissing as he was in everything else he did.

Kali splashed AJ as she climbed from the pool. "I'm starved. Where's that chicken?"

Snapping her gaze to her friend, she reddened, worried that Kali had read her thoughts.

Glancing back to Luke, who stared at her like he could, in fact, read her thoughts, she saw that his eyes glowed with a warmth that defied the temperature of the water.

A Nerf football came sailing toward Luke. He sprang out of the water to catch it.

For an executive, Luke had a very firm body. Tanned, lithe, just enough muscles to prove that he worked out, but not so bulky that he'd maintained a rigorous schedule at a gym. He was the type of man who could hold someone close without smothering her—as if he were to show up at the Gruene Hall, he could hold his own with fast songs and slow ballads until the end of the night, when the band closed down.

AJ dunked herself under the water to cool the thoughts of the last time she'd two-stepped with a man—a man who, halfway through a friend's wedding reception, turned to AJ and casually lobbed a comment about how he'd been offered a once-in-a-lifetime opportunity to tour with an orchestra, and that he owed it to himself to leave Nashville and chase his dream of being the new crooner who'd restyled Frank Sinatra's classics.

A dream that, apparently, no longer needed the encumbrances of an almost-fiancée.

He'd said he hoped she would understand that getting married would wreck his image of a sexy crooner. His publicist said he needed to be single to get buzz for his albums and women swarming his shows.

Albums created with studio time she'd funded by working two jobs and giving him access to her credit cards.

As she came up for air, she heard Kali squeak.

Ripped from a night she rarely allowed herself to replay, AJ climbed out of the water and sat on the edge of the pool, trying to keep emotions in the box she'd taped shut eight years ago. Following Kali's gaze, she saw an official Kendall County vehicle cruise near the park.

Shivering, she remembered why it was always safer to play the good girl.

Jake caught the football Luke tossed, and then they both reacted to hearing tires crunch the gravel parking lot.

"Damn," Jake muttered as he stared at the squad car. "Someone must have called us in. We've only been here ten minutes."

Luke caught AJ's gaze, and she felt like they communicated on some private line of thought—neither of them enjoyed being on this side of a lawman's radar. She didn't know what his level of experience was, but there'd been a few times she'd seen her father carted home in the back of a blue sedan, and she knew that it wasn't something she'd ever aspire to experience.

Still, this was not a federal offense. She would not employ her panic default. Those ten minutes in the pool were some of the most delicious she'd enjoyed in a very long time, and if she had to pay a fine, so be it.

She glanced again at Luke, as he pulled himself out of the water, and saw that his legs were just as muscled as the rest of him. She bit her bottom lip.

Yep, these ten minutes had been worth it.

Chapter Twenty-Two

Luke had more experience with officers of the law than he cared to admit. It was the stain one acquired cleaning up after celebrity brawls. Still, standing in a pair of wet swim shorts was not the position of strength he liked to be in when having to negotiate with a deputy.

Thankfully, Jake was the one who felt most comfortable, slapping the officer on the shoulder, calling him by name, and suggesting this was all a simple misunderstanding, designed to indulge the whims of a pregnant woman.

AJ fastened the towel tighter under her arms. She'd rearranged the cover-up so many times it amazed Luke it wasn't in knots. Though he appreciated what his new friends were trying to do, it was time to fess up.

"It's my fault, Deputy. I planned this afternoon as a surprise for AJ without realizing the pool was closed. Kali and AJ arrived first, so Kali couldn't turn back without giving the surprise away, and she's too nice a lady to ruin something she knew was important."

Kali smiled with relief. "Thanks, Luke."

He wished he felt better, but this was one of those times when the truth would not set him free. He was sure it would involve a perp walk.

The deputy turned his eyes on AJ. "You knew nothing about this plan to break into the Comfort pool?"

"Kali told me I was being kidnapped."

"Kidnapped?" The deputy echoed. "Well, tonight just keeps getting better and better. I'll call in this disturbance to the Comfort PD and let them sort it out."

At that point, Kali and Jake talked over each other to the point it sounded like cacophony to his ears. Luke found AJ's gaze and tried to apologize without words. There was a smile in her eyes that made him think she might not be all that angry about this turn of events.

In all the years and all the circumstances Luke had found while pursuing a potential client, nothing had prepared him for Comfort. He shivered, wishing he could wrap himself in a towel like AJ had done. But he'd had to appear unaffected so as not to give the deputy any room to doubt.

He hoped his lips weren't blue.

AJ framed her hand over her eyes, protecting against the last few spikes of sunlight, asking, "John, have you had dinner yet? Luke brought chicken from Popo's for our picnic dinner."

The deputy pulled down the lenses of his silvered Ray-Bans. "Fried chicken?"

Luke released his tense breath. "And their famous potato salad. I pulled out all the stops. We'd be glad to share dinner and laugh about this silly incident."

"Thanks for the offer, but I need to touch base with dispatch. I was just going on duty when I saw you all here." He glanced around the group. "Who wants to ride with me in the squad car if I have to haul you off to the jail?"

Kali gasped.

"Just joking," the deputy said with a chuckle as he walked back to his car.

Kali walked over to hug her husband's waist and whispered to Luke, "Great idea, Luke. Really, smashing plan for such a memorable night."

"How was I to know the town had a lifeguard shortage?" Luke reached into a bag for a towel, found one, and then scrubbed the terry cloth over the goose bumps on his shoulders. "I'm not local."

AJ draped her arm around Kali. "It was a lot of fun until the deputy showed up. Besides, a perp photo will give me a little street cred with my parents."

Kali groaned, but then her eyes lit up. "No reason we couldn't eat the chicken while we wait to find out our penalty, right?"

Luke knew he'd found a group of people he could enjoy when he met them at the coffee shop—Kali's ever-present need for food confirmed it. This vacation was turning into more than a loosening of his work bindings; it was a reconnection with all the things he loved best about life. Food and friends, at the top of that list.

As he watched AJ unpack the picnic basket, he amended his list. There was something far more interesting about this time in Comfort than BBQ and fishing trips. She must have felt him watching her, because she glanced over her shoulder and smiled at him—and not the smile she gave to everyone else. This one was just for him, and he knew it.

A loopy grin drifted across his face, and he knew he must appear the biggest goof but couldn't help it.

He was falling in love with a lavender queen, and there wasn't anything that could stop him from enjoying every moment of the ride.

The deputy hurried over to where they stood in their wet swimsuits. "Hey, I'll let you all off with a warning because I've got to get to the interstate. Someone called in a report of an old lady driving the wrong way on an access road, and I'm the closest one to the exit ramp."

Chapter Twenty-Three

When welcoming new plants to the garden, remember it's important to water them in by hand until they're established. — "Lessons from Lavender Hill"

AJ jumped from the backseat of Jake's truck and followed the deputy's stride as he marched over to Inez's Cadillac, pulled over onto the grassy berm of the access road, heading west on the interstate. Ethan was standing next to Inez, his arm draped around her shoulder, and AJ offered a prayer of thanks.

No one seemed injured.

"Ethan?" AJ called out, hoping he could explain this nightmare.

"Hey, AJ!" He waved. "I saw your gran driving the wrong way on the access road, so I whipped around, followed her up the ramp, and forced her off the road, into the ditch. She's okay. Sorry about the bumper."

AJ gasped, grabbing her throat. Running toward her grandmother, she could tell Inez was furious—her blue eyes were blazing. But the anger was misplaced. Ethan saved her life. The damp flip-flops picked up dried grass and grit from the road, and her wet swimsuit was showing through her

Lavender Hill T-shirt, but she reached for her grandmother to hug her close.

"Someone could have driven right into you," AJ said, trying to control the panic. "What were you doing?"

Inez pushed free from AJ's embrace. "I was going home, and this fool boy drove me off the road like he was a maniac. He could have killed me. This deputy better arrest him and charge him with a stiff fine."

The deputy was asking Ethan questions about the incident, but AJ looked at the directional sign and knew there was no logical reason for her grandmother to be heading west on I-10, particularly not against the flow of traffic. She squeezed her eyes closed, wishing—praying that this wasn't the beginning of the end for the woman who'd been her harbor in a stormy childhood.

A firm hand gripped her shoulder, and Luke leaned close to her ear, asking, "Is there anything I can do?"

She exhaled and felt a tear dampen her lashes. She shook her head no, but her heart was screaming otherwise. "I'm not sure what will happen, but let Jake and Kali take you back to your car. There's no reason for us all to stay here."

"AJ, I need to talk to your grandmother." The deputy nodded toward Ethan. "He's given his statement, and I must take one from Mrs. Worthington, too. Would you mind stepping away?"

"Why?" She panicked. "I can help her. She's my grandmother."

"She also can't produce a driver's license, and I need to find out what else isn't adding up." The deputy motioned with his head. "You all need to take a breather over there, near Ethan's car."

Covering her mouth, AJ knew her hands were quaking. "Ethan?"

Ethan reached for her arm, pulling her toward the road's shoulder. "Come on, I'll show you how I got her to pull over before she got on the interstate. I wish someone had filmed me. It was cooler than anything."

Luke followed, but Ethan was doing all the talking, motioning with his hands how he'd flagged down Inez before he cut her off and forced her into the grass. A million horrible images flashed into AJ's mind before she could ever utter a silent thank you to the angels that protected both of them from a disaster.

Luke handed her his cell phone. "Do you want to call your parents?"

Staring at his phone, she tried to think of how she'd explain the situation to them and realized that there was no good way to speak without barking at them. Today was her father's turn to pull Inez duty.

After she calmed down and found out where he was — and why he'd left his mother alone — she'd insist they get that appointment with the internist booked. Waiting on Roger to take control was not working.

"Would you call my dad, please?" AJ hoped Roger would be honest if this news came from Luke. "I'm not sure I can remain civil right now."

Luke nodded, becoming efficient and compassionate in one breath. His hair had dried in weird waves, and his swim trunks clashed with his polo shirt, but he'd become so valuable to her in such a short time she wasn't sure how she would navigate the rest of this without him.

Jake walked up to Ethan. "You're a hero, man," he said, slapping his palm against Ethan's shoulder. "A freaking, awesome hero. Wait till the kids in your youth group hear how you saved Mrs. W from not driving headfirst into an eighteen-wheeler."

AJ's stomach clenched, and she put a hand over the vein that was pulsing under her forehead. "Can we please not broadcast this story? The women in this family have entertained the gossips enough this summer."

Ethan's grin was wide. "Man, I'm still on an adrenaline rush. If I hadn't seen her make that weird turn at the overpass, who knows what might have happened?"

AJ put her hand on Jake's arm. "Would you mind taking Luke back to his car at the pool? Kali's probably starving, and I don't know how long I'll be here, but I can get a ride back to town with Ethan when this is over."

"Yeah, sure," Jake said, nodding. "Is Luke talking to your dad?"

She turned to see him pacing beside the access road and gesturing with his free hand. "I hope so. Someone needs to get Dad to wake up and pay better attention to his mother."

They all stepped farther onto the berm as a farm truck came barreling down the access road, whipping them with an air current fueled by diesel. AJ held her hair back and knew that she looked like a mess, but appearance would be the least of Worthington family problems in the immediate future.

AJ walked over to Inez's Cadillac and looked in to see what was in the backseat, maybe a clue where her grandmother was going. She opened the passenger door and saw the contents of a familiar purse that had spilled to the floorboard. As she bent down to pick up the odd assortment of hairspray, faded airline vouchers, and prepackaged crackers, AJ saw two things that wouldn't belong in her grandmother's purse—five $100 bills paper-clipped together and a folded piece of notepaper usually kept in a cookie jar back at Lavender Hill.

The paper crinkled with resistance as it was unfolded, and in some bizarre moment she'd not want to admit to anyone, the computer passwords blurred like they were being washed away letter by letter.

She wiped her lashes, surprised by grief. Why had she fooled herself into thinking these last few months were a blip in Inez's personality? Why had she waited so long to acknowledge the decline right before her eyes?

AJ ran her knuckles across her cheekbones, fighting the urge to give in to the watershed. Inez wouldn't want that, and she probably wouldn't believe the diagnosis even with the evidence explained.

Glancing up at the sky streaked with late afternoon orange and the fiery red stroke of a day's long goodbye, AJ squeezed the next wave of tears back under her lashes. There'd be time for crying, but it wasn't here. And it sure wasn't now, when some of the fastest tongues in Comfort could comment as they drove by.

Though the whys of this theft of a woman so bright, healthy, and vibrant raged through her brain, AJ folded the paper and tucked it into the back pocket of her shorts. She kicked the tire just to release vinegar in her blood, but she would conserve her fury until they knew exactly what they were dealing with.

"I don't know what you're so upset about," Inez grumbled, as she ambled over to the side of the car. "You're not the one facing jail time."

"They won't lock you up, Gran. We'll call Sheriff Weston and explain ... the situation."

Inez threw her hands up in surrender. "I don't need special privileges. That's reserved for the July Sands of the world. I'm due what I'm due."

AJ looked into her grandmother's eyes.. "You want the ladies of Comfort to see you walk into jail handcuffed?"

Inez's temper cooled. "Well, that would make Sunday school awkward, wouldn't it?"

"I'd say it would." AJ reached her arm around Inez's shoulders, squeezing a hug from a woman not known to give them easily. "I'll drive your car back home, since you don't have your wallet."

"I ... do to ... have my wallet. I showed all my papers to the deputy."

AJ glanced toward the man writing out a ticket. It looked like he was holding Inez's evening bag, the one she used to carry to formal events in San Antonio. "Well, then maybe we got excited over nothing."

"I'll say so, missy." Inez turned and waved at Luke. "But if you and Mr. Hot Pants want to take my car on a ride up to bluffs and have a little quiet time together, I'm not opposed. Not opposed at all. You're old and I want a great-grandbaby."

Chapter Twenty-Four

Comfort, Texas   March 12, 1957

George walked out to the front porch, his eyes downcast. Inez stopped singing her quiet song to comfort her toddler. She would have snapped her fingers to shock her husband from his gloom, but she was holding Roger and trying to keep him from squalling.

With a sneer, she said, "Let me guess, she said no."

George pursed his lips. "She was embarrassed for me. Apparently, I was so shameless to ask if there would be any inheritance, now that my dad is not long for his reward."

Inez didn't know what reward was coming for a man who hadn't a kind word to say or two pennies to share, but it had been her idea to drive to Comfort today. She regretted that they'd not waited for the funeral.

On the upside, she'd packed a cooler. They could stop by the butcher on the way out of town and see what he had on sale. Prices were so much lower here than they were in San Antonio.

Money. Everything came back to the bottom line—or the lack.

They were so close to being able to put in a bid for the new Chevrolet dealership, but it would take a bank loan just to cover the franchise expenses. She'd hoped — even prayed — that George's parents would want to help him attain his dream of owning a car dealership, but once again, she'd underestimated how much the Worthingtons hated her for ruining their only surviving son.

George lifted Roger from her arms, tucking that sweet little head close under his chin, and stepped off the porch. "It's best we go on home now. Momma said I had no business going to the hospital. Daddy wouldn't know if I was there or not, and she didn't want to put a burden on the nurses for having to entertain me."

Inez's arms felt bereft of Roger's weight. "Are you two kinds of kidding me, George Worthington? If you want to go see your daddy, you get in that car and go see the man."

George walked over the dirt like he was on his own death march. "It's best I don't. That way, I remember him how he was before the stroke brought him down."

A fury took over Inez's senses, and she had half a mind to march into the stuffy house and give that old woman a tongue-lashing she'd not soon forget. Telling George that he'd be in the way of the nurses — what a bunch of bologna.

Though indignation burned underneath her skin, Inez paused.

Maybe it was some of that Sunday school training she'd been listening to since they took little Roger to church, but more than likely it was good common sense reminding her that this moment wasn't the real fight.

The battle would come when the family attorney read the will. If there was anything that amounted to an inheritance, besides this dried-up, two-bit farm.

She patted her newly bleached hair and made sure the curls had held their shape in the humidity. Inez Worthington wasn't the same little good-for-nothing tramp George had drug home all those years ago. Oh no, they had beautified her as befitted the wife of one of the best car salesmen in the city. And as much as she wanted Mrs.

Worthington to envy her stylish dress and shiny new shoes, she wanted to protect George's interest in the family inheritance even more.

God only knows how long his mother would keep sucking oxygen, and if she didn't give him the money this summer to buy the dealership, then maybe she would the next year, or the year after that.

Inez could be patient. She'd learned just how long girls had to wait to get a break, and she would not blow this opportunity.

A grin spread across her cheeks.

She had the one thing Mrs. Worthington loved even more than George, and that would be the best bargaining chip of all for Georgie to get the money he needed to set himself up as the Chevrolet King.

Inez hurried down those shallow steps, revolted by the scent of cow dung drifting over the fence. "Hey, don't you set Roger in the back seat. I bought him one of those cushions to sit on, so I can strap him to something while you go speeding down the road."

George leaned his head out from the car. "You mean this contraption that looks like a throne?"

Inez smiled and glanced toward the dining-room window, where she knew Mrs. Worthington watched their every move. "Exactly."

Chapter Twenty-Five

In the overall picture of your garden, consider the benefits of vines. Clinging, draping leaves can provide natural shade for a patio or disguise imperfections in a fence or divider. — "Lessons from Lavender Hill"

"I can't believe we haven't talked since the—" Kali air quoted, "Inez incident."

AJ sighed, holding her double-espresso latte closer to her lips. She needed the afternoon shot of caffeine to keep up with the whirlwind spinning around her property. The calm inside Cup of Joe came with the added benefit of air-conditioning, a jazzy soundtrack, and scones baking in the nearby kitchen. But most of all, her friend. Kali had agreed to meet without needing any sort of lure.

"There's been so much going on, and I'm about at the end of my rope," AJ said.

"You're in the middle. You can't quit now."

AJ glanced to the ceiling, remembering that Kali had nursed her beloved aunt through the final stages of cancer. "I don't know how to do this. I'm not like you. I can't do illness. I'm more of a maid-slash-cook than a nurse."

Kali propped her chin in her hand. "You can do exactly what you have to do. We all can."

AJ shook her head, seeing failure in every one of her attempts since driving her grandmother to the big house. "You know, Gran never wanted to live with me at the farmhouse, even when she first moved to Comfort. She developed insomnia sleeping in my home, kept carrying on like someone was watching her. That she was being judged by a woman in another room. It was spooky." Sighing with the blur of those first few weeks, she regretted she'd not taken the time then to better understand her grandmother. "Now, she lives in that cabin on the property, and my dad is supposed to be watching after her. Not that he's been much help—as evidenced by how he didn't even stop her when she said she had things to do. Things like running away."

The whisk of the overhead fan spun those words around in a circle, and AJ wondered how many more times Gran would try to leave.

"But I can't move her back in with me; Mom is there. That's a recipe for disaster."

"What does your dad say?"

AJ sipped the espresso for clarity. "Dad says this is all getting overblown and that we all need to chill out. He says I can't control everyone and make them behave." She'd pondered that thought again and again, wondering if wanting to control the people around her was her fatal weakness. "And, who knows? Maybe he's right."

Kali reached across the table and squeezed AJ's hand.

"My aunt got delusional toward the end," Kali said. "We thought it was the morphine. But your grandmother is still rational—on most days. Has your dad gotten her in to the see the specialist?"

AJ set her mug on the table and watched the steam swirl up from the coffee on a fairy dance. "First Dad had to help her remember the password for her ATM card so she could pay the bail, and that was a chore. Luckily, he remembered the date for his father's birthday, and that worked. We then found out Gran has an ungodly amount of money in her checking account, and now I'm worried that my dad has found the pot of gold he's been searching for ever since having to declare bankruptcy. Then we heard a blistering lecture from about three different law enforcement officials about taking away her driving privileges. Since she's on my insurance, I've had a call from one agent that my rates were being jacked up because she's on my policy, oh, and I'd better be grateful I wasn't being sued for allowing a dementia patient behind the wheel. Apparently, I'd have zero assets if she'd hit anyone."

"Have they diagnosed her?" Kali asked.

"She hadn't been by then, but she is now. Dad and I took her to San Antonio yesterday, and the neurologist said it was a wonder she'd gotten away with hiding her impairment. The doctor looked at us like we were willfully blind — and maybe we have been, I don't know."

Kali folded her hands around her coffee mug. "I am so sorry, this is awful."

"Well, that's not the end. We hired Walter to go to her cabin and install locks she doesn't know how to work — so she won't just leave the house in the middle of the night — and she's taken to Walter like he's George Worthington reincarnated. I can see the resemblance, but really it's been embarrassing for poor Walter."

"Maybe you can hire him to be a caregiver when your parents leave."

AJ grimaced. "Oh, you're under the mistaken impression they're leaving? No. I'm not that lucky. Mom says the conversations with Luke have inspired her and that she's experimenting with some lyrics for the first time in years. And Dad? Well, Roger Worthington has discovered that maybe he likes driving a tractor, and he's plowed under all the fields I normally lease out. And to be clear, no I did not ask him to do that. He took it upon himself to fire up the engine and go connect with the earth — or some such thing."

AJ watched Kali's mouth hinge open.

"I've stopped paying attention when he goes off on his rants about coming back to his roots and discovering his inner rancher, because I don't believe him. He's always had a weakness for women who will support him, and I think I might be the latest."

"But what about going back to California?" Kali asked.

"Yeah, that's a good question. Until a few weeks ago, he seemed to have such a nice life there that he didn't need to call and check on us in Comfort. Not until Gran told him that story about Mom coming back to steal the property."

AJ let her gaze wander to the others carrying on with their normal and blissful lives, while her world slowly tilted off center.

Kali blew out her breath. "I'm exhausted for you."

"I'm exhausted for me, too." AJ wasn't being entirely truthful. There had been wild moments of hilarity brought on by Luke and his antics to get her to shake off her anger and tour him around the Texas Hill Country. He'd proven to be the antidote to the insanity at her farmhouse, and she'd grown quite fond of his … wit. "But on the upside, I've written better notes for the gardening manual. I've titled it *Lessons from Lavender Hill.*"

With a wariness she rarely had, Kali looked distrusting. "I'd like to see proof."

AJ shrugged as if she was apologizing to a teacher for not producing a homework assignment. "I borrowed my mother's notepaper, and she snatched it back this morning. Said she'd edit my remarks, and that if I ask her really sweetly, she'll jazz things up."

"Your mother is doing your homework?" Kali pushed back from the table. "Do you know how pathetic that is?"

AJ chuckled. "We're communicating and doing something creative together. I will go with it because it's … healthy? Besides, it's fun to hang out with her again. In some weird way, dealing with Gran has given Mom some freedom to not feel under my radar, I guess."

Kali checked her watch. "You don't have a radar. You care. There's a difference."

"It's really the only bright spot in what's been a horrible few days." AJ sighed. "Well, maybe not the only spot, but the most noteworthy."

Standing, she knew she'd have to hurry to make it to the shop before her staff sold the petunias at half price. The heat was making folks short tempered, and she'd heard more excuses for not coming to work than in any year prior.

Kali grabbed her arm. "Oh, my word. You're dating Luke English, aren't you?"

Gravity must have released her. Her body had already lifted with the mention of his name.

"Dating? Don't be absurd." She was sure her neck was turning pink and giving away the truth. She'd been spending every evening with him.

"I've never heard you use the word absurd in your entire life." Kali's gaze radiated across AJ with a surgeon's precision. "You're not leaving until you tell me everything. And I mean *everything*."

AJ wished Anna and Lacy had made the coffee date, because they'd have deflected the attention and let her have another week to figure out what her heart wasn't able to articulate. Falling for a guy who was making himself virtually indispensable didn't sound romantic, but it was her best rationale and the one she was repeating to herself in the mirror every morning.

Besides, Luke's days in Comfort couldn't last forever. He had a career in Tennessee. He'd have to eventually report back to his office and his client list of beautiful singers. Suddenly, she didn't like the taste of her coffee — there was a bitterness she didn't remember.

Leaving the mug on the table, she said, "There's nothing to tell. Everywhere I turn, he's there. He's become a life coach for my parents, and he's got Penny thinking of how she can market her cookies to customers. He suggested that I should give away samples from a platter at the Lavender Hill register, and I halfway like the idea."

Kali shoved AJ toward the freestanding fan that was recirculating the stale air-conditioning in the coffee shop. "That's not what I want to hear, and you know it."

There was no way she was telling Kali about their late-night walks through the lavender fields and catching fireflies—it was too easy to imagine more to the walks than companionship. And that's what Luke had become: a friend. Reluctant though she was to entertain the idea when he had arrived, she trusted that he wasn't like any of the other music executives she'd met over the years and that he really had her parents' best interests in mind when he spun what-ifs into the air.

Yes, she thought, friend was a good catch-all for what they'd become. It didn't include the strange hum she felt when he watched her doing ordinary things, or the way her skin sizzled when he accidentally brushed past her, and the dreams of him were not worth giving oxygen to in repeating, because she was not falling in love—that much she knew.

Kali stood in front of the fan, hogging all the cool air. "I can do this all day."

AJ turned her back to the coffee bar, leaning closer to the breeze, trying to cool her throat with the minuscule amount of air blowing around Kali's shape. "There's nothing to say. He's not the ogre I thought he was when he first showed up. He's a nice guy."

"A nice guy?"

"It's not an insult. He's kind and thoughtful. You should see the way he treats my grandmother. She's not happy being handled like china, but he finds a way to make her go along and not get as angry as she does when Dad tells her what to do." AJ grinned, thinking of how they had to convince Inez that her Cadillac was still in the shop, getting that front bumper repaired. It had been Luke's idea to tip the mechanic to leave the car untouched for another week. Time for Roger to figure out how best to take the keys away permanently. "And, it's been nice to have the advice of someone who has been through this already in his family. Yes, that's it, he's really … helpful."

AJ heard a deep cough behind her shoulder and turned to see Luke standing so close she knew — just *knew* — he'd heard every word. Groaning, she said, "Seriously?"

"You're welcome," he said with a wink. "Although I'm not doing this for the Boy Scout badge. Unless that badge comes with a candlelight dinner."

Kali's gaze ping-ponged between Luke and AJ.

"I'm leaving." AJ felt boiling lava flow from that secret place in her heart. She wanted to flee to someplace private, a refuge for putting words back into a box, but he was blocking her exit. "And you probably have a plane to catch."

"Saturday." He gave her no room to run. "So, I still have three days until my vacation is over. Free for dinner?"

"We eat dinner together every night."

"I can make a reservation that doesn't include your parents."

Kali grinned. "This town really was your idea of vacation? Most people go away to someplace with a little less mildew on the storefronts."

Luke gazed into AJ's eyes. "I liked the atmosphere the moment I saw it."

Locked boxes in her heart opened in synchronization, and hurts shriveled into nothingness with the exposure to Luke's praise. She shoved him back. "And that's why he makes the big bucks, Kali. He can charm shine off the sun."

Kali stepped away from the fan. "Jake does enjoy fishing with you."

"Thanks, I like him, too." Luke held a package wrapped in birthday paper. "I have a gift, AJ. Will that let me buy you a cup of coffee?"

Kali smiled like this confirmed everything AJ hadn't said.

"I've already consumed enough caffeine to keep me fueled for a while." AJ knew the itchy, pulse-racing feeling zipping through her bloodstream had more to do with proximity to him than anything the barista had prepared. "And, it's not my birthday."

"Do I need a reason to give you a present? You've been feeding me for over a week and letting me have office space in your house, so it would seem fitting I pay you some fee."

She didn't know why his offering to reimburse her sent fire across her nerve endings, but it just did. She expected no kind of reimbursement. The guest luster had faded the day he offered to mow her yard. "If that is a check, I will tear it up."

Kali nudged her. "Your birthday is in October, which he would know if he knew the story of how you got your name."

"Shhh—" AJ didn't want to go there. Her parents wrote the story of her name in a song, and citing that was off limits to everyone who might be inclined to tease. "Grab a cup of coffee, Luke, and you can meet me at the shop."

Kali chuckled with wicked delight.

"I wish I could, but I promised July I would drive her to Fredericksburg this morning to meet the counselor she wants to consider for her next round of therapy."

AJ put a hand against her heart. "Do not joke around with me about that. You know that professional help is at the top of my wish list."

He handed her the gift. "It was entirely her own idea. She said she wants to figure out why she kept repeating the same mistakes and thought it was time to face up to some facts."

She wrapped her arms around Luke's neck and squeezed him close. "Do you know how long I've wanted her to want that?"

Luke folded his arms around her waist and pulled her even closer. "Years?" he asked, nuzzling her throat.

His lips felt warm against her skin. Her nose filled with the fragrance of his cologne, and she noted perfectly layered undertones of tuberose and leather. Opening her eyes, she realized that most of the customers in Cup of Joe were watching them with fascination—Kali included. AJ pulled back and caught the package before it fell to the floor between them. "Thanks, that was, uh, fantastic news."

He grinned. "My pleasure."

"Well," Kali demanded. "Open the present."

Still tingling with a million feelings she didn't want to label and a scent that had surprised her nose-blind senses, AJ fumbled in getting the tape undone from the paper. She moved away from the fan and set the package on an empty table. Peeling off the paper, a linen-covered journal and a Montblanc pen stared back at her from the tissue. She glanced at him, wondering what he meant with this gift.

Luke brushed her body as he collected the discarded wrapping. "I saw you hunting around for something to write on as the ideas for your gardening guide flowed, so I found this journal at the 8th Street Market."

She held up the expensive pen. "And this?"

"That's my most lucky pen." He caught her gaze as one of his hands circled her grip holding the pen. His thumb rubbed the initials carved into the clip. "I'm giving it to you because I believe you have important things to say and, sometimes, having something beautiful to write with is all the inspiration an artist needs to create."

Flushed, she pulled her hand free. "I'm not the artist in the family."

"You'll never know if you inherited the magic of words if you don't practice." He leaned forward and kissed her cheek. "I believe in you, AJ. You will do big things."

Chapter Twenty-Six

A garden doesn't come into its own until the sun shines on it. —
"Lessons from Lavender Hill"

AJ pulled the choke on her truck and goosed the engine
with gas. After a hiccup, it started and began its rumble
down High Street. She put one hand over to hold the warm
bag of sandwiches she'd picked up from High's Cafe as she
prepared to turn. Her brain was barely registering the
overflowing planters filled with begonias and petunias, or
the banners fixed to the light poles advertising Comfort's
annual street fair, because every time she left Lavender Hill
and drove into town she searched the sidewalks for a
glimpse of Luke.

He'd been staying at Comfort Commons, and according
to local gossip, he spent a lot of time at the library, sitting on
the porch of High's Café talking to ranchers, and poking
through the local shops, buying gifts for a long list of people
back in Tennessee.

She'd not seen him since he presented his gift to her
yesterday, and Penny had been quick to tell her he'd driven
to Austin to meet with some record companies.

Turning the steering wheel to take the back roads, she
wondered what Luke had thought of Austin—if the more

laid-back music scene appealed to him, or if he was missing the sophistication of Nashville instead. Just who were those people to whom he was sending gifts? And did he have any more vacation days?

AJ bit her lip, knowing exactly why Luke English had dominated her thoughts for the last twenty-four hours.

He was not the guy Inez would call "all vine and no watermelon." He was a keeper.

She imagined what he'd say if she ever told him how much he meant to her. Considering how she felt at first, it was a shocking reversal. Pulling up to the side entrance of the red-brick church, she parked the truck and let her hand linger on the handle before she threw the door open.

Was she falling in love with Luke?

Or was this just a harmless flirtation because she'd been in a relationship drought since Cullen?

Climbing out of the truck, she reached back for the lunch orders her mother had asked her to deliver. If she didn't wipe the silly grin off her face, everyone inside would guess her secret, or at least suspect she'd sipped Cupid's Kool-Aid. Working her shoulders back to a more relaxed posture, she stepped across the sidewalk toward the church's side entrance. This was not a crowd that had any business second-guessing her intentions. They were some of the worst gossips in town.

"Knock, knock," she called out, walking through the robing area to the small sanctuary with its beautiful raised ceiling and stained-glass windows. Holding up two bulging sacks, she announced. "I've brought lunch."

Ethan turned around and motioned for the six teenagers in the praise band to quiet their instruments. The auburn-haired woman in the middle was the last to cooperate, but then she always was.

"Perfect timing," Ethan said, coming over to give AJ a side hug. "We were just saying we were starving."

One boy piped up, "Yeah, and there's nothing here to eat except communion crackers. I know, because I checked."

"Your mom had to call in a lunch order," another kid said dismissively.

AJ guessed that having a mom call the shots was pathetic, even if that mom was super famous. She met July's gaze and saw the joy bubbling behind her mother's eyes. July might be sitting in a church with a bunch of puberty-riddled musicians, but she was happier here—with Ethan—then she'd ever been at the store. Hard though that was to accept, it was a reality that couldn't be denied.

"Happy to help," AJ said, realizing that maybe she'd been too quick to think she knew all the answers for rehabilitating her mother.

Ethan rummaged through the sack, pulling out sandwiches and setting them on a pew. "July and I have been messing around with arrangements to some of her older stuff, and we thought getting these young guys involved would help share the fun." He glanced up and found July's gaze. "Isn't that right?"

July smiled, and there was a light in her eyes that had not been there at breakfast. "I enjoy being around young performers—they kick-start my juices."

Her mother looked younger just holding the guitar again, and sitting among the teenagers had put color in her cheeks that had been missing for weeks. If AJ needed a clearer message that her mother wasn't really retired—no matter what press releases might have suggested—this was it. Her heart sank—just a little—realizing that July needed more than fresh air, sunshine, and family.

Because she couldn't resist, she looked over at the boy holding drumsticks and asked, "Had you ever heard my mother's music before today?"

His face flooded with red shades. "Um, no."

AJ grinned, feeling freer than she had in a long time. "Well, you will love the songs. Mom has a way of turning the simplest melodies into strings of notes and lyrics that once they're in your head, you can't forget."

"Kind of like magic," Ethan suggested as he opened a bag of potato chips.

"Or wormwood," AJ offered. She reached into her purse and pulled out the special vegetarian wrap the cook had put together for July. Walking it over to the chair where her mother sat, she offered the spinach-tortilla wrap. "I can still remember tunes she'd make up to sing me to sleep at night."

July wrapped her fingers around AJ's wrist and, with eyes as wide as saucers, asked, "You're not mad at me for being here, playing music?"

She and July still had a lot of bridges to build, but AJ had been wrong to funnel all the songs of a thirty-year career into a storage box. Part of respecting her mother meant acknowledging that music was organic to her, not something that could be set aside. "Not mad, Momma. I'm actually proud of you for giving something of yourself to these kids. They will learn more from you than from any teacher they might have at school."

July's eyes filled with tears, and AJ had to look away. Her parents weren't the only ones who leaked these days.

Ethan stood back while the students pounced on the sandwiches. "Can you stay a while, AJ? We're cranking out some good harmonies."

She glanced at the light streaming in through the stained glass and knew that the church was glad of the company. "Wish I could, but I also picked up lunch to take up to the cabin for my grandmother. Penny is in the city doing the shopping, and my dad is—I don't know, somewhere— reconnecting with one of his high school friends."

July harrumphed. "I bet that friend has a small waist and big bo—"

"Don't go there, Mom," AJ warned. "You are surrounded by impressionable young minds. They need not know your opinions, just your music."

July chuckled. "You're right. Nobody really cares what we think. They just care that we show up, right?"

Ethan put out a hand to stop the flow of conversation. "That sounds like something we could use to develop a lyric!"

AJ punched his arm. "Already done, bozo. Mom and Dad had a song called "Doing Life." It was a big hit for them back in the day."

Ethan pursed his lips like he was thinking through other ideas. "Still, I feel like July and I might be on to something, a song we can write together. A song set in Comfort."

"You mean, a Comfort song?" July bent over her guitar and draped her fingers over chords that danced to life with her masterful touch. A few more brushes of her fingers and new combinations of notes rose to tickle the heavy beams holding the ceiling together. She hummed along with a tune only she heard in her head, and a few words played on her lips. "The story isn't over yet ..."

"Yes!" Ethan leapt to his chair and picked up his guitar, quickly folding it on to his lap as he tried to expect where July might go next with the sketching out of a melody.

AJ scanned the kids' rapt expressions. She'd seen that starstruck look hundreds of times on the faces of musicians invited to her parents' farm in Tennessee, as they would sit in the living room making music—and in some unscripted moment, one or both of her parents would create something new, and within minutes symphonies of notes rained down from the sky and formed into a song. She'd pick up her dolls and go outside to play among the gnarly roots of the magnolia tree, creating her own world. Today, she would slip out of the church and drive the two miles to her grandmother's cabin and rock on the porch with another woman who knew the loneliness that came from living with songwriters.

AJ slipped out of the church and made her way back to the truck, trying to remember the details of some of the stories Inez would spin from her dad's childhood.

Inez had a string of Roger stories she'd whip out for fans and reporters, all of them casting her son as a misunderstood genius. That he couldn't hold a band together was due more to artistic differences than his lack of structure. And all the times she and George had financially carried Roger and his bandmates were due more to the fickleness of the music industry, not that Roger was drinking his paycheck and spending his royalties on parties.

Inez was Roger's number-one fan, until the day he met someone who knew his songs better than he did. The night a tall, leggy, auburn-haired beauty walked into a Memphis blues club with a guitar strapped to her back and an itch to give Roger Worthington's songs a heart they'd never had.

They'd played together on stage that night and looked into each other's eyes as if everyone else in the world ceased to exist. The legend was that July jumped in Roger's Jeep that weekend, and they headed for Texas, destined to never look back. And they wouldn't have, had Nashville music producers left them alone. But their voices mixed lyrics together too uniquely to be given to dance halls and barrooms. A recording studio refined their mystical sound, and the Billboard Top 40 changed their futures.

And Inez had never forgiven July Sands for becoming the muse that inspired Roger's success.

There was more to the enmity, there had to be, AJ just had never bothered to ask. As long as she could keep her mother and her grandmother from spending too much time together, she didn't have to referee their arguments. Not knowing the rest of the story hadn't bothered her, until now.

Driving through town, she wondered if other families had this much dysfunction. Ethan's family seemed normal. Even her almost-fiancé had a loving relationship with his parents.

So, maybe there was some curse given to those who chose a career in the music industry.

She'd have to ask Luke. He would know.

AJ parked her truck under the shade of a live oak tree at the cabin where Gran lived, and where Roger had taken over the second bedroom. She climbed out, reaching back for the cooler of icy Coca-Colas and her grandmother's favorite chicken salad. Her grandmother had sacrificed so much to hold their family together; it was a wonder they didn't talk about it more. She wasn't sure what happened along the road to divide them all—besides the divorce—but whatever it was, it had been defining.

She should have brought Beans with her. Inez was fond of the dog, and he'd be good company. He was remarkably unfazed when her conversation shifted midsentence.

"Hello," she called out, walking up the steps to the porch. "I come bearing lunch."

She glanced to the garage to see if her dad's rental car was around. The potted plants needed to be watered, and she could see the blinds were still drawn.

AJ reached down to twist the knob, but it didn't give. Panic flew at her heart. She'd called her grandmother from Comfort to tell her she was bringing lunch. Inez had said she'd be waiting on the porch. Rapping her knuckles against the wood, she called, "Gran? Are you okay? Can you hear me?"

AJ leaned her ear against the door. She glanced down the porch and could see the window-unit AC was dripping water, so someone had cranked the air high. Just as she was about to walk around to the back door, the whoosh of wood and hinges stopped her.

"Well, it's about time," Inez said, putting hands on her hips. "I was about to call the sheriff and send a car out for you."

With relief, AJ checked her watch. "I said I'd be here at one, and it's one o'clock on the nose."

Inez held open the door. "Hurry up. We've got business to discuss."

AJ slid into the cool room and glanced at the window unit to see the thermostat rolled to its coldest setting, as she set her tote bag on the floor. "You're comfortable, Gran? It's not too chilly for you?"

Inez paused from moving magazines from the tabletop. "Feels good."

Shrugging, AJ glanced around to see quilts piled on the sofa and a ski jacket tossed over the back of the recliner. If that's how Inez wanted it, she wouldn't complain. There were plenty of issues to go around. Fighting about the thermostat didn't need to be one.

She set the cooler on a chair and pulled out the cans of soft drinks and the quart of chicken salad. "I'll get the plates."

Inez grunted and headed back to the bedroom.

AJ returned from the kitchen with mats, plates, silverware, and cups filled with ice. Arranging it all like she'd done since she was a child, she watched Inez come into the living room with grocery store sacks in each hand. They were bulging, and AJ would have offered a hand had she not known how resistant her grandmother was to receiving help.

Inez set the bags on the sofa and walked over to stare at the table. "You want me to clean up?"

"Well, you can help after we eat. Look," she said, lifting the quart of chicken salad and scooping some onto Inez's plate, "I brought your favorite."

"But we ate already."

AJ stalled and felt a new worry circle her heart. "No. We haven't."

"Yes, we did. That's why I went to get the money. I've got something I need to talk to you about. And the Bible. We need to find George's Bible, because I might have stuffed

193

Benjamins in there too. No one ever looks at the Bible anymore."

AJ's gaze whipped to the grocery sacks. "What money, Gran?"

Inez collapsed onto the chair. "You remember how Mrs. Worthington was always so miserly with George? How she made him beg for every penny she gave him?"

With surprise, AJ scanned her memory bank and realized this was new information. Inez had always refused to talk about her mother-in-law, besides the basic details. She wouldn't know anything at all had her dad not told stories about his grandmother and how she doted on him when he was a little boy. "I don't remember that about her."

"Oh, she was awful. Even after George's daddy died, she would keep the inheritance from him. It's like she didn't trust us to use the money wisely. She wanted it all to go into the property, but we wanted it for the dealership." Inez sighed. "She knew it, too."

AJ had never spared two thoughts for how her grandparents came to own the three dealerships they'd had in San Antonio. All she knew was that when Roger filed for bankruptcy, part of the deal was that he couldn't be the executor of his father's will, and that had funneled old Worthington money into a trust for AJ.

"Tell me more about her," AJ asked, pushing the plate in front of Inez. "Does Dad look like her? Am I like her too?"

"Sadly, I think we both turned out like her. Don't hold on to people too tight, AJ. It never works out the way you think it will." Inez's eyes grew misty. "But to answer your question, Roger took after my side of the family. She overlooked his coloring because that baby could charm her out of every bad mood. It didn't take George and me long to figure out that if we wanted anything from her, we had to send in Roger to ask for it."

194

No doubt how Roger had learned his ways of manipulation, AJ thought. "I can't recall seeing a photograph of her."

"She didn't want her picture made, said it was too vain." Inez slid her fork into the chicken salad. "It wasn't until Roger was a teenager I finally understood why she was so sour, and—for a blink of an eye—I felt bad for not making more of an effort to be nice to her, but by then the patterns had been set. We were enemies from the day we met. And when she died, I felt nothing but relief."

AJ poured Coca-Cola into her grandmother's glass, trying to figure out how anyone could hate Inez. Granted, she was stubborn, but AJ had only ever known love and support from her grandparents. "She was born melancholy?"

"All her sons had died in the war, all save Georgie." Inez ate a bite of food. "Roger was the sun and moon in our house, and I would have died had anything happened to him. So, to have lost three sons—well, it must have been more than one soul could take. It's no wonder she was meaner than a one-eyed snake."

AJ leaned back, wondering about this woman and what she must have been like. Her granddaddy was an angel, and she assumed his family would have all been that way. Clearly, she'd been wrong.

"And that's why I cashed his tuition checks and saved the money for a rainy day."

Spinning her attention back to her grandmother, she sputtered, "What?"

Inez chewed happily, as if lost in her thoughts.

Glancing around the room for some clue to this past life, AJ looked at the bookcases and end tables, hoping that there was a box of journals or old letters that would make sense of a past she'd only now discovered. "What tuition, Gran?"

"Roger's." Inez refilled her glass. "Mrs. Worthington insisted that Roger go to the best private schools in San Antonio, she said if we would be so worldly to live in the city, then he'd be the smartest kid in our social set. Well, you know your daddy, and school smarts aren't his thing. Even with his grades she kept leaving a monthly check on our desk. We were more than able to pay the bill by then, so I'd go to the bank and cash the check and instead of taking the money to the provost, I'd hide it around the house. For a rainy day, you know?"

The temptation to open those grocery sacks was almost more than AJ could take. "How much money did you hide, Gran?"

"I think that's about seventy-five thousand, give or take some."

Covering her eyes with her palm, she tried processing this information. "Are there any other bags of money stashed away?"

Inez paused, dangling the fork in mid-air. "You know, I don't remember. I tried to find it all when you moved me out here—so I'd have money handy if I needed to go shopping—but for the life of me, I can't seem to think if that's everything. Have you found Granddaddy's Bible? Something is in the Bible."

Gulping for air, AJ stood and walked to the sofa. She pulled back one corner of a sack and saw stacks of hundred-dollar bills bound by rubber bands. Her stomach clenched. Her gaze dove to the bottom of the bag, trying to stay calm as she mentally figured out what to do with wads of forty-year-old money. "We'll drive into town in a few minutes and open an account at the bank." A bead of sweat dripped down her spine. Would the tellers question why they suddenly had so much cash?

"Oh, no we're not." Inez scooped more salad onto her plate. "Banks aren't safe. My daddy said they'll go under in a heartbeat, and bartenders always know that kind of thing. That's why we always kept cash in the house. Mrs. W was sure this was just one more way I was as stupid as dirt, but look who has the money now."

AJ glanced at her grandmother, blissfully unaware that she'd said more in ten minutes than she had in years. Sitting back down, she looked at her grandmother, realizing that she was ill prepared to deal with this roller coaster. She had a lot to learn about her grandmother and navigating what might be revealed because of the dementia. "So, uh, what was it you wanted to talk about? The money? Your mother-in-law? Granddaddy?"

Inez stared at AJ with a blank expression.

"You said you wanted to talk about something important," AJ prompted.

"I did not."

Closing her eyes for a quick moment, she prayed for understanding. "Okay, we'll come back to that, so tell me more about Mrs. Worthington."

Inez laughed bitterly. "She hated me the moment she met me. Called me a tart. And, I guess I was. No bigger than a flea, I was singing in nightclubs when George rescued me. Don't you know, I was in every way opposite from what she had in mind for her precious boy, and she never let me forget it."

After offering AJ a refill from her can of Coca-Cola, she added, "And I finally made my peace with that much hatred, until the night Roger brought home a girl. All the sudden, she —"

"Hello, how are my favorite ladies?"

AJ jerked from Inez's memory-laden conversation to her father standing in the cabin's doorway. His smile was broad, and he had his hair pulled back in a ponytail so she could see his beautiful brown eyes.

Whipping back to her grandmother, she put her hand on Inez's arm, saying, "And. What happened?"

Inez rose, holding her arms open for Roger. "My sweet baby, I haven't seen you in the longest time."

Roger's voice sounded pinched. "We ate breakfast together four hours ago."

Leaning back into the chair to recover from the moment, AJ regretted her dad's timing. There was so much she wanted to know—things she'd never considered were missing from her reference. George's mother. Was she really that hard, or was Inez remembering things wrong? And Inez's father was a bartender? Inez sang in nightclubs? Who was this woman? How could she have gone her whole life never bothering to ask about the past?

"We come bearing barbecue," Luke announced, following Roger into the cabin.

When AJ turned around to greet them both, she had a moment where she totally understood memory loss. All the questions she had about her grandmother's life story trickled to the end of her tongue and escaped into an abyss. Her heart kicked up. Her skin sizzled. Luke had changed her thoughts from chaos to anticipation with four words.

"You brought lunch?" She asked.

"From Austin," he said, smiling as if seeing her made him happy. "Roger and I made a quick trip to meet some folks."

Since yesterday morning, something wonderful had happened to Luke. She was sure he looked exactly as he had all week—his business shirt hanging out over a pair of old jeans and well-worn boots—but his face had this sun-kissed glow, and he seemed so comfortable in his own skin she couldn't even remember how uptight he'd been when he first arrived in Comfort.

Her memory tried to recall the scent of his cologne—sandalwood? No, tuberose. And timeworn leather. She smiled remembering how the scent lingered in a mind already maxed out with a catalog of fragrances. Her heart galloped ahead of her thoughts, and her palms perspired. She gulped, hoping that she didn't look like a bashful teenager had taken over her body.

Luke winked, as he walked into the living room looking for a place to set an aluminum-wrapped pan.

The cash! AJ glided backward toward the sofa and reached for the grocery sacks, hoping she could bury them in a closet until a better idea came forward. Fumbling for the plastic grips, she knocked a bag over, and a thumping pile of cash bricks tumbled to the carpet.

"That was supposed to be my secret." Inez stood and folded her arms across her chest. "Why did you spill the beans?" she accused.

Shrugging because she didn't know what else to do, AJ bent and swept wads of hundred-dollar bills into a bag. Her face felt flooded with a heat that had nothing to do with guilt and everything to do with a man who was now thinking she brought so much crazy into his world, he'd best forget they'd ever met.

Roger hurried over, his knees groaning when he bent down. "Let me help you there, darling."

"Oh, well, you were bound to find out—nothing ever stays a secret in this family." Inez collapsed into the chair again. "But you can't have my money. I'll know if you snitch some to cover your bar bill."

"She will never let me forget that she bailed me out of the eighties," Roger derided.

"Don't you mean a particular date?" AJ asked.

"No, the whole decade is a blur," he said, with a twinkle in his eye. "Except the October you were born. I was terrified I'd drop you, so I stayed sober for a month. I really tried to be a father, but I'm too much of an ass."

He handed her all the bundles, and she tied the grocery bag shut like they sealed for shipping. Fragments from her childhood sorted behind her eyes, but the only thing she could latch on to were the images of him standing outside various tour buses, holding her against his side. The first legitimate memory she had, that came equipped with sound and color, was after they'd moved to the farm in Tennessee, and he'd bought chicks for her to name.

Clatter was coming from the kitchen as plates and utensils were found, and Luke walked back into the room. "I found the most fantastic barbecue place on Eleventh Street, and once you taste these ribs, you'll want to go back with me tomorrow to stand in line with all the other diehards." Luke held a fork and offered it to Inez. "Do you want to sample?"

AJ rocked back on her heels, stunned that he wasn't even questioning why thousands of dollars were sitting on the sofa like they were Ben Franklin throw pillows.

Roger ambled over to the table. "One of the guys in my old band plays at a club near there and swears that more people go to Franklin's than come to hear his gig."

Luke put his hand on Roger's shoulder as if he was consoling. "I've heard your band members play solo over the years—I'm not surprised."

Roger chuckled, and AJ almost fainted. Her father could not laugh about anything that might reflect badly on him. A reason he stopped attending award shows. AJ glanced around the room, searching for a place to hide the money until she could talk Inez into opening a bank account, but her gaze kept landing on Luke as he and Roger were discussing the music culture that was so keenly suited to independent artists.

She walked over to the table and watched them nibbling on ribs while discussing the many evolutions of Willie Nelson.

Inez tugged on AJ's shirt and said, "Your father was so jealous of Willie. He almost refused to perform for the governor once because the governor requested Roger cover one of Willie Nelson's songs."

"Yeah, I remember that. Someone called dad out as being un-American."

"Well, I'm sure he sang his way back into their good graces."

AJ bit back her smile. "Did you know you were singing the other day? In the park."

"I don't know about that."

"Well, you were good. Even Luke heard you."

Inez quirked her brow. "Luke thinks Beans has talent, so that's not saying much."

The smell of spicy, warm beef had swirled around the room, reminding her she'd been so stunned by her grandmother's stories she'd forgotten to eat. "Would you sing for us now?"

"Ha," Inez's laugh was bitter. "I don't sing."

Luke picked up the thread of this conversation and tugged it. "You knew all the lyrics to "Mr. Sandman" the other day, and I bet if I start it, you'd finish it."

Roger looked up from the rib clutched between his fingers. "I don't even know the words to that song."

Luke wiped his fingers on a paper napkin and hummed the refrain.

"Stop embarrassing yourself," Inez growled. "I told you I don't sing."

"But you told me you sang in a nightclub. That Granddaddy rescued you." AJ watched Inez's expression, hoping she'd tell the rest of the story.

"Momma would never darken the door of a nightclub. I should know. She never came to see my shows unless I was in a dance hall or at a fairground."

Inez stared at Roger like she was trying to put his words into context. "I was your biggest fan."

Roger leaned down and kissed his mother's hair. "I love selective memory."

Luke caught AJ's gaze and lifted one shoulder as if to say, *What can you do?*

"Now, who's taking me to the bank?" Inez asked. "AJ says I have to put this money in an account or she's taking me to the woodshed."

"I did not say that." She defended. "But we need to move fast before she forgets what she found."

"Like your passwords," Roger offered.

201

"I tell you again, I did not take those," Inez insisted. "I don't know how they ended up in my purse."

This was the same awkward conversation they'd had in the neurologist's office when he'd asked for examples of Inez's recent behavior.

"Forget it," Roger said, wiping his hands clean. "I'll take Momma into town. I've already got a car outside. Luke can ride back with you."

AJ had to swallow the distrust she felt regarding her bankrupt father around piles of uncounted cash. There were too many other hurdles they'd had to climb over together; she'd let go of his history with mysterious holes in his pockets. What was it Inez had said?—Don't hold on to people too tight. She'd guess that applied to her parents as well as Luke.

"Gran, you want to finish your lunch before you go?" AJ finger combed her grandmother's hair.

"I told you I already ate." But in a softer voice she added, "I wouldn't mind a to-go cup of the Co-Cola. I know Roger is going to want to put all that money in an account with his name on it, and I'm going to need the soda to keep me sharp."

Roger shot his mother a disparaging glance.

Luke stayed silent, but his expressions were lively, and AJ was sure he had an opinion on how to handle this. She respected that he left them to feel their own way through, even though he could probably have sorted this conversation into a better maneuver and have them behaving toward an effective plan of action. There couldn't be much difference in dealing with a teen superstar and an addled senior citizen.

AJ reached for her phone. "How about I call Keisha and see if she could meet you both at the bank? She was saying the other day we needed to figure out a financial path for going forward, and part of that was figuring out Gran's assets."

Inez stomped her foot. "Nobody better be thinking of putting me in a nursing home. I will stay right here."

It stunned her what her grandmother could hear, process, and react to in one minute, and be clueless to in the next. The spinning wheel in Inez's mind must exhaust her, too, because more and more, a vacant stare replaced the usual spark and vinegar. But at the moment, Inez was *in* the moment, and was not happy about having her cash taken over by people who were imbeciles — or words to that effect. The argument between mother and son lost volume as they walked out of the house and loaded the grocery sacks into the trunk of Roger's rental car.

"AJ," Roger bellowed back toward the house. "Does Momma have an ID in this purse?" He lifted the designer bag like something nasty weighted it down.

"Open it and check," AJ said, leaning her shoulder into the cedar pole that held the patio roof in place. "If there's a red wallet inside, it should have all her important papers. I wrapped it with a thick rubber band to keep her from picking out the ID and insurance papers."

"This is Comfort," Inez said as she slapped her hand on the roof of the car. "The Worthington name still means something in these parts. They'll know who I am."

Roger rifled through his mother's purse like he was sure something inside would bite him. "It's here."

AJ sighed with relief. "Lucky you."

He helped Inez into the passenger seat, tossed the purse at her, and shut the door. As he walked around the bumper, he turned to AJ and said, "Your turn next. I can't deal with this."

"None of us want to deal with this, but we'll do right by her, because she took care of us when we were falling apart." AJ stood upright and dusted her hands against the back of her shorts, murmuring, "Some more spectacularly than others."

Roger groaned as he fell into the driver's seat and slammed his door.

"I assume you are referencing the 1990s in that remark," Luke said, moving next to her. "Did your dad end up here in Comfort during his fall from grace?"

She turned to him, oddly comforted that Luke knew most every situation her parents would have faced, good and bad, and he didn't run screaming in judgment. It was like he'd seen it all before, and the gruesome fallout didn't disgust him. This realization soothed lingering doubts she had about his motives. He didn't fawn over her parents. He didn't indulge them. And he didn't act like he could solve their problems either.

He'd treated them as he would a friend; enjoying their company, teasing them about their foibles, and meeting them where they were, without forcing them to change.

She watched him as his gaze followed the car and its dust contrail as Roger sped down the driveway, and then remembered he'd asked a thoughtful question.

"Dad ran from his parents much like he ran from Mom and me. He's always acted as if there was a ghost here at the farm that would chastise him for putting his shoes on the sofa." She turned to appreciate the car disappearing over the crest in a newly tilled pasture. "I seem to be the only person, outside of my grandfather, who has good memories of the house. And I've never known why. I mean look, it's so beautiful here with the rolling hills and that creek weaving between the live oaks. I totally understand why the settlers took one look at this valley and stuck their stakes in the ground."

When Luke didn't respond, she worried that she'd gone on too long, and turned to face him, planning to change the topic. But when she caught his gaze, the fascination in his eyes had nothing to do with limestone hills and scrubby landscape—he was staring at her. And he was grinning.

Chapter Twenty-Seven

Luke watched AJ's lips move, but all he could think about was how could he walk away from this woman on Saturday. She'd bewitched him the moment they talked about compost like it was a coffee menu, and he'd been her slave ever since. He'd called one of his oldest friends last night and asked him how he knew when love was love for the long haul. His friend had teased that there is no such love, it's as much a commitment as it is a crazy rush of adrenaline. After they had talked about the prospects for the Atlanta Braves, he'd ended the call and thought about his feelings for AJ.

Even this morning, she was the first thing on his mind, and he knew like he knew a hit song the moment someone performed it in the studio he was knee-deep in love with a girl who might never trust him. His gut clenched as he watched her talk, and he knew there was no way AJ would ever leave Comfort. God imprinted it in her DNA.

What was he going to do about this girl?

Love her forever.

He heard the whisper as clear as if someone had shouted it from his soul. Without realizing how inappropriate it was, he grinned like he'd won the lottery. And he had. This was the worst time to date someone—her grandmother was three shakes away from a nursing home—but he couldn't help it.

He loved AJ, and somehow, he would make a future work out for them.

If she'd have him.

"What are you smiling about?" she asked with skepticism. "If you tell me I have chicken salad between my teeth, and you're just now mentioning it, I will smack you."

Watching her mouth move was one of his favorite things. "No chicken salad, I promise. But I was thinking about you."

The worry line between her eyebrows deepened. "I don't think I like that. You have insane skills with inventing more ideas for my shop, and I'm exhausted. Once this book is over, and the harvest and street fair are behind me, I will take August off to piddle."

"Is August a slow time for you? Can you take vacation then?"

"Vacation?" She said the word as if trying out a foreign language. "I'm in retail. We never get time off. There are lulls, high season, and then there is the market. Kali drove me to Dallas for the spring market, and I was so overwhelmed by products and salespeople I vowed to quit the business right then. Then we had to go to the gourmet kitchen supplier on another floor, for Kali's business, and it reminded me why being in retail is so exciting."

"I work with vendors on the supply side of those markets, and it's terrifying for them too." He stepped an inch closer, thrilled to watch her eyes react as he shortened the distance between them. "I was wondering if you could come see me in Nashville. In August. You know, so we could stay in touch."

Her eyes softened. "We can stay in touch by talking on the telephone."

"The telephone? How about we Skype instead? I prefer to see you, you give away so much more with your eyes than you ever do with your words."

She looked down, as if trying to hide her gaze from him. Her fingers found the cross necklace and lifted the silver chain. "Tell me about this, you seem to wear this every day."

"Aw, so you're studying me. I like that."

A pale pink color stained her cheeks, and she dropped the cross.

He reached for her wrist, sorry that he'd embarrassed her. "It was from Roni. She gave that to me at our wedding, saying I was sacrificing myself for her and that if I were aiming that high, I should try to remember the other ideals Jesus taught. She was fond of pointing out how impulsive I was and that jumping into situations without thinking everything through would get me into the worst trouble. If she could have seen the way I've chased my career, she'd have bragged 'I told you so.'"

AJ met his gaze, reading his thoughts. "She loved you."

Luke's memories of Roni were as comfortable as his favorite sweater, and he felt no pain when he thought of her—just a regret that she couldn't have lived longer on this earth and really known true happiness with a man of her dreams. He'd been a pale substitute, but he'd made her comfortable until the very end.

"And I loved her," catching a whiff of that old feeling. "If I have any good qualities at all, I learned them from watching her navigate cancer. I promised her I wouldn't remain the world's youngest widower, but somehow, it's been years since I've been in a serious relationship."

AJ grew quiet, and just as he thought she'd turn away, she leaned on her toes and kissed his cheek. "You're a good man, Luke English."

"That sounds like an improvement over your first impression of me."

She grinned. "Well, actually, my first impression of you was quite ... memorable. It was what happened when I saw your reaction to my mother that sank my interest."

She was moving away, like she was going inside, and he reached for her arm. "I know this may seem ... a little fast, but I can't keep this down any longer. I like you, AJ. A lot. You're ten kinds of amazing, and I feel so alive when I'm with you."

AJ stilled, as if she waited for the inevitable "but."

"And if that doesn't freak you out," he said, meeting her toe-to-toe, "I'd like for us to see each other, intentionally."

AJ paced the patio like she was running the traps on his words. Her shorts had a mud stain right across the backside, and the slash fascinated him to the point he didn't even tell her about it because he knew she would run for her truck. She was as beautiful to him when she dug in at work as she was when dressed for a party. She had a will that was as strong as iron, but she didn't use it like a battering ram—it formed a level of perseverance unlike anything he'd known with other women. This core trait drew him in a way that made him think if she ever fell in love then she would put her man in the center of the same dedication she put her family and her business.

He'd never been loved like that, and it stunned him how hungry he was to know what it felt like to receive that level of devotion.

"To be clear, AJ, I'm not expecting a declaration, but I wanted you to know how I felt. You can go dig in your lavender beds if that would help give you something to do while you try to figure out how I could use this to further my case with your parents."

Her eyes were guarded when she spoke. "My parents have spent more time with you than they have with some managers from their careers. If they will plot a comeback with you, there's nothing I can do about it now."

"Could you ever be happy for them if ... they plotted a comeback?"

"I don't know." She let her gaze settle on the hillside. "Could you watch someone you love get back on a bucking bronco while still broken from their last ride?"

With those words lingering in the air, she walked into the cabin. It didn't take a whiz kid to know the truth behind her worries. But the vision he had for Roger and July was ninety degrees different from anything they'd already attempted. He saw them pursuing new material in a much less structured environment, and the independent music industry was a good fit for them. They could stay relevant and be vibrant with their talent and influence, but do it in a way that suited their temperaments. Everything he'd learned in these day trips to Austin had validated that there was space for them in the Texas music scene, and it didn't need to look like the train wreck cluttering their wake.

He didn't know how to convince AJ of that, since for her it seemed the music business was a one-size-fits-all disaster waiting to happen. She'd not want to hear his personal career ideas, either. Roger wasn't the only one energized by the Austin music industry. But before he cast his dreams into the open, he owed it to his company to talk to them first.

And that meant driving to San Antonio on Saturday to catch that last flight home.

Glancing at the vista that so entranced AJ, he wondered if he could live here. Could he give up the restaurants, the nightlife, the parks, and river, to live in a place where coyotes still roamed the streets? Running his hands through his hair, he felt the overlong hair curling around his ears, and knew that he'd already changed. If he didn't get a haircut before Monday, his assistant would brand him a stranger.

He chuckled. It felt good to shake off expectations he'd clung to since he'd begun working in entertainment. He'd reached all his goals: corner office—check; industry accolades—check, check; portfolio beyond his wildest dreams—check, check, and check. But his only real friends lived in Atlanta, his condo was nearly unchanged in the six years he'd lived there, his calendar was a repeat of every year since he'd made vice president, and the only surprises came courtesy of hearing what other people were doing.

It was time to re-invent himself.

The clatter of porcelain and silver rattled his thoughts, and he knew AJ was cleaning up from lunch. His feet were moving before he even had a strategy in place. Winning AJ might be the most unscripted thing he'd ever done.

In the honey-colored kitchen outfitted with 1970s fixtures, he hunted through drawers to find a roll of foil and wrapped the leftover ribs in aluminum, setting them in the refrigerator. Inez's collection of food products looked similar to his days in a fraternity house. Takeout boxes of an indiscriminate age, candy bars in the vegetable bin, soft drinks in half-open state, and the only things remotely close to fruit were the plastic containers filled with bits of pie.

He closed the refrigerator and stared at the odds and ends taped to the front: phone numbers written in large, bold ink; a reminder of daily chores; a Bible verse; a postcard from someone who'd traveled to Mexico.

"Will you kiss me?"

He spun around to face her.

Her gaze shot to his eyes. "Too soon?"

Finding a pocket of oxygen again, his brain kicked back into gear. "Honestly, I didn't see that coming."

She smiled. "Maybe you haven't been the only person wondering if the energy between us is something worth exploring."

To his utter embarrassment, he felt like a fourteen-year-old who just got a yes to a prom date with the head cheerleader. His knees were weak. Trying to play it smooth, because he was a veteran executive who'd escorted Grammy winners to their awards shows, he rolled his shoulders back and said, "I'm rather good at kissing. You should know that going in."

She laughed. "I didn't know people bragged about that."

"Well, considering we're still getting to know each other, I wanted you to have that bit of information. I mean, ladies have commented."

Covering her mouth to stifle another laugh, she tried to look serious. "And that counts as empirical evidence?"

"That's really for you to decide." He winked and took a step closer. "I'm a willing student if you find gaps in my skills."

A delightful rose hue fanned across her cheeks. "I won't be much of a judge. I'm far less experienced than you."

"Hard to believe. Someone has told me every single man in this county has been in love with you."

She stuffed her hands into her pockets. "A complete overstatement. I haven't dated a lot since I came to Texas."

The door to her past had squeaked open. He would walk inside while he could. "And before Texas?"

She drew in a difficult breath. "Before Texas I was engaged to Cullen Smith."

He whistled. "Cullen Smith who is on tour with Diana Krall?"

"Is that what he's doing these days?" AJ looked down at her clogs. "I stopped checking his website several years ago. He's living his dream. I'm living mine. It didn't seem prudent to keep replaying how things would have gone had he actually put a ring on my finger."

He did some quick math with what he knew of the performer and realized that big dollar signs were following the crooner. Even more interesting to Luke was why he'd let AJ go. "How did you meet him? He's been based in New York for years."

"Cullen was at Vanderbilt on a piano scholarship, and we had art history together. He was a big fan of Mom's, one thing led to another, and we dated for two years. He'd already taken me ring shopping, and we talked about where to stage the proposal so he could get all the props just right, and then … he dumped me."

"You are leaving out a few key details, I'm sure."

AJ picked up some mail from the counter and thumbed through the envelopes. Her silence didn't worry him, he knew that she was the Worthington who thought before she spoke. His only hope was that Cullen Smith hadn't left a scar too deep for him to overcome.

She set the pile back on the counter and said, "A producer friend of Mom's offered him a once-in-a-lifetime recording deal that involved an immediate tour with some Glenn Miller-styled orchestra. His manager said he should ditch the girlfriend. Being attached would be bad for album sales."

Luke had seen the marketing material—someone had styled Smith as a '60s-era sex symbol. "He is attractive. My assistant swears he single-handedly made suits popular again."

AJ sighed and backed up, as if bringing his name into the room had stolen her interest in kissing.

Luke hated the loss. "So, a widower and an almost-bride, you know, we're a lyric waiting to happen."

A small smiled played on her lips. "That is why I never wanted to get involved with someone in the music business, the future never includes faithfulness and longevity."

He stepped closer. "Don't brand me with that Smith brush—I can't carry a tune in a bucket—and I'm notoriously monogamous. You know my story. I take the vows for 'in sickness and in health' very seriously."

She turned, and he reached for her arm. "Wait. I'm glad we've covered the portion of a relationship where we compare our past love lives, but AJ, I'm not like Cullen. I'm not like Roger Worthington. You will always be more important than a song."

Something wonderful happened in that kitchen. AJ wrestled with her conscience—maybe her heart—but whatever it was, when she came to a point where she'd made peace with the past, she smiled. And it wasn't an ordinary glory. She beamed. "I will quote you when you tell me we can't meet because of some concert or a meeting with a reclusive artist. I rather like being more important than a song."

Luke felt a whole songbook from ages past roll off his shoulders. He brought her close and would have hugged her, but he couldn't stop reading her eyes for the codicil. She'd require proof. "So, about that kiss."

She lifted onto her toes.

He put a finger against her mouth. "When I kiss you, there won't be questions about my integrity lingering in that beautiful mind of yours. You'll be so thoroughly kissed that you will wonder how one perfect moment could surpass every other kiss in the known world and how soon we can repeat it."

Chuckling, she stood on her tiptoes so she could let her mouth hover inches from his. "That's quite a promise."

"Lady, I aim to deliver." His gaze shifted to her lips, and he brushed her mouth with his lips. "But it won't be right now."

Gasping, AJ dropped to her heels. "What?"

"Sorry to disappoint you," his breath seemed to have struggled from the basement of his body, but he would honor AJ Worthington if it was the last thing he did. "When I kiss you, it will be the beginning of a promise meant to be kept. I'm not teasing you along. I'm not using you to get to your parents. I'm not lying to you to keep you distracted from the truth of my actions."

"I believe you," she said breathlessly. "My parents respect you, but neither of them is leaping at your marketing suggestions."

"Well, now that hurts." He wrapped his arms around her waist and held her close. "But what you and I are creating is something special. And I can tell it will take a grand gesture before you believe that all my motivations are toward you and not those older Worthingtons."

"Would it help if I said I don't need any gestures? I'm a lot easier to convince than I previously thought."

He bent to nibble the skin under her jaw. "Don't taunt me, AJ. I'm fragile."

"That makes two of us."

His lips found her earlobe, and he tugged the skin with his teeth. "And that's why I'm not going to kiss you."

She gulped. "You talk a lot."

"Occupational hazard." Luke pulled away and released his arms from her waist. He reached for her hand and folded her fingers into his grip. "We'll wait until the moment is right. I won't have you second-guessing me. I have it on good authority you don't trust words."

Her eyes narrowed. "That might be an overstatement."

"Or not." He moved over to hold the front door open. "See, I've never really understood why you're so committed to rescuing people adept at navigating life."

"You mean, my parents."

"They seem to fall under example A." Then he walked over to the window unit and turned the thermostat back to a level suited to nonlaboratory status. "But Keisha tells me you took her and her son in when she was going through a divorce. Jake says you let Kali use your kitchen to perfect her goat-cheese-making methods before her house was remodeled, and a woman named Anna swears that you're the person people go to when they need overflow space for their out-of-town relatives, so apparently, this list is extensive."

Her skin flamed again, but he continued, "Ethan told me that the church secretary has you on speed dial."

She glanced at him as if prepared to defend herself, then bent down to retrieve her bag from the floor. Fishing out her keys, she said, "You already know this, why poke me at my weak spots."

"And the farm?" Luke spanned his arm toward the window that overlooked the creek that used to run through Worthington family acreage. "Or what was left of it, you alone repurposed into a lavender farm so you could employ folks in an area that doesn't seem to have a lot of diverse economic opportunities."

"I don't understand what you're trying to say. I'm a nice person. I do kind things. That's not usually treated as a crime."

Luke stood with her on the porch, his hands on her shoulders, gripping her like she was fine china. "I'm not judging you. I'm in awe of you. But I haven't figured out what makes you tick either."

"You're making too much of this."

"Am I?" Luke followed her to the porch steps. "Or is it because everyone in your life has left you, and the only way you think you can keep people around is to do nice things for them?"

"I'm sure you're insulting me."

As he glanced at the hanging basket overflowing with multicolored flowers, he finally figured out something. He closed the door behind them. No one ever returned the favor for AJ. No one seemed to do for her what she so easily gave to others.

With a tenderness that surprised him, he realized that the one thing he could do to prove his love for her was to come to where she was. He wasn't sure what that looked like at the moment, but he would use that long flight tomorrow to figure it out. "I am coming back to Comfort, AJ. I've found something here that is too good to ignore."

"It's all right," she said, fumbling for her keys and dismissing their tender moment. "I knew you'd have to go back eventually. This was just a vacation for you, right?"

"It was a shift in my universe, but let's call it a vacation for now."

"I'm late for work." She hitched the bag onto her shoulder. "Safe travels. I'll pass your regards on to everyone. They'll miss you. I'll … miss you."

The brow over Luke's eye rose like it had a spine of its own. "I am coming back, AJ."

She kissed his cheek. "No worries, Luke. You're a busy man. It was great to know you. Though I never dreamed I would say this, I appreciate what you've done for my family."

He cupped the echo of her kiss with his hand. "You're a weird one, Autumn Joy Worthington. But lucky for you, I'm incredibly attracted to weirdness. And don't run, because you're my ride back to Comfort."

Chapter Twenty-Eight

Adding composted manure to the soil around your plants will shock them into good health. –"Lessons from Lavender Hill"

Monday morning, AJ turned on the table lamps bracketing the sofas as she walked through the living room. She twisted the switch on the twin buffet lamps anchoring the dining room too. Bringing light into the darkness was one of her favorite morning rituals. The house smelled fresh, and the shadows were cool after a sleepless night.

A late-night walk through the lavender fields hadn't been nearly as comforting as usual, but Beans had been good company, and he didn't complain as she ranted to God about why every time things looked up, a left hook would send her world spinning again. She hadn't asked for her mother to descend on the farm this spring, but she'd adapted. And the consequences of Inez's disease were probably something she should have recognized sooner, but she was not without options for dealing with that surprise. The thing that hurt so much was that her surprise brush with romance was snatched away as quickly as she accepted its potential.

How could she have been so stupid to let herself imagine a change of heart regarding Luke? Dumb enough to feel a pain in her soul for what could have been.

Stepping into the kitchen, she glanced through the open door and saw her mother curled up asleep on the sofa tucked into a corner of the sun porch. Beans guarded July from his vantage on a pile of quilts.

Remarkably, she didn't feel panicky that her mother had stayed up late writing lyrics—based on the notepaper spilled onto the floor. She paused. Was she really feeling this calm about the one thing that she swore was a deal-breaker with July?

Waiting, AJ expected an eruption of dismay, disappointment, or at the very least disgust. None followed. Her heart was just as still as it had been when she walked through the butler's pantry. She picked up a notebook and set it on the table without any of the righteous anger she would have predicted.

Maybe she'd made peace that her mother was never going to be the TV mom of the afternoon specials. July was a musician, and without the thrill of creating, she was just a shell of a woman. AJ thought about the last month and the fun they'd had without forcing cookie baking into the mix. She smiled. Accepting her mom as she was—calluses from guitar strings and all—was as much about AJ growing up as it was her mother retiring.

Walking back into the kitchen, she filled a teakettle with water and set it on the range. AJ rummaged in the silver caddy for a stiff black tea, supposing she'd known all along that she'd be the one to bend. Separating July and music was like asking the moon to stop making shadows.

Beans nudged her hip.

"Hi, there, boy." She scratched his ears then opened the back door for him. As he lumbered down the porch steps into the darkened yard, AJ took a moment to notice tiny yellow darts streaking across the horizon.

Light was breaking through the blanket of morning, and she took comfort from the routine of sun, moon, and stars working in reliable synchronization. Maybe stepping back from her dream of reforming July—and Roger, too—was nothing more than accepting life for what it was.

Giving grace to people, as they were, was the better use of her time.

She reached toward the bowl of Penny's peaches and wiped one on the hem of her shorts.

The people of Comfort had been good to her when she rolled into town angry, betrayed, and lost all those years ago. They'd not questioned her sanity when she plowed cow pastures into lavender fields, and they'd indulged her when she gave away bouquets of lavender stems at craft shows and church suppers.

She breathed deep the morning air and bit into the peach.

The kettle hissed, and she hurried to the stove to lift it off the burner before it blew its whistle. The ritual of the tea steeping gave her a few minutes to find the journal Luke had given her. Though it wasn't her habit, she would try to spend a few minutes on the front porch thinking and writing and hoping something sensible came from the exercise.

"AJ?"

Startled, she turned to see July rubbing her eyes. Yesterday's sundress hung wrinkled around her mother's shoulders.

"Hey, Mom, why don't you go on upstairs to bed?"

July brushed at the creases in her dress. "I don't even remember lying down."

"Apparently, you were burning the midnight oil." AJ moved toward her mother. "Come on, let's get you back in your own bed."

July stepped back, banging into the doorframe "I'm not a child. I can put myself to bed if I'm ready to go."

"Suit yourself." Bruised, AJ turned away to put the tea on a tray. Why did she keep trying to take care of people who didn't want her help?

July took the peach from AJ's hand and bit into it, saying, "Men aren't as simple as we've made them out to be. I think women like to tell themselves that men are shallow because it makes us feel superior, but most of them are complex."

AJ turned around and watched juice drip from her mother's chin. When had her mother lost that look of hollowness? "Oh-kay. Not sure how we made the leap to that conversation, but I'll take your word for it."

"You're upset that Luke left Saturday. You thought you had him all figured out, and he's surprised you." July wiped her chin with a dishcloth. "I wanted to say something after dinner, but you were still too prickly."

AJ stood, not at all ready to have this mother-daughter talk. "I'm mad at Dad for not depositing Gran's money at the bank like I thought he would. I didn't buy his story that it was too much to turn in at one time."

July chewed the peach and shrugged. "Well, if that's what you want me to believe, I'll go with it. But we both know you got attached to Luke, and now he's left you. Unlike Cullen, this guy might return."

AJ hated her mother's observant nature. "I'm going outside to do writing for the manual, so if you'll excuse me."

"Right, you will put down quips about what makes your gardens so great."

"Something like that," AJ didn't like the patronizing tone coming from a master songwriter, but there was nothing she could do about that. There were boxes of childhood creative attempts that proved she didn't inherit her parents' genes. "I don't judge you for your music. Please don't judge me for my gardening."

"Your gardening is a gift unlike anything I could create. I don't know where you got the green thumb, but it's a beautiful thing. If you can articulate how you do what you do, then I'll be the first in line to buy your book."

"But you were mocking me." AJ's wounds were way too close to the surface. "And teasing me about Luke, both of which were too close for comfort."

July sighed with the weariness of years of regrets. "I'm sorry, baby. I don't always know where my meanness comes from, but it's wrong to take it out on you. You're the only in this family who has a heart."

"You have a heart, too." AJ balanced the tea tray. "I wasn't raised by wolves."

July smiled. "We had good years, didn't we?"

AJ had to admit her childhood wasn't a total train wreck. "We did."

"Can we start over?" July asked, setting the peach hull down on the counter. "I mean really start fresh—like with a clean slate? I don't want to keep feeling like I have to make up for the mess of the nineties every time I'm around you. Can you forgive me for being a selfish bitch and let's move on?"

"This may be the first time you've asked me to forgive you."

July pushed a strand of hair behind her ear. "I took a while to accept that I'd done as much harm as your father. My failures were rather spectacular, and I've only recently come to terms with the idea that those failures were feeding my desire to be creative again."

AJ had never expected these words. A quick glance confirmed that this wasn't a dream—the dog was scratching at the back door.

She latched on to one old pain that she wanted explained. "You helped Cullen with his career. You put him in front of the producers."

July's brow arched. "So, you want to go there?"

She might regret the honesty. "Yes."

"I did help him. He'd begged me from our first meeting. I'd resisted because I didn't want to get between you two, and then for reasons I don't remember, I called in a favor and got him some studio time with a guy out of New York." July sighed. "It was supposed to be a short-term fix for getting that kid to shut up."

"Your fix ruined my life."

"It was as much my shock as yours that Cullen had real talent," July said. "Turns out when he set his keyboarding aside and concentrated on his vocals, he had real chops. I heard he recently played the Napa Valley Jazz Festival and had fans eating out of his hand. Guess I can pick 'em, can't I?"

AJ had deleted Cullen from her social media accounts when she moved to Texas, and she was glad to be in the dark. But she wondered, if after all this time, would she still have a reaction if she were to meet him again. "Actually, though I didn't know it then, his leaving turned out to be a defining moment for me." She looked through the window to see dawn coloring the fields with gold streaks. "I'd never have all this if I'd stayed with him."

"He was too much like your father," July added, as she walked toward the sink to rinse her hands. "He would have broken your heart. At least that way, he did it before you had a child to raise and income to split."

AJ considered what her life would have looked like if he'd taken her with him. "You know that was my decision to make, not yours."

"Then I'll ask you now, please forgive me for sending that self-centered, two-bit hustler off to be someone else's heartbreak?"

The silence softened the grief, left room for a goodbye to a long-held grudge.

"You've had a lot of therapy, haven't you?" AJ asked, wondering what else she'd misjudged in her family's dysfunction.

Her mother smiled with a strange mixture of serenity and sleep. "Tons, for all the good it's done me. If your father is a rolling stone always chasing something, I'm the one stuck in the rut, doomed to repeat all my mistakes. And though we were creatively bad for each other, I think our breakup actually made us work harder for our music. I've heard some of the lyrics he wrote in the last few years. He's good. If he had the right advice, he might even have a hit."

AJ sipped her tea and let the heat scar her tongue. The pain was a good starting place. It helped her remove the assumption she'd had any clue about what had ever motivated her parents. "And you? Are you writing again?"

"You won't like my answer, but yes. I can't seem to quit the melodies in my head. And being here, being with you, has helped me see that I have to unleash my talent. Even if I don't do anything more than pursue songwriting, I've got to keep creating. It's in my DNA."

"My greatest triumphs have come after my deepest falls, too, so maybe I've been a little harsh, insisting that to stay with me you have to give up your music."

July ran her fingers through her hair. "Oh, AJ. To go back and redo my life, that would be a gift of unspeakable value. I've made a hash of so many things."

"I wouldn't say 'hash' per se." AJ knew what she could write, if she ever took Luke's advice about venting onto paper. "You never forgot the way back home."

"And you've always kept the door open for me." July sighed and folded her arms into herself. "I will get it right this time, AJ. This time I'm starting over for real."

AJ saw tears rim her mother's eyes. "I have confidence in you."

"Why?"

She hadn't expected to defend her statement. It was way too early and lacking a caffeine supply to be more than polite. But she could tell by the water clinging to her mother's eyelashes that a good answer was important. She drew in a tentative breath and said, "Because in all the years past, when you came here, you never wanted to pick up the guitar. You wanted to drink and forget a deal that had gone wrong for you or forget some man who'd broken your heart." She pointed toward the guitar on the floor of the patio. "You must have dug that one out of the attic."

"I did," July said sheepishly.

"And to my knowledge, you've not hid a stash of whiskey in the bathroom."

July leaned over the sink and watched sunrise color the horizon with feathery pink. "The hardest thing I ever did was walk off that stage four weeks ago and vow to quit the hard liquor. But I swear, I've felt liberated ever since. It's like someone set me free, and I can reinvent myself. That's both terrifying and freeing."

Quitting performance was harder for her mother than walking out on a marriage and a family had been, but she'd always known that a microphone was July's greatest lover. That's why AJ feared the road so much. She never knew when her mother would be dumped, or what she'd be like in the withdrawals. But now, with the sun streaking light into the kitchen, she saw that her mom would be just fine.

She was stronger for her broken places.

AJ met her mom at the sink, set the tray on the counter, and wrapped her arms around July's waist. She settled her head on her mom's shoulder, much like she'd done when she'd been a brokenhearted teenager, wondering why boys were jerks. "You still looking for a friend?" she asked.

July clutched AJ to her body. "Oh, in the worst way."

"I love you, Mom."

July squeezed with intensity. "I love you too, Autumn Joy."

AJ smiled against July's unruly hair. "So, I guess this is a breakthrough?"

"I guess it is." July rubbed tears from her face. "We both know I was a lousy mom to you, so if we could just be friends, I think we'd figure out where to go from here."

Like someone had just gift wrapped her private wishes, AJ sighed with a strange bliss. "You've got my friendship, Mom. You always did."

July's smile lacked its trademark lipstick, but it was still just as wide. "And we'll figure out what to do with your dad as we go along, okay?"

"Ok." AJ scooped July close again and buried her nose in her mother's hair. She itched for a pen and paper. Pulling out of the embrace, she said, "I've got to go. See you at lunch?"

"You don't have to explain anything. I understand the need to work."

AJ gathered the notebook and a pen and walked through the butler's pantry toward the front of the house. She may never see Luke English again, but his imprint on her family would last for a while. Thinking of Luke made her smile. And that was a sweet bombshell.

Somehow, he'd created a bridge for July, and he'd left AJ the means to write and think through the methods she'd used in the gardens.

As the screened door banged shut behind her, AJ stared at the pink shades rippling across the hilltops and knew she'd not waste the gift.

The thing that stunned her the most about all this stirring of the dirt in her mind was that it wasn't so different from what she'd had to do to make room for flowers. One had to remove the rocks and the weeds before they could till the soil—much like she was trusting others again for the first time in ages.

AJ opened the notebook and tapped the edge of the book with the pen. She sat down on the top step and held the pen close to the page, scribbling a few words about looking at rocks and weeds and imagining what would grow. It was the dream of better things that gave a gardener that spirit to persevere through the hard work. Staring at the dawn, she dialed back to those long-ago days when she walked the pastures, kicking at old cow patties and shale, visualizing rows and rows of blooming lavender. Bending over the book to write, she poured out those memories and let the dreams seep onto the page.

Beans collapsed at her feet, as if he knew they would be here for a while.

Chapter Twenty-Nine

Annual plants give the gardener a boost of impact in beds or planters. They are one season beauties and have to be replaced year after year, so don't get attached to their color. — *"Lessons from Lavender Hill"*

Pulling weeds from the begonia bed a week later, she yanked a stray mustard vine from underneath a pink bloom. How this got here was anyone's guess, but wasn't that just like her garden? Stray seeds were almost always a gift from the birds.

Wheels crunched gravel in the front parking lot, and Kali's SUV pulled to a stop inches away from the new arbor. AJ glanced down at her dirty arms. Sweat was dripping along the back of her neck, and she had a bandage on her hand from a run-in with a rosebush.

Kali stepped around the front of her vehicle, looking fresh in her loose white top and tan shorts, her baby bump giving her a glow that could not be purchased.

Another woman climbed from the passenger seat. She wore work boots, skinny jeans, and a silk blouse that looked five times more expensive than anything AJ kept in her closet. The woman's glossy dark hair was styled in an elegant French twist, and tortoiseshell sunglasses sat perched on her nose. AJ shrunk into her jean shorts and T-shirt, feeling wholly inadequate to interact with the woman who was sizing up Lavender Hill's prospects.

Kali waved. "Hey, AJ! We stopped by for a quick minute because I wanted you to meet Colette Sheridan, and I wanted her to see the property you and I have been daydreaming about."

AJ pulled a bandana from her pocket and wiped sweat from her face. Miss Sheridan was the name of the San Antonio architect Kali had been bragging about recently. AJ remembered hearing about the restoration work on a Comfort-area ranch where there was no limit to the money being invested. She stood and winced. Her thighs ached from weeding.

Peeking at the abandoned house next door, the one she and Kali had discussed converting into a tearoom, she could imagine the hoot of disdain this architect would make when told the idea they'd cooked up for expanding Lavender Hill and combining it with a sales outlet for Kali's Provence Farm products. She stopped next to the potting shed, hoping the dirt fragrance would overpower her own. "Forgive the nails," AJ said, offering her hand in greeting, "I've been pulling weeds for hours."

Kali turned toward Collette, as if to explain, "AJ does have a staff, but she's enough of a control freak to do all the odd jobs, as well."

"You get my respect then. Not only are you in retail, which is such an unpredictable business model, but you also have such a physical job." Colette smiled. "And what a delightful place to spend your days. The lavender fields were obviously a project with passion."

AJ glanced beyond the potting shed toward the rows of lavender almost at peak, as they rounded the acreage behind the shop and disappeared over the hilltop. "Well, I dreamed about doing a lavender farm for a long time. And now it's sort of grown out of control."

Kali leaned her hip against a picket fence. "Did you know Colette has been living out at the construction site in an RV? She's practically a neighbor."

"It's just for a few weeks," Colette corrected. "The upside is I take particular delight in aggravating Beau Jefferson to keep him aware of the building timetable."

Something about the way the architect said Beau's name made AJ's ears perk. Beau had a colorful history in Comfort, and AJ was one of many women who'd admired his rugged good looks. But, as a contractor, he was hardly the type to attract attention from a woman who probably had season tickets to the symphony. "I've hardly seen Beau since he's been back in town, except for a few times at the coffee shop, but if he has a building deadline, he'll meet it. He's a man of his word."

Kali folded her arms on top of her belly. "I invited Colette here today to see if she thinks our tearoom idea has any legs. I picked up a key from the realtor so we can take a look at the house next door. Figure out if there's room for the small restaurant. I think we should expand the plan for parking also, because your customers are parking out on the road, and we'll need more room closer to the tearoom."

AJ realized Kali had spent significantly more time thinking about this idea than she had.

Colette shaded her eyes as she studied the two properties. "So, you're thinking of ways to combine the two locations, right?" she asked, sounding like she was calculating concrete costs while she spoke. "Make this destination viable all year long?"

AJ had the feeling that the idea they'd drawn one afternoon in the coffee shop, sketched out on a paper napkin, was about to get shot down. She followed Colette's gaze to the yard next door. Bare spots and weeds broke up the withered grass around the ranch-style home. She'd already given so many years to building Lavender Hill, was she really willing to add something else?

She could almost hear Luke saying, *If you want to have any fresh surprises in your career, you have no choice but to branch out.* But did she want the surprises of starting something new? Something bigger?

No, no, no.

Rubbing her earlobe, AJ almost missed hearing Colette's assessment.

"We'll know more when we get inside the house, but I think you two should expand your idea of a tearoom into more of an events area. A place people could host receptions, parties—" Colette motioned with her arm toward the lavender farm. "Maybe even a place for outdoor weddings. We could keep the shell of the house and build out from there."

Kali covered her mouth with her hand. "Oh, my word. What an incredible idea."

Colette shrugged, as if she whipped out magical solutions three or four times a day. "It's an option. And it could generate more year-round revenue than a tearoom that might just rely on customers from the garden store."

Kali's face looked brighter already. "There aren't many places for wedding receptions or family reunions in Comfort. Something like this might bring new traffic to town."

How did a few short words send AJ's calm sailing like a paper airplane caught on an airstream? "You're seeing something big?"

Colette smiled at AJ. "I'm seeing something with flexible spaces."

"And multiple uses," Kali squeaked. "We'd make a lot more money this way."

Kali obsessed about making money. She'd also been the one to urge AJ forward with ways to expand income potential with the garden center: new products, the book idea, and, most recently, a tearoom. Kali was a born entrepreneur.

Colette's voice rose as she described ways an event venue could connect the two properties, allowing for AJ's already beautiful hills of lavender to be a center point to the new structure. AJ wiped sweat from her eyes and narrowed her gaze to see if she could see what Colette was seeing.

Luke would be able to see an event center in the middle of a barren yard. He was like Kali and Colette — visionary. She was practical. Give her seeds and she grew plants. She did not imagine books, lyrics, venues, or any of the other wild visions the Lukes and Kalis of the world did with a snap of their fingers.

AJ swiped away the honeybee investigating her throat, knowing a truth as plain as if someone had said the words out loud: Luke would love this idea of a second venue.

His voice was already circling her brain, pointing out the marketing advantages. How she could link the two properties and turn a visitor's first trip to Lavender Hill into a return with relatives and party planners. He'd probably see some correlation to her gardening book, too, since he was fixated on her telling her story.

Luke.

That tall, handsome man with an easy smile and impeccable taste. Her heart lifted just thinking about him. Like he'd ever been very far from her mind since he left for San Antonio. How was she ever going to forget that for one moment in time, she'd let herself think she could have a second chance at romance? That someone like Luke English would trade all the glitter and glamour of the music industry to live in dusty, old Comfort, Texas, and be happy with her.

Her palms were cracking with drying mud. Or maybe it was regret. Either way, thinking of Luke had a way of making her skin seem too small for her body. And her heart race. But she wasn't in love.

Love had turned her inside out once before. This was not that nausea-inducing emotion.

Luke was just a nice guy, and men like him were rare creatures.

Actually, he was more than just nice. He was creative and spontaneous. He'd been unquestionably kind to her family and friends. He'd been generous with gifts of his time and talents and in applying his insight to her sticky family dramas.

That made him sound like a paragon of goodness. She bit her lip.

Who was that nice without asking for anything in return?

She stared at the blue sky. All Luke seemed to want ... was to be with her.

He wasn't using her to gain access to her parents—he'd had them from hello. No, what he genuinely seemed to be after was a sunbaked girl with dirt under her fingernails.

AJ's heart lifted from its locked-down bolts, seeming to hover over a flight path.

And she'd let Luke leave without ever telling him how much she appreciated his—kindness.

Her gaze descended back to the crusty earth where it belonged.

She wasn't in love. She was in awe that someone had been nice to her.

Colette and Kali were talking fast, their ideas stepping over each other, but AJ saw Luke's twinkling eyes and remembered that he'd helped her overcome her blind spots toward her parents. And, he'd given her his lucky pen to help with the writing process.

But mostly, he'd helped her laugh again.

No, she wasn't in love. But she would miss him. Forever.

The lavender fields were blowing their beautiful purple stalks, it would be harvest season soon. She looked across the sea of periwinkle and thought if someone could photograph this scene, it should be the cover of the book.

The book was a good project.

But it would not be enough to forget a man with twinkling eyes and a smile that made her forget why she was so anxious about her parents. If she was half the woman Luke thought she was, it was time to do something bold.

Whipping around, she saw Colette and Kali walking toward the car. "You're leaving?" she called out.

Kali turned back and squinted into the blinding sunlight. "Well, you hardly showed any interest in developing the property."

AJ waved her hand toward Colette to emphasize her alliance. "I'm not opposed to buying that space, it's just that it's a little soon to decide about building an event center. Let's think on it."

"Two days ago, you said a tearoom was terrifying." Kali's brow rose over her eye. "What makes you so open-minded now about the idea of an events center?"

She had a tendency to think in terms of what she could control—what she could guarantee she could accomplish. Spreadsheets were her road map. Responding positively to a spontaneous idea was not her preferred business model.

It might be time to consider that there was a lot of life out there that wouldn't fit within her palms, and maybe that was okay. AJ sighed and put her toes on the edge of the proverbial high dive. "I don't know. I see it now. Colette's great at describing things."

"I am?" Colette pulled off her sunglasses. "That wasn't much of a description."

AJ stared at the neighbor's barren yard pockmarked by anthills and prickly pear shrubs and imagined blue salvia and brown-eyed Susan lining a flagstone trail, wild rosemary clumping around a small pond, and roses climbing a trellis—besides the surplus lavender fields billowing out from a party patio. Once she wove that property into hers, she could expand both businesses and have a compound of buildings and gardens that would produce more lavender—and the lucrative lavender oil—and a place to host people year-round. She liked entertaining. And Penny could be the caterer.

She could almost feel Luke nudging her shoulder, whispering *yes* into her ear.

"All this time it's been right beside me, and I didn't understand what the potential held," AJ said, with some awe and a little dismay she could be so blind. "I always underestimate the outcome of things. I'm way too cautious."

Colette gestured toward the forty-year-old cowshed behind her shop where AJ stored distilling equipment, bottling supplies, and tractors. It leaned to the left and had a gaping hole where the hayloft doors had blown off.

"That barn," Colette asked. "Is it useful?"

"Only to me," AJ said. A line of sweat had dripped between her shoulder blades. Thinking about how she'd cobbled together old buildings and recycled equipment must make her look like a junkyard shopper.

"It's got good bones. We could use that as a footprint to build a bigger barn with huge windows overlooking the lavender fields and steep eaves to give a majestic feel," Colette said. "We could save the original house, paint it white, and use it for a bridal dressing area, and maybe light catering, and build a new barn-style hall there between the two properties." She pointed to a place that was little more than a gulley for rain runoff. "We'd give it an outdoor entertaining space that echoed the feel of Lavender Hill and copy your gardening methods so that clients feel like they could access the lavender hillside as a backdrop for their events."

Kali's jaw hinged open.

AJ read Kali's expression and glanced around the grounds of Lavender Hill with both dread and excitement. This dawn-of-destiny moment felt like the long-ago conversation when she explained her idea of the garden store to her grandmother, repurposing the Worthington family farm. Thankfully, Inez had a bold streak and a will to see AJ removed from Nashville and the toxic fiancé who had stolen AJ's joy.

AJ's skin prickled as a cloud drifted over the burning rays of sun, dropping the intense heat. "If I had access to the acreage that accompanies that house, I could expand the lavender gardens to surround an outdoor entertaining space. The fragrance would amaze guests at the event center, it would make a great backdrop for photos, and during harvest it would add to my overall inventory. I could even set up a distilling demonstration, if someone wanted to see that."

Colette nodded like she was in sync with AJ. "I love that idea, particularly if we could build a pavilion overlooking the lavender fields, and then a casual space for a firepit, too. Can you burn the stalks you don't use? Wouldn't people love to buy the bound lavender stalks for kindling? My word, the smell would be sensational."

AJ squeezed her fingers together, keeping the excitement in her belly contained to the casual observer—Kali exempted, since she seemed to be able to read minds with little provocation. And she had history watching AJ make fists and fumbles with her personal life. "I'm interested in this, Colette. Really interested."

Kali wiped perspiration from her brow. "How could we put up that kind of capital? This is a far leap from remodeling the house into a tearoom."

AJ whistled for Beans to follow her across the driveway, as she walked onto the drought-stricken land that bordered her property. "I invested what I had left of my grandfather's inheritance in a very successful startup. It's not much, but with the profits I'm making at the shop, it might help us make the leap to going into business together."

"You have capital to invest?" Kali cupped her baby belly like the infant was leaping with joy. "You drive a ten-year-old truck."

AJ fiddled with the gold hoop in her ear. "I don't need shiny things. Those were important to my parents. That's not my style."

"Except for your Sub-Zero refrigerator and Wolf stove."

"Well, yes, except for those." AJ had spent a lot of time — after breaking up with Cullen — re-imagining her priorities and learning who she was. It revealed cooking and gardening to be talents she had and a source of passion she'd never tapped. Moving to Comfort had unleashed all that and more. A head for business, an understanding of what people wanted to see in their yards, and a work ethic that had never been tested. "The thing is, I should develop the land around Lavender Hill." She turned back, appealing to her friend who had witnessed this emergence from the Tennessee cocoon. "But it would be a lot more fun if we did it together."

Stuttering, Kali said, "But you haven't even finished your book."

AJ instantly imagined the notebook and scattered papers where she and July had sat at the dining room table a few days ago and talked through the logistics of writing out a gardening manual. July insisted that taking over this task was payback for all the hospitality AJ had offered over the years. AJ reminded her mother that helping with work was more in keeping with just being a mom and daughter. Knitting together their efforts with words was a lot easier than talking through history that neither of them wanted to revisit.

Maybe her life was finally falling into place.

All those years of sacrificing–in part because of need, but also because of running from her parents' fame — had come back around. She was in a happy place and had a good career path for the future.

Her parents were healing.

Her grandmother was close.

She was blessed with incredible friends and a purpose in life.

And for a moment in time, she'd known Luke.

Happiness bubbled under her ribs like a wellspring that had come uncapped.

She glanced at Kali and admitted, "Mom's helping me with the writing, Dad has taken a boatload of photos we've been using to block out the progression of ideas, and by working together, we'll have something to offer Elizabeth soon. It's all going to work out in the end."

Kali spun to face Colette, incredulity replacing her previous skepticism. "I don't know who this woman is. She looks like my AJ, but I swear I don't know this language she speaks. My AJ is never this spontaneous."

Colette replaced the sunglasses on her face and chuckled. "I'll come back in a month or so with some sketches of barn spaces that can be multi-use facilities. In the meantime, you two talk to the realtor. Even if you don't turn the space into a venue, you should at least protect the access to Lavender Hill by owning the adjacent property."

AJ watched Beans leap over a dry creek bed and sniff at a suspicious mound in the neighbor's yard. She really couldn't say if she'd follow through to build an events center, but the hope of doing something big removed the hollow space that had formed when she watched Luke pack up his car.

And Luke leaving Comfort left about as big a hole as anything she'd known in a long while. Wrapping her arms around her waist, she hugged her ribs and stared at the mildewed house, thinking if—and it was a big if—she could make something beautiful out of that 1970s brick, then maybe she could discover what else there was to tap inside her soul.

Or maybe what she wanted—even more than redirecting her parents away from the grueling life of mega-stars—was to find someone to share all this prosperity with. Someone who'd made her think again about a happily ever after.

Someone like ... Luke.

Chapter Thirty

Comfort, Texas   April 3, 1968

Inez hurried Roger to the car before her mother-in-law could see how damp they were from huddling under the rain-wet tree, waiting on George. He'd return from Comfort to pick them up any minute. Checking her watch, she saw the ticking hands creeping toward the end of her patience.

She hated being at the mercy of Mrs. Worthington.

It was particularly worse at Christmas, when the old lady was in a perpetual state of depression because all the men in her life—save George and Roger—had deserted her. She could take a few minutes to dote on Roger, her only grandchild, no? All the old matron could see at this point were his terrible table manners, lack of chitchat skills, and total disinterest in anything to do with the farm. And that guitar. It was like an appendage.

And Inez got the blame for it all.

Did it matter that George was so successful with his car dealerships he could barely spare the day for Christmas dinner in Comfort? Or that he'd run her meaningless errands in town so his mother wouldn't have to crank her car and drive out tomorrow? Oh, no. None of those details mattered.

The priority complaint centered around Inez not bringing the beloved pralines from La Fogata's Restaurant. Mrs. Worthington mentioned it three times before dessert. With her dentures, she couldn't even eat the pralines anymore.

Inez wiped water from her hosiery, as her husband's shiny new Chevrolet Corvair cruised to a stop at the driveway.

Inez jerked open the passenger door and slid the seat forward for her son.

"God, she's such a drag," Roger groaned as he collapsed into the back seat. "I don't know why we even come out here. It's like a mausoleum in there."

George cocked his brow as he looked at Inez with accusation. "You've poisoned your son."

"I have not," Inez defended. "He's thirteen. He can make up his own mind about his grandmother. Besides, if you hadn't abandoned us there for three hours, maybe we'd be a little more charming."

George gripped the steering wheel. "You know why I do her errands. And it's the same reason we come out here three times a year."

Momma holds the purse strings. She didn't say the words out loud, because she never wanted Roger to know how dependent they'd been on Mrs. Worthington at the start, or the ridiculous interest rate she charged George for the loan she made so he could buy the first and second dealerships, but Inez was drowning. Every time she came here, she lost some of her spirit; her gears got out of mesh.

George always wanted her to think positive, be one with tranquility by gazing out across the hilltops and imagining the wilderness from days gone by. Or listen for the coyotes at night, as the stars filled the sky. But each and every time they came to Comfort, all Inez could do was take a beating for all the ways she'd never been able to measure up to Mrs. Worthington's impossible standards.

Not even with those stupid pralines.

"Is there a reason you two were walking to town in the rain?" George asked.

Inez glared at him.

"Hey, Mom," Roger said, as he rolled up to sit in the backseat. "Grandma said the strangest thing at lunch today. She said she wants to move to San Antonio to live with us because she's getting too old to keep living alone out here at the farm."

The blood froze in Inez's veins. "She's way too set in her ways to move into the city," she said, carefully controlling her tongue from springing the insults it kept handy. "You must have heard her wrong."

George cut his gaze to the road as he steered the car onto the pavement. "She's not been the same since the dentist pulled her teeth. Momma hates those dentures."

"Dentures are not a good enough reason for her to move in with us, George Worthington, and you know it." Inez whipped her face around to stare out the rain-slicked window and pray that this was all some joke. In the last fifteen years, she'd put with a lot, but that had not prepared her enough to open her home to someone who was so mean she kept hot water to scald the neighbors' dogs. Barracudas, small dinosaurs, yes, those she could consider, but not an old woman with a vindictive streak—not until hell freezes over. "Maybe we need to hire someone to look in on her now and again. I can call a service and see if they have someone looking for a little extra work."

George's silence was thick.

"I heard Daddy say it wasn't such a bad idea. That if Grandma will sell the Comfort house and farm to him, he'd make room for her upstairs at the house in town."

Inez gasped.

Roger reached for his guitar. "Trading land for peace of mind sounds like a song if ever I heard one."

Chapter Thirty-One

Yard work can relax the mind, like therapy.–"Lessons from Lavender Hill"

Kneeling into the mounds around her lavender plants, AJ spread out the oyster shells she worked into the soil last season, snatching weeds, too, as she assessed whether the stems were harvest ready. Tossing a handful of green blades into the old pickle bucket she carried with her between rows, she decided the best time to harvest would be the last week of June. She'd hoped to wait until after the Comfort Street Fair so that she could advertise for attendees to visit the farm and pick their own, but that would be a week too late. Pulling out her cell phone, she dialed her crew chief to set up the workdays.

Leaning back on her heels, she adjusted her hat and stared at the rows that rolled over the hillside like a purple carpet. After the harvest, she'd have to evaluate the fields and determine which sections were spent. Some of the lavender plants were already eight years old. If she acquired the property next door, she could add more inventory, even try cross-pollinating the varieties, and double what she was able to distill into lavender oil. She stood, stretched her back, and whistled for Beans, but he was too lethargic to do more than lift his head and question why they were working outside when there was perfectly good air-conditioning at the shop.

Waving goodbye to the contractor who was repairing a section of her drip-irrigation system, she walked back to the shop, thinking of the coming calendar.

Though he'd been gone over a week, Luke still seemed to haunt her head. Every time she thought about planning something or going out, she'd unwittingly look for him.

She was tired of dreaming about him—picturing him living here in Comfort. With her.

And then there was that niggling matter of desire.

AJ sighed.

She'd been out of sorts for a few days now, and she'd chalked it up to the cumulative emotional drain of sorting out her parents and her grandmother. Ethan had stopped her at church yesterday to ask why she looked so glum, and the best she could answer was that the heat tired her. He asked if it was a perpetual music fest at her house with both parents spending time there, and the sparkle in his gaze showed he'd be willing to jam with them if it would help.

The truth was, there was music in the house. July played her guitar in random fits, sometimes writing notes, other times just staring through the sun porch windows like she was reeling in some far distant muse. It wasn't awful to hear the gentle strumming, nor did AJ feel threatened. It felt almost … natural.

With the exception of her father banging through the front door and demanding attention. More times than not, he and July would end up on the front porch swing reminiscing about better days or arguing about who was going to be the first to unveil new music.

AJ rolled her shoulders loose.

Wasn't this what she'd always wanted—her parents both here?

Maybe her wants had changed. They took up a lot of her space.

Feeling thirsty, she headed to the shop, knowing there would be a keg of peach tea in the kitchen.

As she got closer to the back door, the heat generated by the air-conditioning units rolled in waves toward her, and she glanced toward the empty parking lot. Mondays were hard on her bottom line.

Tires crunched the gravel along the road, and she turned to see who was going by. Beans leapt forward, fascinated by the truck pulling a trailer and turning into Lavender Hill.

Jake Hamilton's truck, with his horse ranch's logo on the side, swallowed two parking spaces as he stopped near the potting shed. He climbed out of the driver's seat, his cowboy hat adding a few inches to his stature. As if he forgot something, he hurried to return to the driver's door and pulled something from the cab.

AJ squinted at the mud on his boots and figured he was working at the goat farm today. She didn't know how much longer they were going to stay in Comfort. Jake was blatant about wanting their baby to be born at his family's ranch near Houston.

"Sorry, I can't stay long," Jake said, slamming his door. "Kali sent me on a grocery store run because she might melt if she doesn't get some chocolate ice cream."

Grinning, she was a little surprised it was only ice cream. Normally when Kali wanted to binge, toppings and hot-fudge sauce were involved.

"Thankfully, I could kill two birds with one stone." Jake pushed the hat back on his forehead. "I hate going to the grocery store."

He handed her a grocery store sack with a wonky red ribbon tied around the top, like she was supposed to know what to do with it.

AJ took the sack and felt the odd weight. "I didn't need you to go to the store for me. Penny was making a run to Kerrville tomorrow."

He held his breath, as if waiting to see what she thought of the gift.

"It's not my birthday," she said cautiously.

"I didn't think it was, but a friend called and asked if I'd deliver this to you today. Said you would know what it meant."

The hair on her neck rose. Their mutual friend group was limited to people who lived within a five-mile radius of Comfort. "Am I to open this now?" she asked, holding the sack from the bottom so it wouldn't drop to the pavement.

"Yes, and I'm supposed to film you opening it," Jake mumbled as he reached for his cell phone. "Don't start, I have to get the angle right."

"Is this a prank?"

Jake glanced at her quickly. "To be honest, I wasn't sure myself. But my source said it was an inside joke and that you'd get it."

AJ had a pitiful experience with inside jokes — particularly the kind that came in presentation form. But then, with lightning realization, she remembered the last person who'd gone to some effort to surprise her. As Jake fiddled with the camera on his phone, she took off her hat, let the mass of hair fall to her shoulders, and finger-brushed the waves. She was not taking off her sunglasses. It was Monday, and she didn't wear makeup on Mondays.

"Did Luke put you up to this?" She tucked stray strands of hair behind her ear, hoping he'd confess, and she could savor that Luke hadn't totally forgotten her as soon as his plane hit the tarmac in Tennessee.

Jake aimed the camera lens toward her. "I was told not to confirm or deny the identity of the sender, just to film you opening the present. I guess he — the person — is expecting a reaction."

That Luke went to this much trouble to plan this gave her a thrill, and she weighed the sack in her palm. "I hate that I have no lipstick on."

"This isn't going to any social-media sites, so don't worry. You look great." Jake poised his finger over the screen. "Okay, on my count, untie the ribbon."

Beans was circling her legs like he was as excited to see if the gift included kibble too. AJ untied the ribbon and opened the sack. She stared at the glass bottle and cocked her head to the side. With more confusion than joy, she pulled up the handle and read the label—"100% pure Vermont Maple Syrup." Forgetting she was being filmed, AJ tried to put this in some context, and it took longer than she'd expected to remember the conversation that would have circled back to syrup.

Staring at the label, she mumbled, "Luke said he was a pancake connoisseur and doubted I could live up to my claim of making the world's greatest pancakes."

Jake stepped closer, with his phone aimed toward her. "Ok, so this is my part of the script. Luke said to tell you … 'You never made the pancakes for him, and that he is coming back to Comfort in three weeks and expects you to live up to your end of the promise.' I think that was my script."

Her head popped up. "Luke is coming back?" She regretted that a lifetime of broken promises echoed that question.

"Scout's honor. Now, you got anything you want to say before I send him this video?"

With her heart circling her ribs, she blurted a befuddled, "Thanks, Luke!" She lifted the syrup like it was a prize. "Bring your dancing shoes. That's the week of the Comfort Street Fair and there will be a lot of two-stepping going on downtown July 3."

Jake turned the camera on himself. "Consider yourself warned," he added. "These people do not mess around with their library fundraiser."

Jake shut the camera off and tucked the phone in his pocket. "Okay, so were you surprised by the syrup? I had to go to a grocery store in Boerne to find something made in Vermont. Who knew he was so fussy about tree sap?"

AJ folded the sack around the bottle and hugged the surprise of his return close to her heart. When he left, she was sure that was the end of Luke English. She thought he'd forgotten her as easily as he had the rearview image of Comfort's city limit sign.

"You've got that funny expression that Kali would say means you're in love."

AJ swallowed and rearranged her features. "Well, Kali would be wrong. You should know better than to trust her opinions on romance since she almost let you go after you two scoured San Antonio looking for that old engagement ring."

Jake held his hands in surrender. "I'm just calling 'em like I see 'em."

Being in love was not something she wanted to think about. She was too old for a silly romance. When she committed to someone, it would be for the long haul. And Luke English—despite his charm, wit, and sexiness—was in the wrong profession to be considered as a lifelong partner. She was never leaving Comfort, and he was knit to Nashville. Even if her heart was skipping along the lavender tops this minute, it was a temporary weirdness. Not a permanent condition.

She'd make that man pancakes. But she didn't hold out any hope that there'd ever be a second breakfast to follow. There just wasn't anything here in Comfort to keep him coming back.

Beans barked to let her know Jake was leaving.

She stepped forward and stopped as he rolled down his window.

"Give my love to Kali," she said, wondering when she'd have time this week to run over to Provence Farms and play with the baby goats. "My mom said she'd like to come see the cheese-making process and visit your barns. We used to keep a few goats at our farm in Tennessee."

Jake nodded. "Things getting better with your folks?"

AJ shaded her eyes and said, "Yes, oddly so. The passive-aggressive behavior has toned down, and we can make it through a whole meal without name-calling. Gran seems a little more stable now that she's on medication, but as far as she knows, her Cadillac is still in the shop. No one has the nerve to tell her she can't drive again."

Resting his wrist on the steering wheel, Jake turned to face AJ. "I know your grandmother will never get better, but I'm glad your folks can help carry the load. It's got to be such a relief to have them around to help."

AJ thought about the chores they'd done around the property and wondered if that was the beginning of a new routine or just a way to burn through some energy that had none of its usual outlets. "Yeah. It's been nice."

Jake tapped the dash as a signal he would back out, and Beans ran a few small circles in what they could describe as his good-bye dance. She caught the dog by the collar. Glancing next door, she saw the property with its for-sale sign glowing in the morning light.

The front door of the shop opened, and AJ turned toward the porch to see who was pulling Beans's attention.

July stood shading her eyes. "Hey, just wanted you to know I'm taking off for a few hours. Your dad will drop me off in Fredericksburg on his way to Austin. Can you come pick me up later today?"

She was short-staffed but would make it work. "Sure, give me about thirty minutes' notice before you want me to meet you." Now, for the real question. "You and Dad are travelling together? Can you imagine what the paparazzi will do with that evidence?"

"There's not a newspaper in the world that would waste their money on us these days." July turned to go back indoors and then stopped. "But I worked on your book notes, and the edited pages are in your office. That was kind of fun. Maybe I haven't lost my touch."

She was sure that anything her mother did to her gardening manual was ten times better than what she could have created. "Thanks, Mom."

"What's that in the sack?" July asked with her hand on the doorknob.

AJ folded the plastic to disguise the bottle of syrup. She wasn't ready to expose her feelings for Luke to a woman who could write a textbook on bad romances. "Just an ingredient for a recipe I'll make one of these days."

Beans sat on his haunches, like he was waiting on them all to return to their senses and go inside.

A small sedan pulled into the driveway, and Beans barked at it. She turned around, seeing her father at the wheel of his rental car. She did a double take when she realized he'd cut his hair.

"Dad?" AJ stepped over to his side of the car. "Is that you?"

He opened his door and stepped out in the sunshine. "Don't make a federal case. I kind of realized lately that I looked like I could be my mother's sister, and that would not help me win any lady friends."

July approached them. "I told you it would take twenty years off you to get rid of those split ends. Didn't realize I'd see your ears too."

AJ switched her gaze from her father's stylishly cut hair to her mother's figure, which had softened in the weeks she'd been eating three meals a day. They both looked healthy, stable, and like the kind of people who wouldn't scare journalists with their bitterness.

"You look good, Dad." Her words were stiff because her father always prided himself on being edgy and unkempt. "And nothing at all like Gran."

"High praise." He folded his arms across his white T-shirt. "Inez and Penny are working at the library today. Getting the information for your booth for the street fair, or something like that. I didn't pay attention because your grandmother said doing that task would put her close to the bank, and she could go in and pull out some money. I about had to hog-tie her to make her swear she wouldn't withdraw any of that money we just deposited."

A consoling breeze blew through the gardens, winding around AJ. "Thanks, Dad. She's been obsessed about that cash. Maybe you should call the bank manager and explain the situation."

"I did that the first day, and I made sure you were the only other person who had access to her account. She still won't let it go, telling everyone that I'm going to steal her cash."

"The doctor says not to take any of this personally."

"How can I not take it personally? I live with her — god-awful as that sounds." Roger watched July walk over to the passenger side of the car like he was appreciating how she moved through the sunlight. "But at least I'm not staying long. I've got a gig in a bar in Austin this weekend. If it goes well, I may stay on Sixth Street for a while."

"Fair enough," she said, knowing it was only greediness that made her want to keep both her parents around, now that they seemed to be friendlier. "I'll see if Penny can stay with Gran at the cabin this weekend."

"She would if you pay her for it." Roger ducked into the driver's seat. "You're the one with the deep pockets, so if you can write the check, Penny — or someone like her — can do the job. I'm never going to rustle my mother into the shower ever again."

AJ watched them drive away and had the surreal feeling of a parent watching teenagers take off for a night on the town. A worry ticked in her gut. Would they make wise choices? Would they come home before dawn?

Beans danced his good-bye moves, as her dad tapped the car horn.

And as if another north wind blew in, she was that girl who lived next door to her grandmother and had nothing more exciting to anticipate than a night of bookkeeping and late-night TV.

She hugged the bottle of Vermont maple syrup.

Maybe the winds of change had blown past them, and better days were ahead.

Chapter Thirty-Two

Pick herbs and flowers when they first blossom and are still only half open. They will open in the warmth of your home. — "*Lessons from Lavender Hill*"

"AJ," Inez called out, "are you in here?"

AJ glanced from the ribbon bunching around a blend of herb stems bound into a posy, one of the many small bouquets she would tie with wire to the wristbands scattered across her worktable. "Back in the kitchen," she responded. Her hands were sticky with rosemary oil, and the fragrances of lavender, eucalyptus, and thyme had permeated the wallpaper.

"Gosh, that's the worst smell ever." Inez walked into the room pinching her nose. "How can you stand it?"

AJ cocked her head to one side, surprised by the tone. Usually, her grandmother liked the aromas when they distilled the oils from herbs. "Well, it's not as strong as what's in the barn this week, so that's something."

Inez collapsed onto a chair that Betty had recently vacated. "I was in your barn last week when the crew brought in all the harvest. I thought my headache would never go away."

"I call that the smell of money."

"Money, money, money. That's all anyone wants to talk about." Inez fiddled with her watchband. "There's someone at my house, and I'm sure they've taken all my cash."

"That's Mary Ruth, she's there to make sure—" AJ wouldn't remind her grandmother that Mary Ruth was there to make sure she bathed and swallowed the medicines. *That* was a sore subject. "That you have company for lunch."

"Well, I don't like her, and if she's there, I'm going someplace else."

AJ had given her a golf cart with an orange safety flag mounted to the roof, since they'd run out of reasonable excuses to keep her away from the Cadillac. Providing her with a low-voltage golf cart that could give her some independence around the property, and high visibility to others, had seemed like a good temporary solution. Now, she wondered if her grandmother might try to take the golf cart into town.

"Come help me," AJ offered, as she lifted a cardboard bracelet toward her grandmother. "We're making wrist posies to sell at the street fair."

"That's ridiculous."

"And yet it's kind of a fun thing to find when so many shops are selling bratwursts and beer."

"I'll take a beer." Inez glanced around the kitchen. "You got one?"

"Since when did you like to drink beer?"

"I've always liked beer. My daddy ran a dive in Gladewater, and he let me drink the stuff to see if it'd gone skanky. Couldn't sell bad beer for full price, you know?"

AJ set her wire cutters onto the table and deliberately studied her grandmother's pristine complexion. "Your father owned a bar?"

"He was a troublemaker, too. Ran a gambling operation out of the stockroom, but he was smart enough to dodge getting convicted." Inez sighed like her breath weighed tons.

"He was a mean old snake, but he was all I had. Until I met George."

"Gran, I've never heard this story." AJ hoped she could keep her talking. "Here, take these snips and clip the heather for me, and while you're at it, where is Gladewater?"

Inez picked up the scissors and stared at the handful of herbs AJ held out to her. "You got any beer?"

"I don't keep beer at the shop."

"That's too bad." Inez set the scissors on the tabletop. "I'm going to town."

Before she could escape, AJ was up and had latched on to her grandmother's fine-boned elbow. "I can drive you. Where do you want to go?"

"Go?"

"You said you wanted to go to town."

"I do. Someone stole my car, and now I will have to get a new one. I've already called the Cadillac dealership."

She'd have to call the dealership and warn them not to act on Inez's phone calls. "Sit down, for now. We can go in a few minutes. I have to get a few more of these made tonight." AJ glanced out the window and saw Betty waving in the grounds crew who came after shop hours to groom the lavender fields. "Maybe we can grab a bite of dinner too."

"I'm not hungry."

"Well, I'm starved," AJ said wearily. "We had a crazy day here at the shop, and I barely got lunch. I still have to go to the grocery store before Lu—before all the crowds roll into town tomorrow."

Inez sat down like a petulant child. "I'm not going with you to a grocery store. I need nothing. Your father has all but abandoned me, and Penny is in a bad mood. She says he's moving to Austin, and it's because I'm not nice to him."

"Are you mean to Dad?"

"He's mean. He takes all my money. I know he's been stealing from me."

AJ rubbed at the vein throbbing under her forehead. "Well, you'd better stay put and let me call the sheriff. He'll want to know about this."

"About time someone said something with some smarts." Inez pinched her nose. "Has anyone told you this place stinks?"

AJ walked through the hallway and out the side door, straight for the golf cart. Ripping the key from the ignition, she stuffed it into her pocket, worried where her grandmother might go. And where was her father? He'd promised he would stay close this week and keep an eye on Gran, since everyone was working double-time getting ready for the fair. The tourism projections were unusually high because of the mild temperatures and a travel feature on Comfort that had run in the area newspapers.

Scanning the yard, she looked for her mother's bicycle. July had promised to help assemble the wrist posies, right after she made a few phone calls. AJ rubbed her forehead, fighting back the headache that threatened.

Where were they?

That she'd stated to think of her parents as "they" was disconcerting. They often holed up at her house, brooding within vicinity of each other. She'd walked in on more than one occasion where they were both playing their guitars in the sunroom. They'd been grumbling and accusing each other of missing the notes, but it was a form of world peace she'd dared not question.

The rev of a motorcycle's engine broke through her thoughts.

Ethan roared into Lavender Hill's parking lot, his motorcycle shining as if recently polished. As he pulled off his helmet, Beans bounded down the steps and greeted him with a sloppy welcome. Ethan scratched the dog's ears and looked around the yard.

"Is your mom around?" He asked, looping his leg off the seat.

She still wasn't used to how quickly Ethan's interest had shifted to her mother, but the sparkle in his eyes was proof of his affections.

"I wish I could tell you. I expected her here about an hour ago."

His gaze perused her shape, from the messy bun on top of her head to her tennis shoes, as if tallying her assets and finding her lacking. She didn't blame him. The days had been long and tiresome with the added responsibility of making products to donate to the library fundraiser. To accommodate, she'd sacrificed time before a mirror.

"So, you really don't know where your mother is," Ethan asked, "or are you just playing hard to get because you want to stand in the way of her happiness?"

AJ wasn't sure if he lumped himself in with the qualities guaranteed to foster July's million-dollar smile, but she'd take her chances. "Mom will do what she wants to do regardless of anyone else's preferences. I should have learned that lesson years ago."

Ethan swished his hair off his forehead. "Don't be bitter. She's got the soul of a poet. You can't corral that kind of spirit."

AJ was about to warn him away from falling for a woman twice his age, when Inez's voice shrieked from the shop's back door. "Cat fight!"

Whipping around, she saw Inez leaning over the railing, staring at something near the barn. The shrill taunts carried over the noise from the road, and AJ realized Inez was not referring to literal cats. Taking off, she wondered which of her employees were arguing, but then remembered the time and realized most of her staff had left an hour ago. As she rounded the back of the house, she saw two women wrestling in the dirt. Feet were kicking, dirt was flying, and screeching yelps underscored curse words.

Shock made her stop when she recognized Penny's blonde hair tightly yanked in July's grip, then the need to end the madness took over. Her adrenaline climbed, and she prepared to run into the fray. Arms reached out for her middle and stopped her like brakes on a runaway train.

"Leave them to it," her father said, holding her tight against his chest. "This has been years in the making. It's time to clear the air."

Chapter Thirty-Three

Don't squish ladybugs, dragonflies or even spiders. They're garden helpers. — "Lessons from Lavender Hill"

July sat on the curb, a wet towel pressed against her forehead. Ethan hovered near, but not too close, as she'd already shrieked at him once to leave her alone.

AJ shook two aspirin into her palm and offered them to her mother. July swiped at them with no gratitude.

"She's more inclined to want alcohol," Roger grumbled.

July's head snapped. "Go to your girlfriend and see if you can make her apologize. None of this — and I mean none — is my fault."

"It's always your fault, July." Roger offered. "You pop off with some smart remark, and all the old insults come to the head. Hell, I'd have flattened you if given half the chance. You've had a bee up your butt all week."

Snapping her gaze to her father, AJ begged him to quit. "No one knows why you're still here."

He grinned like he hadn't had this much fun in weeks. "Lighten up, AJ. Those two have circled either other for years. I'm not ashamed to say it's satisfying having two women fight over you, and I'd like to gloat a little longer."

"Mr. Worthington," Ethan said. "They were more likely fighting *because* of you, not *over* you."

Roger stood taller, his shoulders rolled back. "And who, exactly, are you?"

AJ grabbed her dad by his elbow and pulled him toward the shop's back entrance. "Go, get Penny, slip her out the front door, and put her in Gran's golf cart." She reached into her pocket. "Here's the key. Take her to Gran's place and call me to let me know if she will press charges."

Roger pulled his arm free. "Nobody will press charges."

"Yet."

"Not for something like this." Roger released his breath, and he seemed to shrink an inch. "Penny's been a wreck ever since she found out how much I enjoy being in Austin."

"Austin isn't that far."

"It's not the town I find so interesting." He winked. "I've met someone. And it looks like I'll have a permanent place to stay, so I won't have to live with my mother much longer."

And with that confession, pieces of the travelling-to-Austin puzzle shifted into place. "You're broke and incredibly unfamous right now. I don't understand the appeal."

"Way to swipe, little tiger." Roger huffed. "Turns out, it's someone I met years ago, and we've reconnected. We're both a little older and wiser, and I will chase this for as long as she'll have me."

With the same disgust she'd felt when *The Tennessean* would print photos of her father and whatever date he'd been on the night before, she reverted to the teenager who wanted to run away from home. Except, this was her home.

"Well, you need to take Penny to Gran's and treat her with respect. That woman has taken good care of you longer than anyone else."

"Except your mother."

AJ cut her gaze to him. "I can barely remember the years you two were civil."

"We had ten or twelve great years together." Roger opened the door to the shop. "Then she went berserk and believed the press about herself, and I could never be enough to keep her happy after that."

Being enough for someone. That was always her sore spot.

"Well, way to whitewash all your sins, Daddy." AJ followed him over the threshold. "And how convenient that you have forgotten your bender that lasted my entire third grade."

He stopped and turned around. "You knew about that?"

She nearly rammed into him. "You can't hide that kind of thing from someone who trailed your footsteps."

"Your mother said you'd find out, but I never thought I was that obvious."

Hurricanes were less obvious, but there was no point rehashing that now, when there were two angry women nursing bruised egos. Stepping around her father, she headed to the kitchen where Inez was wetting a towel from the faucet.

Penny, bent over at the waist, was trying to keep herself from hyperventilating.

"I have aspirin, who needs some?" AJ walked toward the table and scooted the scissors out of arm's reach. "Penny?"

"Don't speak," she grumbled. "I'm too ashamed."

"Miss Hot Pants had it coming," Inez said, glaring at July. "That woman has always been so disrespectful to our family."

Penny wasn't technically family, but this wasn't the time to remind Inez of that. "Mom must have had her reasons for going full-body contact. We just don't know what they are yet."

Roger walked into the kitchen. "Man, it smells like a perfume factory in here."

AJ stepped over to the window and lifted the sash, no need to beg for more criticism. "Dad, don't you want to take Penny home now?"

"I'm not going with him," Penny cried. "He's broken my heart for the last time."

Roger rocked back on his heels. "We've never been in a real relationship, Penny. It's always been about the moment for us."

"For you, maybe." Penny looked up at him and wiped the tears from her cheeks. "I gave you years of my affection, and you took it all for granted."

His face aged a few more wrinkles. "You're probably right."

Inez tossed the towel to Penny. "Clean yourself up, girl. No point crying over spilled milk."

Penny pulled the towel against her cheeks and howled. "I've been such a fool!"

AJ left the aspirin on the table. "Take her home," she murmured to her father. "It's the least you can do."

Roger winced. "For the record, the fight wasn't entirely about me getting between these two. Penny was accusing July of deliberately deceiving you. Afraid you wouldn't be able handle the truth when it came out."

Beans's rapid barking interrupted when AJ would have grilled her dad for more information. She turned to see her dog at the front window, his paws on the ledge like he'd take flight if only he could figure out a way through the glass.

Walking to the front window, she pushed the curtain aside and saw a car parked in the haze of sunset. Luke stood next to the driver's door, listening to July, who was gesturing with both hands.

AJ's heart lifted with surprise. Beans wouldn't quit barking, so she opened the door and let the dog loose. She wasn't too far behind. Her blood zinged with Cupid's arrows and when Luke turned her way, his smile lifted all the pressures off her shoulders.

Just like that.

That man, in a slightly wrinkled suit, somehow rearranged her world with the tilt of his head and a gaze that said he wasn't at all revolted to discover her family in yet another emotional chaos. And for that kind of grace ... maybe she did love him.

Chapter Thirty-Four

Luke opened his arms in reflex, thrilled that AJ walked toward him like a homing pigeon finding its roost. Now that his shoes were planted on Lavender Hill soil—after a crazy flight delay and an epic traffic snarl on San Antonio's Loop 1604—it was almost enough to make him forget the madness of the last four weeks. Almost. He still hadn't processed that he'd quit his firm, but the beauty was that it didn't matter. No one at this address would see his impulsive choice as a negative, or that's what he'd hoped.

AJ wrapped her arms around his waist and nestled her cheek against his shoulder. He rested his chin on top of her bun made of spun gold, breathing as freely as any man who'd just found his other half.

Time could stop now, *Please, God.*

He just wanted to stand with this good woman and face every evening allotted him for the rest of his life. The breeze she brought to his soul was the freedom love promised. Liberty to be himself. Her arms didn't judge. She held him as if something made him to fit her shape.

It hadn't been long after he'd met her, but some gentle moment had birthed the peace that she was the one with whom he'd wanted to spend the rest of life.

Whether she had that same feeling for him was not something he worried about. At least not today. They'd have plenty of time to figure out how to communicate with each other, endure each other's moods, and anticipate the rest of their lives. Particularly once these relatives figured out they didn't want to live in a house with newlyweds. AJ was the center of his universe now, and one day soon, he would tell her how she was the love of his life.

But maybe not at this moment.

July's hair was standing on end, she was nursing a busted nose, and that youth director stared through him like aliens had just descended.

Roger was walking down the steps of the shop's porch, dragging Penny in his wake. Luke could feel the tension skitter along the surface of the driveway as if ice had replaced the tar top.

"AJ?" He asked, wishing he could kiss her senseless instead of putting together twisted puzzle pieces. "Did I just walk onto a zombie-movie set?"

Her chuckle sounded more strangled than entertained.

"You have no idea." She pulled back and found his gaze in the evening shade. "Mom and Penny have had a disagreement, and we're still sorting out the details. Back out of this while you still can."

Ethan stepped forward. "I can drive your mother home. Or to the hospital, whichever one she wants."

Begrudgingly, July stepped far away from Ethan's charity. "I can walk."

"I'll drive you home, Mom. Ethan, you need to head back to town, and not a word of this to anyone. Promise me?"

Ethan folded his arms across his chest. "I don't know if I can ever un-hear what your grandmother said after I pulled Penny off July."

"We're all a little scarred by Gran's temper." AJ pushed hair behind her ear. "But, as long as everyone is walking under their own steam, we'll sort it out another time. Let's clear the front of the shop before a news team starts livestreaming the fallout."

Luke had seen fistfights before, just not one between women old enough to know better. July's eyes still glowed with fury, but he'd be willing to bet that might be shame more than anger. As Penny didn't seem to be too happy being shuttled toward Roger's car, he guessed he'd missed some developments over the last few weeks while sorting out crooked tour managers, clients too thin-skinned for their reviews, and how he would support himself as an entrepreneur.

Penny braked before being shoved into Roger's passenger seat. "Tell her, July. Tell AJ, or I'll come kick your sorry ass again."

July stood straighter. "Shut up, Penny. No one cares what you think."

AJ stepped over to wrap her fingers around Beans's collar, keeping the dog from chasing a bat that dipped down to explore the suffering. "What is it, Penny?" AJ asked cautiously. "What is it you want me to know?"

Penny's hair stuck out on one side, and her lipstick had smeared into her cheeks. "You've been cheated. And I don't mean by the money. That's just crazy Inez talking. July, and Roger, too, have ditched you. Even after all you've done for them!"

AJ glanced from her father to her mother, asking a silent explanation for the bizarre charge.

"Tell her the truth for once," Penny shouted. She pointed one bony finger to Roger. "Tell her you two have signed on with lover boy there, and you're both going back on the road with his new record company."

Luke felt like a spotlight had just picked him from a crowd and blinded him with a glare that could sear his corneas. AJ was slow to turn around, but the frost in her eyes was memorable.

"You've signed my parents?"

July cursed. "It's not what you think."

AJ's gaze had shifted from him to her mother, but he was no less cold from the lack of personal contact.

Taking a step back, AJ said, "You're a singer. He works in the business. This isn't algebra." A little muscle throbbed over her jawline. "Have you signed a recording contract with Luke?"

July's posture crumbled. "Yes, but—"

"How could you?" AJ spun toward him. "You knew how I felt about my mother and the industry. How could you go behind my back this way?"

He'd used faulty judgment in not sharing his plans for going into business for himself, but he'd wanted to get all his proverbial ducks in a row before he did his dream casting. AJ deserved to know that he wasn't a flake.

Based on the frostiness in her expression, he doubted this was the time to bring up how busy she'd been with the harvest during the last few weeks, and that they'd talked on the phone only a few times. Their texts were lengthy, but a cell phone message wasn't the place to spell out how he'd set in motion a plan to go into business for himself, helping independent artists create the tools they needed to forge their own path in the industry.

No, she wasn't interested in any of his explanations. She looked as if she wanted to haul him to jail. "AJ, I can explain."

"Don't bother." Her fingers were shaking as she folded them into fists. "You knew from our first meeting how I felt about my mother and the music business, but your kindness to my family made me think you weren't like the average agent. How stupid was I? You went behind my back to sabotage my plans for my mother."

The air stilled. Even the bruises hushed their moaning.

July rolled her shoulders back. "*Your plans*? It's my life, AJ. I hardly need saving from myself."

Roger slammed his hand against the roof of his car. "You're not the parent, AJ. We can do what we please."

"But all I want is what is best for you both," AJ stammered. "You were finally here. Away from it all. We were reconnecting. Finding a new balance and a way forward."

"And you wanted it to stay like that forever … on your terms." Roger shook his head, then said, "You're as controlling as my mother."

Sucker punched, AJ turned on Luke like he was the agent of doom. "You did this. You made them dream they could be stars again."

He wasn't sure how he'd suddenly been cast as the villain. Roger and July—though no poster children for healthy relationships—had at least come to some mindfulness regarding their talent and to the normalcy of Comfort. In their equanimity, they'd become the neon sign he'd been seeking to ditch the corporate life and pursue the dream he'd nursed that first summer he'd worked July's road crew. That they'd been willing to consider stepping out as independent musicians and funding their own creativity was a triumph. There were enough singers and studio musicians in Texas to grow his business as an independent promoter, and having Roger and July on his roster would open countless doors.

They'd begged him to guide them along the path, and one evening while AJ was taking Inez for ice cream, the three of them had a Skype call, fleshing out the loose details of how their skills and talent might mesh. Maybe Penny had overhead that conversation.

"Um," Luke stumbled, unsure of how to respond. "They had the dreams, have the dreams, and I'm the lucky guy who gets to help them build their careers back—if they choose to—but it's not anything that will look like what came before. There are no six-figure contracts and no road tours. We will make it up as we go along."

AJ stared a hole into his forehead.

"I think Penny misunderstood what she overheard," he hurried to explain. "There's still plenty of room for a family, the farm, and easy living. No one needs to get hurt."

AJ spun on her heel and marched away, off into the darkening lavender fields.

Roger held his hand to prevent Luke's urge to follow. "Let her go, dude. She's got a burr that won't come loose soon."

"But how—why—did this happen? I haven't even told her about my business ideas because I felt I owed it to my boss to separate before I started something new."

Ethan sighed. "I should go talk to her. I'm a pastor."

"That and three bucks will buy you a cup of coffee," Roger put his foot on the car's floorboard. "Let's clear out of here before AJ decides she's better off with none of us."

July dusted her hands on the backside of her shorts. "No."

Luke turned to see July standing taller than he'd noticed in a long while.

"I understand her better than you ever did, Roger. I'll help her process what she's given us these last two months. She's a nurturer. It will make her feel better to know she's made us better."

Luke felt like they had backed him into a rosebush. "What about me?"

July patted his arm. "Go get settled in your hotel and stay there until I call you tomorrow. AJ has more practice forgiving us than she has with you."

"But—"

July smiled with wisdom, albeit battle worn. "She'll be merciful, but you must be patient."

Roger sighed before he crawled into his car. "Meet me at The Cocky Rooster Bar. We'll have a stiff drink ready, and you can hear what July and I have been thinking since you've been gone."

Chapter Thirty-Five

San Antonio, Texas August 18, 1970

Running like she was being chased by a ghost, Inez skittered to a stop at the screen door at the end of the utility room and stared through the mesh to see her fifteen-year-old son being chased around the backyard by his grandmother. The old prune swatting at his bare shoulders with a switch. Inez banged her fist into the doorframe and shouted, "You stop this minute!"

Pushing through the door, she took the steps two at a time, determined to yank that switch out of her mother-in-law's hands.

"I mean it!" she yelled. "Every neighbor has heard Roger screaming like a schoolgirl!"

"I caught him stealing money out of my purse." Mrs. Worthington stopped, heaving with exertion, but the switch was beating time against a swath of air. "He deserves a whipping."

Inez read the panic in Roger's eyes and knew that the only thing that had saved him this time was that he wasn't so high that he was slower than his grandmother.

He deserved a whipping, if only for the marijuana he was smoking. But it was too late. She'd spoiled him to prove she wasn't the monster her father had been.

Roger was too handsome, too lazy, too rich to develop any of the grit that had seen her and George through their rough patches. If he would survive in the world, he'd have to find his own way. After she set things right today.

"You put that switch back on the burn pile where it belongs." Inez rolled her shoulders back. She wasn't tough, but a young police officer in Comfort had told her she'd look more authoritative if she positioned her body like a Marine. She'd taken his advice, and it made battling with her mother-in-law a little more even. Inez still lost most arguments, but that was because George wouldn't back her up when she tried to stand up to the bully in the black dress. "I warned you last time what would happen if you chased my boy with a stick, and it's time you found out I mean what I say."

Scorn underscored Mrs. Worthington's tone. "You don't have the nerve to put me in a home. I helped pay for this house. I paid the tuition on that worthless boy's education. And there's nowhere you can send me that I can't find my way back here."

San Antonio sunshine burned a bead of fire into her shoulders, but today was the day she would draw the final line in the sand of this battle. If she would ever respect herself, she had to act on her threat. She doubted George would understand, but she'd stopped explaining this to him months ago.

Turning on her heel, she marched into the house as if she were a general gathering her troops. She didn't bother speaking to Roger. He'd become so surly that his disrespect wasn't worth her effort. The temperatures in the house cooled her skin, but they could not contain her fury.

She'd taken all she would take of Mrs. Worthington bossing them around. George acted immune to the power struggle of the women in this house, but she'd warned him what would happen if he didn't tell his mother to find another place to live. One of them had to leave, and he could choose between which female he preferred.

In typical fashion, he'd hid at the dealership and the country club.

Inez kicked off her shoes and sank her heels into the plush carpeting lining the hallway. She'd paid to have this carpet trucked down from Dallas because someone rumored it to be the same brand as featured in Ann McDermott's house. And what was good for those uppity McDermotts was damn well good enough for her. Gladewater girls may have grown up with tar pits, but they had style.

Throwing open the closet door, she walked into the spacious room and pulled out the suitcase she'd packed after the last argument. She flipped open the lock and double-checked the clothes, six months' supply of cash, and every important paper she'd need to prove that she was the real brains behind the dealerships. George was the face of their business, but he didn't order a line, pay for an ad, or hire a new employee without her approval first. Let him see how he'd fair without her guiding his every movement. He'd track her down before nightfall, and finally, when faced with the despair of having to run his business without her, he'd kick his mother to the nearest nursing home.

It wasn't a win she'd gloat in, because all the society gossips would snip about how Inez wasn't being sweet enough to an old woman who'd lost every relative save those living in the house with her, but by God, those women didn't have to walk in her shoes. They didn't understand how vindictive her mother-in-law was because George Worthington had the gall to choose his own wife.

Slipping her feet into flat shoes, she reached for her purse, her keys, and the family snapshot she'd framed from their last vacation to the coast. Let George wonder where she'd gone. Let him stew that he didn't know the pass code to their savings account or the delivery schedule for the new inventory arriving in ten days.

Once and for all, the family would find out what it means to abuse, and lose, the one person who held them all together.

Inez lugged the suitcase downstairs and through the kitchen to the garage without a single interference from her son, her mother-in-law, or the housekeeper. She'd have preferred a witness to her escape, but she'd swallow that injustice like she'd swallowed her pride every time this family treated her like she was their doormat.

Raising the garage door, she tossed the suitcase into the back seat and climbed into the driver's seat, as grim as any runaway. Jamming the key into the ignition, she decided she didn't have to choose her destination this moment. It would be enough to drive off this property knowing that when she came back — and she would — it would only be after they had suffered mightily — and entirely on her terms.

You could take the girl out of the gambling hall, but you couldn't take the gambler out of the girl.

Chapter Thirty-Six

Pruning your plants is an act of love. — "Lessons from Lavender Hill"

AJ stared out the window of her office at Lavender Hill, both watching a pair of tourists amble through the rows of shorn lavender and not seeing their faces—a strange lack of focus that had plagued her since Luke's return. Her stomach rumbled to echo the discontent she felt the moment she'd lost control of her family's budding health. If she'd ever had control. A reality that woke her to a darker side of her character, the part where she wanted to manipulate people and outcomes to suit her picture of rightness. The morning she'd washed her face and recognized the fright in her eyes was the day she'd walked into her lavender fields and cried for the woman she'd become. Even with that unwelcome reality, she still couldn't fight the sense of failure that she had not stopped Luke soon enough. If only ... no. She wasn't going there again.

Her parents would make their choices. They'd live with their outcomes. She could control only her own attitudes and actions.

That was the mantra she had to keep telling herself, because the urge to scoop them into an intervention was still strong. Strong enough she didn't trust herself not to yell accusations of betrayal at them or blame them for ruining the first chance they'd had at normalcy.

At least normalcy by *her* standards.

Standards she wondered if she'd drawn out of the dirt found under those old magnolia trees at the farm in Nashville, the roots where she'd built rooms and houses for her dolls to live by her rules.

AJ rubbed her hands into her hair, loosening the braids holding back her sun-streaked hair.

"Knock, knock, boss."

Turning to see Betty in the doorway, she wondered how long her manager had been watching her unravel. "Hey."

"There was a woman here who wanted to talk to you."

"Was?"

"She chickened out of telling you what she really wanted to say but left you this invoice."

AJ must have been hiding in her office longer than she realized. "Keisha and I paid all the bills Monday."

"This is from the caregiving service." Betty set the paper on the desk. "The lady quit. Said there were too many people telling her how to deal with Inez — including Inez, who was uncooperative."

Figures. Penny had refused to stay in Comfort a moment longer and abandoned them to fend for themselves. AJ had assigned July and Roger to sort this out, and they'd hired a service from Kerrville. She glanced at the start date and realized three days went fast. And were expensive.

"I'll deal with it," she said with resignation.

Betty nodded and turned to leave. At the doorway, she turned back and said, "Mr. English has called a few times. You still not talking to him?"

She stared at the invoice, the figures blurring. "Not yet."

"Seems this isn't his fault. He's just easier to blame."

Sighing, AJ pulled her chair out from the desk and sat down. "Keep an eye out for the manure truck arriving from Provence Farms. We need them to run the rows at sunset."

Betty smiled wearily. "Got it."

Pulling out the drawer where she kept her checkbook, she picked up the pen to write a payment to the service but couldn't move to put ink on paper. Memories of Luke had chased her all over the farm the last forty-eight hours. It was spooky. He was here in Comfort; she didn't need to conjure him from the locked rooms in her heart. But she couldn't throw off the sense of him any better than she could manage the odd dance with her parents. They were acting somewhat normal, but there was an undertone in the atmosphere, and it grew stranger every time they dodged her or came late to dinner. No one wanted to talk. They had tacitly agreed to pretend the meltdown at the store had either not happened or wasn't significant enough to revisit. Both of which were lies.

Leaning back in her chair, she told herself—yet again—that this was the way they'd always dealt with conflict and she wasn't going to change them. Could she live with that?

She picked up the pen, knowing she'd didn't have a choice. The only thing she could do was the thing she should have done years ago.

"AJ?" A woman stood at the door. "Is this a good time?"

"Elizabeth." AJ dropped the pen. The stack of yellow notepads on the corner of her desk wore a sudden spotlight. "You're early."

"Am I?" She walked into the room, checking her watch. "I thought I was late. Traffic in Austin was thicker than I had expected."

Glancing to the clock on the wall, AJ realized the day had gotten away from her, and she had so much still to do. There were stacks of festooned wristbands in the kitchen still needing to be packed in plastic tubs to transport to the street fair tonight. "Can I get you something to drink? We hired a food truck to come out today, and they left us a few gallons of their lavender tea. I plan on inviting them here more often. The customers love their products."

Elizabeth's eyes widened. "Do you think they'd let us put their tea recipe in the book?"

She shrugged, remembering the young woman who'd been so pleased that her tea was a huge hit. "Maybe?"

"I also want to talk to your friend, Kali, about her lavender-infused goat cheese. Anytime we can showcase how the lavender has other uses is good for your bottom line."

"It is?"

Elizabeth shook her head. "When you talk like that it makes me think you've ditched your writing assignment again."

AJ wobbled as she reached for the three pads that comprised all the text she and her mother had crafted. Those late-night memories were sweet. July had teased that pulling words from AJ was harder than anything she'd ever done. It wasn't that the words felt simplistic, but so much of what she did here and in the gardens was instinctive—a nuance that streamed through her brain in a free flow. She'd regretted she didn't have a horticultural degree she could reference for expertise. All she could do was dig out the books she'd sourced when she was researching how to turn fallow land into a lavender farm.

She hoped it was enough.

Like she was handing her baby to a surgeon, AJ held the notepads toward Elizabeth. "Is this what you've driven here to find?" She tugged the pages back. "You must promise not to judge me too harshly and that someone with expertise will review these and make them sound sensible."

"Oh, perfect!" Elizabeth exclaimed as she snatched the notepads and scanned pages. "Good work, AJ. These are better than I expected."

It was too soon to think Elizabeth really liked the work. She might give out blanket statements to soothe her clients. "Use my desk to sit down and read. I don't want to be around when you get to the dull parts."

Shaking her head, Elizabeth checked her watch again. "I'll have to take these with me. I don't want you to see me weep with joy because you made the deadline. Barely, and not without an ulcer, but I think we can get this to the printer in time for the publicity circuit."

AJ clutched the doorjamb. "You mean I didn't ruin your plan?"

"Ruin?" Elizabeth tucked the notepads into her purse. "You always undersell yourself. And besides, I might have fudged the timeline. I do that because every one of my clients runs behind, so I keep two schedules. A real one for me, and an artificial one for people who swear they can't write."

The clatter of wind chimes falling to the floor would not have been enough to break her shock. "I was never in any danger of breaking our contract?"

"Something sold me the first time I came to this place. Maybe it was the views or the fragrance in the air, but I knew we would have a hit book. I made room for leverage. We're using an Austin book printer, and his wife drove out here last month and told him he'd better not mess up the process because she wanted to get the first autographed copy."

"I'm stunned."

"Don't be. You made this happen, AJ. You're the garden goddess." Elizabeth froze and then held a finger in the air as if it were an exclamation to her thoughts. "That could be our title!"

"I've been calling the book *Lessons from Lavender Hill*."

"Okay, that's interesting too. We're going to tell your story, along with the photos and recipes, and when I'm done, the whole book will feel like a tribute to your lavender farm and a 'how-to' on doing life." Elizabeth breezed past AJ. "I'll offer you suggested titles after I read your text, but I won't be shy if we need to add pizzazz and more content."

"Of course," AJ said, with almost tangible relief. "Tell me what I need to do next."

AJ watched the publicist glide down the hallway. "When will I hear from you?" she called out, feeling a sudden panic that Elizabeth would think the text was elementary. "A month? Six weeks?"

Elizabeth stopped at the room filled with art and candles. "I'll be in touch after the Fourth of July holiday. We'll talk about an editing schedule. The photographer has been here four times, snapping photos of flowers, greenhouses, and the lavender fields, but we still need to get that cover shot. Get your hair and nails done next week, I'll want him to take your portrait too."

Dread wove around her belly. July and Roger were naturals before the camera, but she was tortured by self-consciousness and the notion she was not glamorous enough for a book.

"I'll need you to decide how you want to dedicate the book and any acknowledgments." Elizabeth patted the side of her leather purse. "Then, one day, months from now, you'll have a beautiful book in your hands."

A terrified tremor passed through her heart at the thought the book would be real and propped on a stand somewhere in the shop where she'd pass it every day. People would read the pages and judge her for the silly things she'd written or the details she'd left out. "I'm not ready for this."

Elizabeth smiled. "It will be a keepsake and a testimony to your work ethic and creativity. Trust me, you'll be as proud of your work when you see it in print as you are when you look out across those blooms."

Glancing through the window to the hillside boasting acres of *Lavandula intermedia*, AJ knew she'd have to let these anxieties go. She'd come to terms this summer with the realization she couldn't control people any more than she could control the health of her plants. Maybe she'd believe that after things settled down.

"I'm going to channel all those crazy thoughts into the fields when we begin pruning the lavender, and maybe then I'll believe you." No, AJ thought. Not even that would help. "On second thought, send the books to stores up north, and then I won't even have to sell them here."

"I'm quite sure we won't be able to keep them stocked fast enough. But you go enjoy your neuroses," Elizabeth said with a chuckle. "I'll go make a book."

After Elizabeth left, most of the customers had disappeared, too. With the promotions for the street fair plastered around the garden center, all the tourists had moved to downtown to await the start of the ceremonies before the dance began at sunset.

A half hour later, AJ sipped a cool glass of tea as she and Betty sealed shut the last tub of wristbands to be sold from the Lavender Hill booth.

"The crew called to say they set up the same spot you had last year for the fair, and I sent some potted plants to hold down the banner and tent posts. I'm running home to shower and change," Betty said, refilling her to-go cup with tea. "I'll take the late shift for the booth. You got some help for the first few hours?"

AJ nodded, trying to remember who would work the booth and then realized that in the eruption of her personal life, she'd forgotten to recruit a roster of helpers. "I'm covering the first few hours."

"But you need to be out socializing with the mayor and event chairman. You need to put your dancing shoes on and go have some fun for once."

"I know what I'm doing."

Betty paused. "I don't think you do. You've let this business with your folks get under your skin, and it's thrown you. Let them be who they will be, and you go be you. And while you're at it, snatch up that hunky Luke English and don't let him leave. Y'all are too cute together to let that potential go to waste."

If only Betty knew how badly that relationship had burned.

A horn beeped from the drive. "That's Jake and Kali," AJ said, reeling back her thoughts. "Once their guys get situated for the fertilization of the fields, they will help me get these things to the street fair. Dad has taken my truck because he said he needed to do some heavy lifting."

"I saw him in town today. Seems a man that old can buy his own darn truck."

AJ watched Betty pick up a tub of wristbands and carry them to the side door.

She wasn't ready for tonight.

The crowds. The watermelon snow cones. The face painting. The street fair was Comfort at its best, and she was in too sad a state to enjoy any of it.

The rap on her side door snapped her mind back from a packing list for the booth, and she glanced toward the hall to see Kali peek her head around the door.

"Jake's backed his trailer up close. Have you got everything ready to go?"

"Thanks, and yes," AJ said, pulling her rolling cart loaded down with the tubs and sale fliers for the shop. She saw Kali's cute maternity dress and shoes—she was more interested in dancing than working her goat-cheese booth. With Kali's due date six weeks away, they'd already turned over the day-to-day operations of the cheese factory to their employees. She and Jake were leaving next week to "nest" at their horse ranch in Brenham. "You're not working your booth tonight?" she asked.

Kali patted her baby bump. "That might be the smarter plan, to stay off my feet. But I've heard rumors the tunes will be memorable this year. And I don't want to miss a thing."

AJ glanced at her jeans and halter top. "Maybe I should have dressed up too, but I forgot to hire staff for the booth. I'm working until Betty arrives later."

Kali smiled. "You look great. But take your hair down. Those braids are for working. Tonight is about partying."

Patting the woven hair, she felt for the bands tying the ends. She wasn't in the mood to celebrate, but she didn't want to fight Kali either. She just wanted to forget that she'd flirted with hope and change this summer. "I'll brush this mess out in the truck." AJ turned the lights off in the shop and locked the back door.

"The realtor says our offer is still good," Kali said, waiting for AJ in the driveway. "Are you ready to push the 'send' button on buying that property?"

She glanced across the dry creek bed to the overgrown yard of her neighbor's property. What had seemed like a fresh idea a few days ago now seemed dreadful. Luke's betrayal had taken the wind right out of her creative soul.

"I don't know, Kali." AJ swallowed. "That's such a huge risk. My grandmother is going downhill fast. And with your baby almost here, we don't know how your world will change, either. This would be the worst time to start something new."

Shaking her head, Kali propped her hands on what she had left of her hips. "Coward."

Towing the cart toward Jake's trailer, she ignored the taunt. Ignoring things was her superpower, and it would be what got her through tonight and the days ahead.

Jake stepped over to lift the cart and winked at AJ. "Don't give in to her. She's become bossy these last few weeks."

AJ grinned with a confidence she didn't feel. "I know her weakness for ice cream, and I'm not afraid to break out the Blue Bell."

Kali draped her arm over the truck's bed. "But the event center is a great plan, AJ. No one else would have anything like it for miles around."

She'd done some midnight research, she recognized that the business model would probably make money right out of the gate. But all the things that had seemed so doable weeks ago now looked like ashes of a fantasy.

Colette had tossed a few kernels for the dream, Kali watered color and possibility into the dirt, but it was the memory of Luke that made the whole scheme seem plausible—like the day she'd found old lavender seeds and wondered if they'd sprout in the limestone soil of Kendall County. Ideas this big took huge amounts of faith.

Bringing an event hall to life would also take a determination, a grit, she didn't have to spare. A cloud drifted over the sun, cooling some sting in her thoughts. Luke had come to Comfort and quickly caught them all up in a whirlwind of hope. But the thing about hope was that it needed faith to breathe. And her faith was as hard to find as those first few lavender plants ten years ago. Maybe it was gone for good.

Chapter Thirty-Seven

Galveston Island, Texas   August 23, 1970

Inez played with the paper umbrella in her margarita and ignored those men at the other end of the bar—the band of bachelors celebrating the end of freedom for one of their own. A mariachi band approached from the patio.

It had been a mistake to drive to Galveston.

Five days ago, she was sure George would hightail it down here to beg her forgiveness. Now she wasn't so sure he'd even missed her. When she'd called to ask the housekeeper to send her the box of additional clothes she'd left in the hall closet, she'd found out that Roger had skipped school to go to some concert in Houston and old Mrs. Worthington had taken the bus to Comfort for the week to be part of some commemoration for soldiers. No one. Had. Stinking. Missed her.

Figures. Her timing had always been off.

She tossed the last of the dregs down her throat, slapped a ten-dollar bill on the bar to cover her tab, and marched into the humid night to fume. Her flip-flops weren't much for making a statement, but down here no one seemed to care. She'd combed out the tease in her hair but missed all the height and the ever-present scent of hairspray. Her reflection in the Hotel Galvez mirror didn't look familiar.

Climbing down the storm wall, she sank in the sand and tried to take pleasure in the grittiness sliding over her toes. The stench of rotting fish wafted from the shoreline, and the slap of water against the pier reminded her that there was a big world out there that didn't care one fat nickel for a middle-aged mother who had lost her way. Plodding through the sand took so much effort, she kicked her flip-flops off and left them where they landed.

The real insult was that, in the last five days, not a single man had tried to pick her up. Sure, she'd held on to her figure over the years, but there wasn't enough cold cream to erase the wrinkles life had drawn into her forehead. If anyone noticed her at all, they'd think she was a pitiful has-been and would have no idea of the power she held in San Antonio. She'd thought there was more to her than the aura of her social circle. But the proof was here at the beach. Without her heels, hairdo, and high-end clothes, she wasn't worth a second look.

Inez folded down and sat on the cold, damp sand. Staring into the inky darkness of the Gulf of Mexico as it washed onto the shores of this skinny toenail of Texas, she felt as insignificant as the ghost crabs popping up to skitter across the beach.

Sifting sand through her chipping red-polished fingers, she wondered what she'd have to do to reclaim her glory.

No one outside her family knew she'd left town. The staff at the dealerships would have thought she'd been hopping from one car lot to the other, as was her habit. And someone else was running the symphony fundraiser this year, so she was off the list for those planning the next meeting.

She glanced up at the velvet sky.

It's not like she'd burned any bridges.

She could pack her things tonight and start the long drive back to San Antonio, be home by breakfast.

She wouldn't have gained anything for her truancy, but she'd probably not lost much ground. Still, though, the thing that had propelled her from her home would still sit there at her kitchen table, taunting her every time she tried to control the chaos Roger created. Oddly enough, she was ready to admit that thing didn't wear black, nor was it draped in a small strand of pearls.

The thought bedeviling her had everything to do with filling a hole that had formed in a little girl's heart about a hundred years ago.

She couldn't make people do what she wanted.

She'd never been able to get daddy to see her as anything other than a nuisance. She couldn't make Mrs. Worthington appreciate how much she'd improved George's life, and she sure couldn't get that child of hers to care about anything other than himself.

About the only thing that had worked her way was how good she was with the business. But the pressure of doing the managing behind George had weighed her shoulders into her rib cage.

And her heart felt shriveled to the size of a prune.

Inez's throat screamed for a drink, but she wanted no more alcohol. What she wanted ... what she needed ... was someone to love her. To value her.

Security. Trust. Companionship. Pleasure. Just words, but they represented everything she'd ever desired but had never been given. Running away from Gladewater hadn't helped and running away from San Antonio hadn't done the trick either. The blare of a honky-tonk overwhelmed any comfort offered by the waves, and she'd never felt more alone.

Desperate.

She wanted to be appreciated for who she was and what she did for her family.

And George. How long had it been since he'd looked at her with any real feeling? And she couldn't even remember the last time he'd crawled into her bed. Inez let her gaze wander over the cottony tips washing up to the shoreline. That man of hers was good-looking, rich, too. This wasn't the first time she'd wondered if there was another woman keeping him company.

Jealousy stung her with its whiplash and scowled her face. More wrinkles, but she couldn't help it. She worked too hard to stay pretty, stylish, and indispensable to be set aside for a younger model. Not today. Not ever.

George may not love her anymore. And God knows Roger could barely tolerate the sight of her, but she would go home and reclaim her place as the most important woman in their world. No two-bit floozy would sneak into her family and undercut her role as the mother. She'd fight with both fists if she had to. If some girl thought she could walk into her house and get between her and her men, well, she had a long, hard think coming.

As Inez stood and dusted gravel from her bottom, she had the oddest feeling that Mrs. Worthington was smirking. Like she was standing on that boardwalk, leaning over the railing, and reading Inez's mind, saying, *See, now you know how I felt.*

Inez propped her hands on her hips, stunned by the mirage.

How had that happened?

A sudden breeze shifted the humid air. Shivering, she glanced at the sky to wonder about the change in temperature. A thin stretch of cotton wove through the night sky, as if rain clouds were blowing in.

The change would feel good.

She wasn't a praying woman, not much of one anyway, but she'd latch on to a seed of faith that if Roger ever married, she wouldn't trap him into being beholden to her like George felt to his mother. She'd die before she twisted another girl into the knots she'd had to live with.

Once, of course, after he dropped the foolish idea that he wanted to go into the music business when he grew up. That was no life for her son. Stage lights and microphones created a false image. Now that she'd buried that part of her life, and absolutely no one in San Antonio knew she could even carry a tune in a bucket, she was a firm advocate for desk work. Roger would inherit the car dealerships one day, and he needed to get started working in the shop. Learning the ropes of basic mechanics would teach him the value of selling quality automobiles. And, once he was a manager, and a daughter-in-law came into the family, Inez would be the sweetest, kindest mother-in-law the city had ever seen. They'd crown her queen of the family table.

A smile broke the lines grooved along her mouth.

That was the lesson she'd take with her from Galveston.

She was not going to repeat Mrs. Worthington's mistakes.

She might not be able to change the past, but she could— if God would let her—change her future. Dusting sand from her fingertips, Inez rolled her shoulders back and marched toward the pier.

The time away had been good. A refresh. That's how she would sell it to George.

Chapter Thirty-Eight

You can find the best first aid ointment in a garden. Aloe produces a gel that can heal most simple skin wounds. — "Lessons from Lavender Hill"

AJ toyed with the arrangements of the wristbands she was displaying under the shade of the tented booth. Other vendors had stopped by to see what she was selling this year, and already two ladies had insisted she let them buy the tiny wrist corsages before she'd even unpacked them from the tubs.

Since it was a fair, there were no doors to keep customers away from High Street's many entry points, but most of the tourists traveling in for the party and dance were still finding parking, and she had a few minutes to tweak the burlap tablecloth and the centerpiece of a mason jar overflowing with lavender stalks and aromatic flowers. A trio sang through a sound check from the stage set up in front of this year's sponsor, the farm and ranch insurance office. They had brought a steel guitar and were practicing lively swing tunes. She could see the accordion near the foot of the man at the electric keyboard and couldn't help but smile. Nothing said Texas Hill Country music better than a squeeze-box.

Sausage was sizzling from a nearby grill, and AJ remembered she'd snatched a bite of chicken salad about five hours ago. Her stomach rumbled. It would be a busy night, and she should wander around now to collect her favorite treats and beverages. Betty wouldn't arrive until closer to dark.

Asking the artist at the booth beside hers to keep an eye on things, she stepped around the arrangement of potted lavender and lantana that helped anchor the tent poles. A handful of city officials were inspecting food-service areas, and there was already a crowd at the beer tent.

The town sparkled in the afternoon sunshine. Generous flower baskets hung from all the streetlights. Shop keepers had brought out the glitz to lure folks into their stores, and the vendors represented the best of Hill Country flavors, wines, and crafts. Edison bulbs outlined the dance area staked in the middle of the street, and the light poles pointed back toward a raised chandelier crafted of steer horns, ivy, and tiny lights.

She looked twice at that chandelier and wondered if she couldn't create something similar for the event hall. It didn't have to be steer's horns. She could use old rakes and shovel heads and have it wired for lights. And what if she planted ivy to grow from an inside wall, creating a backdrop of green inside the hall? How cool would that look? Her heart raced, and her imagination flowed as if someone had opened a faucet.

"A nickel for your thoughts."

The faucet slammed shut.

She closed her eyes to erase the image of a festive hall, filled with guests at candlelit tables, and the tuxedos on the small chamber ensemble playing background music for a wedding celebration. That baritone had swiped her brain clean of all scenes. The ricochet of his voice to her heart created its own reckless chaos.

AJ swallowed. This would be the first time she'd seen Luke since Penny revealed his fraud. And she wasn't prepared. It was foolish, she knew. Kali had said he'd be at the fair, that he was excited about the bands performing tonight for the dance. But in that weird moment of strolling down the street, surrounded by pickup trucks, people wearing cowboy boots and cutoffs, and the heat of the sun opening her senses to the world around her—she'd forgotten to be sad.

She'd set aside her anger and absorbed the surrounding goodness. The Mayberry illusions had fooled her heart.

AJ turned her head, ready to steel herself to his sophistication. An outsider among the locals. But the man standing behind her shoulder was not the stranger who'd snuck into her garden two months ago. This man was as comfortable in Comfort as any other rancher. His hair had outgrown its style and was still damp from a recent shower. The black T-shirt and jeans were both lived in and yet fitted for his body. His sunglasses hid his eyes, and his boots were caked with dirt. Luke English belonged to this moment.

And he'd never looked sexier.

With a croak she said, "My thoughts are too expensive for you."

Luke grinned, showing off his orthodontist's expertise. "I like a girl who knows her value."

She couldn't help hoping he didn't hate her after that meltdown at Lavender Hill. If he did, he might turn to some beauty and forget he'd ever met a lavender farmer. Her mind pictured him in a tuxedo with a beautiful brunette smiling back from some gala photographer's snapshot. That another woman might steal him away caused her a rare flare of heartburn.

Her mouth went dry. Her fingers tightened into a fist.

She turned her head and settled her gaze on his chin, which had not seen a razor since he'd arrived. He watched the trio warm up the stage with their classic country tunes and grinned. As if he enjoyed the moment. No, she decided, she did not want to be around if another woman decided Luke was a worthy prize. She'd have to hurt that person, and she wasn't normally inclined to violence.

The better days of the summer, the ones where they laughed and flirted and became friends, pushed away the hurt, and she searched the memories for clues for going forward. Even if she never saw him again, she had to let him know that she didn't hate him.

Far from it.

"Luke, I'm sorry." AJ wasn't sure where those words were coming from, but she let them flow, regardless. "I might have overreacted the other night, and I didn't give you a chance to explain. I'm usually a rational person, but ever since I met you, I seem to go right to my worst behaviors, and I'm embarrassed by how unfriendly I've been. I've avoided you this whole week."

His gaze shot to her, even though he didn't shift his position. "Well, that was unexpected."

"I don't recognize myself either," she said, letting her eyes find something familiar, like the trio tapping their toes to the timing of their music. "Four months ago, I had everything figured out. I knew what the summer would produce. What my sales projections would perform, who among my staff would quit by July, and what I wanted to plant for fall. And then my mother showed up. And Gran went downhill. And then, you and my dad landed on my doorstep. It's been some weird mash-up of all my worst fears. And I've behaved badly. I didn't know I'd become such a control freak."

He turned his body toward her, his hand hovering as if it were waiting for permission to touch her arm. "I never meant to cause you so much stress. I only wanted what's best for everyone—myself included. I may have gone about things wrong, but please never look at me again like I am the devil incarnate."

A herd of teenagers scurried past them, laughing and trying to dance to the old-fashioned song. AJ stuffed her hands into the pockets of her jeans, remembering a lifetime ago when she would have been one of those carefree girls in a minidress, trying to be cool enough for the guys who were way too fast.

Tiny puffs of smoke wafted over from the sausage grill, and AJ smelled charred dreams in its wake. Maybe she was feeling morbid, but she knew she would lose Luke. She accepted that now. Someone else would get to spend the future with him.

Dictating how people had to act, had to live, had backfired. This street fair wasn't a party, but a funeral for all that she'd dared hope.

AJ shook her head, sending her ponytail swishing along her shoulders, bared to the sun by a halter top. Depression was not her cup of tea. July liked to taunt that Worthington DNA didn't allow for anything but optimism. But that wasn't true. She fell to the blues like anyone else. It was just that the bone-deep work ethic that forced her out of bed every morning didn't cotton to slowing down, even when life fell apart. That's why she could plow her emotional recovery into the garden and endure most of life's setbacks.

Including the one where she wore the bride's dress.

"Let go, AJ," Luke breathed. "You look like you're carrying the weight of a
million problems. Let them go. They can't be that bad."

"That means letting go of you, too."

He choked. "Why?"

"Because we want different things," she said with the solemnity of a minister. "You love Nashville and want my parents to dive back in. I like farming and running a shop. We want the total opposite outcomes."

"But do we want different things?" Luke took a step back, his smile flattening into a reprimand. "You don't know what I want because you've never asked me. You've been defensive since the moment we met. Have you even asked your parents what they're planning to do about their future, or have you decided that if they're playing their old music, they must go back to the Grand Ole Opry and Tennessee whisky?"

Her cheeks stung like someone had slapped her. "I don't need to see the playbook to understand what happens at the finish line."

"Oh, so you're an expert in the music industry? You keep up with the trends in traditional and independent publishing? You know what's exploding with the onset of iTunes and YouTube?"

"Well, no."

"Then don't judge." Luke's face flushed with temper. "You don't know what you don't know because you have demanded no answers. You've tucked your chin down and carried on with your farm, as if the wind would blow all this confusion away."

"That's not—" she almost said "true" but stopped herself.

"You know I'm right. I've watched you for a while. I'm learning your patterns. You own the corner of passive and aggressive. You fascinate me, but you frustrate me, too."

Bristling at being scolded, she rolled her shoulders back.

"Ask me, AJ. Ask me why I came back to Comfort. Ask me why I'm doing business with your parents and any other independent artist that has strolled into my virtual office."

Her throat filled with cotton and question marks. She'd been so consumed with her own surety and—she admitted—arrogance, that she'd never considered that there could be a different explanation.

"You can't do it, can you?" He shook his head. "You can't let yourself trust another person. Is it impossible to imagine that someone else might have good instincts and solid advice for your parents? What, exactly, are you afraid of?"

Speechless, she wondered.

Luke shoved his hands through his hair, sending the curling ends into disarray. "I don't know why I keep thinking you will wake up and see me standing here with my arms opened wide. I must be so stupidly in love I continue to think you will love me in return and want to be with me. Talk to me, AJ, and find out who I am beneath the business card."

She stared, astonished that she had hurt him.

Luke sighed. "How dumb does one guy have to be to not see what's right in front of him? Are you even capable of change, AJ?"

A million fighting words circled her brain like butterflies flying against a wind tunnel, but her tongue wouldn't cooperate. *He loved her?*

"Yes, of course I am." She wanted to be that person. "At least I want to be."

"Then why can't you allow others to grow and change?" He took off his sunglasses and stared into her soul. "I'm not perfect. Your parents aren't perfect. But please don't write us off without at least giving us a chance to prove that we're older and wiser than we were at the beginning of the summer."

As he backed away, her soul called out. But old pains silenced its cry — scars from broken trust, forgotten promises, and selfish desires that had stepped all over the tender roots of her faith years ago.

"Luke!" She forced herself an inch forward, lifting her hand to flag him down, but a lemonade cart rolled between them, lumbering with weight and a mulish teenager who wasn't moving fast. Luke blended into the crowd that had formed under the shade trees beside High's Cafe.

"Luke," she whispered. But she knew he'd not heard her — wouldn't hear her. She dropped her hand. Searching the crowd, she could no longer see him among the throng of guests at High's party tent. Her eyes squeezed shut, and she swiped at a tear that escaped. This was neither the time, nor the place, to come to terms with flaws in her character.

With the surprise of sudden lightning, AJ recognized the silvery head of her grandmother darting between couples in line at the beer tent and panicked. Inez? She searched to see who was following the darting woman. Where was her father? AJ took off, trying to catch Inez, all the while cursing her father for ditching his responsibility yet again.

"Gran, stop!" AJ circumvented a couple. "Please, stop!"

Forgetting the Lavender Hill booth, AJ followed Inez down the street. For an old woman, she moved fast in those flip-flops.

Reaching into her back pocket for her cell phone, AJ glanced at the screen to see if she'd missed a message about Inez on the loose. But there was nothing but the screen-saver image of a lavender field in full bloom. That split second away from watching her quarry was too much. Inez had vanished in the crowd.

She paused at the corner of High and Eighth Street and looked both ways along the road, trying to determine where her grandmother would have hidden. Farther down on the right, near Front Street, was the large storefront of Eighth Street Market. Inez was friends with the owners. Maybe she'd gone there? She started to take off in that direction, worried that her grandmother was too easily disoriented to find her way back.

"AJ!"

She recognized that voice. "Not now, Ethan," she called over her shoulder. "I've got to find my grandmother."

"Kali has her."

Whipping around, she saw Ethan standing near Cup of Joe's entrance, decked out in a white Western shirt, starched jeans, and a straw cowboy hat that nearly swallowed his head. "What?"

He pointed to the other side of the street, where Inez stood patting Kali's baby bump like she had all the time in the world to chat.

The breath whooshed from her lungs as AJ folded at her waist and let despair roll off her shoulders. "Safe. I'm so glad she's safe."

Ethan walked over to her where she stood. "Jake was going to snatch her as she ran by—everyone knows to keep an eye out for Miss Inez."

"That means the world to me," she said, standing and bracing her arm on the light pole. "Seriously, I'm not cut out to manage her and my parents in the same summer."

His smile spread on his face. "And that's why I'm here."

A frisson spread along her spine. Ethan's appearance looked ripped from the screen of a Hallmark movie about cowboys and love gone wrong. Hadn't he learned that July Sands wasn't going to linger in a town without a stage and a sound mixer?

But there *was* a stage, she thought. Tonight.

Who had brought Inez to town?

As if he'd read her mind, he said, "Your parents are here."

The worries for Inez morphed into something darker, more turbulent. Something fused with the memory of every wrong turn she'd made in trying to rescue her mother from the road of fame and never-ending performance. "My parents are where?"

Ethan swiped the hat from his head and used it to gesture to the tourists wandering High Street. "They're getting ready to perform on the stage, and they're looking for you. They sent me to find you."

The early bars of the melody "Tangled in Delight" carried over the loudspeakers, and she could hear her father barking into his microphone that the sound levels were set wrong.

That track was their break-out hit.

That melody elevated them from nightclubs strung along the Bankhead Highway to morning radio show interviews and fan clubs. It ran up the charts on country and pop stations so fast, the media branded them as the "it" couple of the '80s. It was also the song, while at their divorce hearing, they vowed never to sing again.

She gripped the lamppost. "Am I walking through a nightmare?" she asked with the temerity of someone who knows they're about to step into a disaster. She glanced about again for Inez and saw her accepting an ice cream cone Jake offered.

"On the contrary," Ethan said, offering her his hand. "I think you're about to see something you never dreamed possible."

Chapter Thirty-Nine

Crowded plants quit blooming. To bring them back to health, remove them from the ground, separate their roots, and plant the smaller, individual clumps in fresh soil. Beautiful new plants can grow from the division. — *"Lessons from Lavender Hill"*

AJ choked as she turned to see the stage over the heads of those gathered in the street. Coughing to open her throat, she felt Ethan pat her back. "I'm stunned," she said.

"I knew you would be," he said, a grin in his tone. "They've been planning this for weeks. I let them use the church to practice and record some of their arrangements. It's been awesome!"

AJ sent him a death stare. Didn't he know that was inviting a monster into the sanctuary?

"They're so pumped about tonight. They wanted to see if they could put aside their differences long enough to perform again and give you the surprise of a lifetime."

"Oh, this qualifies," she said, feeling thirteen again and watching their seething anger as they pretended for the cameras that they were in a Christmas mood and not going to kill each other the moment the director turned his back.

Ethan watched them getting their microphones positioned on the stage, saying, "They said the strangest thing while rehearsing. They said they had to break up to learn how to collaborate with others."

AJ shook her head, not feeling an ounce of the anticipation Ethan enjoyed. She prayed that this wouldn't blow up and ruin the strange balance they'd found around her kitchen table. She tucked her hopes that she and her mother had found a new relationship deep into her heart and locked it tight. If July and Roger were singing together tonight, then something bigger and stranger than she'd imagined had happened, and she was afraid to see what would bloom.

"Well, hell, people actually showed up," Roger said with his trademark moody demeanor. "I had a bet with July that only my mother would come hear us sing, and that's because I had to tie her to the truck and bring her with me."

A chuckle rose from a crowd that grew thicker by the second.

"For those who don't remember me, I'm Roger Worthington, a singer-songwriter who grew up in these parts. This pretty lady to my right is July Sands, a rather famous singer who decided she can't let go singing any more than the rest of us can give up breathing."

He strummed his guitar and leaned close to the microphone. "Just for grins, we tried out our old routine of singing together. Turns out, at our advanced ages, we realized we desperately missed working together and the rhythm we feel when we sing."

Clapping rose from folks at the back of the group, and Roger glanced toward the fans. "Thank you for that, it's reassuring to know we're not new to these fine folks enjoying one of God's perfect sunsets."

Someone whistled.

July stepped closer to her microphone and said, "Welcome, Comfort, we're grateful for the set you gave us tonight. We'll not abuse your hospitality, but there was a reason we asked the mayor to let us slide into this time slot.

We knew our daughter was working her Lavender Hill booth, and we wanted to offer her a blessing for her hospitality in the only way we knew how."

No, no, no! AJ clamped a hand over her mouth to keep fear from spilling from her lips. There was no way this could end well. Scanning the crowd, she looked for Luke, wondering if he'd put them up to this moment. Inez was holding on to Jake's arm and stretching on her toes to see the stage. Nausea gripped AJ's stomach, and she wanted to flee.

"So, if you see AJ tonight, buy one of her wristbands," July held her wrist toward the audience. "Not only are they pretty and smell great, but all the money goes to the library fundraiser so locals can access books and the internet."

"And download our old tunes?" Roger interrupted.

"No one needs to hear that," she said with self-deprecation.

Folks in the crowd whistled and called out song titles like Roger and July were taking requests.

July brushed away hair that blew across her cheek. "For folks that don't know, Roger and I singing together tonight is a small miracle. And we're doing this because we love our AJ and wanted to give her something better to remember us by than the way we showed up when we rolled into town a few weeks ago."

"Some of us used to look better than others," Roger added. He nodded toward his ex-wife. "July never looks bad."

July smiled like it was the easiest thing in the world to do. "Roger and I had made a real mess of our lives, and AJ took us in."

Roger strummed a few more chords. "Let's leave it at we were creatively bad for each other. We broke up a few years ago, and it's taken a while for us to realize that failure was the best thing that could have happened to make us creative again. Unfortunately, in that nasty chaos, we lost touch with the one person who meant the most to us. The single best thing we ever created."

AJ's knees buckled.

"Isn't this awesome?" Ethan clapped.

"Terrifying."

Ethan laughed, thinking she was being sarcastic.

As a little girl, she discovered holes in her heart that could not be filled—feelings of security, trust, and the reality she was not enough to hold her parents in one place. She'd tried to be the perfect child until the day the courts made it clear the family had been torn into two pieces, and she was no longer necessary to act as glue. A part of herself had shriveled then, and from that day until this one, she'd kept love at a distance, both longing to be close again to a person and panicked that the next person she loved would break her heart all over again.

No one would understand this confusion under her skin, and she dared not show its seams to anyone, either. She'd bite the inside of her cheek and keep the tears buried until she could walk her lavender fields and stomp her heartache into the soil.

Ethan nudged her like he wanted her to be in the same glorious concert moment he was enjoying.

She looked at his profile and prayed he'd find what he was looking for out of this crush he had on celebrity.

AJ stepped back, trying to find footing away from this farce. Nothing about their performing together made sense, and she didn't want to waste one second on this shamble when she had issues of Luke and Inez to deal with first. Trapped by fans with beer cans and corn dogs, she waited for the swell to part, and then she'd escape.

Sunset painted High Street and the stage with candied orange hues and a haze of sherbet cream. The crowd seemed to have caught a fever, and they were surging toward the stage. Roger gazed across the audience with a benevolent expression, while July looked up to the horizon with her eyes squinted to see no one but the ghost of a lover who had helped her pen these words.

AJ couldn't take another moment of this strange routine.

Roger hugged his guitar and leaned in close to the microphone, begging the audience to help him. "Somewhere out there, is our little girl, AJ. Someone get her and bring her close."

July shaded her eyes against the glare and spoke into her microphone like she was whispering to an old friend. "She will not be happy about this. And will probably resist."

Ethan chuckled, and wrapped his arm around AJ's waist, pulling her toward the stage. "I've got her," he called out above the heads of the women pressed up close to the platform.

AJ was attempting to tug free of him, but it was futile. Townsfolk had recognized her and were shoving her and Ethan toward the steps with momentum. Her feet were unsteady, and a strange liquid was circling her veins. She was sure someone would say she was nervous or humiliated, but those words were too tame for the level of doubt she'd hit head on.

"You folks make room for AJ." Roger instructed the people near the steps. "She's kind of like a calf that knows it's about to be roped, so go easy on her."

July leaned into the microphone. "Play along with us, AJ. We're trying to make up for all the grief we've caused you this summer."

From the street level, clapping started and chanting for her to oblige her parents. AJ knew she'd look like ten kinds of stubborn if she fought this, but the last time she'd been on a stage with them had been at the Country Music Hall of Fame weeks before her father filed for divorce. These moments were rarely what they seemed.

Climbing up the steps, she tried to step away from her mother's reach. She knocked into the keyboard and sidestepped kicking the accordion. Roger reached out to steady her. She looked into his eyes, begging an explanation.

He smiled like she had nothing to worry about.

Oh, to think that was true.

July turned toward the audience, and while strumming her guitar strings, spoke into the microphone, "Many of you know our baby girl, AJ. She owns Lavender Hill, and that's a destination here in the Hill Country." She glanced back at her daughter, her gaze raking over the skinny jeans and a halter top showcasing a figure that was both strong and beautiful. "She's not a baby in years anymore, but she will always be our baby girl."

July strummed while thinking through her next statement.

"Roger and I have been here in Comfort for a few weeks, some might say hiding out, but otherwise recuperating from our broken dreams and the knots we tied with our own mistakes. AJ, as those of you who know her, took it all in stride and welcomed us home like we had every right to walk through the door of her heart and dump our baggage, too."

July picked a few more notes and paused for effect.

"That's what love does. It doesn't ask a lot of questions. It doesn't wait for explanations that meet the requirements for justice, it just ... does. AJ has always been, and will always be, a safe harbor for those that she loves. And we, her father and I, are more humbled than we could ever express for the love she's given us all these years. We nearly trampled her to death with our tragedies, but she's so sincere, she crawls back up from the road tracks we left on her back and loves us even more."

Roger moved toward his microphone and rearranged his guitar.

"And that's why we wanted a lot of witnesses," July continued, "when we sang her our pledge to be true to that love and to honor her for gifts of grace and perseverance.

This girl has grit, y'all. And this is the song Roger and I wrote for her shortly after our Autumn Joy was born in October 1986. This is our way of reminding her how much we love her."

Reaching back for the keyboard as a support, AJ gulped down the flood of tears that had been hovering under her eyes since that night Luke returned from Nashville.

Like someone was playing a highlight reel of the last twenty-nine years of her life, her parents began the notes of a lullaby they used to croon to her at bedtime.

Autumn Joy, how sweetly you came to live from a moment past.
No blustering wind, no stormy sea, just a breeze that would always see
What a difference love makes to broken souls and runners fast,
The child that bends and laughs and always wants to please.

There were more stanzas, but AJ had turned away and was hurrying toward the back of the stage, desperately looking for escape between the blurring swipes of her lashes. There was a break of light between tall stacks of speakers, and she leapt to the sidewalk, almost falling with the weight of unshed tears.

Years of internalized pain, unleashed by sunset and a song never meant for public scrutiny, fought against the composure she wore like armor. It was her song, her gift. And they were going to make it a confession.

A pair of hands reached out to provide balance for her ankles. Brushing away the help, she wanted to run, until her fingers sizzled with the contact of the Good Samaritan's arm. Startled, she looked up into the brown eyes of the one person who could have orchestrated this display.

Luke's gaze was neither contrite, nor was he offering her sympathy. He looked untrusting. Like he was waiting for her to bite.

Luke had been the influence that had turned Roger and July into being decent human beings again. This man. With his talent, insight, discernment, and timing, Luke had become the hero in her parents' recovery story.

And he'd be the hero in her story too—if he'd still have her.

Chapter Forty

San Antonio, Texas   March 5, 1984

Inez stared at George like he'd caved before they had even drawn the battle lines. How dare he let this trollop into their house? There wasn't much one could do about the girl holding hands with their son, particularly when they seemed joined at the hip.

Inez stepped away from the sunshine radiating through the opened door and took an inventory of the adversary. Skinny and effortlessly wearing Goodwill clothes as if they were couture. Too tall for Roger, that was for sure. Her hair needed brushing, and her eyes were dilated. Strung out, most likely. In her other hand, she was clutching a guitar case like it held her fortune.

Damnation.

A musician.

Roger had called his daddy last week to say he'd met someone and she would revolutionize his life. Inez rather hoped that meant the girl was an accountant.

"Momma, I want you to meet July." Roger stepped away from hugging his father to drag his latest girlfriend across her new carpet. "She's amazing!"

Inez knew firsthand what went on in those nightclubs. No woman singing before drunks was ever amazing. What this two-bit singer was ... was easy. Cheap. And dispensable. She'd leave before the month was out.

Inez rolled her neck to force her blood to flow again. A ghost whispered in her ear, reminding her of another singer who'd arrived at a Worthington household and received no welcome.

She slammed the door shut on those memories and chided her conscience. Roger had been raised differently than George. They had raised him with every advantage, and once he got over this foolishness about being a performer, he would step into the role she had carved for him at the dealership. Advertising. That was what would make Roger happy. Take over her feeble attempts at TV commercials and put all his writing skills into making some snappy jingles that would sell cars.

Forming the smile that had won over the Junior League, Inez held a hand toward the girl and disguised every prejudice. There'd be time later to pull Roger aside and remind him that bringing a girl home to San Antonio did not have to signal wedding bells.

George was patting Roger on the back, so he missed seeing how the girl named July—if that was even her real name—cut Inez cold. She didn't take the hand that was offered but set her guitar case on the floor and let her gaze bounce around the hallway's chandelier and paintings.

"This house is so pretty," she said with awe. "I had no idea Roger's home was so grand."

Inez could hear the whir of an adding machine behind the girl's eyes.

George closed the door. "Oh, all this is my wife's doing. She's the one with the glamour bug. I'm a country boy at heart."

He'd pay for that, Inez thought. They were both highly respected members of local service clubs, and they vacationed in Mexico a whole lot easier than they ever did in Comfort. But this was not the day to remind George Worthington of the man he'd become. There were tentacles that needed removing.

"Let's move into the living room. I have cocktails ready." Inez gestured to the room to the right, hoping they'd wiped their shoes on the doormat.

Roger sighed as he fell into the deep cushion of the sofa. "Mom, we're starved. Can we go into the kitchen and make sandwiches? We had a late show in Luckenbach, and I had a tire blow out on I-35. Took me an hour to get the spare on."

Inez ground her molars, imagining what her friends would say if they'd seen him sitting on the side of the interstate. "Go sit down and let Daddy serve you a drink. I'll make something and bring it in."

"I can help you," July offered as she studied a framed photo of Roger at his high school graduation. "We want something simple. A peanut-butter-and-jelly would be fine."

"Roger doesn't like peanut butter and jelly," Inez said, remembering the hot lunches she'd insisted the housekeeper make him every day.

July turned around. "He does now."

And with the tone in that girl's voice, Inez knew this would be a long struggle. Two women fighting to control the love of one man. There would be bruises.

"Yeah, Mom, PB-and-J is good for me."

"We're grilling steaks for dinner," Inez said, plotting how she would win against youth and beauty. "You can wait a few minutes, can't you?"

Roger threw his head back into the sofa cushions. "I told Dad July was a vegetarian. Why are you making steaks?"

Inez remembered the days when her daddy was so poor that the only things they ever ate were peas and spinach. Just because it was trendy to despise beef did not mean she would give an inch. She'd earned those steaks, and she would make sure they enjoyed every bite. "She can have a salad. The rest of us can enjoy filets."

Roger stood, propping his hands on his hips. His glare turning accusatory. "You will be difficult about this, won't you?"

Inez rolled her shoulders back. "It's what I prepared. I'm not the one turning it into a battle."

George stepped over next to his wife. "Son, your momma worked hard on dinner. Let's not make a scene."

"She has a housekeeper who worked hard. I bet Mother was at the car dealership all day. Like she's been my whole life."

Inez did not need to turn to know that The Musician judged her with Roger's words. The years Inez had spent at the manager's desk were the very reason they could afford steaks tonight. She would not back down or apologize. In this business, every season had its risks, and she'd been the one to come up with creative solutions to outwit the competition. Did anyone thank her for this insight? Or their luxuries? Of course not.

No one had ever guessed that she had a compulsion to work that could not be quenched by staying home. Even the Junior League hadn't cured her. She didn't know where this desire to work came from, but she was tired of it controlling her life. If Roger ever did right by his family, maybe she'd feel like she could retire. A new generation could keep the business going.

"Roger, don't talk like that to your mother." George took a step toward the hallway as if he'd bolt if Roger pushed back again. "Let's sit down and meet this nice young lady. July, is it? What an interesting name."

Inez controlled the resentment rolling over her nerves. All she'd wanted was for Roger to announce he was quitting this foolishness and choosing to settle down. Walking in the door with a wild-haired hippie did not signal an end to the music. It seemed instead as if he'd taken yet another leap farther away from them.

Well, she'd learned a long time ago the way to deal with the Worthington stubbornness and this was no different. She'd have to be smarter and pace her reactions. This July woman didn't look like she had sticking power. The furnishings might attract July to the family wealth, but a few years of picking up after Roger's habits and she'd be hightailing it out of here.

Then, even if it took a lifetime, Inez would have the dream she held most dear. Roger would come home, broken of his pride, and fall into her arms with all the love and gratitude she'd longed to see. He'd thank her for running interference between him and his grandmother, with the principals, even that judge who'd wanted to throw him in jail for driving under the influence. Finally, he'd acknowledge that she'd loved him best.

But first, she had to deal with this girl in peasant clothes and pray she wasn't already pregnant. "Cheese crackers," she announced. "I'll be back in a second with something to tide you over until dinner."

Before Inez could take two steps, the heavy tread of her mother-in-law's footsteps crossed the threshold. The ever-present sizzle of disdain circled around her. Dressed in a pale gray, Mrs. Worthington entered and surveyed the people gathered. A few seconds ticked by, and Inez almost felt inclined to say something—anything—to break the dismay of what the old woman would say when she saw the girl Roger had dragged home. George started to reach for her, but his mother shook off his attempt.

Instead, Mrs. Worthington held her heavy arms forward and said, "My precious boy. Come give me a hug and introduce me to this beautiful creature. I've missed you so much I thought I might die."

July glanced at Inez and winked. It was not, as some might think, a tribute of solidarity. Inez read the action as an insult. A master manipulator set a new order in motion. Roger was too weak to resist those moth-riddled purse strings. And July had chosen sides. Inez had lost again.

Chapter Forty-One

Most plants would rather have their roots watered than their leaves. — "Lessons from Lavender Hill"

"Is that my Roger singing?"

AJ glanced away from Luke's stiff posture to see her grandmother standing with Kali and Jake as they drew close to the stage.

Luke looked unsure of what to say, but Inez walked around the stack of speakers to stand behind the drum kit and stare at the duo harmonizing about the miracle of bringing a new life into the world.

"That's 'Autumn Joy,'" Inez said with thoughtfulness. "I haven't heard that song in years."

AJ wasn't sure if her grandmother recognized the people on the stage, or the verse of a song familiar from an album that July and Roger released before July became the darling of Top 40 radio stations.

Luke glanced at AJ for some direction. AJ shrugged, not sure what to do with her grandmother.

"July and Roger always had a magic no one else could duplicate," Inez said as much to herself as to anyone close enough to hear. "They are every bit as good as those Carpenters."

"Gran?" AJ put her hand under her grandmother's elbow. "Let's step inside the air-conditioning."

Inez turned beady eyes to AJ. "Get your hands off me, lady."

There wasn't a shred of recognition in that gaze, and AJ felt punched in the gut. She released her grip and dropped her hand, unsure what to do next.

"You look like someone has hit you upside the head with an ugly stick," Inez scowled. "Mascara is running all over your face."

AJ wiped under her eyes and saw black makeup on her fingertips. "It's been an emotional night."

"I'll say," Inez turned back to watch the stage. "Those two owe me five thousand dollars for covering their studio fees. They'd better pay up."

AJ glanced at Luke for some guidance; all he did was offer her a handkerchief. Taking the linen, she cleaned her cheeks and said, "I'm sure you can see them after the show."

"George, tell this woman to leave me alone." Inez looked over her shoulder to spear Luke. "I'm so tired of having to deal with their fans. Let's get AJ and go home before the traffic backs up."

With eyes as wide as saucers, he nodded and played along. "Yes, ma'am. I'll get the car."

Panicked, AJ caught his gaze and begged him not to leave.

Luke stepped closer to AJ's side.

Roger wrapped the melodic notes at the end of the song with a guitar solo worthy of any high-priced concert and then leaned into the microphone and called out for AJ, turning this way and that until he saw her.

Feeling tonight couldn't get any more twisted, she waved to him and hoped he'd worked through all his public apologies because she couldn't take one more trip down memory lane. As she watched, July turned to find her, standing with Inez. July and Roger glanced at each other and communicated in a second what song they'd do next.

July leaned back to give a cue to the man with the steel guitar, while Roger leaned into the microphone again. "Folks, I think many of you know my mother, Inez, as she's been in and out of Comfort for longer than I've been walking on this earth. Tonight, she's here, and since it may be one of her last shows to see, I'd like to do one of her favorite songs. Not that July or I wrote it, or even recorded it, but every time this song came on the radio, Momma would sit down, shushing those around her, and fall into this song like it was her lifeline. Sometimes, we all need a moment to forget the world and fall into a song. I know July feels the same because we've been talking about the power of music this week and practiced this song. It's a cover, and we'll give it our best. For Inez, who always gave her best for us."

July stepped back to her spot on the small rug placed near the mic and started a soulful strum of her guitar.

Inez looked at AJ with skepticism. "Why did he call out my name?"

"He wants to thank you for all you've done to make him a world-famous singing star," Luke said. "He's dedicating this song to you and telling everyone you're awesome."

Inez rolled her shoulders back. "Well, I *am* awesome. It's about time he realized that. Talk about an ungrateful boy. I never knew another child so willful."

AJ shared a smile with Luke. Reaching out, she wrapped her hand around her grandmother's, surprised that their fingers knit together as if there had not been a break in the years since they'd walked down the River Walk hand in hand. A new wave of tears formed under her lashes, and she unashamedly let them flow.

Roger sang the words to a song that many in the audience didn't recognize, but the haunting melody of the "Sounds of Silence" quieted those who might question. Inez moved forward. Wonder spread across her face, and the angst that had set her eyes in stone fell away. She looked fifty years younger as she stood starstruck, staring at Roger. It was as if she didn't recognize his gray hair, gaunt cheeks, or the ravages of life woven into the lines of his face. He was that rangy, handsome Texan who was frequently mistaken for Kris Kristofferson.

AJ didn't know this song had such a hold on her grandmother, but it was bliss to watch the disease lose its grip on Inez for the five minutes it took for Roger and July to inhabit the lyrics and melody. Roger nodded to his mother and had to have seen the awe in her expression.

If what the doctors said was true, this gift was more precious than any speech he might make to the woman who'd forget words ten minutes after someone uttered them. AJ squeezed the bony fingers, grateful that her father was creating this blessing and sharing it so freely with those who'd wandered into Comfort. It was as if something beautiful had happened inside the heart of Roger Worthington this summer, and he couldn't help but express it in the only form he knew how — with a sound mixer and a guitar.

That July was letting him control the stage was a gift too. Her career had soared so much higher than his, but on this raised platform, she was an equal partner in this harmony of moments. There was no introduction, none of the usual off-handed bragging points or plugs for upcoming events. They were two singers entertaining folks at a community fundraiser.

As AJ's gaze swept the collection of cowboy hats, ponytails, and ball caps, she saw her friends, her employees, customers, and other shopkeepers as enchanted as any of the tourists who'd been surprised by the quality of musicianship.

Luke tapped her shoulder. "I can take Inez home."

"I'll take her with me, but first I have to check on the booth," she said, wishing she could walk away from the responsibility. "I never expected to be away from it as long as I have."

"Surely, you have someone who can take care of that."

She heard management expertise in his comment and knew she'd fallen short of what he'd do if this had been his project. It would be easy to bristle at him stepping into her territory, but she let it go. Tonight was too full of mystery to let pride ruin the thread connecting hearts and healing hurts.

"Betty will be here soon, then we'll leave."

Luke escorted them to the sidewalk as Roger and July sang another of their famous duets, their tones climbing and sliding around notes with a truth that had not been part of their music for many years. Inez followed willingly, loosened from the grip of rage that had been so long a part of her demeanor. Every few minutes, she'd look back to the stage as if double-checking the denim clad singers perched high above the fans. AJ squeezed her fingers, reassuring her that this was as real as the touch of their skin.

Kali and Jake met them on the other side of the crowd shoved in close to the stage, a place where there was some breathing room.

Kali wrapped an arm around AJ. "Are you okay? That was a tearjerker. I don't know how you stood it."

"Really, as much as I hate the spotlight, I'm more torn up by the sweetness than the surprise."

"We grow stronger for breaking apart."

Kali and AJ turned, stunned to know that Inez not only heard the conversation but had something profound to add.

"What?" Inez asked with her characteristic sass. "That's the next line of the lyrics in this song. I've heard it a time or two."

Wrapped by a cool breeze, AJ listened to the song rebounding between the speakers and heard July's voice

316

drop an octave with the next line of the verse. Her grandmother had been right.

Jake shook hands with Luke. "So, was this what you'd thought it would be?"

A screen dropped over Luke's expression as they walked closer to the sidewalks where the vendors had their booths. "Sure, it's great to see the folks of Comfort turn out for the fair."

"I mean, July and Roger singing together in public." Jake flagged down a beer tent waiter. "You said it would be magical, and you were spot on."

AJ put her hand on Luke's arm to stop him. "You set this up?"

"They told me what they were going to do, but I didn't organize it." Luke returned her gaze. "This performance was all their idea. It was the only way they knew of to prove to you they were too young to give this up. And they needed to prove to themselves that they could be together as artists, not enemies."

The audience whistled and clapped loudly when Roger and July finished a song and began strumming the intro to another fan favorite. An exhaustion wrapped around her heart. She would have to believe him instead of relying on the old ghost of doubt.

"I wanted to be as far away from you as possible when they took the stage," Luke said. "Because I didn't want you to look at me like you're looking at me right now."

Kali slapped Jake's arm. "See what you've done?"

Jake shrugged. "What did I say?"

"Nothing, you did nothing wrong." AJ pulled her grandmother closer to her side and away from the beer tent. "We Worthington girls will go sit down and try to figure out what we've been through in the last few minutes. You can join us at the booth or not. Your call."

"I'll go buy us some beer," Jake said, sidestepping his wife.

Kali rubbed her belly. "Ginger ale for me."

AJ hurried with her grandmother in tow, not daring to look back to see if Luke would follow or not. She needed to think through what Jake meant and Luke's involvement with her parents.

Inez's flip-flops slapped the pavement. "Slow down, honey," she said, as they came to the Lavender Hill booth. "There's no reason to run away. Running solves nothing."

"It buys me a moment to think back to what's happened," AJ said, homing in on the folding chair tucked behind her display.

"Baby, we can never go back. We can only go forward," Inez said breathlessly. "And you can start over as many times as you like."

AJ pulled the chair nearer the breeze and settled her grandmother into the seat. Once she was sure Inez would stay seated, she reached into the cooler and handed her a chilled bottle of water. Dipping a handkerchief into the melted ice water, AJ wiped her overheated cheeks. There were remnants of mascara on the linen, but she felt better for the bracing shock against her skin.

"Hey, lady? You going to sell me one of these posies?"

AJ turned around to see a wrinkled man in overalls standing on the other side of the table, holding two wristbands in his paw-like grip. "Yes, they're five dollars each."

He handed her a twenty. "They're worth twice that much. Keep the change."

She took the money and folded it into the coffee tin she'd brought to manage the cash.

"You're their girl, aren't you?" he asked, turning back like he'd been itching to ask. "The one they were singing to a few minutes ago."

This man would be of the age to know the tabloid stories. Chewing her bottom lip, she tried to find a tepid phrase she could use to dismiss the digs that would be part of the unraveling of this evening.

"That must have been special," he said. "Few people have a song written about them. And it wasn't half bad either."

AJ's head snapped up. He'd left before she could thank him.

Inez huffed. "Those old-timers. They don't know how hard I tried to get Roger to stick with his music. It was the only thing he was ever any good at."

AJ rearranged the display as she let her grandmother's odd words repeat through her brain. They had never discussed the stories of Inez and Roger or Inez's own history. No one ever teased about the gems of childhood. It was as if someone had wiped the slate clean of Worthington details. And she'd been so self-consumed, that she'd never asked.

Not asking questions seems to be the fault line in her relationships. From Cullen's treachery, to the actual reasons for her parents' divorce, to her grandmother's backstory, to Luke — *especially* him. She didn't want to go one more day denying that they had something worth exploring, and if stepping outside of her shell to investigate what made someone else unique was the way to accomplish that, then she'd go full Sherlock Holmes.

"Gran." AJ watched Inez studying the water bottle as if it was some invention. "How did you meet Granddaddy?"

"Who?"

Her grandmother hadn't even unscrewed the cap. Taking it from her hands and opening the bottle, AJ returned it to Inez. "George Worthington. How did you meet him?"

"I don't know George."

Betty walked up to the booth, surveyed the situation, and almost turned around to leave. AJ latched onto her arm and held her hostage. "I need you to work the sales," she said. "I've got to deal with Gran."

Betty's brow arched, and that movement spoke volumes of her opinion, but she helped customers choose the wristbands they wanted to purchase, while AJ came up with a plan.

"I'll take Gran to Cup of Joe's. She needs to drink lots of fluids, but she seems drawn to the music tonight, too." AJ saw her parents stepping down from the platform, handing Luke their guitars while they navigated the steps.

Betty waved AJ off, saying, "Go dance a two-step for me. You know how much fun it is when Pat Green takes the stage."

AJ didn't think she could endure much more in one evening, but she knew she needed to talk to Luke. And she would not let him go to sleep tonight without clearing the air between them.

Chapter Forty-Two

San Antonio, Texas   May 12, 2006

Inez held George's hand against her lips, not so much kissing his pale, blue-veined fingers as breathing in the scent of his skin. Committing his essence to memory. The doctors said his passing could be any day now, and they had increased the morphine drip to make sure he felt no pain from the cancer that had eaten through his colon.

There had been a quick progression from the time of diagnosis to this bed at University Hospital. The season had revealed many surprises, doctor visits, and tests that upended their ordinary world. The dealerships were for sale because she was too overwhelmed to think of managing them without him by her side. Roger was flying in from some third-rate tour in Australia and hoped to make it in time. AJ was taking finals at Vanderbilt, and they'd not wanted to confess how sick her beloved granddaddy was until she'd wrapped up those business classes. July was ... well, God knows where her ex-daughter-in-law was these days. Probably shacked up with some dancer in the Pocono Mountains.

July was not worth the effort of remembering.

So much pain flooded with that name. That was one of the few things Mrs. Worthington and she had ever agreed upon—July Sands would lead Roger Worthington on a merry chase, and it would not end well. And it hadn't. Thank God, her mother-in-law had died before the tabloids got ahold of Roger and July's breakup.

The rhythmic beeping of the oxygen machine beat in time to the chaos in her mind. And that beep, beep pulse of George's heart followed her when she went downstairs for coffee, drove home for a shower, or sat in the drive-through line at Chick-fil-A, waiting on a sandwich for her and a milkshake for George. It had become the melody of her memories.

She could still remember how brave he'd been at the club in Austin, rescuing her from the mob and certain rape. There had been no clue that night that their world would spin together, and they'd have over fifty-two years of living ahead of them. She sometimes wondered, back in the days when she thought she had a choice, if she'd had it to do all over again—would she?

George's role as a knight in shining armor peaked that night in Austin. After he graduated, he became a man who loved the path of least resistance. She was the go-getter. The society maven. The one who starred in the TV ads for the dealership.

She glanced over to his face, so handsome still—even as death hovered over his eyelids and eased the creases sunbaked into his skin. She rather suspected that was why she'd always had such high expectations for him; he just looked like someone who'd take the world by storm. Thankfully, even if he didn't live big and brash, he'd taken her advice about dressing for success, because he always looked well turned out. Though, if he had a choice, he'd probably insist on wearing his overalls to the grave. Those were the first thing he'd put on every Friday after work, and he'd wear them straight through until he got ready for church on Sunday.

Inez set his hand under the blanket to keep it warm, knowing, without a doubt, she would not bury him in overalls.

She'd blamed his mother for all his flaws, but the only person who could really have made George change was George. And he'd been content to be himself from their first days together until their last. He'd lived his life as a believer in Jesus and treated the good book like it was his personal road map. His mission must have been a short list, because once he rescued her and got his son into a church, he seemed to have sat back like he had it made. George was a simple, uncomplicated man. Though she didn't like his contentment, she respected him for owning his true self. It made the letting go of regrets a lot easier.

Her list of regrets was long, twisted, and had red notes in the margins. His ... few. George had been faithful. He had integrity. And he was a valued businessman. There was a lot to be said for a man like that.

Standing, she leaned over to kiss George's forehead.

Straightening the strands of hair over his balding head, she regretted that she'd been such a difficult woman to live with. He'd deserved someone easier. But, for reasons she still didn't understand, he'd chosen her.

Tears fell between her lashes, and she wiped them fast. The doctor was stopping by soon, and she didn't need black tracks ruining her makeup. She'd been crying into her pillow for weeks now, and she'd hoped she was past this sudden leakage of tears. AJ would weep when she saw George all tied up to these tubes. Those two were thick as ticks on a dog.

She reached for her purse and found her cell phone. Checking the time, she guessed AJ had finished finals by now. After she made this call, she'd ask the travel agent to order AJ's ticket on whatever airline could get her here the fastest.

AJ. Inez had been the one to nickname that tiny doll baby, because she thought the birth name, Autumn Joy, sounded too hippie-ish. Lord, she'd never heard the end of grumbling from Mrs. Worthington over that name choice, either. Not only was July too showy, too artsy, she would spoil the baby and raise her to think the world revolved around her little finger.

Despite the dire predictions, AJ had been a dream child. Mrs. Worthington had doted on the baby, until a heart attack finally accomplished what Inez had longed to see happen. Her dying words had been for Roger and July to have more children.

Maybe if Inez had been more confident in her mothering, she and George could have had more children. But Roger had drained her with his willful spirit, and she'd told George they were "one and done." He grieved their small household, often rewinding stories of the never-before-told antics he and his brothers created in the halcyon days of pre-WWII Comfort—stories that would send Mrs. Worthington into a depression for all the sons she'd lost.

Inez moved over to the window, staring at the busy street below while she waited for the call to connect to AJ. This would be one of the hardest things she'd had to do since the doctors gave them the terminal diagnosis. That girl had locked down emotionally after her parents' divorce, and George had become her confidante. He was the only one who could draw a conversation out of her these days.

Inez wondered if she could fill the gap George's death would leave, and if they'd figure out a way forward without him there to be their glue. With Roger gone to Timbuktu, it would be her and AJ at the Sunday table. What in the world would they talk about?

An image of that formal dining room, still turned out with 1980s fabrics, popped into her mind, and she knew all the cocktail parties, all the Thanksgivings, all the dinner parties would end with the funeral.

For the first time in her entire life, she'd be alone.

She swiped her cheek and drew her fingers through another puddle of mascara.

She'd seen what happened to her friends who were widows. The sound of silence must be terrifying.

AJ's breathy voice answered the call, as if she were walking from one building on campus to another. "Gran?"

A flood rushed Inez's heart. "Honey, I'm calling with some news, but first, how did your tests go?"

"Not bad. Not great. I guess Dad told you that Cullen and I have broken up, right?"

Roger had not told her anything of the sort. If it didn't affect Roger, it wasn't a priority. "No, I'm sorry, I hadn't heard. That boy wasn't good enough for you, anyway. Singers can't be trusted. I should know."

As the hurtful pause continued, Inez knew she'd said the wrong thing. She squeezed her eyes shut, wishing she could dial the words back and change her tone. "I need you to come to San Antonio as soon as you can, sweetheart. It's your granddaddy. He's taken a turn for the worse. And he can't go to heaven until he can tell you good-bye."

Chapter Forty-Three

Herbs can grow almost anywhere there's sunshine and soil. Use them in a vegetable patch or patio pots or have them grow beside your sidewalk. The sudden fragrance surprises people in the best way. — "Lessons from Lavender Hill"

Periwinkle colors washed the sky and distant lights twinkled as if the stars peeked in on those gathered on the makeshift dance floor. Children with melting snow cones and old men shooing dogs away from the bratwurst stand added an air of happy danger to those spilling out from the beer tent and wandering the shops open late for the fair. AJ tried to appreciate the humidity drifting away and leaving pleasant temperatures in its wake. But she couldn't. Inez was dragging her feet.

"I see Mom and Dad heading our way," she said, trying to cajole her grandmother. The pairing of her parents in the same sentence still sounded wrong to her, but there was a rightness she would explore if those songs tonight really meant they could start over. "And they're smiling."

"Let me go, missy."

"Not on your life," AJ said, wrapping an arm around Inez's waist for an added buffer. "We've got to get you home."

Inez glared at the people crowding her. "This is not my home."

"I know, I should have said the cabin."

"I don't live in a cabin. I want my Cadillac."

AJ pushed a strand of hair behind her ear, fallen from her ponytail, and approached her parents. "Did one of you forget to find a sitter for tonight?"

Roger ran a hand through his hair. "Mom wanted to come, said she'd behave."

AJ looked at her father and questioned whether he understood how serious the dementia had grown. "You can't trust anything she says, the doctor warned us. She's been all over the town, and I almost lost her. She needs a vitamin drink to recover from this outing."

July sighed. "You're welcome, by the way."

AJ blinked and looked at her mother standing under the warm glow of a streetlamp. "Excuse me?"

"For putting our hearts out there for the entire world to see and hear," July said, folding her arms over her chest. "We exposed our vulnerability, and you haven't even thanked us for apologizing for being the worst parents ever."

"Yeah, I broke the divorce decree, and it felt so great to thumb my nose at those smug attorneys and sing "Tangled." I wish we'd done the whole song. I hated that we signed that clause saying we wouldn't perform the song." Roger glanced at July. "You were flat at the start, but I covered for you."

Stunned, AJ rocked back on her heels, staring at her parents. They looked exactly the same as always, and yet there wasn't the usual bitterness in their eyes. She would take a leap of faith and believe performing together tonight signaled a peace that would become their new normal. Or so she'd hope.

"Thank you, Mom, Dad." Her heart was in her throat, and she swiped at the tears formed by exhaustion and forgiveness. "I'd love to talk about what this all means when we get back to the farm, because I want to think we're all moving forward and finding a new way, but first we have to get Gran somewhere secure."

"I don't know what you're talking about." Inez tugged out of AJ's grasp.

AJ brought her around to stand between her and her parents. "You brought her, please take her home."

"This is not my home." Inez shouted.

"Your home is where your bed is, Inez." July snapped, reaching for her mother-in-law's arm. "And right now, it is here."

"I'm not going with you. I don't even want to see you."

July glared at Roger. "She's your mother. Deal with her."

AJ glanced to the right and left, wondering who was judging their family fight. "Please." Her voice broke. "I've got to stay with the booth, and I really need to talk to Luke. I blamed him for things that were really blessings in disguise."

July groaned. "It was *our* idea. Roger and I planned this after I saw your expression when I played guitar with those kids. I knew we had to do something big to set the past right, and Luke tried to talk us out of it. He said embarrassing you was no way to prove a point. Do not give him credit for our debut."

Roger nodded. "And to be clear, we are going into business with him. He's quit his job in Nashville to manage independent artists, and we will be his first clients."

"If he takes us on," July added.

"Yeah, that." Roger said. "He said he's not signing us to a contract if you're opposed to the idea. So, don't trip us up.

We're healthy and ready to go to work on some new material."

"You can do whatever makes you happy," AJ answered honestly. "You two looked so natural on the stage. And I was floored by your tribute to me and the song for Gran. I admit, I feel like I'm walking through a dream."

"A good dream, I hope?" Roger asked, wrapping his hand under Inez's elbow.

"The best." AJ glanced across the street to see Luke locking down her parents' guitar cases behind the stage. "I'm sorry I wasted so many weeks fighting this. You two truly deserve to go back out there and see what you can make with your talents. As Luke said from the beginning of all this, you're not done performing."

Roger grinned. "Yeah, this feeds the soul. I couldn't believe how well everyone responded."

July smiled. "I saw folks singing along to our songs. That hasn't happened in a long time."

Sticky-fingered children passed between AJ and her parents. "Will you take Gran home now? I really need to talk to Luke before he flees here thinking we're the strangest people he's ever met."

July leaned forward to kiss AJ's cheek, but before she did, she whispered, "He's not going anywhere. For him, home is where you are."

They hugged quickly, and as AJ regained her breath from her mother's promise, she asked, "Are those lyrics to a new song?"

"They're the words to your Comfort song, the one being written tonight." July stepped aside to let Inez and Roger pass by. "If you'll let Luke into your heart."

Wiping at her cheeks, AJ couldn't answer. She offered a weak smile, hoping that Luke was in a forgiving mood. She watched her parents and grandmother blend into the crowd, being stopped by fans along the sidewalk. Drawing in a ragged breath, she knew she had to grab that stardust overhead and take the first step. In her whole life, she'd always waited on the whims of others, but like it was a choice written into a long-ago plan, she knew she had to claim her future. There was a lifetime of love hanging in the balance.

A ballad being sung by the new set of performers brought the dancers hurrying toward the dance floor, and AJ scurried to get out of their way. She eased around the stack of speakers to see Luke talking to a sound technician. She debated whether she should interrupt, but then Luke turned. And when he did, her heart skipped. There was dust on his black T-shirt, and his hair was mussed by the breeze. There were no lines of stress around his eyes, and his smile came easily. Though she could hardly process the change, he was happier now than he'd been when they'd first met. She'd bet the farm on it.

"Hi," she offered shyly.

He tipped the man to take the guitars to a secure place and walked over to her. "Hi, yourself."

Whispers from their past conversations flew at her, and she wanted to dodge the accusations and harsh words, but she had to own them. "I'm sorry, Luke. I was so wrong about you. And I can't even explain where my heart was that I was blind to the good you brought to my world, but I hope you'll forgive me."

He glanced up to the velvet sky and let his gaze drift back to her with a smile in his eyes. "There's nothing to forgive. You were absolutely in the right. I can only hope one day you'll feel as protective of me as you do your parents and your grandmother."

"Don't pretend, Luke. I hurt you. You said as much."

He reached forward and cupped his hands around her shoulders. "You love people in a big way, Autumn Joy. I want to be one of those lucky people who has a place in your heart."

Tears blurred her eyes, but she held his gaze. "You will have the biggest place, if you're willing to put up with all the crazy I have going on in my world right now."

"As one author of that crazy, I say 'thank you.'"

She leaned on her toes and gave in to the urge to brush her lips across his. "I love you. I think I have almost from the first."

He didn't give in to the temptation of her kiss. He held his hand out, like he was offering her more than his palm. "Dance with me."

The band had started one of their hit slow songs guaranteed to move couples closer together. She gravitated to him and placed her left hand in his. He pulled her with him to the floor defined by the shadows cast by twinkle lights.

As he spun her around to face him and drew her close, she felt her skin light with fire. The charcoal of her past was the tinder for this new flame, and its strength stunned her. She stepped into his embrace like this was a dance she'd been born to follow. One of his arms slid behind her waist, the other caught her right hand and held it close between their ribs. They swayed, then sidestepped, then circled. Some say dancing is just a conversation, and she hoped that was true. What she wanted to say to him was that she'd be willing to spend the rest of her life dancing with him, if he would have her.

A few folks jostled into the space, forcing them to close the inches between them. AJ almost couldn't choose what to say, if she got up the nerve to speak. His cologne and body heat tickled her nose, his hand rubbed patterns into her back, and she wished this song would never end.

"Luke," she finally said, heedless of the outcome. "I'd like to start all over. Begin a real romance with you and treat you with kindness instead of questioning everything you did and said."

His chin grazed the top of her hair. "I don't want to start over again."

Squeezing her eyes shut, she tried to stop the flood of pain that raced like a volcano over her fragile peace. "You don't?"

"Um, hmm," he said against her hair. "I want to marry you, AJ. Sooner rather than later, if you don't mind."

Her knees buckled. "What? I thought you were angry with me."

He stopped as people danced around them. "I will not say that being in love with you has been a picnic. But I knew—almost from the moment we met—that I wanted to be with you more than I ever wanted a predictable life. I'd love to live with you forever, if you'll have me. Crazy and all."

Panic screeched to a stop, and lavender blooms replaced the hot lava. "You mean that?"

"With my soul," he vowed. "Whatever your parents do with their lives has no bearing on us. We'll start our own family, and they can do whatever they want—okay?"

She nodded, still stunned that what she thought would be an uphill battle to convince him she cared was a war already won. "Yes, if that was a proposal."

Luke stared into her eyes, his smile warming his face with the slow burn of a fire that was coming off kindling. "Do you remember the day you wanted to kiss me, and I said you'd have to wait?"

Embarrassment flooded her cheeks. "I remember."

"I told you that when I finally kissed you, it would be worth waiting for, right?"

A sizzle started under her ribs and quickly scorched her nerve endings. She wasn't good about expecting spring blooms either. "You bragged, but I haven't as yet seen anything that lived up to the hype."

"I'm in marketing, we like to build expectation." His eyes twinkled as his head dropped closer, his lips hovered over hers, whispering, "It makes for a better impact."

If he didn't kiss her soon, she would shatter.

His lips claimed hers in a searing touch that left all other explanations, questions, and unresolved issues forgotten. She fanned her hands behind his neck and returned his kiss with the urgency that had been humming through her since she'd heard the words to "Autumn Joy."

The wheeze and whiz of fireworks exploding overhead didn't interrupt what was the best kiss of her entire life. Neither did the change of a ballad to a rocking cover of a Willie Nelson hit cease their melding. The crowds danced around them, spectators cheered the colors bursting overhead, none of that changed the melting of two hearts into one.

And now AJ knew her Comfort song—it was Luke. Just him. His faith in her, and for them, was a lyric that would never fade. With time, she'd memorize the melody too.

Epilogue

Luke stood on the porch of Lavender Hill, glancing across the horizon. Turning the collar of his jacket up to keep the chill away, he studied the metal frame on the property next door. It was early yet in construction, but the shape of the oversized barn was clear, and the little ranch house was prepped for the spray of white paint over the bricks. The new roof and black-framed windows already made the house look ten times better than it did the day AJ and Kali closed on the property.

"We're sold out of Christmas trees, if that's why you're here," Betty said, climbing the steps behind him.

His gaze took in the potting shed that last summer had held composted soil and a few months later boasted holly wreaths, twinkle lights, and native trees — or what remained of them. "I bet I could find a Charlie Brown tree in the corner."

"You'd be right. If it doesn't sell soon it's going to be kindling in my fireplace." Betty crossed in front of him and opened the door. "You coming in or planning to go over and light a fire under that work crew?"

"I'll let the contractor take care of that. He's got Kali breathing down his neck, so he doesn't need my two-cents worth." Luke wiped his shoes on the doormat bedecked with reindeer. "AJ called to say the UPS driver left her two big boxes. She wanted me to come for the unveiling."

Betty's brows drew together as she led the way indoors. "I wonder what came. We're not expecting more inventory until the spring."

Colorful ribbons decorated the ceiling in the front room. Carols played through the speakers, and the fragrance of warm cider carried in from the kitchen. Though most of the Christmas decorations had sold right after Thanksgiving, he still felt that if he turned too fast, he might knock over a display of ornaments.

Luke patted his coat pocket, double-checking the security of the jeweler's box tucked deep inside. He'd wanted to put a ring on her finger the day he moved to Comfort, but between getting his office established, starting a business as an independent music promotor, and working around AJ's schedule, there'd not been a good time. Moving Inez to an assisted-living facility in Boerne had winded AJ, and then the holidays hit. But tonight, he was going to follow through on the promise he'd made to her at the street fair, and they were going to set a date. Kali had secretly suggested Valentine's Day, but he was going to negotiate for New Year's Eve.

"Is July here?" Luke asked, as Betty peeled off her gloves and set them behind the check-out counter.

"No, she's gone to get her hair done and check on Miss Inez." Betty unbuttoned her coat. "Never saw that coming, but July has turned into a regular visitor. And AJ is glad to know that someone is looking in on her grandmother every day."

"Roger will be back from Austin next week. He said his girlfriend is spending Christmas with her kids, so he'll bunk at the cabin until New Year's." Luke folded down his collar and unzipped his jacket. "That ought to be interesting— Roger and July together for Christmas. I guess we could call that the ultimate test of reconciliation."

Betty's gaze rolled to the ceiling. "Be a gem and take AJ out of town for a week. Even though they're somewhat peaceable, she'll still need a break from walking on eggshells."

"Who is somewhat peaceable?" AJ asked, stepping into the room.

"Your parents," Betty said emphatically. "That's who."

Luke admired AJ standing under an ornament of mistletoe, wearing suede booties, skinny jeans, and a cashmere cardigan. The pale pink sweater suited her blonde hair and brown eyes. She'd had a stylist cut five inches from her hair, and many days, like today, she straightened it. He smiled, thinking she was the most beautiful woman he knew. He stepped closer, knowing he couldn't let good mistletoe go to waste.

AJ was smiling at him as he approached.

"Oh, you two are like teenagers," Betty grumbled. "I wish you'd go ahead and get married."

Luke stopped in front of AJ and kissed her quickly. "Please ignore the lady at the register. She might have frostbite."

"I heard someone say a blue norther was coming in over the hills tonight. Might bring snow." AJ's eyes glowed with delight. "Who wouldn't want a white Christmas?"

He wanted a million Christmases with AJ and would take them in any color they came as long as they were together. "You said you got a package?"

She grinned. "I did, but I wanted you to be here when I opened the box."

Betty stepped away from the counter. "Do you need me to inventory it?"

"Not yet," AJ said, reaching for Luke's hand and pulling him along the hallway. "We'll be back in a minute."

A sizzle raced under his skin. "I'm strangely turned on by a woman who takes charge."

She chuckled as she led him into her office. "Most would say you're just strange for turning your back on Nashville, but I'm so glad you're here. I wouldn't want to have this moment with anyone but you."

He saw two large boxes sitting on her desk. "It's a little early to exchange presents, but I'm happy to show you mine if you want to show me yours," he said, wiggling his eyebrows.

She slapped his shoulder affectionately. "Hold one end of this box."

He watched AJ reach for scissors. "Don't you recognize the name of the sender?"

"Yes, but it's what is inside that's the surprise." Deftly, she cut through the tape and pulled apart the cardboard. Dragging out packing paper, she laid her hand on the glossy stack below. "I don't know if I can do this," she said, looking nervously at him. "You may have to."

Luke narrowed his gaze on her. "It's your book, isn't it?"

"Yes," she said, bundling the paper in her hands. "Elizabeth told me to expect the delivery. It's a limited run, just to make sure there aren't any errors we missed."

Luke grabbed her shoulders and kissed her. "Congratulations! This is a historic moment."

AJ's arms and the wad of paper were caught in his embrace, but she didn't pull away. "I know, that's why I wanted you here. I'd never have found the confidence to start writing if you hadn't shamed me into it."

"Shamed is a little strong," he said, releasing her and reaching for a book. "I like to think I inspired you through tough love."

AJ chuckled. "I still have your pen. I'll use it to autograph copies — assuming anyone actually buys one."

He let his fingers fit around the spine of the book. Because the production work had gone on while he was untangling from his career, he'd never seen the rough draft or any of the cover ideas. Even so, he his heart was swollen with happiness for her. At least one Worthington woman had decided to write a book this year.

"I changed my mind," she said, taking the book from his hand. "I want to be the first to open it."

AJ studied the glossy cover drenched in watery lavender shades.

From Luke's angle, he could see it featured a sunset image of AJ walking through the lavender fields. She wore a silky blue dress, and a wreath of lavender crowned a riot of blonde curls. "You're a lavender queen," he said with awe.

"Actually, we decided to stick with the title *Lessons from Lavender Hill,* because the book reads more like a textbook than a memoir."

Tears were glistening in her eyes. Whatever category the words fell into, they represented her heart on the page. All those who loved her knew what the heft of those pages meant.

"No, *you're* the queen, AJ. Blossoming in all your glory." He picked up another copy of the book. "This is beautiful."

She swiped her lashes with a fingertip. "It's a little much, but I like that Beans is trailing along behind me. He'd appreciate knowing he made the cover."

Luke set the book on the desk and pulled her into his arms. "I'm so proud of you. You are amazing."

She gulped tears and leaned into his hug. "You haven't even read it yet."

"I don't need to—but I will—it's a thing of beauty to see a dream come to life."

"But this book was Elizabeth's plan, not mine."

"You, AJ. You're living the dream. You are in every inch of this place, and this book is a snapshot of what you've created. I love you."

"I love you too," she said quietly.

He held her close, breathing in the fragrance of her hair. She was in his arms, and God willing, he hoped he'd never let her go. The jeweler's box in his pocket rocked with his heartbeats, and he wondered if he shouldn't fall to his knee right now and reveal the diamonds. But no, this was her moment. He wouldn't steal any attention away from what was rightfully her triumph.

AJ pulled back and reached for a tissue. "So, I did struggle with some of the details," she said. "The hardest might have been whom to dedicate the book to."

"I imagine," he said with a nod. "You've had all your best people in your life these past six months. It would have been hard to choose."

She reached for the book. "It wasn't the challenge you might think," she said, flipping through the pages until she came to the one filled with white space and two simple sentences.

He read the inscription. *To Luke, for making all my tomorrows brighter. Marry me, Christmas Eve?*

Gasping, he looked back. "Is this a misprint? This can't be printed in all these books."

"No misprint." AJ's face flooded with color. "All the bookstores — all the world — will know how I feel about you. I may not be able to write a song, but it turned out that I can rock a meaningful sentence. Will you marry me?"

Luke patted his jacket, feeling the box. "AJ, I was going to give you a ring tonight and insist we set the date!"

Her eyes filled with fresh tears. "I guess I'm more impatient than I realized. I just needed to get Gran settled and then figure out how to get you to the church when we could most likely organize our families to attend. Christmas seemed like the logical time, since we're both in a slow season. Mom and Dad are in charge of the party afterwards. They were so happy with their results surprising me at the street fair, they wanted to wow you with our reception. And they've invited your family, and Roni's parents, too. They're going to be mad that I've let this secret slip. But I guess I've told everyone — at least those who read this book."

He glanced again at the page, stunned that she'd done something so bold. She'd become a woman full of the best kind of surprises. "I want to spend the rest of my days loving you."

"And growing lavender?" she asked, as she walked into his embrace.

"Whatever it takes to live with you forever and ever."

"All I need is you." AJ leaned onto her toes and let her lips hover over his. "Say yes to Christmas Eve?"

"Yes."

One Final Note

Dear Reader,

I hope you enjoyed this novel. I fell in love with the mystique of Comfort, Texas, years ago, and it's always felt like fertile ground for weaving stories of women discovering their grit. I've walked through the Texas Hill Country for the story of Kali and Jake in *Emeralds Mark the Spot* (a free novella available to those who register for my newsletter at www.kimberlyfish.com) and in the novel, *Comfort Plans*. If you've read *Comfort Plans*, you may recognize a few characters from that story meandering through the pages of this one, too. It's my secret pleasure to see the characters become friends and do life together.

There are two other novels set in Comfort in the works, and it's my hope that they will debut in the near future.

To stay informed about these and other book releases, please register for my newsletter at www.kimberlyfish.com or follow me on social media: Facebook at Kimberly Fish, author; Instagram at Fish_writer; Goodreads, BookBub, or Litsy at Kimberly Fish. If you'd like to peek into the inspiration boards for the novels I've written, you can find them on Pinterest at Fish Tales. If you are so inclined, please leave an honest review of this book on the site where you purchased it so that other readers might be encouraged by your thoughts.

If you also enjoy historical fiction, I wrote two WWII novels detailing the exploits of female spies and the mayhem of the Texas home front during the war. You'll enjoy the sassy characters and oil-rich settings in *The Big Inch* and *Harmon General*. Both are available as paperbacks and e-books, and *The Big Inch* is also available as an audiobook.

Thank you for spending your valuable time with this book!

Kimberly

October 2019